THE HALF SISTER

Also by Catherine Chanter

The Well

THE HALF SISTER

Catherine Chanter

CANONGATE

To my parents, with love.

Published in Great Britain in 2018 by Canongate Books Ltd,
14 High Street, Edinburgh EH1 1TE

canongate.co.uk

1

British Library Cataloguing-in-Publication Data
A catalogue record for this book is available on
request from the British Library

ISBN 978 1 78689 124 2

Typeset in Dante MT by Palimpsest Book Production Ltd,
Falkirk, Stirlingshire

Printed and bound in Great Britain by Clays Ltd, St Ives plc.

In rivers, the water that you touch is the last of what has passed and the first of that which comes; so with present time.

– Leonardo da Vinci

NARRATIVE VERDICT

INQUEST TOUCHING THE DEATH OF VALERIE STEADMAN
Inquest concluded July 2016

Valerie Steadman died as a result of crush injuries to the pelvis and chest. Valerie Steadman would have died instantly as a result of these injuries and the delay in the arrival of the emergency services is not deemed to be a factor in this case.

On the night of April 12th 2016, Valerie Steadman was staying at Wynhope House as a guest of her half-sister Diana, Lady Helyarr. She was sleeping in the guest room on the top floor of the East Wing known as the Tower.

At 3.25 a.m. on the morning of April 13th, there was an earthquake of magnitude 5.4 (Richter scale) at a depth of 2.3 miles, the epicentre of which was approximately 3 miles from Wynhope House. An earthquake of 4.7–5.6 occurs in the UK every 10 years, an earthquake of 5.6 or larger every 100 years. Six buildings within a 10-mile radius of the epicentre suffered significant structural damage rendering them temporarily uninhabitable, a further 38 buildings suffered minor structural damage and there were a total of 3 fatalities attributed to the earthquake. Both the main section of Wynhope House and the adjoining Tower remained standing although structural damage to the joists joining the two parts of the residence was apparent.

At 3.37 a.m. on the morning of April 13th, there was a lesser aftershock of magnitude 4.6 (Richter scale). The combination of the two tremors and the disturbance to the foundations of the building caused by the recent excavation of a basement extension led the Tower to separate from the main house and collapse. The quality of, regulations pertaining to, and planning in regard of, the excavation are subject to a separate inquiry.

Valerie Steadman's body was located beneath the rubble by the Fire and Rescue Service at the bottom of the staircase in the Tower in the area immediately inside and adjacent to the ground-floor front door at 10.09 a.m., April 13th.

The door leading from the first floor of the Tower to the first-floor landing of the main house and the door leading from the ground floor of the Tower wing directly onto the drive were both locked at the time the earthquake occurred. Despite an extensive search by forensic services, the key to these doors has not been found.

Minor bruising and cuts to Valerie Steadman's knees and shins were commensurate with a fall on the spiral staircase in the Tower and were acquired prior to death. Bruising to both hands on the knuckles and damage to fingernails on the right hand were consistent with injuries likely to have been sustained while trying to open one or both of the wooden doors.

As the doors were locked by person or persons unknown and for reasons not established and as there is no clear indication as to why the key was not readily available to expedite the deceased's escape between the first and second shocks, and bearing in mind that had the doors been unlocked the deceased may have escaped alive, the consequences of the doors being locked are both significant and enduring and therefore the jury in this matter records a narrative verdict.

Peter D. Merland
HM Coroner

Chapter One

Over half of the sitting room is now a bright, brilliant dazzling yellow; the rest is rent grey. Whoever designed these flats in the 1970s in Bracknell never thought about the fact that the windows are too high to let you see out unless you stand up and too narrow to let the light in when the sun is low over the tower blocks opposite. It can get you down, if you let it, but this place where they have arrived is so much better than the prison they have escaped. Valerie has been singing along, but now she picks up her mobile and turns down the volume on the radio.

'Sorry, who did you say you are again?'

Less than two minutes later, because that's all it takes, she is perched on the edge of the imitation leather sofa as if she has somewhere to go, knowing that there is nowhere to go from here, noticing that the Spring Sunshine has rubbed off from the paintbrush to the remote control to the cushion, the news leaving its fingerprints all over her life.

'Oh, Mum,' she says. 'Not Mum. Not now.'

There is no point in singing any longer. Valerie switches on the telly. The reporter is ill at ease, looking over his shoulder as if he is about to be attacked, but in fact the destruction behind him is something to do with a tsunami, not a war. It is all a long way away and the news leaves the victims picking through the wreckage and switches instead to people chanting the name of their new president and celebrating in their thousands, a young man with a child on his shoulders cheering to the cameras above the surge and the swell of the chorus. 'This is what hope feels like!' he shouts. That's how Valerie's come to think of herself recently, a woman with the weight of her young son on her shoulders, a load that both grounds her and leaves her light as air and dancing. Leaning against the kitchen counter with her first cigarette for a long time, she studies this, their safe place, and imagines her mother visiting at last, hesitating at the door with potted-up purple crocuses from the supermarket in one hand, making up for lost time in the other in a what-might-have-been parallel future.

Valerie kicks the stepladder, which knocks the paint pot, which tips out a slow curl of a yellow tongue that licks last week's paper spread out on the carpet, and a thin black cat springs from its sleep up onto the coffee table, rippling the scum on a cold cup of tea and sending part of a half-finished jigsaw of Elvis crumbling over the edge onto the floor.

Some time later, the slam of the back door tells her Mikey is back. 'I'm home.'

Half in and half out of his anorak, the child first notices the smell of fresh paint and the proportion of the sitting room which has turned yellow while he's been at school, and only then registers the fact that his mother is crying. Dropping his reading folder, he joins her in picking up the pieces of the broken jigsaw.

'You all right, Mum?' he asks.

He doesn't want to repeat the question or hear the answer, so he says nothing more, kneels on the floor and presses the cardboard joints back into their sockets, the two of them together quietly reassembling the letters above Elvis's head – Promised Land. He hands her a glittery bit of the star's suit, she slots it into place.

'Come and sit here, you!' says Valerie, patting the sofa.

She budges up a bit, he sits cross-legged at the other end, picking at the hardened piece of glue on his school trousers which has not come out in the wash.

'What's happened?' he asks. 'Is it him?'

It is a physical pain in her chest, the knowledge that this is the first thing that occurs to him, only nine years old and looking over his shoulder. 'No, love, no, and it's never going to be. Where is he?'

'Australia.'

The day he looks at her when he says it, that will be the time when she knows he really believes it. 'Paul's gone and he's never coming back.' She pushes his hair out of his eyes. 'But I have got some news. You know your nanna from Bristol? She's passed on.'

'Where to?'

Valerie struggles to control the muscles in her face. 'I'm sorry, love. What I mean to say is your . . . A doctor from the hospital rang up. Your nanna's dead. I've lost her.'

Mikey has lost a lot of things, like his swimming trunks for instance, and he has managed to get by without telling anyone that all term, but he's never lost a person he loved, although for a long time it seemed to him his mother was hard to find. But now she's lost Nanna and won't ever get her back, he senses the depth of the sinkhole which has opened up in the half-grey half-yellow room and tiptoes as close to the edge as he dares.

'Sorry about Nanna,' he says, staring at the television where people are running screaming from the sea, dragging their children behind them, everything wobbling as if the world is built on a boat. He changes the channel to their favourite daytime game show where the jackpot stands at £2,500. This should cheer her up.

'Don't cry, Mum.' He hugs her. 'You've got me.'

'I've got you, all right,' she says. 'And Solomon.'

He'll be out soon, she reminds herself, then they'll be a family, nights in together with a takeaway and a box set, days out together with a picnic at a beach as golden as this sitting room. They will skim stones across the sea in summer and throw snowballs in winter and who can ask for more?

'And Jesus,' says Mikey.

'And Jesus, of course,' she says, 'Sol wouldn't want us to forget him.'

'What happens now?'

Valerie doesn't know. 'Now' seems to be an unnatural combination of blank days stretching on and on in which there is nothing to be done because nothing can be done, and a terrible urgency to arrange the things she imagines need to be arranged: clear out the fridge in her mum's house before things start to smell, feed her budgerigar, caged and peck-peck-pecking at the stripped millet, call the undertaker, order the flowers, but how she'll pay for it all she has no idea. Money is tight since she walked away, but it has been a small price to pay. There is one person who has money and then some. Her sister. Big sister. Half-sister. Diana.

Valerie blows her nose. 'You get on with your homework, I'm going to phone your aunty.'

'The rich bitch?'

'Don't you dare use language like that,' says Valerie. 'I should never have called her that.'

'You said you haven't spoken to her for years and years and years.'

'I haven't. I didn't stay in touch with her or your nanna. Paul didn't like it, did he? And Diana never called me.'

'And you said she wasn't a real aunty. You said she was only half an aunty.'

'She's family, Mikey, and family matters at a time like this.'

People often assumed that the final straw with Paul must have been him beating her or something violent like that, but they were wrong. It was the joke notice he bought from a gift shop and nailed to the kitchen wall: 'Never Forget, As Far as Everyone Else Is Concerned, We Are a Perfectly Normal Family.' Family, there is no one else left now who understood her childhood except Diana, no one to mourn with except Diana, and not just her mum, but mourn all of it, the graveyard that was their family life back then. She takes a deep breath. No reply. *Leave a message*. Silence taps its fingers with impatience until she abruptly rings off. Your mum passed away, you can't do that on voicemail.

'How did she get to be so rich?' Mikey asks later. He has brought his duvet and Penguin downstairs and put on *Titanic* because that might help. He likes the height of the waves and the sinking; she likes the kissing bits and cries at the ending, but, like most stories, this has a boring part at the beginning before it all goes wrong and that's where they are up to now.

'She married it, didn't she?' Valerie corrects herself. 'To be fair, that's not totally true. She walked out the house when she was sixteen and that was the last we saw of her, more or less, but I think she worked her own way up the ladder even before she met Sir Moneybags.'

Later, there is trouble on the deck, the first mate is looking out through his telescope. Valerie calls her sister again. It's getting late, but she hasn't got her mobile number. There's still no reply.

'Why did she leave?'

Shifting her position on the sofa, Valerie considers the question. 'Truth is, Mikey, I don't know. I never really understood.'

They are jumping now, the passengers, choosing to hurl themselves into the churning sea, rather than die behind locked doors.

'Anyway, maybe me and Diana can make up again.'

'Doubt it,' says Mikey. He reaches for his mother's hand under the duvet, even as fingernails are slipping from the edge of the lifeboats. Nobody comes. Even though they are shouting across the icy sea, help me, help me, nobody comes.

Chapter Two

Positioned by the Aga in the kitchen at Wynhope House, Diana is eating grapes when the landline rings the next morning. She is irritated because they were sold as seedless but she finds that she is having to spit pips into the sink before she can answer.

The conversation with Valerie propels Diana over to the long window where she stands rigidly, looking out at the magnolia flowers, plump and pink against the burned amber of the listed coach house on the far side of the lawns. With the phone to her ear, she knocks on the glass to scare the squirrel from the bird feeder and watches all the long-tailed tits take flight, then she sits awkwardly on the edge of one of the chairs. She says very little. She says, 'Well, thank you for letting me know anyway' and 'Who phoned you?' And then she says, 'And I suppose I'll have to pay for everything.'

The call is over. Diana shakes her head violently from side to side as if to dislodge something disturbing her vision, runs her hands slowly up over her closed eyes and through her hair and clasps them tightly together for a moment before breathing out, a controlled breath through pursed lips, the sort that kindles fire from embers. When she opens her eyes, the subtitles on the morning news are describing several hundred dead in a tsunami and the image shows yet another body being passed from rescue worker to rescue worker, hands above their heads, a crowd-surfing corpse.

My mother is dead.

In the wide wood-panelled hall, she pauses out of habit in front of a gilt-edged mirror. There is nothing wrong with her lipstick, nor with the lie of the jade necklace against her pale neck; it is not those things which made her hesitate, rather it is the bewildering combination of being more alive than she realised before, and yet older, and, yes, at forty-one statistically half way between death and birth. For a moment, time fractures and who is who in the mirror and when unsteadies her world and she almost starts to cry. In the doorway to the morning room, she hesitates. Despite its name, it is only in spring that the early sun streams through the large window as it does now, it is an alchemist, everything it touches turns to gold, the logs in the basket, the antique globe on the desk, even Edmund, his tanned arms, his auburn hair. The back of her husband's head is all she can see from here.

She clears her throat. 'That was Valerie!' she announces.

In the leather armchair, he is sprawled with one leg cocked over the arm like a gorgeous boy, but he is scrutinising the financial pages with the casual interest of an older man who can afford to lose a little. He barely raises his eyes. 'Oh God! Valerie! Your sister? What does she want? A blank cheque?'

As if to catch her as she passes his chair, he reaches out his arm, but she slips away and stands with her back to him at the round mahogany table in the bay window, rearranging the yellow tulips.

'My half-sister called to let me know that my mother has died.' Diana sidesteps his awkward hug. 'And for Christ's sake, Edmund, don't treat me like the grief-stricken daughter. When did I last see her? Years ago. It's a bit of shock, that's all, Valerie ringing up out of the blue like that.'

The flowers are thirsty. She picks up the vase, but then has to sit down quite suddenly on the sofa and the tulips tip to the floor, a dribble of stale water trickling along the embroidered pathways of the Turkish rug. As Edmund replaces the tulips they feel curiously false, as if it would be hard to tell plastic from the real thing. 'You sit there,' he says. 'Monty will look after you, won't you, old boy? I'll fetch us a drink.'

A black Labrador gets to his feet and rests his heavy head on Diana's knees. Her hand reaches out to stroke him, offering him soft repeated condolences which she cannot accept herself. She can hear her husband collecting a bottle from the sideboard in the dining room.

'Damson gin. Best medicine!'

The sleeves of his shirt are rolled up to the elbow and usually she likes him like this, the holiday tan against the city white cotton, but today it all feels faintly absurd, the pseudo workmanlike uniform, and when the hairs on his arms brush across her, she thinks she is noticing too much. Diana drinks urgently; Edmund sips. They do not speak. She holds out her glass, he takes it from her, leaves it empty on the tray, and speaks before she can ask.

'She wasn't ill, was she? If we'd known . . .'

'If we'd known, what?' She cuts him off. 'We would have driven down to Highbridge every weekend to take Lucozade and hoover the stairs? Anyway, it was a heart attack.'

He doesn't touch her, his fingers close in on themselves and he occupies them, playing with the empty glass. 'How is Valerie?'

'Sobbing and hysterical. Probably pissed.'

'Perhaps she's sad.'

Getting to her feet, Diana collects the glasses, uses a tissue to dab at a spot of spilt gin. 'Of course, I'll have to pay for the funeral since we're so stinking rich and she's still, what did she say, getting things together after leaving that man who beat her up. What was his name? Peter, Paul?' She replays the conversation. 'To be fair, she didn't actually say stinking.'

Following her example, Edmund sets things in order in the morning room, checks the date before folding the paper.

'Ash Wednesday,' he notes, poking the log back into the grate, regretting the fact that they hadn't had pancakes; his mother could toss pancakes so high they stuck to the ceiling.

'What's that?' Diana has already left the room.

'Nothing.' He follows her into the kitchen. 'When do you think the funeral will be?'

'Don't worry, I don't expect you to come. Now don't just stand there fiddling with your car keys, you go on to London. I'm fine.' She waves her fingers at him. 'Off you go and play with your money.'

It always rankles when she says that, but he never retaliates. After all, she's probably right. His investments are well looked after by the grown-ups he has employed to manage his businesses, his appearances at the office not much better than a child wanting to help wash the car, and probably equally as unhelpful. Nevertheless, after kissing the dog goodbye, Edmund leaves the house and says good morning to the bronze statue of the boy in the middle of the lily pond as he does most mornings, then he crosses the lawn and heads towards the garages. The builders have finished work on the tower, and the ridiculous underground swimming pool is dug if not watered. He is pleased that the quiet morning is finally all his, undisturbed by the clatter and clang of the scaffolding and the army of strong men singing along to the radio. Usually in March, daffodils and white blackthorn against winter trees would connect him to the present, but today is all about the past. Death follows each footprint left in the wet grass. Forty-one years ago in October, he was ten. Rain and a headmaster's study and the mute video of the Firsts playing rugby in the mud and the slanting rain beyond the window, and there was a great-aunt he barely knew confirming his mother was dead. Then five years after that, playing tennis with himself against this very stable wall and counting each hit, seventy-four, seventy-five, seventy-six, he might have even got to a hundred had it not been for the crack of a shot, that second literally split. Like the atom, he thinks, a decision was taken and then the one irreversible moment when destruction was loosed upon the world and nothing could ever be the same again. Everyone had been just a little embarrassed at the service, as if, rather than committing suicide, his father had dropped a bit of a clanger. He has never attended a funeral since.

When he reaches the stone bridge towards the end of the half-mile drive which leads from Wynhope House to the road, Edmund stops the car and, disregarding the red mud on his city shoes, slides down to the river. It has rained heavily overnight and the stream is sullen. Cupping his hands in the coloured water, he baptises himself all over again, allowing the cold flood of mourning to pour over him; it still does this, bursts the banks even after all these years.

In the time between leaving his estate behind him and arriving at his office in London, the first-class carriage transports him through a no man's land of suburbs and sprawling new housing, neither countryside nor city, neither the weight and warmth of his encompassing history nor the ice-shining gleam of his future returns. Something grey and in the middle where everyone else lives, but he doesn't seem to belong. In the office, he stares out over the Legoland structures around him and thinks that nothing is for ever; he watches a barge moving slowing down the Thames beneath him and thinks perhaps some things are. Mounted on the wall, the small television is permanently tuned to *News 24*, not so much for the disasters tumbling and flooding and exploding and terrorising the world in the background, but for the market summary which streams along the bottom of the screen and for the red and green graphs in the corner like a life-support machine, showing which way the world is heading.

Twenty-four hours gone, and Mikey writes about his dead granny in his English book as part of a 'telling stories in the first person' exercise. His teacher asks him if it is a true story, then says she is sorry, he must be very sad, which he isn't but doesn't like to say so. Valerie posts it online and watches the sympathy scroll in, a black tide arriving in waves over the screen. Over lunch, Edmund tells his accountant; he hasn't planned to, but the news has filled him up with thoughts of dying and they spill over the edge and soak into the conversation about profit and loss. And Diana stands alone at the front door at Wynhope. She is not wearing quite enough given how cold it is for March and the bronze boy is a poor substitute for a listening ear.

Chapter Three

In the following week, between buying some new red slingback sandals for their week in the Maldives and preparing for a dinner party, the ridiculous, overwhelming sense of loss Diana experiences at unexpected moments bewilders her, swamping her without warning in a deluge of sadness, although she cannot name what she has lost, nor does she really have anyone to share her loss with. In the glasshouse, for instance, cutting lilies for the hall table, yellow pollen falls on her cream mohair jumper and she realises that moment will be stained for ever by the death of her mother. Having walked away from home long ago, she never expected this death to matter so much. It is some days later that the idea comes to her that she can invite her half-sister to stay after the funeral; the boy can come too if necessary. She shares the idea with her one and only confidante. Sally is something of a saviour; in her sixties, two facelifts down and loaded up with money from her last divorce when she took the chief executive of an oil company to the cleaners, her friend is a breath of fresh air, at least that's how Edmund describes her.

At the kitchen table, the two of them flick through magazines and make small talk until Diana decides it's late enough, opens a bottle of wine and shares her idea.

'So that's the plan. Reconciliation. What do you think? Good idea?'

'Well, since you haven't told me what it is you need to reconcile, it's a bit hard to say. But, as my lovely niece would say, what's not to like?' says Sally. She points at the picture of the Red Sea on the front of the Sunday Supplement Travel Magazine. 'If it goes well, you can pop along and help out the Israelis and the Palestinians.'

'Reconciliation's probably the wrong word,' Diana says. 'Apology, that's maybe what I mean.'

Pulling out the chair next to her, Sally pats the seat. 'Ah, so the truth will out. Come, sit, what sin did you commit, sister?'

'Well, let's say a sin of omission.'

'How fascinating. I've often wondered when we get to the pearly gates how they'll weigh up the bad things we've done and the good things we've failed to do. Which is worse, do you think?'

'Seriously, I want to apologise because, when I walked out at sixteen, I knew what I was leaving her to. Perhaps I should have stayed and looked after her.' The drizzle that falls against the window is soundless and smears the glass, the world outside as smudged and speechless as the past.

'And look where you've ended up. I still suffer from kitchen envy every time I come here.' Sally indicates the sheer beauty and technical perfection of the room in which they are sitting. 'Well done you, you're the one that got away.' Emptying her glass, Sally finds her umbrella. 'The only thing I'd say is that it can be very difficult making up. You get psyched up, throw yourself at their feet and then it all backfires. Believe me, I tried it several times with the ex. I'd say go for it, but it's not a one-night stand, darling, it might takes months, years. And with those words of wisdom' – Sally kisses Diana once on each cheek – 'your priestess needs to hit the road and pray that God in the form of a policeman with a breathalyser isn't waiting at the end of your fabulous drive.'

The next morning, Edmund wonders if Diana has changed her mind, now she's had a chance to sleep on it. God knows he hopes so.

'Valerie's all I've got left,' says Diana, swilling the Alka-Seltzer round the glass, watching the tiny white crystals cling to the edge, the vortex of water in the middle. 'She's the only one who can . . .'

Edmund spoons the dog's meat from the tin into the bowl. 'Who can what?' It never fails to make him feel very happy, watching the dog eating his breakfast.

'Oh, I don't know. Clean slate, that sort of thing. Things that can be said, once and for all.'

Like Monty whining at the door, Edmund wants to get out. Although he and Diana have travelled widely in their three short years of marriage, the past is a country neither of them is particularly comfortable in visiting, the passports to those places hidden deep in drawers that are overfull and difficult to open. Hovering at the back door, he calls his questions through to her: 'What sort of things?'

'It's a very long time ago and you don't want to hear all that.'

He hugs her. 'Silly billy,' he says, 'And here's Monty.' He ruffles the dog's ears. 'He doesn't want you to be sad either, do you, Monty?'

The next day, Diana makes the call, almost as if Valerie is there beside her, sisters in their stockinged feet supporting each other through their memories, and she will say I am sorry and Valerie will say none of it was your fault, it was all his, I believe you. No reply. She has to leave a message because phones are not allowed in prison and Valerie is visiting Solomon.

Chapter Four

On the way from the station to the prison, Valerie sits as she always does, if she can, on the top floor at the front of the bus. The next stop is the shopping centre where the road goes under the walkway from the multi-storey to the supermarket, all the people in the air above her crossing from one side to the other. It seems unreal that your mother should be dead while you're on the number 52. Through the glass windows of the first floor of the department stores, figures are swimming between racks of clothes like goldfish. She bought her mum a cardigan from there last Christmas, but in the years Paul kept them apart her mother put on weight and it didn't fit. Finally, the bus picks up speed, out through the town, the drives of the houses getting longer the further out you go. Take Diana. She has the longest drive of all. Valerie smiles to herself. Solomon would say you shouldn't judge people by the length of their drive.

At HMP Brackington, the ladies' room is packed. Relatively speaking, she is a new girl at all this but she'll never become an old hand; Solomon is over half way through already. She puts her pound coin in the locker and is about to close the door when her phone beeps.

'Can you and Michael come to stay at Wynhope the night after the funeral? Hope so. We can catch up again after all this time. Di.'

Of all the things she is expecting, this is the least likely, but her number is up on the board and she barely has time to process the invitation before she has to start the long, humiliating security process which divides her from Solomon. Through one door. Locked behind you. Feet astride on yellow footprints on the floor, like someone has stood in a great big pot of her Spring Sunshine. Arms outstretched. Sniffer dogs. Another door. Locked behind you. The only time Mikey came with her he said it was a bit like his computer game Lockdown, all about getting to the next level; she should never have brought him, even on a family day. It makes her angry that he should even have to think about prison at his age, that Paul should be free as a bird and Solomon locked up. Anyone who knows what a peaceful man he is would realise that he'd never assault a police officer on a protest march unless the police officer assaulted him first, but who was going to listen to his side of the story? And what about people like Diana's husband, sitting around sucking his silver spoon and never worshipping anything other than money, never campaigning for anything other than himself? Bet he's not squeaky clean, but they wouldn't send him down, would they? She wonders what he is really like, this Edmund. If she says yes to the invitation, she will know soon enough.

When Solomon hears the news about her mum, he cries, even though he's only met her the once, and Valerie ends up comforting him across the gap between the bolted-down chairs. It is seven years since he's seen his own mother.

'My long-lost sister Diana's invited us to stay the night after the funeral,' says Valerie. 'I just got a text.'

'In her stately home? Well, that's a yes from me. I'll apply for a pass right away.'

'Oh, stop it, Sol.' Valerie manages to laugh. 'Why's she done it, do you think?'

'After everything you've told me about your family, sounds like an olive branch.'

'I don't know. Even if it is, she'll want to be raking over the past.'

Around him, row upon row of visitors and prisoners bend towards each other at the blue plastic tables like chess players. The past and poorly thought-out moves are what have got most of them here in the first place, one way or another.

'What is the worst that can happen?' he asks.

They pull their hands apart, clasp them together again under the table. She can feel him turning the ring on her finger. He should be out in three months, the church is keeping his job open for him, the flat will be finished. This is what hope feels like, she thinks, and tells him what she'd seen on television, how it reminded her of Mikey sitting on his shoulders in the park last summer.

'You know I'd do anything for him,' says Solomon. 'If anything ever happened to you, I'd be there for him.'

That evening, hands behind his head, lying on his bed in his cell after lockdown, Solomon's thoughts are a flickering screen obscuring the prayerfulness he sought. He wants her now, not just for the sex, although he wants that too, but he wants her so he can be someone for someone again, a gentleman for Val, a proper father for Mikey. In the photo he keeps, Mikey is running after a football, the little boy's face screwed up with determination. He scored, but it was as if the kid didn't know how to celebrate. Out in the fresh air, he didn't look as geeky as usual, just frizzy hair and stumpy legs and nine years' worth of wariness.

Turning to his Text for the Day, Solomon tries to focus: 'They that visited us required of us mirth, saying Sing us one of the songs of Zion.'

So Solomon begins to sing quietly to himself. 'Were you there when they crucified my Lord?'

No, comes the reply from the bottom bunk.

'Were you there when the stone was rolled away?' Solomon laughs, but he has the good grace to sing silently, only to himself.

On the bus going home, Valerie texts back: 'Thx Di, Mikey and I would love to stay the night. X Val.'

Chapter Five

On the morning of the funeral Mikey wakes up with the day lying awkward beside him. He hates the idea that school will go on without him, the lining up, the working out, and, even worse, he already hates two days' time when everyone will look at him and wonder where he's been, or everyone won't look at him, like it hasn't mattered that he hasn't been there. His mother says staying at his aunty's is an opportunity to put things right. What things, he doesn't know. What he does know is that stuff doesn't often get put right, not overnight.

Downstairs, the cat is waiting to go out. Having found a packet of crisps in the cupboard and the remote down the back of the sofa, he flicks through the channels: a quiz show, a chat show, a stupid cartoon for little kids, a cooking show, a shopping show. Finally, he finds a nature show all filmed underwater where the fish bulge at the camera, silenced thousands of feet below the surface of the sea. Even the voice of the man explaining the fish sounds as though it belongs in a different world, and Mikey finds himself on the side of the fish. The cat comes back, he finds three more jigsaw pieces of Elvis's boots, eats another packet of crisps and hides the empty packets, and then it is the nine o'clock news. He watches long enough to see more pictures of buildings being swallowed up by the sea because that is interesting, how an earthquake can make waves which grow bigger and bigger, and he wonders how far things can tip without actually spilling over and whether if the world tilts as it goes round and round and Australia is upside down, why don't they all fall off the edge? He leaves it all behind and goes upstairs.

'Mum? We're going to be late for the funeral.'

'Put the kettle on, Mikey,' she calls from the shower.

He brings her mug of tea to the bedroom and sees her straightening her hair which isn't that colour really and getting a brand-new black dress out of the cupboard and snaking it down over her bra and pants like it is a second skin. So that's what you wear to funerals, he thinks, sort of the same as what you wear to go clubbing only a bit longer. She has got him a new jacket with a free footballing tie. He doesn't even like football.

The cemetery building looks like a church, a library and a swimming pool all rolled into one. Mikey feels nervous; in the gents' there is a large man in black at the other end of the urinals, crying and pissing at the same time. They're early, but there are already so many cars the parking is full and there is a sign directing people to an overflow.

'Have they all come for Nanna?'

'Don't be daft, they're for the one before, every twenty-five minutes,' she explains. 'There's thousands buried here.'

Thousands? Thousands dead in the tsunami, that's what it says on the news, but that's in another country, not here. Under every one of those stones, a body? When the rabbit Paul got him died, Paul said if he was a normal boy he would cry, but it was an ugly rabbit and he'd never wanted it anyway. Stiff with its eyes open and its head at a funny angle, and how in the nightmares he never tells anyone about, the rabbit turns into his mum. Other dead things, not including the enemy on Lockdown who don't count: a mouse in a trap; a black-and-white cat, perfect by the side of the road except for a thin line of bright red blood running from its whiskers to the dull leaves in the gutter; and something else, a bird in their old house thudding against the French windows, falling onto the carpet, still alive when he stretched out its wings, still twitching when he pulled its legs. He doesn't know why he did that, doesn't want to think about it now.

'There's Diana'

Between the pink cherry trees, between the cars parked like toys on either side of the road, a black hearse is rolling towards him. It stops, the coffin is sliding out on a tray and propped up beside it like a doll is a tall woman, also in black, with dark glasses which make her look like a spy.

The sound is turned down, the murmuring around him of the little gangs of grown-ups when they don't want you to hear, the sudden and unexpected fluttering of a flock of fat pigeons, traffic droning beyond the cemetery walls, and their spiky heels grating on the gravel as they scratch towards each other.

'Valerie, you haven't changed a bit.'

'Nor have you, Di.'

It's her then. That makes sense. She doesn't look like she's part of their family, but she does look rich. Stupid kissing, kiss, kiss. Not him, no way.

'Lovely flowers, Di!' says his mum.

The white lilies sprout from the coffin like a tropical jungle.

'I'd love them to have been Wynhope lilies,' says his aunt, 'but I'm afraid Edmund insists on keeping them for our private chapel, so I had to place a special order in London.'

She sounds rich too.

'And you must be Michael.'

'Say hello to your aunty, Mikey.'

Paul used to say his mum sounded common, but Mikey thinks she sounds just fine. He kicks the stones and studies the grit and the dirt that lies beneath the pale pebbles.

'Mikey!'

The boy and his aunt face each other. Behind them there is movement, the silent movie of the undertakers manoeuvring into position, the bare branches of the beech trees shifting in the wind and tissues falling like snow, soundlessly from sleeves onto soft grass, but the boy and the aunt are frozen.

'Well, go on then, Mikey.'

But having not said hello, now he can't find hello. Hello has gone and left nothing in its place. He takes a very deep breath as if to find hello, but his new for-the-funeral jacket is very tight and the new for-the-funeral tie is pressing on his throat and they won't let hello back up again from wherever it's hiding.

'Hello, Michael!' says Diana.

So, she had the word all the time.

Inside, there is space and light and whiteness and windows, and at the same time it is all mixed up with blackness and rumbling music and the coffin on a stand with the lid nailed shut. No one would hear you, even if you screamed. It strikes him as odd that although a lot of people die in Lockdown, you never see them buried. He can put that right if he becomes a person who makes computer games and he is wondering about that when suddenly, without warning, the coffin disappears. It is extraordinary, like magic, black magic, because there is a lot of black. His mum is right, all the people come in the front door and leave out the side except the dead person, who slides through the curtains and that's that.

Chapter Six

Lunch is in a bankrupt country house where they'd made a business out of dying, plastering fire exit signs on the wood panelling and selling egg-and-cress sandwiches to mourners. It is every bit as ghastly as Diana has predicted; she is so relieved Edmund has not been forced to mingle with the half remembered remnants of her suburban past, it is bad enough for her. The old women cluster around the child as if mere proximity to youth can provide an antidote to the funeral, and of course it is all about Valerie, poor Valerie, hugs and kisses and condolences for Valerie; most of them barely remember that there was another daughter called Diana, or if they do, it's for all the wrong reasons.

It strikes Valerie that probably both she and Diana are out of place here, for different reasons. If anything, Diana looks more lost, giving orders to the girls in black uniforms serving the tea rather than listening to the old folk with tears behind glasses and memories clasped in handbags. Valerie does try, she says things like, have you caught up with my sister Diana, she's over there; oh yes, Diana, they say, I'll see if I can catch her later. When it is all over, waiting for her sister in the empty hall, sprigs of green cress on the parquet floor and coffee spilled in saucers, Valerie realises it isn't just her family that Diana turned her back on all those years ago, it was her younger self. As Mikey slips his hand in hers, she knows it isn't such an easy thing to do, to step away from your childhood.

The automatic child locks on Diana's 4x4 snap shut. Behind her, Mikey is asleep on the back seat. Valerie is also exhausted, she closes her eyes and allows the bland music on the radio and the hypnotic beat of the windscreen wipers to iron out her crumpled grief.

'Wake up, they're playing our song.' Diana is singing along to something. Valerie doesn't recognise it, but she doesn't say so. When the song is finished, Diana apologises that Edmund is not going to be at Wynhope when they get there. He has to be in London, apparently.

That is a strange decision, not to go to your mother-in-law's funeral, even if you didn't invite her to your wedding, but blearily Valerie concludes it probably wasn't the right sort of funeral, not his sort of people.

'He worshipped his mother, but she died of cancer when he was ten and then his father was so depressed afterwards that he shot himself when Edmund was a teenager.'

The Google search Valerie did on her phone the night before brought up images of a country house, a good-looking tanned man with an oversized cheque for charity in his hands and a smile for the camera on his face and several old newspaper articles about a death at Wynhope House which she didn't bother to read.

Diana explains. 'He doesn't really do funerals any longer, and who can blame him?'

Do not judge and you will not be judged, that's what Solomon would be saying; he's fond of that verse even though he's the most unjustly judged of all.

Diana is moving the conversation on: who was at the funeral, faces half remembered, names forgotten. 'How much had you seen of her?' Indicating left, Diana pulls off the slip road and keeps her eyes fixed in front of her. 'Mum, I mean.'

Arrows on road signs propel them through complicated junctions, traffic lights slow them, stop them, send them on their way, time runs away behind them leaving only tyre tracks on damp roads.

'Not enough. It's difficult to explain. Paul, he was a very controlling man, he cut me off, from her, and from you, I suppose.' Crying does not seem acceptable in the Range Rover. 'To be honest, I don't think she forgave herself for not spotting what was wrong and coming after me. I wanted to tell her I didn't blame her, but now of course . . .'

The right turn is badly judged, the oncoming car honks and Diana swears. 'I don't remember her coming after me either. Or did I miss her running down the road, pleading with me to come home?'

'I think she tried, but Dad wouldn't let her.'

'Did she ever talk about me?'

The roads are smaller now, the twists and turns wake Mikey up, and Valerie whispers over her shoulder that they are nearly there. She hopes he's not going to throw up.

'Well?'

The silence stretches before them the length of the dark lane which is overhung with trees still black from winter and tall hedges rusted brown with last year's leaves leaning in on them.

'Thought not,' says Diana.

She was never as quick off the mark as her sister, couldn't just come up with the right words at the right time. Once, when she was very young, Diana told her she had to pay her for every word she ever used because Diana was the one who owned a dictionary. This isn't an easy day for thinking or speaking, but it is too late now because Diana is saying here we are and ahead of them elaborate wrought-iron gates are swinging open to Wynhope House.

Swivelling round, Mikey watches the gates close behind him. He remembers he needs to ask about the coffin and the curtains, but probably not now.

'Where's the house, Mum?' All he can see is grass, trees, sheep, birds, sky and an endless narrow road between painted railings.

'Here!' says Diana. 'We've arrived.'

In front of the child, the house is enormous. One, two, three long windows; a dark green front door with a porch on pillars; one, two, three long windows on the other side; upstairs, almost the same; and then another layer of smaller windows on top of that with their own little roofs. Pointing at the top floor, his mum winks and whispers to him that those are the rooms where they lock up the servants; in a louder voice she tells his aunt that the place is amazing, beautiful, she's never seen anything like it.

There aren't any words Mikey can really think of to describe it, so he doesn't say anything. To him, the whole house looks like when you cut things out of paper and unfold it, both sides of the snowflake the same. Except. Except over on one side is a tower, just like a tower in a book with pointy bits and church windows and stone faces. It doesn't match. It is as if a king thought about building a castle and then got bored and stuck a house on the end, or the other way round, someone built an enormous house and someone else has come along and spoiled it with the tower. He isn't sure which. He likes the way the tower stands up for itself, as if it knows it doesn't belong and doesn't care, but he is also unsettled by the way the tower clings to the main house like an unwanted child, an embarrassment. Someone Paul would call a mistake. He hopes he isn't going to have to sleep in the mistake.

'But if I'm honest,' his mum is saying, 'that tower is really ugly.'

Diana winks at Mikey, although he has no idea why. 'Just you wait until you see the inside.' She opens the front door. 'Hello?' she calls.

Who is she expecting to answer? His uncle Edmund's away and she doesn't have any children. His mum told him that Diana didn't want any because she didn't like them and that Edmund had the snip. What, cut it right off? he'd asked and Valerie laughed, snip-snip-snipping towards his flies with her fingers. He thinks that bit is made up, but having met Diana, he thinks the other bit about her might be true.

'I'm in the kitchen, Lady Diana! I'll be right with you.'

The hall where they are standing has a staircase wide enough for six people and here, next to him, is a huge mirror with a gold frame reflecting back the pictures of the old men with beards and black jackets climbing the stairs. They are all dressed for a funeral, as well. In fact, everything is like a funeral, from the vase of flowers which smell like the cemetery to the polished floor which is black and white. He slips off his trainers, placing them precisely by the door, ready to make his getaway.

'Well, now there's a well-brought-up young man.' A woman appears from a door on his left; she strikes Mikey as much more normal than Diana, with her flowery shirt over huge boobies and dangling earrings made to look like daisies.

'This is Mrs H and she is a darling,' Diana says, 'and if it wasn't for her, I don't know what we'd do! She is our very own national treasure.'

So, his aunt owns people as well as things.

'Call me Grace,' says the lady. 'If you like, I can take this young man to the kitchen for a little something and get you both a cup of tea?'

Little something, yes, cup of tea, no. Apparently Diana and his mum need a drink. That is something else he could say, if anyone would listen, that it probably isn't a very good idea to let his mum start drinking, it doesn't go well with her medicine.

'That's the drawing room, where they've gone,' says Grace.

There's no sign of any art going on in there, but there are other things that interest Mikey: gold curtains, for instance; a piano, he'd like to play now that Solomon has taught him 'Amazing Grace' all the way through, hands together; a real fireplace with proper smoke and what Scouts might smell like if he is ever allowed to go.

Grace continues the guided tour. 'And this we call the morning room,' she explains.

The whole day has been about mourning. Even the picture above the fireplace shows a man with a pony struggling up a purple mountain bent double by the weight of a dead stag.

'What a heavy thing to have to carry on your back,' he says to Grace.

28

The sitting room is a bit more friendly. It has a huge telly for a start and the kitchen is familiar, at least from adverts, so he's happy to sit there and eat toast. The smaller telly in there is showing a zoo where all the animals have escaped because of the flood and they're running wild through a town and it's something to do with the waves he'd watched only this morning in his own house, but that was then and there and this is here and now. Wynhope. He can't wait to get back home. Butter? Nod. Jam? Nod. Strawberry or raspberry? Shrug. Expect you've had a difficult day. Nod.

'Monty wants your crusts,' says Grace.

'Hello, Monty,' says Mikey, tentatively feeling the dog's ears, and he feels sad that he left his penguin at home.

Everything Grace says confirms his initial impression that she knows what she is talking about. He wants the toilet and to get out of his horrible jacket and no sooner does he think that than she says I expect you want to know where the bathroom is, and if I'm not wrong, I expect you want to get out of that jacket.

'That's the thing about funerals,' she says as she takes him down a passage with too many raincoats and giant fish gasping behind glass frames. 'Everyone's always so uncomfortable. I expect even Lady Diana's kicked off those high heels.'

Right again. Back in the drawing room, his mum and his aunt are standing with glasses in their hands and no shoes on their feet, staring into the fire. Mikey brings a china statue of a racehorse and jockey from a little table in the sitting room to show to his mum. He's been imagining the speed of it, the thrill, crouched low like that on the back of a horse and all dressed in red and green and galloping away, away. Paul used to bet on the horses and sometimes he won but mostly he didn't.

'Don't drop that,' says his aunt. 'Your uncle would be very upset.'

'No, he wouldn't, don't you listen to that,' says Grace.

'Ah, Mrs H! Did you make supper for seven?'

'Just like you asked,' replies the housekeeper.

'We'd rather eat at eight if that doesn't put you out.'

His aunt is doing that thing when you can smile and stare at the same time, rubbing your stomach and patting your head. Grace is going round the big room straightening the curtains; it's a fuck-off sort of tidying up.

'If that's what you want,' she says, with her back to Diana.

'You are wonderful,' says his aunt, 'thank you.'

That is something else teachers do. Put your gum in the bin, Michael, thank you; it's their way of saying you have no choice.

As Mrs H flounces out of the room, Diana is thinking two things: one is that Mrs H is a bitch and she will get the better of the woman if it kills her; the second is why on earth has she suggested eating later, it will just spin everything out. It isn't like her to change her mind on impulse, but with the heightened perception that is brought on by wine and funerals, Diana is brimming over with the yearning that is both grief and hope. Outside, the failing light is transforming the gardens into something quite insubstantial, as though she might reach through the dusk and touch something forgotten.

'I put it all back a bit because we've just about got time for a look around,' explains Diana. 'It's such a beautiful evening.'

It is colder than they expected. Valerie borrows Diana's jacket, and they laugh at the fact that they are both size five when it comes to boots and how daft they look with them in their funeral dresses. Once outside, they stand on the drive and look back at the house. Diana apologises for what she describes as 'the mess' to the side of the tower. The terrace looks immaculate to Valerie, who wonders if she is meant to contradict her sister and say no, no, not a mess at all, it looks simply lovely, but you never knew with Diana quite what she understood or what she meant or what she wanted.

'Obviously we're going to plant up the whole area, but the builders only finished recently and now there's some delay about getting the tiles from Italy.' Her guests are clearly confused. 'Sorry! I should have explained. It's the most wonderful project. Edmund knows how much I love swimming, I always loved it, didn't I, Val? I was quite good at school,' she tells the boy. 'Anyway, he said he'd build me a pool, but neither of us wanted to ruin the park with some ghastly shed, and since we were going to restore the tower, we, or rather I, had the brainwave of excavating under the tower and putting one there. Everyone's doing it in London, why not here?'

'I thought you said you belonged to a health club,' says Valerie.

'I do, and it's fine, very cliquey, but fine. Anyway, it's so much nicer swimming alone.'

She's lonely, thinks Valerie, Diana never did find it easy to keep friends.

'A swimming pool?' Mikey is asking. 'Under there?'

He doesn't know why Diana is laughing at him and her reply doesn't make sense either.

'We couldn't go under the main house because that's Grade Two listed, so we extended it out from the tower under the garden.' She performs a little tap dance on the brand-new flagstones. 'It's here, invisible, but right under my feet.'

Staring at the ground, Mikey tries to imagine a whole blue swimming pool deep beneath them, dark and unbroken. The pools he has been to smell of cleaners and echo with shouts and screams and the sharp whistle of the lifeguard, but this buried pool must be a very quiet place.

'Can we go swimming?' he asks his mum.

Valerie shrugs. 'Don't ask me, this is way out of my league.'

Diana beckons him over. 'It's not ready, there's no water. Look, you can see.'

Squatting down, Mikey presses his face against a glass panel which is a sort of skylight into the earth.

'When it's finished, then you must come and swim, won't that be fun?'

Although his mum is agreeing, Mikey thinks it would be scary, lying on your back in the water with the weight of the whole heavy world inches from your face and nothing to hold it up and, besides, he'd have to own up that he's lost his trunks. His mum is walking away, making some comment about how much it must all have cost and Diana is saying an arm and a leg. He can tell by the way his mum is changing the subject that she doesn't think it's worth that.

'Come on, Mikey,' she's calling. 'Take a picture of us. Use my phone.'

Lining them up in front of the round lily pond, Mikey clicks, checks the screen and shows his mother.

'You'd never know we were sisters, just looking at us,' says Valerie.

'Half-sisters,' Diana reminds her. 'You've got your father's eyes.'

Giggling, Michael points at the screen. 'It looks like the statue behind is about to hit Diana on the head,' he says.

Leaning over the boy's shoulder as she looks, Diana realises his smile reminds her of Valerie when she was young. Maybe it would be nice to have a relationship with her nephew, now that her mother is dead and she herself has no children. There are no moorings on either side of the river and she is adrift in the present. A little awkwardly, she squeezes his thin shoulders. 'I hope he isn't going to clout me.' She laughs. 'That bronze boy will grow up to be Hercules, the strongest man in the world.'

'I know about him from school,' starts Mikey, but his aunt isn't listening, she's telling her own story. She probably thinks he's stupid, but she's wrong, he knows lots of things, he just doesn't always say them.

Perhaps she can buy the boy a child's book of Greek myths for his birthday? Tea at Wynhope, cake with candles on the kitchen table, Edmund singing, Michael unwrapping the gift.

'Zeus's wife was so angry at the news of the birth of Hercules, she sent snakes to the baby's cradle to kill him,' Diana explains, 'but the baby Hercules was so strong he rose up and killed them. That's the snakes you can see in the boy's hands.'

'Bit like how you felt when I was born, I expect,' jokes Valerie, then immediately regrets it.

'All gone,' says Mikey, swirling his hands in the still water of the ornamental pool.

Their reflections are erased by the ripples shimmering in the last of the light, but the awkwardness is not.

The quiet moment offers an opportunity which Diana takes. 'I'm sorry I got all prickly in the car, it's not easy thinking back. Obviously there was just Mum and me for a while, after Dad died, and we were happy. Do you know, I don't remember Dad dying? I think I remember the police knocking, telling Mum someone had run into him on the hard shoulder while he was attending a breakdown, but it's a false memory. I only know it because I was told it. I wasn't allowed at the funeral. All I really remember feeling was that I was happy, there was Mum and me and I was happy. Then it was like your father and then you gatecrashed my party and trashed the house, at least that's how it felt.'

Then she's off, striding slightly too fast, leading them past the tennis court, telling Michael that his uncle hasn't really enjoyed tennis for a long time, but she's sure he'd love to bowl a few overs with him, and he'll be back the next day in time for lunch. She turns to Valerie and asks if she likes the white narcissi.

'We'd love a garden, wouldn't we, Mikey?' says Valerie.

'As I said, you must come and stay, especially when the weather's lovely. Edmund would love someone to play with and I could do with some company.'

Hope comes and goes in their conversation like a song or a siren heard from a distance, in the wind. Arm in arm, they walk on in the company of questions unasked, rounding the corner into the arboretum, expressing delight at the things that are easy to love like spring flowers and pink sunsets. Mikey sticks close. These trees are nothing like the park, no kids playing their music on the ramp, no benches, no bins where you can shovel the dog shit. He pulls on the catkins hanging from the hazel branches and the two women watch him.

'Why didn't you want kids, Di?'

'Usual thing to start with, I was more interested in my career than baby puke. I had nothing, remember that, I was sixteen, starting

33

from ground zero. It took one hundred per cent of me, making it, moving up, photocopying girl, receptionist, letting agent, estate agent, property portfolio manager – that's when Edmund employed me. That's when we met. And I did make it, Valerie, all this didn't just fall in my lap, you know.' Diana pauses as she takes in the extent of her very own country house. Other people might think she married it, but in her own way she knows she earned it. Suddenly she remembers who she is with and why. 'What were we talking about?'

'Kids,' says Valerie.

'Oh yes, kids.' Diana pulls her coat closer around her. 'So I didn't have time for relationships. There were men, typical men, just not worth it. Certainly, I never met anyone I wanted to have children with. Then there's our childhood. I thought if I can't even remember being happy as a child, then how can I ever imagine having happy children?'

'Mikey looks okay, doesn't he?' says Valerie. 'Things don't have to repeat themselves, Di.' After years of feeling more ignorant than her sister, Valerie now believes it is possible that she understands more than her; not Greek myths or Latin words for clumps of trees, but things that matter like love at all costs and never giving up.

'Then when I met Edmund and things got serious, we obviously talked about it – vasectomy reversal, sperm donation, adoption – but do you know what?'

'No, tell me.'

'We realised we didn't want children – as a positive choice, I mean. There's only ever been one moment when I felt a sort of flutter of what might have been, but other than that, we're happy as we are. Edmund's everything to me.' Realising the truth of what she says, Diana grins. 'Call me greedy, but I'd hate to share him with anyone other than the dog, that's hard enough, isn't it, Monty?' She claps her hands and shoos the dog off into the shrubbery. 'Go on, hunt somewhere else, you jealous old thing, you.'

Sisterly talk, thinks Valerie, sitting as sisters should sit, and Mikey running in from the wood to join them, beautiful, standing in the centre of the orchard spinning time on a broken sundial. On the old wrought-iron bench, Valerie turns ripe words over in her hands. One thing she has learned in life is that there are things better said than left unsaid and this moment will not come again.

'Look, I don't know what you want to happen today, what you want to talk about. All I can say is I know it must have been hard for you, your dad dead, me the favourite, and yes, my dad was a bastard at times, I recognise it now of course, the way he put Mum down, the way he bullied you, but . . .'

'Bullied?'

'Well, yes, bullied.'

'Is that the word you'd use for it, is it? Bullied?'

Pulling a branch down from the apple tree above them, Diana examines the buds, little lips, tightly sealed. Dull word, bullied, like sullied. Not the right word at all.

This bench is wide enough for three and there is space in between them. Their eyes fix on the rows of skeleton trees joining hands in the dim light. The boy hits the sundial with his stick over and over again. As she gets up abruptly, Diana tramples the garish daffodils at their feet. Suffocating the last of the daylight, the thick evening is blurring the edges of things, the blue tits and the wren are mute, surrendering the space to the rooks and damp disappointment.

Leaving, Diana calls out to her sister huddled in a borrowed coat like a tart on a park bench at the end of the night. 'Just forget it. I'll go and check on supper. You take your time. Come on, Monty, home.'

They stay together: Mikey watching the robin on the wall watching him, Valerie hearing the word 'bullied' hit her like a ball on a wall, thud, thud, thud. Why just walk off like a teenager? Go on, then, shut yourself in your room and turn the music up. She was Mikey's age when Diana walked out; what did her sister expect her to understand about family life at that age? What does she want from her now? And, yes, 'bullied' is the word she would use, whatever vocabulary Diana decides to impose on their childhood story.

As her anger subsides, Valerie concludes that, despite appearances, she has it all compared to Diana; she would not swap all the listed country houses and underground swimming pools and grass tennis courts and banks of daffodils in the world for what she has: her son, her Solomon, the past put to bed and a second chance. As she and Mikey find their way back, they pause in front of the tower, chinks of light shining through the windows on the top floor like eyes through a helmet. It looks like an army man, thinks Mikey, but he wonders what's keeping it standing to attention, now that they've dug up its boots. Valerie tells Mikey that, if she had to, she would climb to the top and stand on the battlements to fight for him, and he says he'd get a sword and a horse and he'd defend the tower with his life for her.

'Seriously, Mikey,' she says, 'nothing beats telling the truth. Nothing worse than secrets and lies. That should be our motto. No more secrets, no more lies.'

Marching round the pond, stomping his feet on the flagstones as he salutes first the tower and then the bronze boy, Mikey finds a sergeant-major voice, chanting for the benefit of the swarming starlings, 'No more secrets, no more lies,' he sings, punching the air, 'no more secrets, no more lies.'

Chapter Seven

'That's downstairs,' says Diana, leading the way a little unsteadily. 'Now let's see where you're sleeping.'

The large glass of Merlot downed on her return to the house was probably a mistake, but at least now, dealing with bricks and mortar, she feels a renewed resilience. She is still pleased she invited Valerie, she has just rushed into the past too quickly, knocking things over as she went. It's difficult with Michael around, she doesn't know how much he knows.

'When we have house parties, we use the coach house,' Diana explains as they climb the stairs. 'Edmund's elderly aunt was in there when I arrived. She's the one who looked after him when he was a teenager, after both his parents were dead. I said to Edmund, she needs to go, it's not as if you can't afford a decent nursing home. You weren't going to catch me mashing her banana and wiping her bum.'

'That's what I get paid to do at the care home,' says Valerie.

Valerie has a job? Diana thought she lived on benefits. Propped up against the banisters, Diana laughs rather hysterically. 'Not my thing at all. If I ever reach that stage, put me down. Seriously, pop a little something in the wine and wave goodbye.' She opens a bedroom door and turns on the light. 'Now, this is one of the spare rooms, but we don't want to give you that. Did you ever watch that? *Who Wants to Be a Millionaire?*'

Valerie can imagine the programme appealing to Diana. Quite apart from the money (and she's certainly come into the money), her father used to call Diana a know-all, then Diana would say she'd be the one with the last laugh and here she is, laughing.

'This room's lovely, Di!' says Valerie. 'I'd be fine in here.'

The pale shade of olive green turned out better than Diana hoped when she redecorated. Stroking the fine silk bedspread she traces the embroidered feathers of the red parrots, down the climbing stalks of the emerald blue flowers, the smooth and knot-less surface of wealth. She is good with colour and fabrics; the rental clients always came back to the properties she used to manage for Edmund's property company and they commented on how the flats were furnished in impeccable taste. They, like her, were nearly always outsiders, and she knew how to construct English class for the foreigner: how to have the sense of a Labrador waiting for a walk in the grounds, without the hair on the furni-ture; how to have the touch of history, without the handcuffs. She misses work, she acknowledges privately, as she straightens the bed. Valerie and the boy are standing behind her as if there is a red cabled rope across the landing so she resumes the role of tour guide.

'Michael, you're in this room at the top of the stairs. There's a brand new duvet with footballers on it, just like your tie!'

The words 'but I don't like football' are just a swallow away, but she's still talking.

'And in case you like reading, Uncle Edmund dug out a couple of old books he had when he was a boy.'

Robinson Crusoe. Mikey doesn't open it because but he doesn't want his mum to be sad that they don't have many books any longer. The social worker only had room in her car for the things that really mattered, and when he puts it down Diana reaches her own conclu-sions about the literacy skills of state-educated children. Perhaps she can help him, when she gets to know him better, pay for a private tutor, take him to libraries.

'What's up there?' Valerie peers up a much narrower staircase.

'What Edmund calls the nursery, although, as you say, not much use for that. Don't worry, no mad women in the attic, but we do have our very own gothic tower.' Imitating a trumpet, Diana strides in front of them. 'In Victorian times, Edmund's relations made a lot of money and didn't know what to do with it. So what's new!' She shrugs. 'They built the tower as a sort of joke. You can get in through the door you can see from the drive, and eventually that will be the way down to the pool, but if you follow me' – she speaks in what she hopes is a conspiratorial whisper which might appeal to a child – 'there's a secret entrance!'

At the end of the landing, at what looks like a wood-panelled wall, Diana slides one section to the side and behind it there is another door with an ornate key. A light reveals a short stone passageway and, beyond that, a spiral staircase.

'Jesus, Di!' says Valerie. 'I've had enough of visiting prisons.'

'Trust me,' says Diana.

'Can Monty come?' Mikey asks his mother.

'Monty stays here, on guard,' says Diana. 'Sit, Monty, stay.'

The boy whispers in the dog's ear, 'Bye bye, Monty.'

The sound of chattering fades as the grown ups disappear from view. He is small for nine years old, the steps are steep, and he struggles to keep up. The staircase goes round and round, like a helter skelter, except he is trying to go up it, not down, and his socks keep slipping on the stone. He can touch both sides of the staircase at the same time. Every now and again there are little candles on ledges, but almost no windows, and he only passes one door which turns out to be a bathroom, so he has to go on up. Above his head, the underneath of the steps look like they might go on for ever and take him somewhere he has never been before. It isn't like Lockdown, though, he won't be able to cheat to get out. He half expects to climb until he reaches the sky and be rescued by an army helicopter, but, no, here he is at the top with a door to a bedroom with a massive four-poster bed on one side of him and on the other, a wall. Just a wall. It seems wrong that the spiral ever has to end.

'Now, Val, I simply insist.' Diana is moving round the hexagonal room, putting on the lamps and drawing their attention to one fabulous feature after another: the rich red velvet curtains with gold cords matching the swags which drape the bed; a great tapestry hanging from the ceiling – can you see the hunters on their horses, Michael, and the hounds at their heels, and there's the deer ahead, they're going to catch him, don't you think?

'And here,' says Diana, pointing to a framed piece of embroidery hanging on the opposite wall, 'they call this a sampler. A little girl in Victorian times did it. Look closely, at the bottom it says "Edith Carlton, eighteen twenty-four, aged ten".'

All three of them study the picture, a river flowing through an idyllic parkland with a house much like Wynhope in the background, harps hung in the weeping willow trees in each corner and lines in green thread beneath.

'By the rivers of Babylon, there we sat down, yea, we wept, when we remembered Zion. We hanged our harps upon the willows in the midst thereof,' Diana reads out loud.

To Valerie, there is something indescribably moving about the sampler; there has been so much weeping recently, she can feel the water running like tears and the little girl, only the same age as Mikey, seated on her own in a dim light, stitching sadness into the cloth.

'It goes on a bit,' Diana is saying. 'It used to hang in the drawing room. Can you imagine something so gloomy when I'm trying to brighten the place up? Edmund likes it, though, something to do with the ancestors and Antigua. He calls it the Wynhope Psalm, so this is our compromise, to hang it in the tower.'

'Was she a little slave girl, this Edith? Or was she the child of one of the plantation owners?'

'I've no idea, Val, I've never thought about it,' Diana replies. 'Does it matter?'

His mother starts to sing one of her old reggae songs, 'By the rivers of Babylon, where we sat down,' and his aunt is joining in, 'and there we wept', and they dance in a silly way and they laugh when they run out of words. At one of the leaded windows which ring the room, Mikey opens the latch, letting in the evening air, and the song is blown away behind him. He can see out and hear different things. Over the giant Christmas trees which fringe the edge of the park, great black birds are ganging up, swirling and screeching in circles, waiting for everyone to go to bed in this vast, half-empty house before they attack. Taking refuge on the high bed next to his mother, he picks at a loose thread on the bedspread. He can tell she doesn't want to sleep there and feels within himself the tight tummy of responsibility.

'I like Mum to sleep closer to me,' he mumbles, all in a hurry.

'What did you say, Michael?'

'Nothing.'

'You let your mother enjoy a bit of the luxury she deserves.'

So she heard him the first time.

'Don't you worry about Mummy. We'll leave the door open at the end of the passageway onto the landing and she'll be fine, I promise,' she says. 'Now, I'll just check the bathroom.'

They are alone together at last. His mother looks so lovely there, on the great bed in her little black dress, her toes curled up under her and her eyes huge and smudgy black. He can tell she's crying, so he lays his head on her lap, he tells her he can sneak up there and sleep with her when Diana has gone to bed, but she sniffs and wipes her nose on the clean towel and says she's just being a silly billy, it's the funeral and seeing Diana and she's just so sad about Nanna, but it'll be fine, he's not to worry. He doesn't believe her. On top of the chest of drawers there is a large blue-and-white china bowl with a jug in it and a potty by the side. This will make her laugh. Mikey picks up the potty, puts it on the floor and makes a big thing of pretending to unzip his trousers. It works. His mum hides her face in the pillow, sobs turning to laughter; only he can do that, she always says to him, only he can make everything better.

'Oh, Mikey,' she gasps, 'Stop it! She'll find out!'

And there she is, at the door, believing for one hideous moment that the boy is actually going to pee in her porcelain and the sheer physicality of him fiddling with himself appals her.

'That's worth a lot of money,' she cries.

'It's just a potty,' says the boy. 'For pissing in.'

'Don't talk to me like that. If you're not careful you'll grow up as crude as your grandfather.'

'What does she mean?'

Taking the potty, Valerie thumps it back on the chest of drawers. 'Don't you dare, ever, speak to my son like that.'

Truth hurts, that's what Diana wants to say, but looking at them wound round each other like ivy, she sees they are insuperable, inseparable, this mother and son. Perhaps she overreacted, she isn't used to small boys, so she retrieves the voice she keeps for other people's grandchildren. 'Do you remember the little door on the way up, Michael? That's Mummy's own proper bathroom! You can always do a . . .' Diana hesitated. Pee pee? Wee wee? Piss? She doesn't even have the language for them. 'You can always use the toilet there, if you need to.'

As Diana demonstrates the little bathroom, saying how they'd had a devil of a job with the wiring and how the builders didn't dare disturb the tower too much in case it came apart from the main house, Mikey goes on ahead, down the spiral staircase.

'Joshua fight the battle of Jericho, Jericho, Jericho,' he sings as he jumps from step to step. Doesn't he sing well, his aunt is saying, trying to make up for things, but she's a long way away now. 'And the walls came a-tumbling down.' Stuffing his socks in his pockets, down he goes, each bare foot on the stone feeling like something separate from everything else.

The candles are lit, but now he can see they're just lightbulbs which flicker like flames. He counts them, eleven, twelve, thirteen . . . then there is the door to the in-between passage, but the stairs keep counting . . . fourteen, fifteen . . .

'It doesn't go anywhere, Michael.' That's her again. 'The door at the bottom's all locked up!'

And it is, because, suddenly, in front of him is nothing but another great big, flat, hard, cold wall. He runs his hands over it and feels the difference between the bricks on one side and stone on the other. Just as he had gone up as far as he could, now he has gone down as far as he can. Something about the wall at the top and the wall at the bottom spoils everything. The door is locked. His aunt appears out of the shadows behind him.

'Look,' she says, trying to be all friendly. The key fits the lock first time, she pulls heavily on the door, and light comes cheating into the tower from the lawn which is lit up like a prison camp in a war film when the spotlights come on when you try to escape; it's luminous green and strange. It seems impossible somewhere so wide, so open, so bright can exist on the other side of this small blackness.

'And this is where the builders have made a new hole and the spiral staircase will go on down and down to the pool. They've bricked it up to be safe.'

Wine breath. She locks the door again. It's so dark he can't see her or her new wall, but he can feel her, like she might spark if he poked her, he can hear her telling him to follow. He doesn't want to stay at the bottom of the tower all on his own, but he doesn't want to do what she tells him to do either. Just for a second, he sits down. He might stay there and they'll all forget him and he'll knock a hole through her bricks and go all the way down to the empty pool and lie down there and die down there like the people in the graves at the cemetery and then they'll all be sorry. He's sure he wouldn't be the first body to be found in her ugly tower. He hoots like an owl.

'Hello,' he calls out to the ghosts. 'Hello echo.'

Chapter Eight

Even the kitchen would have been nicer than this, thinks Mikey, but they're eating in the huge dining room because Diana wanted to do things properly for them. The table is much too big for three people and it all smells like air freshener, but it might be the real flowers. There's no ketchup and the lasagne is slimy and everything is made of silver so he can see his reflection bent out of shape wherever he looks. His mum is drinking too much too fast; it's a long time since she was properly drunk so he feels sad and a little scared. Diana is probably drunk too, but she is fixed together tightly, so it isn't so easy to tell if she's falling apart. It hasn't taken long. All evening it's been the same: one moment arm in arm, giggling about the seesaw in the park opposite where they used to live, and the next squabbling like girls in the playground. Brothers and sisters always argue, that's what his friends do, but they just argue over stuff; maybe that's what they're arguing about, stuff, because Diana has a lot of stuff and his mum doesn't have much stuff at all.

'Just because I made something of myself and you haven't,' Diana is saying.

She can't have made all this, she must have bought it.

'Lady Muck!' says his mum, reaching for the bottle. 'You wait!'

If Solomon was with them it wouldn't all be down to him.

'Off you go to bed, Mikey! Give your mum a big, big kiss!'

Over his mother's shoulder, Mikey can see his aunt raising her eyes. His mum's neck smells of smoke, but that's only because today is difficult and just one probably won't kill her. Once he made a secret list of all the things that could kill her and then crossed them off so they wouldn't. He's the one who'll do the killing, he'll kill all her enemies, like Diana, for instance, rat-a-tat-a-tat-a-tat-a-tat in his head goes his imaginary machine gun.

As he leaves, he overhears his aunt say something about him not being much of a talker. In the hall, with full on acting, he rat-a-tat-tats his aunt again, then he crouches on the bottom stair straining to hear what they're saying, letting the ticking and the tocking of the grandfather clock match his pulse. The dog is shut in the kitchen, which is sad for them both. When Mikey's been there what he thinks is probably a very long time and their voices are getting louder and his heart is beating faster than the clock allows, he struggles with the golden knob on the dining-room door which slides round between his hot hands and sneaks back into the room. Opposite each other at the table, his aunt is leaning forwards, jabbing her finger at his mum's face. He doesn't think they'll hit each other because they're both women, but he isn't sure. When there was a girl fight at school, Ali said, 'They scratched each other's eyes out.' 'Really?' Mikey asked him. 'Really,' Ali confirmed.

Sifting through his word bank of phrases, Mikey selects something a child might say at a time like this. 'Night night, then, Mum!' he says. 'Thank you for supper, Diana.'

Neither of them even notice he is there.

'Are you coming to bed soon, Mum?'

His aunt is bending down, picking up something from the floor and his mother is lighting another cigarette from a candle, the wax dripping onto the table, the flame that close to her hair. He is a nobody.

'Fuck,' he says.

'What's he doing out of bed?'

'Mikey, go back to your room. Now. I'm not joking.'

'Fuck.' He slams the door hard behind him, it's the rudest and worst thing he can think of saying. 'Fuck you,' he shouts as he runs through the horrid hall in his slippery socks and up the stairs, and there is the door wide open and the bedside light on all ready for him and he throws himself under the duvet and pulls it over him until there is nothing of him showing. If anyone comes creeping through the house to kill him, even if the black birds from the forest come pecking on his window, they won't even know he's there, he's that invisible, that quiet. And if he has to leave in a hurry, he still has his funeral clothes on and his rucksack packed and his trainers are ready by the front door. He knows how to escape, he does it all the time on Lockdown.

Downstairs, his exit provides the right-shaped space for the argument to grow. Valerie can physically feel the size of the tumour between her hands.

'Charming little boy you've brought him up to be,' says Diana, sweeping crumbs across the polished surface of the dining room table into her palm.

'You're just jealous,' Valerie slurs. 'Even you haven't been able to buy children.'

The heavy curtains are letting in a line of light from the security lamp outside. Diana corrects them and then resumes drip-feeding her abuse. Words spit from her like unpalatable food – chav, pissed, failure – they land on Valerie and dribble down her dress, adding to all the other stains where Paul has spilled his filth over the years.

'We're not so different after all. We've both been in the gutter, it's just that your gutter is better decorated than my gutter.' Valerie stubs her cigarette out in the butter dish. 'And we both live on estates, so that's hilarious when you think about it.'

'For Christ's sake!' Diana tips the bottle before noticing it is already empty. In the kitchen she finds another Rioja in the everyday wine rack. The dog stretches, comes to her, but he is pushed away. Her head is swimming, she runs some water into a glass and gulps at it as if it might provide something different. Beyond the kitchen window, nothing but the night, no neighbours, the rest of the world is kept beyond the stone wall which marks the boundary of the estate. She is a grasping, selfish cow, her half-sister, always has been. When they moved house, Valerie must have been five, she was what, twelve? And there were three bedrooms in the new house: one double for her mum and stepdad; another double, with a window over the park, a built-in washbasin and a fitted pink carpet, like you'd think a teenager would have; then there was the little room, a single bed crammed in a corner, head next to the toilet wall so she could hear him farting and coughing up his phlegm, and that was her prison. Well, who has the best place now? Out of nowhere, she wonders what they did with her room when she left, whether they burned the poster of the ballerina she was going to be when she grew up.

After struggling with the corkscrew Diana realises it is a screwtop. Back in the dining room, Valerie has gone and she realises she should never have asked her to come to Wynhope. Life was always better without her.

In the downstairs loo, Valerie is clinging to the washbasin. They're inching around the unsayable, Valerie feels its heat; she should just chuck on the petrol, watch the whole lot go up, at least that way they can start again with whatever is left in the ruins. Having splashed cool water over her face, she returns.

'She got swallowed up, didn't she?'

It's not clear to Valerie what Diana is going on about.

'Mum, I mean. He just swallowed her up, she was never the same after she married your father.' Like water from a stiff tap, the words, when they come, splutter across the table. 'Your fucking father and then you. Fucking father, that's funny, that is.' Diana looks a little mad, appreciating her own puns. 'All Mum had to do was say something, but she never did, did she?'

'Spell it out, what exactly was it she was meant to say?'

'You know.' Using the table for support, Diana inches towards her. 'Do you think I wanted to sleep on friends' sofas, give up sixth form, live out of a plastic bag?' Her voice is raised to cover the enormous distance between them. 'There was Mum, little Val, the bastard – your father – and no room at the inn for me. So I left. He locked the front door, so I climbed out of the window and jumped. Is that so surprising? Then I made something of myself, without you, without any of you. And you know full well what he was like, you, tucked up safe and sound in your pink nylon sheets.'

The meringue didn't taste as good as Valerie expected; she scraped the cream onto her plate. 'You've been watching too much daytime telly. Everyone's at it, aren't they? Abuse this, abuse that. My dad did a lot of bad things, but he never did that and you know it.'

'You're telling me he left you alone after I'd gone? The way you behaved afterwards, dodgy relationships and unwanted pregnancies, shoplifting, abusive partners . . . I bet you go around fantasising about setting fire to things, just to see the engines arrive. Textbook. I know, I've read all about the signs.' Diana waves her hand in a circle as if to imply that the extent of Valerie's depravity is at least the size of their house.

But Valerie is hardly listening, she's thinking how it is true that her father never left her alone, he wrapped her up so tightly in attention that she could barely speak. But not that. He divided them all, that was true as well, he drove Diana out, demonised their mother, sanctified her and, yes, he was a controlling man, she recognises that now. But not that.

'I knew,' she begins, and as soon as she says the words she wonders what she knew for certain. 'I knew, I think, that I was spoiled, sitting in the front seat, staying up later, better presents under the tree, everything always your fault. But whatever it looked like to you, I didn't like it because I wanted you to be my best friend. What was I meant to do, Diana? I was so young.'

'You're avoiding the question. Once he'd finished with me, did he start on you?'

'No.'

'And after all this time, you're still saying nothing. Keeping mum, that hits the nail on the head, doesn't it, Valerie? You're still claiming you never knew what was going on?'

'I was a kid, Diana. When you left, I was Mikey's age. But the reason I didn't know what was going on, as you put it, is because nothing was going on, was it? Let's say it like it is, shall we? Use the proper words. My dad was not a paedo. He did not sexually abuse you in your poxy little bedroom. Truth is, you were always looking for someone to blame for what you were like. Controlling, bitchy, always falling out with your friends, causing trouble, wanting things all your own way. You always had to be king of the castle. You could never share anything or anyone, not even Mum.' Valerie empties her glass. 'And you always were a liar. Pants on fire, that's what they called you at school. They were lies then, and they're lies now. Maybe you've taught yourself to believe them, but they are lies, Diana, or make-believe, whatever. You need help.'

'What do you think it was like for me?' screams Diana.

'And did you ever stop to think what it was like for us?' Valerie springs up and the plate of uneaten meringue slides onto the carpet, face down; everything always falls butter side down. 'What it was like for Mum, left behind in that street, in school, after all that? It was all lies then and it's all lies now.'

'You still don't believe me?'

Having wiped her mouth with the napkin, Valerie pronounces her verdict as clearly as she can. 'I don't believe a single word you say.'

Punctured, Diana deflates, sags to the floor crinkling in on herself, cross-legged, her dress exposing the tops of her thighs, the years collapsing until she is a little girl again, head down, hands and hair covering her face. Valerie can only just make out what she is repeating, over and over again, in time to her rocking body. You don't believe me. You don't believe me.

Finally, Diana uses the wall to push herself back up. 'I'm going to bed. I should never have tried,' she says, then with renewed venom she remembers her trump card, 'and you, you're all on your owny-o in the tower.' She blows out the candles and leaves.

Like a new baby who throws their hands into the air and finds no one to hold them, Valerie panics. 'Wait for me, Di.' She crawls after Diana, up the stairs, slumps and clasps the banisters, refusing to follow her into the tower. She doesn't want to sleep there, she'll sleep with Mikey, but hands drag her to her feet, push her along the landing, through the narrow passage, up the spiral staircase. She's slipping on the stone, staggering against the steepness of the steps. Her hands, his hands, whose hands, I can fall and she'll never pick me up, she can push me, and no one will ever be any the wiser. Every year women are found dead at the bottom of staircases they know like the back of their hands. Even once she reaches the tower room, Valerie's heart does not slow; there are drunken footsteps on the landing when the lights go out.

Default. On the bed. Curl small. Hug head. Avoid eye contact. 'I'm sorry. I won't be like that again, I promise. Leave the light on, Di.' Valerie reaches out. 'I've been scared for such a long time. Even when I was small I used to kneel by my bed and pray you'd come back for me.'

'Well, surprise, surprise, no one was listening. I didn't come back, did I, and that was the best decision I ever made.' Diana is unpeeling Valerie's limpet fingers from her dress. 'He's dead, Mum's dead, and that just leaves little old you.'

Step by step across the room and away she goes, going, going, pausing, in the doorway, the light of the staircase behind her. One last chance, that's all they have, before it's too late and everything comes crashing down around them. This is her sister, not Paul; to apologise would be a strength, not a weakness. 'I'm sorry, I want you to know I'm sorry, sorry for both of us, sorry that it all turned out like it did. And about this evening and everything else.'

'Too late. You said the only words I'll ever remember and never forgive.' Diana mimics her sister. 'I don't believe a word you say.'

'I feel sick.'

'As long as you don't spoil the sheets, you can choke on your own vomit, for all I care.'

Now Diana is gone and all lights are out. It is an awful thing that has happened this evening, terrible things said by both of them, cats mewling and howling in a back alley, that's what they're like, cowering behind overfilled dustbins and scratching each other from walls topped with broken glass, and looking down from a window which will never open again, their mother, tapping and shaking her head. Valerie needs to use the bathroom, but at the top of the spiral stairs, she realises that she can't find the switch, the stone steps fall away beneath her, probably all the way down into her sister's top-of-the-range dungeon. Paul used to do that, take the light bulbs out, but he hasn't been able to keep them in darkness in the end, has he? Diana is still down there somewhere. Valerie can hear the echo as the door from the passage to the landing is closed. Feeling her way to the window, she pulls open the corner of the curtain and looks down on the silhouette of the bronze boy. The moonlight shines on the child's song hung on the wall. Diana tries to own everything with her posh words – not a ditch, a ha ha, not a picture, a sampler.

'By the rivers of Babylon,' hums Valerie, 'where we sat down.' She loves a bit of reggae and red, red wine. Reggae's always been one of her favourites (second only to Elvis, who is definitely not dead), just the memory of the beat takes her back to the festival where she met Solomon for the first time and knowing he was something else straight away, dancing in the street as if there was no tomorrow.

'Lift up your hearts, with the meditation lift them up.' Without undressing, Valerie falls onto the four-poster bed. The visit has been like a grave robber; it has got out its spade and dug questions out of the ground where they have been quietly decomposing for years, and now the bones demand answers. Why did Diana do it? Why did she make it all up? Did she make it all up? She must have known the future would be impossible for her once she said what she did.

To think of Solomon is to reconnect with his sort of wisdom. What's happened must be forgiven. Tomorrow is another day. All we have is grace and hope. Tomorrow. Maybe there'll be answers then.

'Lift up your hearts, with the meditation lift them up,' she sings drunkenly to herself as the room turns circles around her. Night night, Sol, love you. The thought of him in his cell is terrible, but it's only three months and then they'll be a proper family and the sky's the limit. She can wait. Suddenly, she sits up. She never goes a night without checking on Mikey, she hasn't kissed him goodnight, and him in a strange room in this strange house, but it's too late now and she hopes Diana's left the landing light on for him and the door open, like she promised. Night night, Mum, you sleep now, nothing left to fight about now. Night night, Mikey, God bless, she whispers as she slips under the silk bedspread.

Her tears flow onto the huge goosedown pillows, and the song and her love for her son curl like a kind current around her head until she sleeps as she hums and she hums as she sleeps. 'Let the words of our mouth and the meditations of our heart, be acceptable in your sight, here tonight.'

Her light is out.

Leaning heavily on the closed door to the tower, Diana understands the turn of the key in her hand, hears the click of the catch, experiences its security like a zookeeper closing up for the night, turning his back on the restless beasts and stale cages and stepping out safe into the fresh air. She opens the landing window. The tower which has been like a child for her, coaxed and dressed and spoiled to death, is now polluted by her past in a way that Wynhope has never been in the three short years it has been her home. She was so full of hope. More fool her. Far from settling her slurried mind, the bitter air and the strange sounds of the night unnerve her: the barking fox, the relentless, repetitive bleating of a lost lamb and the breathing out of ghosts. In the centuries to come, there will be some other woman at this window and she will have become the ghost, nothing more than a footnote in Wynhope's history, and her mother buried, even this same day. Her mother is never coming after her, Valerie and the boy will be gone tomorrow as well, taking with them their wheelie suitcase and sniggers and her last chance of ever being validated. So be it. She shivers. Somewhere beyond the stables, maybe in the Cedar of Lebanon, a tawny owl is shrieking.

'Goodnight,' whispers Diana as she creeps past Michael's bedroom door. 'Sleep tight.' She can sympathise with a child who wants nothing more than uninterrupted sleep.

In her bedroom, Diana undresses, holding tight to the bedstead and her routine, slips her silk dressing gown over her white cotton nightdress, takes up her place in front of the dressing table. Wiping from her face the thick layer of pale foundation applied for the funeral, she notices her mascara has run, and with cotton wool she disposes of the evidence that Valerie is able to make her cry. Downstairs, Valerie has stamped their mess into the very fabric of the carpet; however hard she scrubs, everything is stained.

It is stupid to get in such a state. Tomorrow, today it must be now, Edmund will be home. She pulls the curtains across his parkland, his shadow sheep, his whole estate at night, as if by doing so she can bring him back in here with her; for someone who has made their own way in the world for over twenty years, it is extraordinary how she now feels incomplete if anything takes him away from her. She lies with one hand clutched tightly around the key to the tower in her dressing-gown pocket, like a child with a special object, the other hand pulling the empty pillow closer. She is thinking of the things she should tell him when he is back, he will believe her, because tonight of all nights, she realises, you never know when it might be too late, you never know when one drunken sleep might last a lifetime.

Mikey is only small and not used to staying away from home. He didn't want to sleep lost in this strange room in this half empty house in the middle of nowhere with nothing but fields and sheep and sky and trees and birds and poo. Mikey's had three jobs so far in his life: the first is to make everything better for his mum and he's the only one who can do that; the second is to do very well at school; the third is to stay awake, to be the lookout, and to make sure everyone goes to bed in one piece and stays that way until morning.

Here, even the house doesn't know how to go to bed quietly. It creeps around, it stands on the step which creaks, even its stomach rumbles. He is good at only being half asleep, at identifying stumbling on the stairs as the sound of grown-ups going to bed, and it triggered him to slip out from under the duvet and creep to his bedroom door, just to make sure. Which is why he was hiding behind his bedroom door like a spy, watching her, feeling the strange thin air of the countryside from the open window against his hot cheeks. He witnessed her turn the key, he saw her put it in her pocket, even though she promised she'd leave the door open, he heard the rattle of the handle as she checked it was locked, and then a quiet breathing out of something he thought was half way between laughter and cross.

It didn't make sense to Mikey. He was trying to unpick the magic trick with which Diana vanished his mother, along with the fantasy film of false candles and a four-poster bed and a spiral staircase which went all the way up to nowhere and all the way down to a hole in the ground. All gone, just like that, with one turn of the key. The house was fidgeting, it knew he was hiding there in his crumpled school shirt and trousers, it was going to give him away. What he wanted to say was give me the key, I'll look after her, but even when he found the words, he was just not brave enough, never had been brave enough when it mattered, and then his aunt was turning towards him, surely she'd see him, hear his heart beating, but she walked on past and disappeared down the dark landing, like a ghost.

Now he's sure she's gone, he turns on the little bedside lamp and slips out and finds the door which leads to the tower. He wants to say sorry to his mum about the rude words and to tell her he loves her before he goes to sleep. Because he does love her, more than anything. She's better than anyone else's mum and more beautiful, and the two of them together, nothing's going to stop them now, that's what she sings sometimes. He pushes the door as strongly as he dares, he even whispers through the keyhole, 'Mum, it's me', but he knows it's a long, long way to the bedroom at the top of the tower and she'll never hear him even though everything sounds ten times louder in the dark. He was right. This door is locked. There is no key. No light. No mum. Nothing except a hollowing stomach and a racing pulse and the words he hasn't said for cold company as he creeps back to his room and, a little like a dog, turns in circles before he lies down and makes a bed of his duvet on the floor. The lamp throws shadows, transforms his new for-the-funeral jacket into a body and his new for-the-funeral tie into a rope. It's worse than darkness, so he shuts his eyes tight and turns out the light. Why would she lock the door, why would she do that?

Chapter Nine

Wynhope settles down for the night. In the lodge at the bottom of the drive, the housekeeper secures the guard across the fire; outside her husband double-checks the hen house. The fox is barking in the wood. It is a cold night even for April. Wynhope gathers the park around itself, careful not to disturb the rooks who have finally settled in the conifers or the lambs huddled with their mothers under the shelter of the spreading oaks. A badger snouts his way across the front lawn and triggers the security lights. There he is, black and white on the luminous grass and behind him Wynhope; all three floors of the magnificent Queen Anne house are illuminated for the delight of the night-sliding slugs and the sly and musky polecat. Even the damp gravel drive shines. The curious tower wriggles its toes into the clay for a foothold, clings on to the end of the west wing with its bitten fingernails. It is the bastard offspring and knows it, its gargoyles hide behind stone hands and giggle and spit at visitors when it rains.

The badger shuffles off into the wings. There is no one to applaud save the tawny owl biding his time in the Cedar of Lebanon. The plough is low in the Lent sky, the moon has risen above the fir trees, the international space station is passing over Wynhope, unnoticed; it sees sunrise every ninety-two minutes and now is beaming back footage which shows a planet at peace with itself, just the slow roll of the blue globe whispered in white. Soon it will be on the dark side and all there will be is black. A smudge on the lens of the satellite turns out to be smoke over China. Those minute variations in the colour of the sea, azure, cobalt, indigo, Persian? Sunlight on a tsunami. Beneath its crusted skin, the planet's joints are old and stiff, the ice sheets melted from this English bed many thousands of years ago and yet still sleep does not come easy. Maybe the dog dozing in the kitchen opens one eye, or the deer trespassing in the spring wheat freeze, tremble, listen and return to graze, but the people rarely pay attention, perhaps only once in a decade questioning the unfamiliar tremor beneath their feet, or once in a century holding tight to the duplicitous banisters, or once in every five hundred years running from their homes in terror that the earth under their feet has turned against them and the cathedral spire has fallen. That time is now.

Chapter Ten

And it is Wynhope who is the first to sense trouble. There are intruders in the cellar, they are rattling the wine racks, their booted feet are pounding up the stone steps, breaking into the hall and giving the grandfather clock a good kicking until it peals for help. The house is shaken awake.

A helicopter, that's what Diana thinks, but it's too low, it's going to crash. Half awake, she cries out for Edmund, but he's in London and she's at Wynhope. Hot, sweating, drink, menopause, fear, whatever, she is disoriented and breathless from panic. On her dressing table, face creams and foundation, the necklace she wore to the funeral, silver trinket boxes, they are all dancing to a discordant orchestra made up of expensive bottles of scent. Kefalonia, three years ago, honeymoon with Edmund, running from a restaurant, plates of moussaka sliding and bottles of retsina smashing onto the terrace, cries of *seismos, seismos*, as the locals fled screaming into the streets. *Seismos*. Earthquake. Out. Hide. Doorframe. But this is here, now, Wynhope, England. Stumbling down the landing, Diana trips on something, a body, a bag of bones, a boy.

Get out. Get out.

The boy is bumping along the floor, in his half-dream sleep he is lying across the back seat of Solomon's car and Solomon is rescuing him, driving him away from somewhere he does not want to be and his mum's in the front seat singing, but when he reaches out, there is no door and no handle, and he does not know where he is or why the car has become a ghost train, the rails rumbling in the dark, the rough carpet against his face. This is his aunt's house, he remembers, and he does not know where to go so he crawls until his face finds a foot and he curls in on himself like a hedgehog.

The boy. In her panic, Diana has forgotten the boy. Grabbing at his hair, pulling at his legs, he resists, she screams. Somewhere, maybe in the hall, a smash of glass and that energises the child. Together they hurtle down the stairs to the front door, but she can't slide the bolt across and she can't get out, she can't get out. Then. Stop. It's over. The door swings open and they fall out into the blank, unmoving dawn, triggering the security lights, herself and the boy bewildered players in an unscheduled performance. He slips free of her grasp. The wind whips Diana's dressing gown around her, the stones on the drive are mean and she retreats to the lawn to feel the sweet firmness of the damp grass between her toes. Were it not for the relentless wail of the alarm and the dog howling in the kitchen, she would have thought that she dreamed the whole thing. There is no way she can go back in there and rescue Monty, she can't trust the house to keep its word, but imagine carrying the dog's body from the ruins, Edmund would never forgive her. But she and the boy, they're out. She did not think it happened like this, when you're alone; on the news from other countries there are always neighbours running into the streets, hugging each other, counting each other, reaching for their phones and banging on doors. But here, it is just the two of them, mute, as if all words have been shaken out of them. It is so quiet she can hear the hum of the tilted, turning world.

'That was an earthquake,' Diana says, more because she needs to hear herself speak than anything else. 'I know it was. Probably not a real earthquake, just a tremor. We do get them in England, not very often, but we do. And it's over now. Everything will be all right.'

Finding no words of his own, Mikey processes those coming from this woman. He wants so much to hold on to something which is not moving, but he cannot bring himself to touch her. He has something important to say. It is an earthquake, he repeats inside his head, and his brain scans his memory: it finds a children's book with a picture of a volcano all mixed up with doing a sponsored skip at his last primary school which had blackberries in the bushes round the edge of the playground which they weren't allowed to eat. It did all that in a millionth of a second, but then the brain realises the uselessness of this information in the current situation and it returns to the one overriding word pounding inside him, so insistent that he holds his head between his hands for fear it might split him apart.

'Mum.'

Inside the tower, Valerie is consumed by this sudden stillness. It is unreliable, as is the silence which has replaced the inexplicable muffled roar that rumbled up the spiral staircase and blundered into the room. When it woke her, she thought it was a bomb; that is the only thing she has ever seen on telly which might be like this, coming out of nothing and shaking everything without warning. By the light shining in from outside, she can see splinters of glass on the floor and she remembers the sampler, it must have shattered, and then she pieces together where she is and why. At Wynhope. With her sister. Not a bomb then, the only thing she can think of is a hurricane or an earthquake or something from the weather channel but whatever it is, it seems to be over. She's survived. And Mikey?

'Mikey,' she screams.

Her son fills her up, there is no room in her left for anything else other than him, the Michaelness of him, his smell, his voice, his being is all that matters to her, his being safe. Without warning, the light outside is switched off, the bedside lamp isn't working, she is inching blind through the unfamiliar room with her arms outstretched. The steps on the spiral staircase turn their backs on her and twist away beneath her feet. She slips and falls and it hurts, but not so much that she cannot carry on, one hand on either side pressing against the cold walls, reading her way out. At last, a gap. Valerie reconstructs yesterday's guided tour and knows this must be where the passage connects the tower to the house to the landing to the spare room to Mikey. Wood. Door. Handle. Latch. Open, for Christ's sake, open will you.

'Mikey, Diana! Let me out. Mikey, are you there, love? Are you all right?'

In her heart she knows the door is locked from the other side. She might have been drunk last night, but there's no mistaking what she heard. She must go on down to the door onto the drive, and even if that's locked, they'll be out there. Someone will hear her calling, but what if they're not, what if she's alone, what if the house has collapsed and Mikey is, what if, not that, please God anything but that. Finally, there are no more steps. She can go no further. This is the bottom, stone to her left, stone beneath her feet, stone close above her head, damp and slick to the touch and smelling of cellars, and here to her right, rough brick. With a sick lurch in her stomach, she remembers the cavernous pool excavated beneath her feet and she panics, clawing at the vast oak door, tracing the metal brackets of the hinges, finding the handle and grasping it. Although she can feel blood on her knees like a child who has fallen in the garden, she holds on to the fact that she is safe. Only one word matters now, only one word has ever mattered.

'Mikey.'

'Diana! Mikey! Is there anyone there? Mikey!'

From their world, the unlimited outdoors, they hear her. Valerie is calling madly the names of anyone she has ever loved, anyone who might have ever saved her.

'Solomon? Mum, are you there? Somebody help me. Mikey.'

Mikey hammers at his aunt with his fists. Why is she standing like that, a skeleton statue, her bones sticking out from her nightie, her hair thin like a witch and straggling? He is so scared by this woman who is his aunt and by this thing that has happened that is called an earthquake and by the screaming of his mother that dizziness spins him and he has fairground feet. A grown-up should say what they are going to do, but there is no one, there never is anyone to see what is happening or do anything about it. They turn a blind eye, that's what his mum says, but although it's night, he can see, and although he has his hands over his ears, he can hear, and there are no other sounds in his world, only the screaming of his mother and the hammering on the door of the tower.

Di. Unlock the door, please. Di, don't leave me. Mikey. Di, Di, Di.

With his thin pummelling arms in her hands, Diana seizes the boy, holds him writhing like a monkey. 'Stop it,' she shouts at him. 'This isn't helping. I can't bear it, I can't think straight, stop it.'

The stitching on her dressing-gown pocket rips from the seam as he lunges for the key. 'Let her out, let her out.'

The pounding in the tower is violent now. The boy yanks at her, grasping her nightie, exposing her breasts.

'Get off me.' She pushes him so violently he falls.

'Please,' he sobs from the ground, 'it's my mum. Let her out. I'll be good, I won't tell, I promise, please.' His mother's cries are a lurch in the pit of the stomach.

'Mikey.' Behind the thick walls and slit-eyed windows of the tower, Valerie has heard the voice that matters. 'Mikey, is that you? Are you all right, baby? Thank God.'

'I'm here, Mum. I'm coming to get you.' The boy crawls on the grass, gets up, slips, stumbles towards the house. He will get to his mum. He will go back inside the house, up the wide staircase, past the pictures of the old men, onto the landing and turn right because that door leads to the round and round staircase. In his mind there's no need for keys in this rescue mission, there are no locks. He can navigate the first five levels of Lockdown on the computer, all it needs is for him to be there for her, to make it all better; she always says he is the only one who can do that for her.

As lightning pins its victims, simultaneously energises and paralyses them, in a matter of milliseconds voltage snatches away both breath and thought, so Diana is disabled. Something has struck through her, it is not lightning, but she feels the shock of it as if it were lightning. The key brands the palm of her right hand and she holds tight to the burning and relishes the pain: she does not run; she does not save; there is something in the crying and the darkness which electrifies her. The earthquake is over. Let Valerie scream a little longer, if only to know what it feels like to call for help and for no one to come. Let her wait and see.

It is only Edmund's voice in her ear which cuts through her strange hypnosis and challenges this mastery. She hears him so clearly it is as if he is right next to her.

Diana, what are you doing standing like a rabbit in the headlights? Your sister is trapped, the key is in your pocket, save her.

His words earth her and she is released. The toes of her right foot press into the soft earth, the heel of her left foot rises above the wet grass, she is coming, she cries, but it returns, galloping behind her, beside her, overtaking her, hooves reverberating and churning and turning the ground. The boy is ahead of her, he's almost at the house. Diana reaches him just in time, she falls upon him, she saves him from himself.

As the earth trembles beneath Mikey, some new beast falls on top of him and knocks all the air out of him, pins him to the ground, its breath hot on his neck, its heaving weight pressing down into him. Its bare breast slides against his grazed cheeks, he can see the stains of blood on its translucent skin and smells its scented sweat, feels its nakedness. It's much bigger than him, this monster. He can never escape from it. He's trying to say get off, get off me, but it doesn't speak his language. My mum is in there. She needs me. I love her. Without her, I am nothing. There are no words for this. With great effort, he pulls his knees up under his body, the gravel grinds into him but he hardly feels it, he summons great strength to throw the humping thing off his back, to get to his feet, to get the tower, to get to his mum to save her, but even when he is free, he cannot stand because its long nails fix his bare ankle and trick him, trip him again.

The second tremor is weak and mean, the feeblest member of a gang who puts in the boot at the end when the hard work has been done by the others. It is looking for imperfection, senses it in the joists which connect the tower to the house; they don't belong together, never did, the relationship makes no sense, and now even their foundations are unaligned, unearthed. At that moment of extreme stress, there is no resilience. For years, unnoticed, the tower and the house have been bickering, winter after winter the frost picks at the crevices, drop by drop the rain weakens the mortar, then someone starts digging up the past and like a family facing uncertain times, they realise they have nothing keeping them together. With a terrible moan of separation, the cracks between the two structures widen, the house loosens its hold and, unsupported, the tower crumbles to its knees, head in its hands. There is no way of telling what is falling, except there is falling and the sounds of falling, of stone, beams, turrets and gargoyles and wires and pipes, and when it is all fallen, it is anarchy softened only by smoke, stillness and silence.

No more shaking. No more screeching. All the lights are out. No more barking. Only a sort of nothingness, an absence of what has ever been relied upon before. Like the earth under their feet and the sky over their heads.

'Oh God.' Diana drags the boy away from the billowing dust. 'Oh God,' she chokes over and over again.

Mikey allows the holding on and the letting go, but does not know it. He shakes as if the disturbance of the tremor has found its way inside him and he has taken on the spasms of the earth's core as if they are his own.

His fitting is unbearable to Diana. 'What could I have done? Stop it, Michael, stop.'

He cannot stop.

'I was just about to go in and then . . .' Diana's speech is swallowed up by coughing.

His head jerks and his limbs twitch; all thought, all language gone.

'What shall we do?' Diana is oblivious to the age of her partner. 'I can't go in there, what if it all comes again? Where's my phone? I'll call nine-nine-nine.' Suddenly she recognises that this is a child and she sinks down to his level, fumbling towards a hug and failing, pulling at his sleeve and promising. 'She'll be all right,' she says, her teeth chattering. 'People live for days after buildings collapse, in air pockets, things like that. I've seen it on the news. Mummy will be all right. I love her too. If only Edmund was here, he'd know what to do. But it will be all right. I promise you, it will be all right.'

Chapter Eleven

It's true, earthquakes of all sorts are nothing new to Edmund; he is a well-travelled man, geographically at least, so when he was woken up in his city flat by the loose change rattling on the mantelpiece and the gin bottle chiming with the decanter, he recognised what was happening. Turkey. New Zealand. But it was Japan that came back to him as he stood in his pyjamas looking out over the Thames and the night-winking City of London, feeling the subtle tremor slip away. Tokyo was another year, another escape from some unpleasantness or other; then he'd watched skyscrapers actually shaking as if someone had knocked the Christmas tree and he'd wondered if he was going to die there, and he'd hoped, half hoped that it might be so. This was a poor relation of an earthquake.

Kept awake by a nagging feeling of guilt that he should have pulled himself together and gone with Diana to the funeral, Edmund was restless anyway, and now he knows it's pointless to try to get back to sleep and he sits on the edge of the bed playing with his phone. Within minutes Twitter has got a #earthquake and it is not long before an app alert is triggered automatically by significant price movements in British shares on stock exchanges in the Far East. Property. Lloyd's Insurance. Land development companies. Energy. All significantly down. On the news feed he selects the map and with finger and thumb slowly focuses his way through the concentric circles – England, the south, Twycombe – until the epicentre of the earthquake is revealed as no more than a few miles away from home, and as he returns the map to its former size, the circles look like ripples in the river at Wynhope when the surface of the pool has been broken by no more than a falling acorn. Diana's phone goes to voicemail, the landline is unobtainable. Dressing quickly, he keeps one eye on the coverage on the television, disoriented by being here when he should have been there, where everything is happening in flickering orange and flashing blue lights. He feels the unfairness of all those ordinary decisions we take unaware of their extraordinary consequences. Already viewers are sending in live selfie recordings: late-night half-empty beer bottles dribbling across a coffee table; a shelf stacker from a supermarket capturing the moment when all the tins of tomatoes take to the aisles; a webcam proving that animals feel it first as a cat leaps from the sofa and flees through the flap seconds before the room starts to tremble. The narrative runs along the bottom of the screen. Earthquake 5.4 rocks southern England. At least one aftershock. Two fatalities reported so far. Hospitals on full alert. Emergency services overwhelmed and requesting the public not to call unless absolutely necessary. Safety procedures activated at Bindley nuclear power plant. People are advised to remain in their homes if possible.

Edmund's overwhelming need is to get back to Wynhope. Although there have been more times than he can count when he has wished the place flattened, fantasised about fires and coming home to find nothing but dust and a chance to start again free of the past, now that this is a possibility, however unlikely, he finds his own foundations shaking. He is making assumptions that Diana is fine and he is not going to challenge them; Diana is nothing if not a survivor and he is nothing if she has not survived. No news is good news. It might be a cliché, but like so many clichés, there is a truth in it which helps him sleep at night. Let sleeping dogs lie, that is another. He prays for Monty to be alive.

As he drives towards Wynhope, the thin yellow line of dawn is behind him and an imperceptible watering down of darkness lies ahead.

Chapter Twelve

A rumbling in the distance disturbs the dull night – not again, surely not another aftershock, Diana can't stand much more – but this is just a car coming up the drive over the cattle grid, its headlights illuminating the pale trunks of the silver birch trees standing watch in front of the coach house. Edmund? No, he's in London, probably doesn't even know what's happened. It is Mrs H and her husband John. Feeling an unfamiliar relief that everything can be given to someone else to sort out, she runs to meet them as they pull up behind the garages, but the thought of the housekeeper seeing her like this, bedraggled like a bag lady, and John seeing her in the clothes she wears to bed, slows her down. They have coats done up over their pyjamas and a torch. The spotlight exposes everything about her; they would like to do that, she knows, expose everything about her.

'We've got a crack in the back wall at the lodge,' says John, 'so we came up to make sure everything was all right at the house.'

'Mikey, come here, my love, you're freezing. Look at you still in your shirt and your best trousers.'

Gratefully, Diana relinquishes responsibility for the boy to the housekeeper, who wraps her arms around the child and presses her cheek against his face. Mikey allows himself to be folded up in her.

He holds on tight to Grace's coat, and when he is sure she is not going anywhere he lets go, just a little, and struggles to think how he can tell her what's happened, what he saw and what he heard and how his aunt has got the key in her pocket and how nobody knows what's important and how nobody's doing anything, but it's hard to make sense of it all and in the end it's something much simpler he needs to say. He takes her arm and drags her to the drive.

'Please can you help my mum?' he asks her and he points.

'Of course, my love, where is she? Valerie?'

'Oh my God,' says John as he turns the corner and instinctively covers his mouth against the dust. 'What the hell?' He systematically swings the torchlight from the house to what is left of the tower, then on around the garden where the last of the snowdrops blink white beneath the twisted rose bushes, and on past the impenetrable wall of yew hedges, all vaguely shrouded in a layer of unnatural cloud. For John, the image in front of him takes on the characteristics of Belfast in the 1980s: sirens, the smell of sweat on uniforms and urine on the kiddies' pyjama bottoms, counting the men in his platoon and finding the numbers short. He rounds on Diana.

'This can't just have been the tremor, it wasn't that strong.' Suddenly he laughs loudly, incongruously. 'It was the pool, wasn't it? Bloody ridiculous, that pool. Destabilised the whole lot. I said so. That's what's done it. So where's your sister?'

'She was going to sleep in the tower, John,' says Grace. 'Oh my, you don't think . . .'

'In there?' John directs the beam to the wreckage then starts to run. 'She might still be okay.' He shouts, 'Hello? Valerie, isn't it? Can you hear me? Valerie! Valerie!'

'Valerie!' Hand in hand, Grace and the boy catch up with him. 'Valerie, my love, can you hear us?'

The only other sounds are the dog howling from the house and the relentless pulse of guilt inside her head. Valerie is dead, Diana knows it. The key is in her pocket. She hasn't done anything wrong, she was put in a terrible situation, and, yes, she failed in some ways, but it was not her fault. Everyone will blame her, no one will believe her. The familiar phrases beat their logic into the rails like an oncoming train, whining their threat down the track, the time to save herself is now. They all have their backs to her. In one swift and violent movement, she flings the key to the tower into the border behind her. It must have fallen in the shrubs, a shining lie, bright amongst the dark leaves and red berries, or perhaps it fell beneath the camellias. Edmund taught her that yews protect against evil and camellias hate the morning sun; they both have reason enough now.

She joins in with a more confident voice. 'Valerie, can you hear me?'

Everything is failing: the security lights do not come on again, the alarm is reduced to an intermittent whine, Monty howls and stops, howls and stops, and Mrs H is possessed with pointless questions. Whatever happened? Did anyone hear her calling? Why couldn't she get out? Instinctively Diana glances back at the flowerbed behind her, smelling of secrets and drizzle. John is the gardener; she imagines him, fingers probing the warming earth.

'What is it? What's in there? What have you seen?' cries Grace. 'Is it her?'

'It's nothing,' says Diana, turning away, 'there's nothing to be frightened of there.'

'Is the house safe?' asked John.

'The boy will catch his death out here,' says Grace.

'What about Monty?' pleads Diana. 'Sir Edmund will never forgive us.'

'I thought you said you could help my mum.'

After one last check, John makes the decision. 'We can't risk it on our own. It's too unstable. We'll need to wait for help. The coach house is a better bet.'

Scooping Mikey up in his tattooed arms, John carries the boy. He is passive and unresisting in the strong man's hold, head lolling down and neck crooked at an unnatural angle. Diana and Grace follow him in a line, like night travellers.

As they blunder into the barn conversion, Diana is reminded yet again that the flat was someone else's refuge once, until she evicted her, and now she expects these walls to protect her? Aunt Julia was dispatched to a home fairly promptly after they got married and died soon after that. Edmund was right when he said moving from Wynhope would kill her; he sent extravagant flowers to the funeral, apparently it cost less than sending himself. The coach house was left smelling of care staff and bed sores, and Diana redecorated swiftly and pragmatically, painting over the suffering in New World White, which she thought would be nice for entertaining, although this was not the party she had in mind, the pathetic group of them bundling in from the cold night with their chaos for luggage and one person missing.

This is what Diana used to do for a living: walk into unlived-in, high-end flats, check them out for marks on the cream carpets, open and close the drawers in the designer kitchens and count there was still twelve of everything. She was known for her eye for detail, her rigorous control of contracts, it was what helped her work her way up, that and her ability to bring a veneer of class to the most shabby of rental properties, the damp on the wall and the faulty wiring all concealed behind a makeover; now she doesn't know what her job is, except perhaps looking after the boy, and God knows she hasn't got a qualification in that. Mrs H and John have hurried back to the lodge to call the emergency services. She is alone in the shadows with Michael. He is not much more than a silhouette against the window opposite her, pressing the remote control repeatedly, but before she can explain again that the electricity is off, he is turning the light switch on and off, on and off, on and off.

'You'll fuse the house. Then what will we do?'

Then what will we do.

On and off, on and off clicks the switch.

'You'll only make things worse.'

She has nothing to offer him, no bribe big enough, no threat now that will count.

Finally, he gives up, and she can just make out his shape curled like an unlucky black cat in the other armchair. He is very small.

'Do you want something?' she asks.

He doesn't reply.

There must be something. Her hands are so cold as she fumbles around the kitchen, feels the contents of the cupboards one by one: bleach, a mousetrap, a packet of something, maybe ant killer, it's too dark to read the small print. No buzz of the fridge. No radio on in the bathroom. The boy kicks his foot against the edge of the armchair. Sucks his thumb. He passes close to her as he makes for the door and even the air around her changes.

'You must wait here. There's nothing to do but wait.' Her right hand reaches out towards him to hold him, but falls back to her side, paralysed by its history.

The door opens and a hint of daylight and the sour smell of smouldering rubble filters into the room. John and Grace bring with them a refugee survival kit: coat and boots for Diana; for Mikey, a terrible old anorak one of the grandchildren left at the lodge; blankets, an emergency camping light, some biscuits and a flask of tea; and the dog, unharmed. Monty brings not only some sense of hope and energy into the unlit, sterile flat, but the instinctive ability to sense distress. He goes straight to the boy, places his paw on his knee and waits patiently for a response.

The couple are full of updates. They're not sure how long the emergency services will be, it took a while to get through, there were three missed calls from Sir Edmund but they had to leave a message when they rang back, oh, and they had a quick listen to the local radio in the car, there's minor damage in Twycombe, a few casualties taken to the Royal Infirmary, but nothing too awful. Except here. Suddenly, Grace bursts into tears and John is saying not to worry, he's sure the family are all right and it's just the shock making her get everything out of proportion. The camping light flares and their faces leer out of the half-light like skulls in the paintings Edmund took Diana to see in Amsterdam. She is familiar with the trials and tribulations of the housekeeper's family, the daughter Naomi, the grandchildren, Liam and Louisa; she used to be treated to a regular update like a soap opera and shown endless pictures of them on family holidays, usually somewhere very hot. She doesn't have any photos like that, never will. She doesn't need a photo of Liam in his skimpy trunks; she knows him well enough.

A mobile beeps a message alert.

'They're safe,' says Grace. 'Oh no, they're still waiting to hear from Liam. He was out clubbing and hasn't come home. What if something's happened to him?'

What if, Diana wonders, that would be something. Her hand goes to play with her necklace, but she's forgotten that she might as well be naked, so she twists her wedding ring instead and asks to borrow John's phone to try Edmund again.

'All his numbers are in there in case of emergencies at Wynhope,' says John, 'and I think you can call this an emergency.' He waits. 'No luck? He's probably driving.'

Diana hands the phone back to her housekeeper.

Grace's fingers are fumbling as she replies to her daughter's texts. 'It makes you realise,' she says, 'in the end family's all there is.'

Chapter Thirteen

Everything is unreal, from the earthquake itself to this night time dash down the deserted dual carriageway. The whole thing is like a book or a film, and Edmund permits himself the same range of arm's length emotions as he might feel in the cinema – suspense, fear, impending catastrophe – but not really buying into the story at all. Around him, lights form patterns, elegantly lining the banks of the Thames, swarming in clusters around the edges of the parks, and beside him now, the harsh spotlights of the prison. Funny to think that Valerie's boyfriend is locked up behind walls as tall as these. What did Diana tell him, that the man was banged up for assaulting a policeman or something like that? He's inside and I'm out here free as a bird. Truth be told, he is a bundle of nerves. The prison disappears from view; Edmund has known his fair share of white-collar criminals, none of them convicted of anything.

On his journey, there is no evidence of a disaster. The uniform rows of unlit houses, the brake lights on the motorway, the snouts of the woods nibbling at the suburbs, all is as it should be, and Edmund wonders if he's overreacted, if in fact everyone's overreacted. The environment agency and the media are always making mountains out of molehills, red weather alerts for a bit of drizzle, flood alerts for the odd puddle or two. In one of the villages about eight miles from home, a policeman flags him to slow down and he overtakes a fire engine, notices the fluorescent yellow jackets and the acrid smell of smoke seeping into the car, but statistically there could be a fire any night of the year; it doesn't mean anything. Nevertheless, Edmund takes risks on the narrow country road, holding the bends tight and fast, and he makes it to the village in under an hour and a half from the flat, arrives at the lodge, through the gates, up the drive and he is home. As he gets out of the car, he hears the tentative dawn chorus lifting the garden.

Through the flat grey light, which distorts perspective and which you only ever get just before sunrise, Diana is coming down the drive towards him, disordered, lumbering like a crazy woman in a Barbour over a nightdress and someone else's wellington boots and then she is close up and with him, tying him in a tight knot. The only reason he is not overwhelmed with tears of relief at still having Diana is because he has not allowed himself to feel the fear of losing her. It is when he spots Monty bounding towards him that his eyes smart, he releases his wife and falls to his knees.

'There you are, you old scoundrel, what would I have done without you?' His smile acknowledges what is written on Diana's face. 'And you, Di. I was so worried about you too.'

As they round the corner from the garages, he sees Wynhope as it exists in his mind, as it was for his father and the generations before him; the immaculate lawn mown once already this year in perfect concentric circles around the lily pond, and his friend, the bronze boy, two rabbits running from the flowerbed which lines the orchard wall, the front door open, welcoming him home. Then he registers the house as it is. He brings the two together, holding up separate postcards of the same place, before and after the war, or something like that.

'I thought they said on the news it was just a tremor. What's happened? How did it happen?' But then his questions are overtaken with laughter, a sort of inarticulate hysteria. 'I'm sorry, I can't stop,' and they come again, unstoppable soundless cramps from deep within him. 'I can't believe the tower's finally gone. This is what's meant by an act of God.' He wipes his eyes, red from dust and crying. 'God just comes along and does what I never dared do.'

Diana doesn't understand, he can see that, but it is too hard to explain. He tries to pull himself together. 'All these years, my father and that bloody tower. God knows how much I've hated it and, oh, I don't know, all the talk and plans about pulling it down which never materialised because I never quite had the guts, and now – look at it – just sky. Nothing but sky.' Somewhere in that heap is his sampler, which he has been able to recite off by heart since he was a boy. 'Rase it, rase it,' he quotes to Diana, 'even to the foundation thereof. Little Edith was a prophet after all.'

Too late he realises how insensitive he is being; of course Diana is going to be devastated by the collapse of the tower, not to mention the fact that this has pretty much buried the pool, literally and metaphorically. He is sorry, she must be so disappointed, having spent all that time and effort decorating the place, putting her very own mark on Wynhope, that's what she said, but he'll find her another little project, he promises, and if he's honest, he could never really have fallen in love with the tower, however spectacular the curtains. It was always going to take something more fundamental than a new coat of paint to put it right. The sun is rising directly behind the ruin, rays of light colour the drifting dust, and he is struck by its beauty, a Turner watercolour, Wordsworth's *Tintern Abbey*, a place where the past is no longer a series of impenetrable walls and locked doors, but a softer world, a portal to a different sort of future.

He feels a little shaky himself. 'It's quite ethereal in its own way, isn't it?'

Diana is no longer listening, she is stumbling away from him towards the coach house.

'We went to my mother's funeral,' she hisses as she shakes herself free from him, 'or have you forgotten?'

'I haven't forgotten, everything got so topsy-turvy. I just forgot they were staying, that's all. I'm sorry. Where are they?'

'They aren't anywhere. The boy is in the flat. And Valerie, my half-sister in case you've forgotten, was sleeping in there.' Diana flicks her head towards what is left of the tower.

An eye for an eye. He might have known the tower would not give up that easily, and the house standing there smirking with its hands on hips. How angry he is with Diana, that she wanted a pool, because it must be something to do with the pool, that she has been here and allowed this to happen, and above all, that there is a boy, another boy with a body in the tower and a future to be faced all alone. John comes out from the flat to meet him. Edmund feels keenly his white-collared impotence as his handyman talks about tractors and ropes and heavy lifting gear. In the end, though, it is clear that any rescue attempt would not only be futile, but dangerous, and nothing can really be done until the emergency services arrive. As Edmund steels himself to go into the coach house, he acknowledges to himself that he'd rather be tearing at stones than talking to orphans and that both were probably equally ineffective.

Now he hates me. Diana feels it like the moment the wind gets up from the beach and smashes the glasses on the terrace and the summer holiday is over. Maybe he'll always hate me for this moment. He married me because what I brought was order, agreement, no history, no future. And now it's all about the dead, again. Off he goes, running after the boy. That's what it will be like, everyone worried about the child as if childhood itself is a reason. The boy will talk, no one will understand her part, no one will worry about the fact that she has lost a mother and a sister in the space of a week, but then perhaps she can tell them everything and she means everything. She can say let me start at the beginning, let me tell you the whole story. Studying the scene from the doorway, Diana makes out a still life in a dim light of a darker sort than those museum paintings: Mr and Mrs H peering out of the window waiting for the emergency services, where are they, what's taking so long, Michael and the dog both hiding under the table, and great big scribbles in blue biro all along the bottom of the white sofa where the boy is continuing to graffiti his unintelligible message, scarring himself and his story into the fixtures and fittings, even as Edmund, perched on the armchair, is talking to him. He's apologising, as usual. Sorry, so sorry, so bloody upper-class. Down on his hands and knees now, we'll do everything we can for Mummy, promises promises. He isn't getting much response, reaching into the child's hiding place as one might coax a cat from a drain.

Having little success, he gets to his feet and joins her.

'It was pretty bad for me too, Ed,' she says.

'I don't know what to say to him.'

'What did people say to you?' she whispers. They never talk about his childhood, either.

'Sorry, that's what people said. That they were sorry.'

This is it, then. I am not holding him, he is not comforting me, and if Mrs H doesn't shut up blathering on about making up the four-poster bed in the tower and who would have thought it, then I will slap her.

There is no need. They are all silenced soon enough. It comes again. This time they recognise it knocking at the door. At first it is almost imperceptible, the slightest vibration everywhere and nowhere, changing everything and nothing. Hypersensitive, their brains process the immediate, recently gained experience to confirm that the tremor is beyond their control, that they just have to hold their breath as it clatters the cutlery in the kitchen and jiggles the cabinet where the glasses are kept in strict, glittering lines. The tremor is neither strong nor long, barely a few seconds, probably the sort of thing that happens unnoticed several times a year, but that's irrelevant; all that counts is the deep-seated realisation that now, because the ground can move, nothing can ever be relied upon again. Each of them gasps, but the boy screams, he screams the inaudible scream of the iconic picture hanging on walls with a dreadful casualness, in flats and bedsits the world over.

Irrationally, the aftershock even undermines their faith in the coach house and they need to get out. Out is bland daylight, any magic of the dawn gone, just the dripping of the gutters and the dustbins ready for collection and everything as normal, except for the severed limb hanging limp and brutalised on the side of the house and John and Edmund shouting Valerie's name across the picture-perfect gardens and the scream of sirens growing closer on the main road.

For Diana, no one illustrated it like this before, but somewhere inside herself she recognises that this is hell and hell is where she belongs.

Chapter Fourteen

There are old photograph albums in his study that have sepia pictures like this: three in a line at Wynhope, the lord of the manor, his wife, the heir to the estate and the family dog, with the staff standing loyally to one side. A fire engine, an ambulance and what looks like two army vehicles with winching gear drive straight through the portrait that Edmund is remembering and skid to a halt in front of them. Monty leaps to meet them, wagging his tail. Reverting to his army training, John steps forwards and briefs the officers, Diana hangs back, Edmund hovers somewhere in between them.

'Please God they've come in time,' he says.

'I don't think it's possible,' Diana whispers. 'Not the way it came down.'

'Poor you' – Edmund pulls her close – 'I can't imagine how awful it must have been.'

'It was horrible, Ed, horrible. We'd gone to bed, I don't know, Valerie didn't even want to sleep in the tower, I had to practically drag her there and now look what's happened.'

'It's not your fault, Di. If anyone's to blame it's me, I should have had a better survey for the pool, shouldn't have cut corners. I should have come to the funeral, then I would have been here.'

'Might be better if the lad went inside if it's safe to do that,' suggests the man who introduces himself as the lead officer, while his crew and three soldiers are slamming doors and shouting to each other.

The fireman's radio crackles; he confirms their location. Everyone is expecting her to do something with the boy, why her, why should she be any better at this than Edmund?

'Come along, Michael.' Diana relents under the pressure and holds out both hands. 'We don't say no to a soldier, do we? One, two. One, two.'

His weight is that of an inanimate object which has no momentum. Diana pulls more forcefully, catches hold of the sleeve of his borrowed coat, feels the strength of her grasp, tensing the muscles up her arm, even into her jawline and her neck, but he wriggles out of the over-large anorak so she falls with a fistful of air and he stays standing.

'Let me help you, Michael,' she pleads as she struggles to her feet.

'No.' Mikey starts to run to his uncle. 'No.'

'Leave him be,' cries Grace.

But Diana catches up with the child and grabs him again by the arm. His head turns sideways, his mouth is open, and his teeth fasten on her flesh.

'Call your dog off, sir!' shouts one of the soldiers. 'We're going to use our search and rescue dog.'

'Get away from me. I hate you, I hate you.'

'Edmund, please . . . he bit me.'

The world is a cacophony of sounds, the words and requests hit Edmund like stones on the back of his head; he does not know which way to turn.

'I'm sure he didn't mean to hurt you, Di,' he calls. 'Mikey, stand by me here. Monty, come.' He gathers in the child and the dog, keeps them close; they are both quivering. Monty listens to him, head up and eager for the fetch command as if they are at a shoot, waiting for the carcasses to fall from the sky. Over at the ruin, a Germen Shepherd noses between the masonry. It is a long, slow process, unreal to all of them except the emergency crews. This is their third call-out, the ambulance driver explains; one to a chimney crashed into a sitting room where an old lady slept on the sofa to be close to the fire for warmth, another to an explosion where a gas pipe had ruptured.

'And were they all right?' Edmund hardly dares to ask.

The man nods. 'We haven't seen anything quite like this,' he says.

Which is probably why someone is filming it, thinks Edmund. He doesn't ask who they are; nowadays you sort of accept that a filming is part of the happening, and, anyway, John seems to be sorting them out.

Finally, a subtle difference in the body language of the dog and the fire-fighters.

'We've got something,' confirms the handler. 'Positive!'

'Have they found Mummy?'

'Bless him,' says Grace, to no one in particular. Diana is all on her own and the housekeeper takes a step in that direction to comfort her – Valerie is her sister after all, half-sister – but she stops. It isn't as if her offer of support would be welcome even if she made it. Instead, Grace is overwhelmed by the sight of the back of the little boy's head and the tall, tense man beside him, and how dreadful this is for Edmund too, given everything that's already happened here, and she offers up a little prayer. It's not something she usually does, but what else can you do at a time like this, apart from hope that there's someone or something out there who can put things right?

Edmund is a man accustomed to prayer, but ironically he finds himself without handholds, wrestling with the binary future which lies ahead of the boy, just as it did for him, once. With your mother or without. Mikey has stepped just a little away from him and he lets him go. It is a truth that this will happen to the boy on his own. There is no other way.

Chill creeps over her skin with insect feet. Diana puts her head between her knees. I will look up and they will be carrying her out saying, she's alive, it's a miracle, and the nine o'clock news will confirm it's a miracle like the pope does with the confirmation of saints and the healing of sinners, except she can see Valerie as she was when she was small, running in from the garden when her dad gets in from work, face red, bleeding knees and broken fingernails and she will tell on me, all sorts of lies she'll say, about what I did, how it is all my fault. Everyone will believe her. Tracing the tooth marks on her arm, just one budding drop of blood where the skin is broken, Diana prays for Valerie to be dead. Can she really do that? She can. Deep down inside, that is what she's always wanted since Valerie arrived in this world – for Valerie to be gone. Leaning forwards onto her hands, she presses into the grass and pushes herself slowly up onto her heels.

'Ed,' she calls over, weakly.

He doesn't even turn round. 'Darling! Keep hoping.'

'Quiet!' The call went up.

One of the firemen is calling out, he is lying flat on his stomach with his head at a peculiar angle. 'Valerie? We're here to help you now, Valerie.' He is stretching into the bowels of the collapsed tower. 'I've got her wrist!'

The lead officer shouts over abruptly. 'Keep hold of the boy, it's not safe.'

Edmund holds the child tight. 'Wait with me. He's got her wrist, they've found Mummy, we just need to wait.'

'Mum, it's me. It's me, Mikey. Can she hear me?'

'Do we have a pulse?'

A small scurry of stones slides down the fractured walls of the tower.

'Stand back, stand back.'

The waiting. For all of them, the cold waiting will never be forgotten. Having been so sure Valerie must be dead, now Diana chews the very real possibility of her living, a piece of meat impossible to swallow or spit out in company. Mikey is so sure she must be alive, his faith makes him jump up and down on the spot, energised by hope and his unshakeable faith in his mother.

Inch by inch, the fireman is sliding out of the collapsed tower, climbing over the rubble slowly, so slowly, two or three others clustering around him. He is shaking his head. They are turning away, tired now, they seem, all action ceased.

Dead then. After all that. Her little Valerie gone. Breath is snatched from Diana, as if death is catching.

Since he has been wound up like a jack in the box, Mikey is still jumping despite the weight of Edmund's arm heavy on his shoulders, he cannot do anything else. Up and down, round and round he goes, he does not know where to go, which way to turn.

That way is the bronze boy and the wood and a little garden sunk beneath stone walls where you might hide and never be found out; that way, behind the house, just fields and woods and sheep ganging up, and he's never been anywhere like that in his life, he would not know how to live in a place like that, all on his own; and over there, the woods with the giant Christmas trees where the birds were circling and screaming last night, they were the most frightening of all. But past the coach house, that's where the drive goes, he can't remember how it goes or where it goes, but it goes, away from here, all the way to the tall gates and then the road and then the town and then home where she'll be in the kitchen, feeding the cat or maybe in the bedroom drying her hair or maybe in the yellow sitting room finishing her jigsaw. Where does this bit go? Mikey runs. Edmund is calling after him, but he runs all the same, very fast, faster than he knew he could. It is vital he outruns what has happened to stop it catching up with him. The cattle grid stops him. It isn't that he can't balance on the rails or avoid the gaps in between them, it is more that if he does cross it, he doesn't know who he'd be, if he'd even still have the same name. Behind him Edmund is coming towards him, slowly, with his arms out wide.

'Fuck off,' shouts Mikey.

Then he remembers they were the last terrible words he ever said to his mother. Words she said she never wanted to hear him say again in her lifetime. She never will. The stitch in his side is so sharp he wonders if he too will be dead soon. What is dead? He slumps onto the gravel, and with his head in his hands, he feels dead. He has never met dead until his nanna's funeral and now he has met dead twice in two days, but he still doesn't quite understand what it is.

It is the flapping of a flock of fat pigeons when the coffin slides out of the boot.

It is made up of crows. Here, one black crow perches on the back of a white sheep, pecking at its wool.

It is to piss and to cry at the same time.

'Mikey, there was nothing anyone could do. I'm sorry.'

That's Edmund's tall shadow above him. He doesn't mean to lie, but he is lying. Someone could have done something.

Mikey doesn't reply. There is nothing left to say.

The drive on the other side of the cattle grid goes nowhere that matters.

Behind him, there is nothing left.

The truths are heavy as earth on top of him, all breath blocked, all words buried.

It begins to drizzle. Sullen grey clouds loiter over the park with nothing better to do than make things worse, and a listlessness and tearfulness seep into the scene; everyone moves more slowly, the sense of urgency is gone. People huddle, the man has put his heavy camera down, the rescue dog is back in the van, Grace checks her phone again and goes to her husband. She is desperate to reach her daughter, there's still no news of Liam, there's nothing else they can do here. Diana can overhear her quite plainly although the argument with John is conducted in angry whispers.

'We can and we should go now. After all that's happened, are you going to put her family before our own?'

Now Edmund joins them. There is a brief muttered debate about whether the boy would be better off going with them. All three of them turn to look at Mikey, picking at the bark on the cedar tree as if there might be something beneath it after all. Privately, Diana is torn: she wants him gone, she can't bear the way he looks at her; she needs him close when he starts telling everyone, she must be there to translate. She realises she might need to learn to love him, she may be all he has left. Her mind trips over its laces as she moves towards him to claim him.

There is not much that Mikey knows. His mind, which was so out of breath the pain was unbearable, is now out of focus as well, but his instinct tells him he wants to stay with Grace and he wants Grace to stay here at Wynhope. He can't leave here because here is where his mum is, but he can't stay here with his aunt, not on his own. His mum always says he's razor sharp when it comes to people, and he's razor sharp now, recognising that there is no love lost between Grace and his aunt, and if he has to choose he knows whose side he's on. Even the dog looks as though he wants to go with Grace, waiting by their car and wagging his tail. When they drive away without either of them, Mikey realises how cold he feels in his socks and his funeral shirt.

'We need to get you sorted out, young man,' says his uncle.

Back inside the house, a different sort of anarchy greets Edmund, Diana and Mikey: the detritus of that last supper is everywhere even though the Stafford porcelain figurines are still dancing in pairs on the sideboard and the freesias stand upright on the windowsill, just a few petals fallen, confetti at a funeral. Edmund says he does not understand it, how some things can be destroyed, but others left untouched. As he guides the boy towards the staircase, Edmund picks up the pieces of the smashed china horse and runs his finger over the rough edge of its snapped leg.

'My father's, Flash in the Pan he was called. He fell at Hereford and had to be shot. The whole household was in tears over that.'

The boy finds the leg on the floor and gives it to him.

'Thank you, Mikey. Look, it fits perfectly. A bit of glue and everything will be as right as rain.' The words are out before he realises how empty they are. What has fallen, what is damaged, what seemed repairable and what has survived. That is the reckoning, always has been.

Forbidding them to follow him, Edmund leaves to examine the damage upstairs, instructing the boy to sit tight on the bottom of the stairs, just for a minute or two. From here Mikey can see straight out through the front door, which is open because it won't close properly. His trainers are still on the mat so he puts them on. If the house falls down again, he can escape that way and from here he can see the firemen. He can't allow himself to think about what they're doing, just that they're out there and strong, and his mum is still here. And from his waiting place he can see the statue in the lily pond, and the bronze boy and the dog seem like the only two people who matter. Diana frightens him, even the sound of her frightens him. He can hear her in the dining room clinking this and clunking that, trying to clear up the big mess she made arguing last night, like that's all that matters when the firemen are still out there and so is his mum. And maybe she's not dead after all.

Diana is in the dining room, it's true, but she doesn't know why or what to do with the filth. She picks things up and she puts things down again, then because the boy is in the hall, spying on her, she retreats to the utility room where she screws her dressing gown into a ball and pushes it down to the bottom of the black sack, knowing it is the sort of thing criminals do and drags the torn and bloody nightdress over her head. Naked, she sorts through the laundry basket, finds dirty pants, leggings, the cashmere jumper stained with lily pollen and is it only yesterday, the funeral? In the hall, she tries to give the boy a shrunken blue jumper that Mrs H ruined by putting it in the washing machine, but he refuses it and, at a loss as to what to do with him next, she sits at the kitchen window and watches her story being played out on the lawn.

Mikey's glad she's gone. He's lost sight of the men, but he can hear them calling now like people do on the building site opposite his house – left a bit, up here, that'll do – and the same sort of sounds, metal on metal and engines. The more he sobs, the tighter he sucks his funeral shirt. He allows Edmund to lead him to a sofa and tuck him up tight in a blanket and say he'll be back in a jiffy and give him his rucksack in case he's got something he wants in there, but Mikey doesn't open it; he just holds it tight, as tight as he can. It's all he has left even if it is almost empty.

The fire crew inform Edmund of their progress; they have been surprisingly efficient given the unfamiliarity of the task. Normally when he visits his development sites, Edmund wears a yellow helmet and a hi-vis jacket, but it's all too late for risk assessment now. Who knows what the insurance position is, this is probably considered an act of God. Valerie is lying in an air pocket, the beams and masonry crisscrossed above her, except the one monumental block which crushed her chest and her pelvis. It takes a long time to lift it, but once it is winched away, all that is left is her body. To die in the dress you wore to your mother's funeral – he doesn't know why that hits him, but it does. The rain falls harder, hammering against a piece of corrugated iron propped up against the potting shed, puddles forming in the tyre tracks on the grass. Ground, dust, sludge: the earth is losing its identity.

The redundant ambulance crew have left and been replaced by an unmarked van. The trolley stretcher gets stuck in the gravel, Diana could have told them that would happen; Valerie's wheelie case did the same, and what will she do now with her suitcase and everything in it? She can't see the remains of the tower from the kitchen, it's almost as though it is offstage and here is the player, walking across the lawn wearing gloves and carrying Valerie easily, thin as a rake she always was. He lays her on the trolley. The zip gets stuck half way up the bag, caught in her dress perhaps. It delays the moment in which Valerie is wrapped in black for ever. When the van has gone, at the kitchen table, Diana flicks through the messages. #earthquake. One hundred and forty will never be enough.

My half-sister is dead. She counts the letters. People who know her have sent direct messages and she realises Wynhope must be on the news. She snaps the phone case shut and bursts into tears.

The vehicles have left deep ruts in the grass; Edmund presses the edges with his foot, instinctively trying to even things out. There is a deafening quality to the remains of the day. There will be things to be done: reseeding the lawn for instance, calling the builders, although what they'll do about the bottomless pit that is the pool, God only knows. Someone will need to contact the electricity board, is there anything to eat, and ordinary things after that, like catching the train and going to his office and renewing his fishing licence. They'll all still line up along the hours, very close to the edge. And there is a motherless boy on the sofa and he promised him he'd be back in a jiffy, but he can't face it, not quite yet. He is physically shaking.

Soaked to the skin, Edmund stays outside and throws the ball for the dog into the long grass and the dog brings it back to his feet and waits. He throws the ball again and the dog retrieves it and waits. Remember the dead, pay attention to the living, that's what the school chaplain told him. Least said, soonest mended. That was what was called counselling in those days. Sometimes terrible flashbacks return, as they do now even after so many years – the firemen and the police shouldering their padded bodies and helmeted heads against the wood, he can hear it, the counting down, the battering, the splintering of the door. He has no memory of their pulling his father's body from the tower. He does not know if that is because he did not see it or does not want to remember it. There is the smell of Jeyes Fluid, the disinfectant usually kept for the stables, but later thrown over the doorstep to the tower, bucket after bucket of water splashing over the stones like the tide, and the rain runs over his head and down his face, trickling under his shirt, and he wants so much to cry and never stop crying. It will pass. Edmund hurls the ball high into the air, like he used to when he was hoping for a place in the First Eleven; for a moment, it is lost in storm light, but then he spots it again. He keeps his eye on the ball as it falls from the sky and he catches it safely. Again he throws the ball and again he catches it. Just playing cricket in the rain. Once more, he is about to send the ball back up when the boy appears tear-stained and dishevelled in the porch. Embarrassed, Edmund wonders what the child thinks, to see a grown man playing catch with himself in front of the place where his mother has died. As no words come to him to explain himself, he simply holds the ball up in his right hand.

'For you?' he says.

The child nods. Edmund throws it very gently towards him in a long slow curve. It falls towards the two cupped palms and the boy catches it and there develops a song of sorts, a rhythm and harmony on this, the ugliest of days: the silence of the throw, the thud of the catch, a safe pair of hands.

It is a long time since Wynhope has dared to welcome a child.

Chapter Fifteen

That night was difficult. Clutching duvets, candles, food, bottles of water, they struggled back to the coach house, asylum seekers of sorts, and as if to ensure they were not mistaken for the dead they both slept fitfully although the boy seemed virtually unconscious; Edmund said he used to sleep for hours and hours, never wanting to wake up.

In the morning, the spring storm has passed but left in its wake a thin drizzle, greyness creeping soft-sandalled into the main house. The gash in the landing wall has allowed rain to splatter over the carpet and Edmund feels the splintered edges of the oak panelling and its violated passage and tests his weight on the floorboards, then he leans out over the edge, the rubble like rocks on a beach beneath him, strewn with the coloured clutter of day trippers who have swum out to sea and never returned. The remains of the spiral staircase are crazy – Escher architecture going nowhere – and somewhere within him is a dizzying desire to follow their lack of logic and plunge. Stepping back sharply, he catches hold of the banisters behind him. He phones John, hears his own voice sounding unreliable when Valerie is mentioned, and feels on safer ground asking for help with boarding up the gap.

'I would wait,' Edmund says, 'but it's too dangerous with Mikey here. Anything could happen. Oh, and Liam?' He kicks himself for his thoughtlessness. 'Is everything all right?' Liam is fine. John will be over later to make things safe, on a temporary basis, at least.

The council is meant to be sending an engineer to assess the house and the lodge. They are close to the top of a short list because it turns out that for nearly everyone else the impact of the earthquake was little more than slates off the roof and cracks in the brickwork of 1950s extensions and shattered glass in poorly constructed conservatories. Wynhope is a high priority case; there was, after all, a fatality. Edmund is of the view that apart from the tower, Wynhope, structurally at least, looks as resilient as ever; Diana is not sure that the house has ever really put its faith in her , but she is relieved to reclaim it all the same and now she wants the place all to herself.

'For Christ's sake,' she snaps at Edmund, 'take the boy away from here. Anywhere. He needs some fresh air.'

From the back door Diana watches the two figures, the tall man holding hands with the child, growing smaller as they walk away from her towards the meadows. That is what it would have looked like if they had children. He would have taught his son to shoot, spent even more time tying flies on his river, frittered away summer evenings in the garden bowling overs, and she would have been the mother who didn't quite get it, not having had hearty brothers who went to prep school or jolly fathers who drove the horse box to pony club. Well, they were right to have agreed no children; it would have changed everything, and, besides, an aversion to family life is something they have in common: one with parents who loved too much, the other with parents who loved not enough or not at all, or at least not when it mattered.

As soon as they are out of sight, Diana regrets letting them be together. She's sure the boy will talk although she hasn't heard a word from him since Edmund dragged him back from the cattle grid. She wants to speak first so that Edmund will not hate her; she can already see the way he is identifying with the child, but it has been so hard to find the right time. When he gets back, she promises herself, then she'll confess. They must have headed to his precious chapel. Edmund likes to believe, or to pretend to believe, or to believe in his own childish version of belief; people often do when someone they love dies. This Solomon of Valerie's, he was one of those born-again types according to what she said. Will someone tell him in prison that she was killed? She can't imagine the relationship would have lasted anyway. The dead remain dead. She is not a believer. Her father, her mother, her sister: all dead. The absolute finality of that knowledge hollows her out, and she slumps at the table with her hand resting instinctively on her stomach, a woman pregnant only with loss. Who knew stillness could be so strong? That the silence of saucepans in a cupboard could be so loud? Both Valerie and her mother have been absent from her life for a quarter of a century and she never cried until now? How will she ever stop?

The only way she knows how to stop feeling is to start doing; getting things done is what Edmund admired about her when she worked for him. Precisely, with one finger and a tissue, Diana dabs at her eyes before remembering that she is not wearing make-up, then she starts to put things back in the right place. As she opens the cupboard doors, the china inside slides towards her and, despite her frantic attempts to push things back, everything crashes onto the floor. Side plates, soup bowls, breakfast plates splinter and smash onto the tiles. Some things are damaged in ways not yet visible; she realises the shelves must have tilted in the quake. As if possessed by a poltergeist, Diana lurches from cupboard to cupboard. It's common sense that the doors should remain shut, but her need now is to open everything, allowing the glasses to cast themselves onto the flagstones in thousands of crystal shards, inviting the jars of jam and chutney and gherkins to splatter their innards all over the floor, daring the bags of flour to jump and burst and shroud the room in ashes.

So there you are. Diana is sobbing on the floor, blood on her hands and feet, her trousers sticky with what is left. This is what it's like, the shit, here, for everyone to see and no little plastic bags to scoop it up and hide it in a bin. Who can possibly think it right for the boy to stay a moment longer at Wynhope, living in a mess like this, cared for by the madwoman who murdered his mother? Someone needs to take him away for his sake, for her sake, for all of their sakes.

Past the little lake, over the iron footbridge into the meadow, Edmund and Mikey head towards the chapel with the dog who plunges in and out of the water, showering them both as he shakes himself dry and scattering the mallards. Edmund catches the beginnings of a smile on the boy's face, but all along the stream where the fronds of the ferns are sealed like secrets they walk without talking. From time to time the ground beneath their feet is saturated and boggy, and Edmund remembers liquefaction, the sludge which surfaced in New Zealand after the huge earthquake there, the very silted and thickened and muddied stuff of history, sucking on the toes of the children who will inherit the earth. Perhaps it will seep through this meadow grass as well, as if its time has come.

'That's where we're going.' He points across the parkland towards his very own tiny chapel, an early Norman rock of a church, an oak tree of a door to welcome them. 'Isn't it fantastic?'

Mikey nods. He is limping a little through the pasture and trying to keep his trainers white.

'Not the best shoes for this sort of walk,' says Edmund. 'We'll get you some boots of your own. You'll need boots.'

Of course the chapel is still standing, how can he have doubted it, it is built of sterner stuff than the tower, Babylon and all that. The chime of the handle, the push of air on air, and the whisper of peace hushes out from the darkness and ushers him in to the scent of lilies grown in the Wynhope glasshouses and the breath of prayer.

'Monty has to stay outside,' he whispers, 'but you can come in. This is a very special place.'

Gripping on tightly to the dog's collar, the boy hesitates at the threshold.

'It's just a sort of chapel,' Edmund explains, wondering if it is possible that the boy has never been in a church. 'That table with the cloth is like the altar and, just here, this a font.' He is going to ask if Mikey has been christened, but stops himself. The boy and all he represents about contemporary English life are a mystery to him. He runs his hands around the circle of rough stone where the children of the estate, including him, have been named for hundreds of years, but not any longer, for that tradition, like so much else, will die with him.

''I know it's very dark inside, but once you're in, your eyes adjust and you can see very well.'

The boy does not move. It is as if he is deaf as well as dumb.

'You don't have to be a Christian. No one has services here any longer, they've taken down the cross. This is just more' – he struggles to explain exactly what the chapel is for him – 'like my special place. The walls are two foot thick. It's a thousand years old.' The numbers have no effect. Edmund tries again. 'Do you know why I come here? Why I thought you might like it?'

With daylight behind him, the child's face is inscrutable.

'Because when I was a boy, about your age, my mother died. She was ill for quite a long time. But then my father died as well, when I was a bit older than you. He died in the tower as well. It was unexpected, at least I didn't expect it. So, it was a terrible day, like this is. And I come here to talk to them when I'm lonely. I light a candle, that's why there are two candles, can you see?'

There is the slightest nod of the head.

'I thought you might like to light a candle for your mother, now that she's dead. Because she is . . . dead. I'm sorry, I'm so sorry.'

Edmund never dreamed his story could be told so simply, that telling might feel like giving. The chapel only ever seated twenty in its box pews, but since being deconsecrated, it has only ever seated one and he takes his place on the aisle end of the second row back. He is struck by the way he has spoken, such ordinary words coming from nowhere when they were needed most. Maybe the spirit still works here on the tongue, even with the artefacts gone; maybe the place can lay its hands on the sickness he feels in his stomach every time he thinks about Valerie, her inconsequential body lifeless amongst the fallen buttresses. The snatch of the latch jolts him, the boy is pocketing the key, the rook nesting in the beams above him screeches a siren alert, and Edmund is suddenly small and scared again, half a memory of hide-and-seek and teatime and voices counting backwards from twenty in the derelict graveyard. But he is mistaken. In fact, with the key in his possession, the boy is not locking him in, but creeping down the aisle, leaving small damp prints on the tombs beneath his feet. Stopping in front of the empty altar, he crosses himself. It occurs to Edmund that everything he has been told about his sister-in-law and her son may not have been gospel truth.

'You can light one of the candles,' says Edmund. 'Here, let me help you.'

The flicker is reflected in the boy's eyes as they place the third candle alongside the others. It sends a steady incense of grief into the darkness.

Back in the kitchen, Diana is on the phone when she catches sight of the two of them returning. Edmund is looking down at the boy as if he is listening, the boy is looking up as if he is talking.

'We'll keep him until you can sort something out,' she is saying. 'But he can't stay here for long, it wouldn't be right. No, I'm not the right person at all.'

The two of them are standing together in the kitchen door, clearly shocked. She sees herself as they must see her, surrounded by fragments.

'What on earth has happened?'

'It's called an earthquake, Edmund. It's what happened when you weren't here.'

Despite the *BBC Live* updates and emergency contact numbers and hashtag hysteria, for most people the reality of the whole event is more than a little disappointing: the dramatic footage from the CCTV showing the guests running screaming from the Travelodge is less impressive when you know that nobody actually died; the multi-storey car park collapsing like a pack of cards looks terrifying until you realise it is only one corner of one level and the only victims are an abandoned Ford Fiesta and the supermarket waste-disposal bins. People needed to feel part of the tragedy that social media told them was unfolding, this scythe which passed within a whisker of their ordinary lives. They want to leave flowers and write notes and hold vigils, and Wynhope is the obvious shrine. In so many ways, Diana craves attention and visitors, just not this sort of attention or this sort of visitor. The police and the electricity board and the vicar, all of them have some legitimate role in their disaster, but the busy-bodies, the do-gooders from the village with their gifts of packets of long-life ham, and the sightseers who never normally get an up-close-and-personal look at the lives of the rich and powerful or a walk-on part in a national disaster, now get two for the price of one. They are not welcome. Garage flowers are laid at the lodge, coins are thrown in the pond at the feet of the bronze boy, the press call endlessly, and even though Edmund's solicitor friend issued a statement on their behalf, they are insatiable. Online, Diana reads all about it, noting all the things the press have got wrong, not least describing Valerie as her sister. Apparently Valerie was a tragic victim who had only recently courageously escaped from an abusive rela-tionship and started a whole new life with her small son; she was a wonderful woman (said the neighbours), always with a smile, and she loved her little boy to bits, but how the hell did they know, she only moved there recently. Friends (friends?) said she always had a good word for everybody; everybody except me, thinks Diana. She only had one word for me: liar.

Sally is away in the Caribbean, missing the whole thing. Other acquaintances pop in, but can't stay. John's visit is welcome, of course; a temporary cover over the hole in their lives is better than nothing. What was it he said? Something about it needing more than a sticking plaster to put things right and that Grace will come when she can and since the lodge isn't safe, that could be some time. Diana senses that something has changed in the hierarchy but she can't put her finger on it; pity the housekeeper wasn't six foot under the rubble, she thinks.

It isn't until a structural engineer arrives with the police that the solitary constable who is apparently on guard at the gates makes an effort to disperse the vultures. The engineer brings news that the state of emergency in the county is no longer in effect; Diana cannot see how it will ever be lifted at Wynhope. He conducts what he calls a PEBI survey and nobody asks what the letters mean; Edmund wonders how they would all fare measured with a spirit level and a plumb line. Later, the surveyor declares that Wynhope is habitable on a temporary basis in restricted areas pending further diagnostic testing. He hands Edmund a form.

The evaluation of usability in the post-earthquake emergency is a temporary and approximate evaluation, i.e. based on an expert judgement and carried out in a short time, on the basis of a simple visual inspection and of data which can be easily collected – aiming at determining whether, in case of a seismic event, buildings affected by the earthquake can still be used, with a reasonable level of life safety. – Post-Earthquake Building Inspection

'In other words, no guarantees,' summarises Edmund as he leans on the car and signs his name.

'Not in this life.' The surveyor smiles, then perhaps realising the error of his ways, leaves rather hastily.

Meanwhile, the other two officials have introduced themselves as SOCOs, Scene of Crime Officers.

'Crime?' queries Diana.

'Or untimely death.'

The man and the woman with names in plastic labels around

their necks and gloves on their fingers are interested in only three things: the building regulations regarding the construction of the pool, locked doors and keys. They do hope she'll be able to help them.

On the garden bench, Mikey sits with the dog, kicks his feet against the wooden bars and listens. He can help them. Kick. Kick. Kick.

'Michael, stop that.'

He can help them. Kick. Kick. Kick. Kicking isn't enough. He has got words, he can sort of hear them, but they haven't come out for a long time now. Perhaps he needs to practise. In the house, he decides to find a private mirror; that's how Mum said he should learn his lines when he had a solo to sing at school. At the top of the stairs, he taps on John's false wall, which is where the door to the tower was before it all fell down. It's like the *Lion, the Witch and the Wardrobe* film – once there was a whole world behind this wall. Prising his fingers between the hardboard and the stone, Mikey wants to see behind the boarding up. His memory is so clear – the smell of washed towels on the four-poster bed, the potty, his mum's laugh – it's impossible that there's nothing left. Did everything fall with the tower, not just the stones, but the things that happened in it? Did it get swallowed up by the empty pool? If he could only see behind the wall.

'Michael! What are you doing up there?'

As silent as a snake, he slides on his tummy into the bathroom and studies his reflection. He does not think he can talk to himself.

'Michael?'

The narrow stairs that go on up offer an escape route, up to the very top of the house where he can't go any further, and there he finds an empty room and shuts the door behind him and listens. No footsteps. This is his place. It's so empty he can spin in it, run in it, even do a somersault in it. There's nothing in here except him, everything he knows and everything he is. The sloping ceilings don't get in the way; he's too small to bump his head, and although the cupboards along the floor at the end are stuffed full of junk, that's okay, because he can clear them out and that can be his hiding place. Peering through the bars on the front windows, he sees that everything is a long way down and quite small, toy cars and plastic trees and four grown-ups in a huddle like Playmobil men. He can't hear what they're saying from up here, but he knows Diana's lying to them all, even to the police. I would climb to the top of the house and fight for you, that's what his mum said to him, and he said that he'd defend her with his life, like a soldier. But he didn't, did he? No more secrets, no more lies. He can cry but he can't talk. If his voice isn't working, he'll have to think of something else. Rat-a-tat-tat. Rat-a-tat-tat. And they all fall down. Instinctively, he slips the key to the nursery door into the pocket of his jeans.

'Michael's fine,' Diana says, back outside. 'He's playing in his room. And here, I've found some custard creams.' She wishes she could offer the investigators the proverbial cup of tea which would have made small talk so much easier, standing around on the lawn like it's a drinks party. 'Isn't it obvious how Valerie, how she' – Diana swallows – 'how it happened?'

And the investigator is saying she'd be surprised, around each tragedy is a story: old people's hearts stopping seconds before the force eight blows and the tree falls on the roof, hardly knowing a thing, which must be a comfort to the family; a travelling salesman trapped by a fire started by an electrical fault in a hotel which should never have passed planning; three young males from Afghanistan locked up by gangmasters in one room, working twenty-four seven to earn their freedom while carbon monoxide leaks from the boiler. Sometimes these stories even bring people to account.

Snapping the top off the custard cream Diana remembers the Christmas biscuit tin. Valerie always had first pick, always took the custard creams. Out of all the biscuits snug in their red plastic homes, the custard creams were the only ones Diana ever wanted.

'I thought you said Mikey was in his room.' Edmund points to a face at the window on the very top floor. 'Is he safe up there? Shouldn't you be with him?' He raises his hand to the boy in a sort of half-wave.

'Why me? Oh, forget it. I'm sure he's fine exploring the nursery. There are bars on the window, and for goodness' sake, Edmund, don't encourage him down.' Diana recovers herself. 'There's no knowing what he might do.'

Or say. That is a half-thought, a wasp against a window.

The SOCOs begin with the pool. It will be helpful if Edmund can provide them with the drawings, the building regs, all the paperwork, and Edmund says of course, but it may be a day or two before he can sort it all out, he'll need to dig it all out, no joke intended. No laughter. This is a serious business, but the investigators are easily satisfied by his excuses because they have a more interesting hypothesis to explore. After the earthquake, Valerie was alive. She had time to escape before the aftershock destroyed the tower. She couldn't escape because the door was locked and she couldn't find the key.

'It seems we can't find it either,' the officer concludes, blowing on her hands to warm them up. Perhaps Diana can help? Is the door to the landing usually locked?

Like a child faced with jigsaw pieces which don't fit together, Edmund screws up his face. 'You wouldn't have locked it, Di, would you? I suppose you were tired and a bit . . .' He is going to say pissed, but underneath the understanding smile, there is something rather officious about these inquisitors, so he continues in a different direction. 'After the funeral. No one would blame you.'

'Blame?' repeats Diana. 'Blame?'

'I suppose in time we can always ask Valerie's son.'

One theory, put forward by Edmund, is that Valerie might have locked the door herself, particularly if she was up to no good, taking drugs, for example.

Diana clutches at the straw. 'She was certainly off her head. She threw stuff round the room before she went to bed. She could have done anything, the state she was in.'

'Threw stuff?' Edmund is puzzled.

'All that mess in the dining room.'

It's as clear as daylight in Diana's memory: the glass smashed, red wine and meringue on the carpet and cigarette burns on the table, the sideboard ransacked, linen napkins flying like cream doves as Valerie demonstrated the worthlessness of their wealth.

'I thought that was the earthquake.'

'Oh for God's sake, don't you ever listen to anything I say?'

Consulting their clipboards, the SOCOs exchange looks that indicate they are used to being present when things fall apart. The man has been checking the wiring and wonders why the imitation candles in the alcoves on the stairs would have been switched off.

'The electricity went out,' says Diana quickly. 'It's still out in case you haven't noticed, although for some reason the rest of the county appears to have power.'

'No. They were switched off at the wall at the door to the landing,' he insists. 'Odd thing to do if you're sleeping in a strange house.' At that moment, something falls from the sky and hits him on the head. 'What the hell was that?'

That was a toy zebra, now lying on the gravel on its side, like dead horses do. Mikey is leaning out of the nursery window. He throws another animal, a lion on a green plastic stand with a model trainer in top hat and tails next to him, the handle of a whip raised and a thin black lash snaking down to the base.

'What are you doing? Michael, stop that!' shouts Diana.

For a second he disappears, but then he is back. The toys are harmless, it is the manner in which they are thrown that is frightening. The last to leap to a crazy end is a gorilla in a cage, no more than three inches tall, one paw moulded around the bars, the other claws reaching through the gaps towards a tiny plastic key.

The woman picks it up, shakes her head. 'Bless him, he's trying to communicate in the only way he knows.' With a deep breath, she seems to be summoning her professional persona. 'We've finished here for the time being. Apart from the tape.'

The black letters slowly unravel the message on the yellow plastic. Site under investigation. Do Not Enter. Site under investigation. Do not enter.

Chapter Sixteen

The Egyptian cotton sheets and feather duvet used to be her haven, but now even the bed is suspicious of Diana, turning her over and rejecting her, and she finds sleep of sorts only through the combination of pills and wine which keep her unconscious late into the morning.

Mikey still insists on sleeping on the floor. As lightly, as softly as any new mother on tiptoe and tenterhooks, Edmund pulls the covers over him. Later, in the car with the ignition on, he listens to the nine o'clock news. Three days on and the earthquake has dropped from everyone's headlines except their own and only warrants a mention because jitters in the market have hit property and building shares. It may be that his portfolio reads like a death warrant, but he has to admit to himself that they have been lucky. He says as much to Diana when finally, heavy-headed and fractious, she joins him in the kitchen and pours herself a glass of bottled water.

'It could all have been so much worse,' he says. 'Look, the kitchen's as good as new, isn't it?' He would have liked her to thank him for the work he has done this morning, clearing up while she slept.

With her head in the fridge, Diana notices nothing. 'I'll need to chuck everything out today.' There is something about a broken fridge, how dead it is, the quietly rotting contents. Should she say more, this morning? Just let him know that she locked the tower door? He'd call her a silly old thing, but he'd sort it out and then she wouldn't have to have breakfast with a secret.

'Perhaps we could still go away. We don't need to cancel the Maldives, do we? All I can think of here is Valerie,' says Diana, turning away from the rancid smell of the milk she is pouring down the sink. 'Come back when it's all sorted.'

Tempting, but impossible, according to Edmund. Apart from anything else (and he thinks he means Mikey but can't say so), he is going to have to spend a lot of time in London, the Stock Exchange has taken a bit of a beating, the government are talking about a freeze on fracking, which is just his luck and completely irrational (there have been tremors in the UK for centuries before fracking began), and then there's the problems with the Riverside Development, the investors are making all sorts of ridiculous demands for geological surveys.

'Can't blame them,' says Diana. 'When the property developer's own little excavation didn't exactly stand the test.'

'So it's my fault, is it?'

He doesn't want to pursue this. He knows in his heart that it never works out well – builders doing you a favour in return for a contract on a new housing estate, planners and county councillors and heritage officials giving you the nod in return for lunch at a club in London with a man with a title. Nothing's for nothing in this world, that's what his father would have said. 'All power corrupts', that was another one of his, but Edmund never even thought of the bloody swimming pool and power and corruption in the same breath, and now Valerie is dead and a paper trail is required, and he finds himself sick to his stomach and a little shaky because Valerie is dead, died, here, at Wynhope, killed, and the pool is the bottom of the sea and Poseidon its angry god. And then there's Mikey.

Maybe breakfast will help. The toaster isn't working, so he sits at the table picking at the bread then spooning out the marmalade to check for glass. 'We haven't even mentioned Mikey, what are you going to do about him?' he asks.

'What do you mean, what am I going to do about him?'

'All right, what are we going to do about him?'

'Not much until social services come.'

'What, and then send him off with them?' Edmund screws the lid back on. He doesn't think small boys eat marmalade. He used to like strawberry jam.

'Why, do you want to keep him here?'

'I didn't say that.'

'What did you mean then?' Diana stands at the sink with her back to Edmund. Only a thin strip of land separates the back of the house from the fields; whatever Wynhope promises from the front, backstage there is no sweeping avenue of trees leading to a Greek temple on the hill, just wire to keep the sheep out and rusted railings on which John hangs carcasses of vermin, in the way that conquering armies put heads on spikes so that the locals should understand the consequences of their actions.

'I haven't really thought of him staying here for ever.' An image forms in Edmund's mind: how it might have been if he'd had sons at Wynhope, if he'd been brave enough to have something he could risk everything for, including losing it.

Wiping her hands over and over again on a dirty tea towel, Diana rounds on him. 'Where else has he got?'

'Keep your voice down. Just now it was you saying he'd have to go. Now you're saying he has to stay. I don't think you know what you want.'

'No, I don't know what I want, all right? My sister's dead. My mother's dead. It's difficult,' she screams. 'Is that all right with you? For me not to know for once? For your lettings agent to have lost the plot?'

The back door opens.

'Hooray.' Edmund claps. 'Thank goodness you're here.'

Mrs H puts everything right. Isn't she always Little Miss Fixit, thinks Diana: honey nut cereal and fresh milk for breakfast for Michael; two supermarket carrier bags with things her grandson Liam has long grown out of, jeans, T-shirts, Lego. She even has the physique for helping small boys, the boy running into the kitchen and losing himself in her barely contained 40DD bosom. When he leaves the room, Mrs H comments that it isn't right, still not speaking after all this time, but it's a terrible thing to lose a parent, and they seemed close, didn't they? Such a lovely lady and the two of them the splitting image of each other. She knows what she's doing, pick-pick-picking at the scab. The last thing produced is the newspaper, Sir Edmund's day wouldn't be right unless he had his *FT*.

'You certainly know the way to a man's heart,' Diana smiles.

'And so do you.' says Mrs H.

And as if the housekeeper's powers do not end there, just as Edmund opens the paper in the morning room, an injection of adrenaline shoots through the arteries of the house and they all find themselves laughing and cheering at the return of the electricity like children at a magic show. Only Mikey remains unmoved. Upstairs, there is nothing important in the nursery that needs switching on. There isn't even any furniture to speak of, no curtains, no lamps, but Mikey has made this place his own. Monty waits for him on the landing, he is a very loyal soldier. The stairs to the nursery are not as narrow and steep as the ones in the tower and you don't have the feeling that they're going on for ever which is what he remembers about the steps in the tower, that and the wall. Although he tries, he can't remember what it looked like at the end of the stairs or at the bottom or what was on the other side of the wall, but he knows for certain that here is where he wants to be now, alone, at the very top of the house.

The door on the right has two keyholes, probably because that is where his aunt and uncle keep all their money. One is like the lock on his front door at home. The thought, loosely attached to the word, catches in the spokes of his thinking, but he pedals on. Yale. That key went to school with him in the secret inside zip pocket of his anorak so he could always get back in, even if Mum was asleep. What would happen now no one could wake her up? He doesn't know; he doesn't know where they have taken her either, but he thinks she will end up with Nanna in the cemetery along with the thousands of others, but he can't ask. Will he ever go back to school? Or back home? Or did home fall down in the earthquake? He can't ask those things either. He can't ask anything, because his voice has stopped working and he has stopped practising in the mirror because he sort of quite likes it, not giving any more of himself away and not knowing.

His nursery room is through the door on the left and that has locks as well, except he's the one with the key now. From the moment he discovered it when the investigators came, he liked it. It has windows facing both ways. Out of the back, far below him, a lamb has got its head stuck in the wire between the field and the house; it's twisting its neck one way then the other, and the more it struggles, the more it gets stuck. It's a long way down from up here; if you jumped, you'd die unless you had superpowers and could fly. From the front windows, the drive is a grey crayon line across the park and he can't really remember how that ends either. It just goes off the edge of the paper.

Kneeling down, he pays attention once more to the faded box he found in the cupboards under the sloping ceiling. ALL THE FUN OF THE CIRCUS FOR BOYS AGED 7–10. CONTENTS: ONE BUILD-IT-YOUR-SELF BIG TOP, TWENTY MODEL ANIMALS AND PERFORMERS, ONE WIND-UP MUSIC BOX. There is no big top, whatever that is, and the thing that is probably the music box only rattles when he shakes it. Having taken it apart, Mikey understands that it has lost a handle and a spring and he puts it back carefully under the instruction leaflet as if he has never opened it. He does not want to be accused of something which is not his fault. Edmund has given him back all the models he threw out of the window and now he can see there are a lot more than the twenty animals it says on the lid. Someone must have made a bit of a collection. Propped up against the wall, he takes them out one by one and arranges them in a semi-circle around him. The fiercest animals are chosen first: the pair of tigers, snarling, one with his head turned to the right, one with his head turned to the left, then the lions, the troop of three elephants including a baby elephant, and the four white horses with plumes on their heads and acrobats on their backs. They all join the circle around him, evenly spaced. The dead zebra is revived, reunited with its brother, and the boy puts them side by side at one end and then the monkeys, hanging from bars at the other end. The outer defences are nearly complete. He shifts position because of pins and needles, and his sock catches the ponies, knocks them over, but with great precision he stands them back up again on the uneven carpet. The people ruin the circus. They are gaudy and ugly. The girls on the horses have pink blobs on their cheeks and white legs and stiff yellow hair so he prises them off the performing ponies, snapping their thin wrists where they are attached to red plastic harnesses and throwing them back in the box. The lion tamer breaks off easily at the ankles, leaving his feet in black boots attached to the base and the remains of his whip on the floor. The other people, the ballerinas, the grinning clown and the fat man in the blue waistcoat, they are all rejected.

The animals are out of order now. Methodically he works his way round the semi-circle evening up the spacing and turning all the animals so they are facing outwards and he is on the inside. When the fire engine tries to get through, its siren blazing, the animals fight it back. When the plastic army tank advances on the circus, the animals do not surrender. Even when the soldiers in their brown camouflage with their machine guns plan to kill the horses, they rise again and nothing – nothing – can defeat the circus animals. The gorilla is broken free from his cage and appointed as his own personal bodyguard.

The sound of a car door slamming interrupts his game. The woman outside with a badge round her neck is familiar. She's staring up at the house, but doesn't see him; no one would ever guess there was someone in the nursery if they didn't know. They have come for him, he knew they would. His aunt is a liar. He feels sad that Edmund is a liar too.

'I am so sorry about your sister,' says the social worker, who introduces herself as Sarah.

'Half-sister,' says Diana, as she boils plain water for the decidedly plain boiled girl and coffee for themselves. Edmund and Diana both examine this thing called 'the loss', which sits at this table with them all day every day, the size and shape of it, the smell.

'How is Mikey doing?'

For the next few minutes they hand the boy round the table like pass the parcel; hesitantly, never quite knowing when the music is going to stop and you will be left unwrapping the paper, never quite knowing what you might find under the layers.

'Diana, I believe you told the duty team that you're happy for him to stay here,' says Sarah.

'For the time being,' adds Edmund. 'I believe my wife's words were for the time being.'

Sarah pointedly asks Diana what she would like to happen next. Breaking the piece of shortbread onto her plate into smaller and smaller pieces, Diana sweeps the stray crumbs from the table into her palm, then back onto the plate. She eats nothing. She takes the spoon out of the sugar pot and puts it ready for washing up before they have even begun.

'We chose not to have children, we married late and, to be honest, we didn't really want any,' she begins.

Edmund takes over. 'That is why my first marriage ended,' he explains. 'I thought my first wife understood that I never wanted children, but it turned out she thought I'd change my mind when it came to it.'

It could have been so different if he had changed his mind, because they were in love, he and Marguerite, head over heels and terribly young and Wynhope was everything to her, not the money or the status, but the way the poplars blew silver in the westerly wind, the dawn chorus colouring in the arboretum until it became a tropical jungle of song accompanying their early-morning lovemaking, the peace at the end of the day when the two of them sat in the rickety summerhouse and watched the grebe crossing the lake with her babies on her back. None of this would have happened. But they had taken different roads, and that, as some poet wrote, made all the difference.

'And WNT,' he added.

'WNT?'

'Wife Number Two.' The social worker's bound to be feminist and think that's a politically incorrect way of referring to a woman. 'She was the same, but different.' Very different, probably a reaction against Marguerite who was fragile and held the future like a speckled blue eggshell. Children would have been just another asset for WNT.

'The whole world mistakenly believes that a man in my position thinks about nothing other than having an heir.' He downs his espresso in one. 'You're asking all the questions. We rather hoped you might have answers.'

'I don't know how much you know of Mikey's story,' says Sarah.

'Enough.' Diana puts the lid on the shortbread tin.

'Because I thought the two of you had not been in touch for a very long time.' Resuming calmly, Sarah tells them that Valerie was a single parent for three years, then found herself in a highly abusive relationship for four years which was undoubtedly very damaging for Mikey, and that she was extremely brave to have sought help and got out. 'She might not have been particularly rich or empowered but Valerie really was a wonderful, loving mother to Mikey. She moved into a new flat, got a job, she was so positive, so full of hope.'

The words 'wonderful, loving mother' spray themselves in graffiti across the kitchen walls. It's a lie, Diana reminds herself; she witnessed Valerie drunk, sending the boy to bed on his own on the night of the funeral. She does not believe in wonderful, loving mothers.

To Edmund, the words are an epitaph carved on a gravestone,

softened only by lichen. Wonderful wife to George and loving mother to Edmund. He never visits their graves in the village, doesn't even go to the church; he keeps candles in his chapel instead.

Sarah is continuing with her story: how after the refuge the department didn't need to have any further contact with Valerie until she entered into a relationship with a man known to them, that they were hoping to marry, he was a very steady influence on her, and it's such a shame for everyone that the man in question is not in a position to be able to care for Mikey. He would have been a great dad.

'The famous Solomon, I presume,' says Diana.

'An illegal immigrant' – Edmund summarises the position like a judge – 'and in prison. We know. You can leave the icing off the cake.'

'An asylum seeker,' Sarah corrects him. 'He received a prison sentence in January after a scuffle with police in a demonstration outside the Ugandan Embassy. We're hoping it doesn't conflict with his indefinite leave to remain. He's a Christian activist and was a gay rights campaigner in Uganda. It takes a real man to combine those two.'

A real man. So she's allowed a stereotype, thinks Edmund, but in truth he knows exactly what she's getting at. 'It must do,' he acknowledges and then turns to Diana. 'I had no idea, did you?'

Another awkward silence, then the various legal options for Mikey are outlined by the social worker. To Edmund, they sound like the additional conditions you complete when you hire a car at a foreign airport, always more costly than you thought originally and not really covering you for any risk at all.

'Adoption?' suggests Diana.

Too old apparently and too damaged. Edmund is unsure whether Sarah is referring to them or to the boy.

'So, unless you know differently,' says Sarah, 'there isn't anyone else, except you.'

The music stops and the parcel drops and no one is looking to pick it up. Outside, a cloud moves over the sun and the light goes from the kitchen. With the sun, goes the fight. The March wind is whipping up the rain, lashing it against the window. Everything out there is hostile like him and why he felt the need to be so aggressive, Edmund has no idea. The music to this game is not the jaunty pass-the-parcel songs from children's parties when he was small, but the great works which he has come to know since, the requiems and passions and kyrie eleisons which heave and heal in the core of the split soul. It is the exquisite pain of Schumann's *Nachtstücke* played by his mother in the early evenings in a terrible foreshadowing of her own passing. It is to this music that he unwraps the newspaper and string and there inside is a boy. It isn't necessarily what he wants to find, he can see it is going to be a difficult and an unlovely thing, it will possibly ruin everything, but it is what he has won.

'This is all rather silly,' says Edmund, quietly closing the back door against the squall. 'I'm sorry I've sounded so, how would you call it, so, unhelpful, but there's no question, really, is there, when it comes down to it?'

Straightening her paperwork and reaching for her pen, Sarah grimaces at him, a spot-the-banker look, and he feels her disdain running down the front of his shirt like spit.

'Mikey must stay with us,' he says. 'We must at least try.'

The pen, phone, paperwork stay suspended above the open handbag, the social worker looks as though she is not sure she has heard him correctly, but Diana is nodding in agreement.

'Yes, this is the only safe place he can be. Safe.' She finds herself repeating things a lot nowadays, like a stroke victim or a dementia patient, not certain the word matches the intended meaning, or maybe saying everything twice to make up for the boy not saying anything at all.

Which is what happens when Mikey is given the chance to talk to the social worker alone. Wriggling into his interview position at the table, Mikey focuses solely on his KitKat, smoothing out the foil bit, screwing up the red part, and Sarah says how sad she is to hear what has happened to Mummy and how her job is to make sure that he is looked after safely in a family where he feels this and feels that, and on and on she goes, sounding like the television does at home when he's upstairs going to sleep and Mum is downstairs watching a box set.

Sarah shuffles closer to him. 'Your aunty says you haven't spoken since the earthquake. Is there anyone you can talk to at the moment?'

Mikey swings sideways on his chair. The foil is flat and shiny as a river. He went to the river on one of their walks, he liked it, paddling, looking for monster fish under the bridge where Edmund says the water is as deep as secrets. No more secrets, no more lies.

'Can you write something down or draw?'

It looks like a three-year-old's house – four straight lines, a roof, windows – but it isn't finished; he adds an extra storey with another row of windows until it looks a bit like Wynhope. With the felt-tips emptied out on the table, he picks the black and scribbles a mess to the tower side and uses grey for smoke rising up from that mess, then with the red he puts faces in every single window. He chooses green for the garden, brown for an oversized dog, glittery gold for the chapel at the edge of the page and blue for the river. Somewhere in the back of his mind he can hear his mum singing about a yellow brick road, so that's the colour he chooses for the drive, all the way across the page and onto the kitchen table. The only colour left is orange; with that he traces the outline of something that is at least as tall as the house. He is secretive as he colours, taking extra care between the lines.

'Wow, that's some tree . . .'

Mikey looks afresh at the picture, then without warning kicks the chair to the floor, rips the page into pieces, pushes it deep into the rubbish bin and is gone, off, out into the rain. From just outside the back door, he hears them confirming what he already knows. He is staying here. He needs help to talk. What is news to him is that although he is obviously traumatised by the earthquake and the loss of his mother, he has a real sense of family, apparently they can see it in his picture, all the happy faces looking out from the windows at Wynhope.

'Did he say anything to you . . . about that night?' asks Diana.

'Not a word, but he will, one day soon.'

When Sarah is leaving, Mikey throws stones at her departing car and when that is gone, he throws stones at a baby rabbit frozen in fright by the lily pond, and when the rabbit flees, he throws stones, he just throws stones.

Having picked the pieces of the picture out from under the banana skin and tea leaves, Diana places them on the table, eager to make sense of them and understand Michael. Maybe Wynhope can be a home for him. She will need to learn about children, but it is never too late; she could give something back, a different sort of restoration. Valerie is dead, there is a lot to make up for. Sliding the fragments around, Diana matches the line of the nursery windows and the column of smoke, constructing a picture of a possible family future until the last piece slides into place and the tall orange thing with the sticking-out bits is not a tree at all. It is a key.

Chapter Seventeen

Unable to cope any longer on her own, Diana is waiting for her own emergency services to rescue her. At her wit's end, she has called Sally. Edmund is in London, of course. Having volunteered his services in bringing up the boy, he seems to have decided his is a non-executive position and the last month has been one long downhill slide.

It started with their disaster being deconstructed at Wynhope, brick by brick. Once a team secured the site, lifted the beams, stacked the slates and towed away the great stone mantel, the SOCOs searched the rubble for the key for another two days. Crime or Untimely Death? A skip was placed beside the ruin. The bed which had been hanging over the edge of the splintered floor, its sheets sodden and the silk bedspread ripped, was lowered to the ground and unmade; the chest of drawers, the proud supporter of the porcelain potty, dismantled; Valerie's pink wheelie suitcase, unpacked. Like opera bodies, the long red velvet curtains lay with their heads on scorched pillows, their feet in puddles of overnight rain. Even the state-of-the-art towel rail was only finally dumped when the pipework had been examined like intestines at a post-mortem; Diana felt that is what they wanted to do with her, open her up and see what dish she and the devil dine out on. She could have told them they were wasting their time, but she didn't; now Michael was there to stay, it seemed unthinkable to say anything. She didn't want to salvage anything, but Edmund rescued the embroidered sampler, even though the glass was smashed and the cloth looked as though it had been dunked in the Rivers of Babylon themselves and wrung out to dry. He put it in the third drawer down in his father's old desk, his safe place. Finally, all that was left was stone. All colour gone. All softness. Cloth, tapestry, wallpaper, light, everything she had offered to the Wynhope tower, discarded.

It became a sanitised ruin, the sort you might visit on holiday, jagged walls and roofless, a neat pile of slates and gargoyles stacked round the back because someone said they were worth a bit nowadays. Permission was granted to repair the inside of the main house and builders permanently sealed up what had been the landing entrance to the spiral staircase, although, as Edmund said, it was going to be a devil of a job to make good the panelling, listed buildings have to be perfect. Regardless of the imperfections lived out in them, thought Diana.

The entrance to the pool was also blocked up. Nobody felt like discussing its future, although one of the men on site suggested it would make a perfect bunker when the shit hits the fan, and Edmund laughed along with him, agreeing they could put a few tins of baked beans down there and prepare to sit out Armageddon.

Just as Wynhope looked a little more like itself, and even the boy looked a little more like an ordinary child, Diana also tried normality for size, attempting the things that mothers do, but there was always a wall. She called wakey wakey in the mornings and felt the mockery of the wall, laid out clean clothes at the foot of the wall, boiled eggs for the wall; she even tried sitting sit next to the wall to watch daytime television. At times, she was almost provoked to take a mallet and batter down the wall and had to clench her fists to stop herself. All the simple things she'd imagined a mother might do seemed impossible, even the vocabulary mocked her: play, read, stories.

In the early days after the earthquake, like those who have been sick and slippered for a long time, everybody else in the area tried on their everyday shoes and stepped back out into the workaday world. Diana's red slingbacks stayed in their tissue paper in their box in their upmarket bag in the bottom of the wardrobe. Edmund re-established his routine, managing to get up to London, but then returning stressed about the Riverside project, with evenings spent on the phone in his study with a slammed door and a raised voice. She didn't ask too many questions. There had been bumpy rides before in the financial department, but they had a pretty good invest-ment-shaped cushion between them and the hard place. When Edmund was home and available, the boy, like the dog, sought him out, but when it was just her and Michael, it was all about separation. Since she couldn't find the middle path between her desire to feed him or starve him, hug him or slap him, she settled for distance, leaving him asleep for as long as possible, allowing him to spend hours shut away with his circus animals in the nursery upstairs. She thanked God for television and for the computer in Edmund's study. They'd downloaded some game he liked called Lockdown, which looked violent and unsuitable, particularly for a boy who'd had his sort of experiences, but it kept him quiet and at least she knew where he was. When she fed Monty, she whistled and the dog came, full of love and expectation; when she needed Michael for lunch, she screeched from the hall to the nursery, but it was only her new best friend, the echo, who replied and she sat alone in the kitchen, the lunch she'd laboured over congealing on the table.

This morning had been one of the worst. Just the sound of the tyres on the gravel at 7 a.m. quickened her heartbeat. Edmund leaving. Why this sudden need to be in the city all day every day? Hadn't it been a joint enterprise, this rescue of the boy? Why was it down to her and why wouldn't Michael speak, for Christ's sake? And when was she ever going to be able to say something herself? And when would they bury Valerie? That thought started her crying again; she thought she might have stopped crying by now. As she lay in bed, calming down, she resolved to make this the day she got a grip. Mrs H has awarded herself a day off, so it's just her and Michael. To begin all over again. That would be something. And there was something. Someone. A person outside the bedroom door, a shadow across the carpet. It was her. It couldn't be but it was; it held its hand to its mouth as she did, peered round the door as she used to. See, there, Valerie, not a woman, but a child, all the years shrunk back to the beginning. In horror, she sat up and forced herself to recognise the visitor for who it was. It was just the boy.

Later, she did her best to disguise her distress. Breezing around the kitchen to the beat of an unfamiliar music channel which sounded youthful and energetic, she poured out cereal which he didn't eat and blackcurrant juice which he spilled on purpose and buttered toast which he chewed slowly and deliberately, always watching her, tracking her from the kettle to the sink to the larder and back to the table, like a drone. Forcing her earlier plans out from under the weight of his passive resistance, she suggested things to do, but ended up leaving him in front of the television while she stripped his sheets, damp and poisonously sweet with the smell of stale urine, and listened to the rhythmic drum of the washing machine as it made everything clean again. They would need a waterproof cover. She put her head round the door to ask him if he'd like to go into town to go shopping, but seeing him, cross-legged and motionless in front of a natural history programme about sea life with a jellyfish pulsing its translucent tentacles through the ocean, she realised she was too scared to risk it alone. Was she alone? The slam of the back door in the gusting April wind made her jump. The intruder laughing in the bathroom turned out to be the radio. No one could live like this for long.

From the far end of the sofa, she asked Michael if he would like to talk about that night, what happened in the earthquake; she knew she'd like to, she said, she was sure it would help them both.

'A problem shared is a problem halved, that's what Edmund says.'

Diana thought a quote from his hero might convince Michael to join in.

Not so. Louder and louder and louder the boy pressed the volume control until she could not make herself heard above the haunting song of the humpback whale gliding past the camera.

The panic in her voice must have been alarming, given the speed at which Sally cancelled the hairdresser and come straight over.

'You mustn't blame yourself,' she says. 'I know you are, I can see it in your face. And,' she continues, 'while I'm on a roll, for God's sake, call me again whenever you need me. I'm back from the Caribbean now for a while. I need a rest.' She winks.

The sitting room has a chill to it, although the heating is back on; the whole of the old house still shivers in shock at its lost limb. It snowed briefly in the night, the same day the clocks went forward. Even if the boy won't listen to her story, Sally will.

'The thing is I never liked Valerie, not really.'

'I know, you told me. But, darling, my brother drove his Harley into the back of an HGV on the M4, and I loathed him, but it doesn't mean I was responsible for his death.'

A great, cloudless sky of release is only one sentence away, if she can do it. This is the moment to jump. 'But I was, in a way,' insists Diana. 'I was responsible.'

Now, arms wide and hurtling, to fall and feel the truth open above her and guide her safely down. The briefest hesitation, then her friend, out of kindness, pulls her back from the edge. She is getting it all out of proportion and Sally isn't surprised. Diana has so much on her plate, her mother's funeral, this crap with her sister, the tower coming down after all the work she'd done there. And the boy on top of that.

'God, just talking about it makes me want another drink.' Sally tops up the glasses. 'It's not as if you left her to die in a burning building.'

The door which was open is now locked. Diana fastens her secret around her.

Sally makes an offer. 'Tell you what, you piss off and do your shop, and I'll stay here with Mikey. He can't be any worse than my ghastly, dysfunctional grandchildren.'

'You love them really,' says Diana.

'I know I do, totally obsessed, in fact.'

Diana drives, she just drives. It's really only if Mrs H is there to stay with the boy that she can ever get out, and even then she doesn't like leaving those two together. It's a toxic combination. The car – the control and the power of it, the self-contained scented interior with its built-in sound system, sat nav, phone, internet – how it used to appeal to her to travel in her own world around her own world, but now a simple sense of a destination and someone for company would be enough. She recalls Valerie half asleep in the front seat on the way back from the funeral and her eyes lose focus. The layby seems like a safe place to draw breath, she'll crash if she goes on like this. There's a van selling burgers and tea, two lorry drivers in T-shirts are slouched at a plastic table, eyeing up her Range Rover. Posh bitch, that's probably what they're thinking, got it all sewn up. What do they know about her and how she's unravelling?

Not able to face the fluorescent noise of the out of town store, Diana makes her way to the local mini market and pushes the trolley like a pram. The miscellaneous purchases in it are lolling like a semi-conscious child, a cabbage for a head, a bag of frozen chips for a body, banana legs, a vegetative state. She's forgotten her card. The queue behind her at the checkout waits impatiently while she scrabbles for another pound coin; the girl on the till says she can bring it next time, and the eyes of the shelf stacker and the old ladies from the sheltered housing and the teenager with her screaming toddler, all of them are mocking her. There goes the lady of the manor, she's been taken down a peg or two.

'He's an amazing boy,' says Sally as she is leaving. 'Beat me at chess. Totally adorable, I could eat him, but God he's going to be hard work for a while, Di, I don't envy you . . . And no, I know what you're going to ask. He didn't say a word. I'm sure it's only a matter of time. If not, you can always get him a shrink. Harry's children seem to virtually live at the clinic,' she adds as she waves goodbye.

In the hall the hands of the grandfather clock are cutting a bigger and bigger slice out of time, the hours when nothing has been said growing, the hours left when something could be said diminishing. As if to confirm the sense that the world is sealing her up in an impossible prison, the postman brings the formal notice from the coroner informing them that Valerie's body can be released for burial, although the date for the final inquest has not been set, pending further police investigations.

That evening, it is Edmund's suggestion that they write down some ideas for the funeral to share with Mikey.

'The advice online says if you start writing notes, you take away the incentive for mutes to talk, it's called colluding,' says Diana.

'I hate it when you label him a mute like some retard from a Victorian fairy tale. Listen, we're not talking about whether or not he wants fish fingers for tea, Diana. This is his mother's funeral.'

Edmund's document is disputed by Diana like a legal proposition. 'Why have you put buried? Cremated, that's what she wanted. And what on earth do you mean by asking him if there's anything else he'd like to tell us?'

'How do you suddenly know all about the deepest end-of-life wishes of a sister you hadn't spoken to for years? But, leaving that aside, I don't mean anything by the last question. It's just a sort of catch-all. Who knows what he's bottling up? I haven't even seen him cry.'

At the kitchen table, Diana passes Michael a biro, and it turns into a silly little tug of war that makes Edmund laugh. There was an American programme she watched once about a medium who transcribed messages, unseen hands taking hold of her pencil, scratching violent and erratic words across the page. Opposite her, the boy is writing. Yes, he does want to come to the funeral. A little hesitantly, he writes 'Solomon', as a suggested guest, but then scribbles it out with a lightning storm of scratches which rip holes in the paper. Monty? Edmund shakes his head. The boy moves on down his questionnaire. No, he does not want to take part in the service. Is there anything else you'd like to say? It is deliberate, Diana thinks, the way he lets the pen hover over the question, the tortuous progress through the three capital letters. Y.E.S. There is something he would like to tell them, but the implication is not yet. The boy is like his mother, he enjoys watching other people suffer.

'I know,' suggests Edmund. 'When I'm in London, I'll buy you one of those little whiteboards with a marker. Then you can tell us whatever you want, whenever you choose.'

Mikey makes good use of his present. Ha ha, he writes, and gives the board to Edmund, and the two of them sit giggling on the sofa, kids passing notes in the back row of the classroom at the teacher's expense.

The next message is also for Edmund: 'Are you coming to the funral?'

This is a test. Diana is curious to know if Edmund's love for the child has limits. Yes, I'll be there, he writes back, adding a smiley face. No limits then. It is all yes, yes, yes in this house now.

In the end the funeral is a desultory business. Diana has resisted all Edmund's suggestions about contacting Valerie's friends and a stroke of genius prompted her to go on Valerie's Facebook page and exercise her rights as a close relative to get it taken down, but not before she'd been faced with a river of online mourning.

Loved you, Val. You were the best and I miss you more than I can say. Rest in Peace.

You didn't deserve this, but I know the angels will watch over you and keep you safe because you were a brave, strong, good woman, the best mother, the best friend.

Val, against the odds you fought your way to freedom, you were an example to all women everywhere.

No mother's ever had such a wonderful son as Mikey. Who will look after him now?

She played with the idea of what she might contribute, but in the end delete was the only button she needed.

The notice in the paper says the funeral is family only, which means the three of them – and Mr and Mrs H, who according to Edmund are family. No one cries except Grace, not even at the grave in the village churchyard. The press are waiting at the lychgate, eager to cover this high society event with just the sniff of a scandal if someone were to turn over the stones. There is no reception afterwards, Diana has learned that lesson.

Afterwards, back to Wynhope and each of them retreats: Mikey to the nursery, Edmund to his river where he can weep alone, and Diana to the drawing room where the double dose of pills she has taken in the morning finally kick in and she sleeps and dreams about not having enough food at a party and everybody going home hungry. Later, Edmund shakes her gently awake and suggests they should check on Mikey, he's been on his own a long time for a day like this. He used to kiss her if she took a late afternoon nap; she's glad he doesn't try, she has bad breath nowadays when she wakes, something foul within her leaking out.

From the door to the nursery, they can see the toys have been carefully arranged. The cars and vehicles are placed in one straight line over towards the wall, as if they are parked. The bricks are arranged in rows, each standing upright, with two or three plastic trees amongst them. The resemblance to a graveyard is unmistakable – the circus animals are grouped in the manner of mourners, the acrobats and the clowns and the lame lion tamer in one huddle, the chimpanzees and tigers sharing their condolences with the gorilla, and all of them clustered around the large cardboard box in the middle of the otherwise empty room.

'I gave him that box, the replacement china came in it. I thought he'd like to play with it. Not this.'

'Mikey?' Edmund's voice is barely audible.

Diana creeps towards the box, lifts the lid. 'A sheet.'

The crumpled white cotton folds into nothing beneath her hands. Falling back, trampling the mourning circus animals, Diana is caught by Edmund's arms. The box shifts, the sheet grows claws which clasp the sides, and a shape like that of a skull rises up. And there he is, the shroud falling from his shoulders, revealing a thin, pale naked body.

Chapter Eighteen

'Perhaps we should lock up the nursery. It's unhealthy for him up there on his own for days, with nothing but those circus animals for company,' says Edmund, but the boy resists fiercely and Edmund backs down. For once, Diana agrees with Michael.

'It's hard to find anything that makes him happy,' says Diana. 'If you take this away, God knows what I'll do with him.'

'It'll drive him mad,' says Edmund.

'Madder,' says Diana.

'He needs friends. Why don't you visit the primary school, like Sarah suggested?'

'Why don't you?'

Diana hoped that after the funeral her thoughts might be more easily marshalled, but there is still the inquest to come, the police investigations to complete, and the thought of Michael going to the local school, embedded in the community like a spy, is intolerable. Worst of all, there's still Valerie. Louder than ever, Diana can hear her wheelie case outside on the gravel and Wynhope with a sore throat, creaking its welcome. To live with this level of fear is unbearable; she presses her long, sharp polished nails into her skin, the scars across her thighs reminding her of how she used to manage when she was a teenager.

But for Michael to go away to school, that is a different matter.

Fired up with a possible solution, Diana searches online for independent boarding prep schools, distance radius from Wynhope well over 150 miles, too far to do in a day. They can afford it. She treats Edmund's financial hysteria with more than a pinch of salt; flogging one of the hideous paintings on the stairs on its own would more than cover the fees. Her only reservation is that if the boy goes away to school, he might say something, but can you imagine some tweedy Latin master ever believing such nonsense, let alone doing anything about it? Her impression is that private schools are a safe step away from the ghastly conspiracy of state professionals who keep phoning and trying to force them all into therapy. After all, he who pays the piper calls the tune.

'Would you like to go to school?' Diana calls Michael into the study and shows him smiling children playing violins in sumptuous theatres or scoring tries under blue skies and autumn leaves, explaining that it's not possible for him to go back to his old primary.

For the first time, he looks her in the eye and nods. Not talking, exactly, but heading in the right direction.

She seizes the opportunity. 'I know you must be very lonely and unhappy and I'm sorry I can't just make everything better. If I had a magic wand, I'd use it.'

Michael touches her cheek.

'I'm sure going to school would help a little, it's what Mummy would have wanted you to do.'

Her tears are on the tip of his finger. He tastes them with his tongue.

In the evening, upstairs, reapplying her make-up, she watches Edmund walking through the dusk, the tulips forming a guard of honour for his slouched arrival home and she feels guilty at how she has been recently: screaming and arguing, the terrible things she's said, the things left unsaid, how that must have felt to him, exhausted from all his problems in the city. Their increasing distance and fractiousness is all her fault. It's not surprising he's fast becoming an expert in ways to be absent. The London flat still has something of the bachelor pad about it; it's not just now that she resents his bolthole behaviour. The pleasures of having a place to call your own are well known to her. She bought her first flat when she was working in an estate agent's on the south coast, insider knowledge. From the outside it was a dreary place next door to a nursing home, and sometimes when she was coming home from work she would see their faces, the imprisoned sick, staring out at the dispassionate sea, and vowed she would never allow that to happen to her. Inside, she made it perfect, rarely inviting anyone back, spending a long time hoovering. This window has a very different view and Wynhope is home. Edmund must never feel the need to stay away ever again.

'Michael and I have had a good day, haven't we?' She smiles as they sit down, bright sprigs of May blossom on the table and the Sauvignon chilled. She has made such an effort, for him.

Raising his eyebrows in mock surprise, Edmund winks at the boy.

'We've been finding out about schools and I've made a few phone calls.' Diana is unstoppable with her lists of subjects, sports, the overseas trips, not to mention the number who go on to top public schools, just like Edmund.

'Not as if I liked it there,' he says, pushing the lamb chops around his plate, just like a boarding school boy might.

'Well, that's different, that's because' – Diana didn't want to mention the dead word – 'things were difficult for you, darling, but you can't deny how it made you what you are today.'

'And what exactly am I? Today.'

Tension is protein for the boy, she can see it in the way he licks his lips. Diana clears the plates. 'Only that it must have been such a help, knowing everyone who knows everyone in the City.'

Screwing up his daffodil-yellow napkin, Edmund throws it on the table. 'A fat lot of good that's done me now. I'm sorry, Diana, sorry, Mikey. It was a good plan but there's not enough money for school fees. Blame me, blame the ice age, blame who you like, but that's the truth.'

The door slams, the boy doesn't even flinch; he just slides from the table and retreats to the nursery, like it is a well-rehearsed evacuation routine.

It is nothing to do with the fees, Edmund admits to himself. It isn't the cost of Mikey going away to school that he is worried about.

'You can't just pack up a problem and pay matron to sort it out,' he tells Diana later as they get ready for bed.

'Can't I?'

'No, you can't. Not if I won't pay.'

'You're not the one stuck here with him all day.'

'You think I want to be in London?' Edmund slips under his side of the duvet and picks up his most recent copy of the *City Digest*.

'Yes, I do. You pay perfectly good talented people a fortune to run your little empire. You don't need to be there. And you running for the train isn't going to stop the index falling and you know it. They're probably all sitting in the office praying that you miss the bloody thing.' She continues from the bathroom, raising her voice above the running of the taps. 'And don't give me that crap about not affording fees. I can read the financial pages just as well as you. Yes, you've lost money on the fracking and the property shares, but it's a drop in the ocean, isn't it?' She doesn't expect an answer. She gets into bed and turns out her light. 'But what really matters, Edmund, is that wherever you are, I don't want to be here, at Wynhope, twenty-four seven all alone with a mute delinquent for company. I don't want to be and I shouldn't be, for all our sakes. So the local primary it is then and on your head be it.'

The first day of the summer term Mikey slips into his new uniform, looks at himself in the mirror, touches his sweatshirt as if he has woken up from a dream, and then leaves for school without looking back. Diana returns from her first ever school run and makes herself a cup of green tea which she drinks on the bench under the catalpa tree, imagining she has been wheeled there by kindly people and left in the sun, as if no one has any more expectations of her in that present moment than that she should live. Alone at last, the boy gone, Valerie also, she holds something very fragile in her mind: hope. Surely Michael will do better now he is at school? Maybe he'll make friends to play with, maybe he'll play with her. Even if he says something, no one will believe him; in time he might not even believe himself, childhood memories are like that. Swirling the tea at the bottom of the mug, she reprimands herself for turning into a madwoman who has started to place her faith in curing warts with witchcraft and lets her mind wander to the memories stirred up by their first school visit.

With thick tweed skirts and ponies, the women in Edmund's social circle have an entirely different experience of education so she never talks about her schooldays with them, but at the village primary they were back chanting to her across the years, hands joined in one long line swooping across the tarmac:

'Please, Jack, may we cross the water,

to see your ugly daughter,

to throw her in the water,

to see if she can swim.'

She was always the lead fisherman, whipping up the others to net the floundering ones; more picking than picked upon, if she's honest, but that's hardly surprising, she was in survival mode from a young age.

It was a joke how easily this local headteacher was won over by her, her faith in the village school being by far the best place to help little Michael rebuild his shattered life, how the important thing was to keep the lines of communication open. The boy didn't talk of course. Records from his previous schools in London confirm that teachers thought he was really quite bright, but his levels of achievement didn't always reflect that; he was too tense, too tired, too quiet even then.

'But I'm sure he'll be chattering away nineteen to the dozen before long' – that's what the head said, and Diana knew that's why Michael was smiling. You read about cases like that in the papers, children telling fairy stories to the adults and being believed. Or telling the truth and not being believed. She didn't know if the staff realised how much the boy hated her: surely something that strong must smell.

That interview was the Wednesday; the following Easter weekend was a close call as well. It may have been too late for her to tell the truth, but it was never going to be too late for the truth to announce itself. Sally arrived out of the blue with a bag full of expensive chocolate eggs and the boys were full of excitement. Naturally Diana volunteered to hide them. Working her way around the gardens under the cheating eye of the bronze boy, she slipped the brightly coloured sweets in the dank gaps between the stones surrounding the lily pond, pressed them into the close soil between the tulips in the stone urns, and lastly she went into the orchard where she and Valerie sat and talked, once. She rested an egg on the broken sundial.

'In the east I rise, in the west I fall,

Again tomorrow I shall call.'

Such misplaced faith they had in the unshakability of their world, her husband's ancestors.

'Warm, cold, warm, hot, hotter,' she called across the spring garden as they searched, her words steering them well away from the camellias and the yew hedge.

The key. Alone at last on this day, which is not just the first day of term, but the first day of some measure of freedom for her, Diana realises how completely everyone else's voices have left Wynhope. John has cut his hours now they're not at the lodge and it's been declared uninhabitable, and Mrs H is more taciturn than ever with her. Edmund's voice is only over the phone more often than not, and when he's home, he talks a different language, if he talks at all. She's given up even expecting to hear Michael. This silence is all hers, she owns it. Picking her way through the site of the ruin,

Diana lets a forgotten brick thump from her hands onto the mud, one dull lump no longer of any significance. Standing above the now defunct skylights into the pool, she peers down and acknowledges this is an empty tomb. No gardeners, no news. Turning her back on it all, she waves at the bronze boy, a silly habit picked up from Edmund who salutes the statue in the way that other people appease magpies to ward off bad luck.

One for sorrow, two for joy, three for a letter, four for a boy.

In the border, she parts the aquilegia with great care, slides her hand under the yew bush: dry earth, needles, roots like fists, thorns for fingernails, the cold key. Quite bewildered by the smallness of this thing which has grown so big in her mind, she weighs it in the palm of her hand, then, having locked Monty in the house because she doesn't want anyone watching her, she sets off for the river.

Once there, it does not seem such a simple thing, to throw away a key, and the river pushes at the banks of her confidence. She thought it would be carried away downstream, but of course it will sink. The rapids are more shallow than she remembered; it will shine its guilt through the water. It is nearly summer, the reeds are fast-growing and green, and the small islands in the river have inlets and harbours where beachcombers might find messages. The pool is deep enough, but what if Edmund hooks it, fishes up an answer to a riddle, and brings it home alive and wriggling for the truth? It's always been his river.

Back in her bedroom, on her own territory, Diana opens the drawer where she hides some of the things she never talks about. Here, at the back, is the pregnancy test kit, for instance. She could have thrown that away, but she didn't. Edmund is a man who prefers not to take the lid off those things he fears, he'll never look here. He isn't the reason she bought the kit, of course – that will never be necessary – and only one of the tester sticks has ever been used. He has such little faith in his physical self and she loves him all the more for that. In the early days of their relationship, people in the office used to gossip about whether she was more than a companion to the boss and they were simultaneously right and wrong. She opens the box with all the hasty, hot-faced guilt of an adolescent.

That Mrs H's grandson would brag to his mates about what happened, Diana took for granted, but she never dreamed he'd tell his family. It's hard to see how it ever happened, two and a half years ago, when things weren't so different from now: Edmund always away on business, the honeymoon days at Wynhope over, and something lumpish and dull-coated which she could only assume was routine squatting outside on the doorstep every morning, waiting for her with its chin in its hands. Like now, she missed going to work. Like now, there was little or nothing to do in the house – Mrs H and the cleaners did that. There was little or nothing to do in the garden – John and the contract gardeners did that. There was little or nothing to do socially that she could control, being at the mercy of other people's seating plans. The only thing she had rights over then was herself, so she spent a lot of time polishing, plucking, trimming and perfecting her self, although she knew there was never likely to be a great physical return on that investment.

Then one day, there was Liam, earning some pocket money in the summer holidays by helping out in the garden, hedge cutting. All she really wanted was someone to talk to, but with his ear guards on he didn't hear her. The sunken garden sucked the heat into its belly, the humid air was swollen with plump bees and sickly with the scent of fat roses, and purple lavender brushed against her bare legs – the whole garden was a brothel. His body was beach brown, and when she touched his arm, just to get his attention, her fingers slid on his sweat. She offered him a beer, he asked for Coke, then she drank too much wine. That's how ridiculous the whole thing was, ridiculous but gorgeous. He was taut, pumped like the thoroughbred she stood next to in the paddock, the first time Edmund took her to Ascot. It didn't occur to her that she was the first to break him in, fluid bodies and fullness amidst the drystone walls and geometric perfection of the box hedges. He was less beautiful when it was over, tucking his flaccid cock into his off-white pants and running down the drive like a guilty kid. The hedge trimmer was heavy when she tried to put it away; there was oil down her legs which wouldn't wash off. Afterwards, she stood in the bathroom in a shower of partial understandings: she didn't regret it, didn't know why she did it, wouldn't do it again, didn't even particularly enjoy it – she rarely did – and as she wrapped herself up in a soft white towel, she thought it was something she needed to do just once, now that she was married to a man. No one ever gets to have all of anyone.

It wasn't long before Diana noticed the change in Mr and Mrs H. I know that you know that I know that you know. Should she tell Edmund before they did? That's always been the dilemma: to speak out or not. The following weeks were counted carefully, Diana imagining all his pent-up boyhood sperm inside her, then there was that one moment in her life when she experienced the briefest, ridiculous regret that there was no blue line and never would be. She didn't say anything, John and Mrs H didn't say anything either, not directly, and Edmund didn't know. What you don't know can't hurt you is one of his favourite clichés.

Wrapped up in the instructions, the tower key is hidden in the pregnancy test box, the box pushed to the back of the drawer, the drawer closed.

It all adds up to a Jenga tower of secrets and lies, and wouldn't Mrs H just love to see it fall. Over the next few days Diana notices that the housekeeper is already undermining what little authority she has with Michael with the swagger of a woman who has brought forth the fruit of her womb (of course, when you've had them yourself), but also of Edmund (you should have seen him with our Louisa, before your time). And when Michael is with Mrs H, the boy materialises in much the same way as he does when he is with the dog. He touches her if he wants attention; he lets her wash his bleeding knees; he accepts food from her; he allows her to help him with his spellings, difficult, different, deliberate. More than that, the two of them are developing some way of understanding each other, even without language. Mrs H chases the giggling child around the hall with the end of the vacuum cleaner – 'I'll get you, young man' – and another afternoon she was singing songs as she pushed him on the rope swing John hung from the cedar, Diana throwing open the sash window, not knowing if it's the crows or the boy, but she can hear screaming. She often hears screaming.

'To think they never found the key.'

Someone is always moving her keys. Diana strongly suspects Mrs H; it's the sort of deliberate malicious thing she would do. If not her, then the boy. If not him, then she fears to think who or what; up until now she's never believed in poltergeists.

'Won't it be something when the laddie starts to talk? The truth will always out.'

No more secrets, no more lies, Michael writes on his whiteboard, and Mrs H thinks this is an excellent motto to live by. 'Did Mummy teach you that? I thought so. She was a good lady, your mother, and never forget it.'

Having decided to get a bit more of a grip on things, Diana has decided to go back to the health club. She checks her sports bag and in there finds the boy's whiteboard with just the one word on it.

Liar.

Hastily she erases the letters and returns it. Head on the table, elbow over the words, Mikey writes something new then wipes his sleeve across the board. Now you see it, now you don't.

'You and your secrets,' says Mrs H.

Who is she referring to?

Swimming seems like too much bother, so instead Diana sits in the steam room where she is dizzy and light-headed, and all it takes is a quiet rumble from the sauna pump and she's back at Wynhope, the tremor building beneath her. It's difficult to make out what is what, because of the steam, but she can feel the drops of moisture on the damp lawn under her feet, and hot and cold with fear she registers a child screaming on the other side of the door and the locker key on her wristband. Bringing with her a brief gust of cool air, a woman materialises in the mist opposite her. Valerie will never let her be. Even far away from Wynhope there will always be those thin arms and nail varnish and one twisted leg sticking out from under a towel.

'I've cut the quote of the day out of my magazine for Mikey,' says Mrs H when she gets home. 'We've stuck it on the fridge, haven't we, Mikey? I'll read it out. "Never trust someone who lies to you. Never lie to someone who you trust."'

Chapter Nineteen

Mrs H has gone one step too far, in her opinion. Diana waits for her opportunity and it presents itself on a plate less than a fortnight later. She was asked to pop into school to see the head. Edmund said it was probably nothing serious; he couldn't stand anything being wrong with the boy, or with her, or the computer, or the wine, you name it. On the increasingly rare occasions he spent time at home he wanted it to be nothing more or less than a refuge and if it wasn't, he was furious with her. But it wasn't a refuge, was it, with its fallen tower and silent orphan, it was a madhouse. The school thing turned out to be something about a poster Michael had drawn in his 'All About Me' unit.

Task: Five things someone should know about you.
1. I come from the Mandela Estate.
2. I do not know my dad.
3. Someone I know murdered someone else.
4. Diana and Edmund are fostering me.
5. My mum was killed.

'The head's wondering if he should be in touch with social care,' Diana tells Edmund and Mrs H as they examine the poster, the childish proclamation slanting chaotically away from the margin, incongruous on the immaculate dining-room table. 'Edmund, are you listening?'

'Fostering. That's a sad way he's described it,' says Edmund. 'But I suppose it's hard to find the right words for complicated family relationships.' He notes Diana's annoyance. 'What do you mean, social care? It's not exactly a, you know, an allegation.'

'It's a disclosure,' says Mrs H.

That's the word Diana was looking for as she drove home; all she could think of was 'confession', which was altogether different.

The housekeeper gives her diagnosis. 'It's not normal.'

'He's not normal,' replies Diana, but nobody is listening to her.

'I don't see what the problem is.' Edmund explains that the boy has done exactly what the teacher asked, ending up with the sad, but incontrovertible fact that Valerie was killed.

Looking at it with fresh eyes, Diana realises it may be one writing task, but there are many ways of understanding it.

Mrs H is less convinced. 'It's clear he has something he wants to tell us,' she says.

Enough. Mrs H is a bitch. She should have forced Edmund to get rid of her ages ago. Diana returns to the dining room to have it out with her and there she catches her housekeeper with her mobile phone, the tell-tale click of the camera, the phone slipped back into her trousers as quick as a pickpocket with slick fingers.

'Were you taking a photo of Michael's work?'

'What would I want that for? I was just checking my messages. Louisa's not been too well and Naomi's been keeping me updated.'

'I'd prefer it if you didn't spend so much time on the phone while you're working.' Diana has crossed a line and knows it. Mrs H's response is that she will need to leave on the dot today and will not be able to collect Mikey from school. Upstairs, Edmund is muttering something about getting changed and the two of them going down to the river. He doesn't speak clearly any longer; it's as though he's mainly talking to himself, but, even so, she knows he doesn't mean her.

'I'm a bit worried about Mrs H,' Diana calls through the wall to the dressing room. It's easier that way. Edmund has a strange upper-class loyalty to those people others would call employees.

'What about her?' He comes into the bedroom, buttoning up an old, frayed check shirt. He is starting to look a little frayed himself.

'She's had a bit of an attitude since leaving the lodge.'

'Such as?' Edmund is caught up with his own reflection.

'For example, just now, spending yet more time on her bloody mobile, fussing about her grandchildren, and when I commented on it, she flounced out saying she has to leave early and won't be around to pick up Michael later.'

'Mikey.'

Running her hand along the bedspread to effect a perfect crease in front of the pillows, Diana stops herself retaliating. 'Whatever. Anyway, she's as much use as a sick headache, sometimes.'

'Can you do without her?' Opening a packet of indigestion tablets, Edmund finds it empty. 'Now they can't live in the lodge and their salary isn't offset by their rent . . .' He opens the window to release a bee; its buzz is replaced by the white noise of John on the mower outside. 'I only mention it because you seem to be saying you won't mind if she goes, or at least reduces her hours.' The pill packet goes in the bin, his hands go to his stomach. 'But I don't want to make things difficult for them.' Quite suddenly he sits heavily on the bed. 'I don't know how I'll manage, everything's felt so difficult since Valerie.'

Standing over him, Diana massages his shoulders. 'It's probably better for them if it's a clean break,' she says. 'It'll make it easier for them to find something else if they want to, although they might not need to. They'll get their pension soon and might have left anyway. And we'll cope without them.' She smiles confidently. 'You know I'll do whatever I have to for the two of us to be happy together.'

When the last day comes, Mikey hides in his nursery, Edmund hides in his office in London, and Diana tells the housekeeper she doesn't expect to see her at Wynhope again, it's better for the boy that way. No cards, no phone calls, nothing.

The car is inching forwards when Mrs H lowers the window. 'I know something awful happened that night, it was written all over your face,' she says. 'You should have learned your lesson. The truth will always out.'

Jumping to one side, Diana only just manages to avoid being blinded by the grit thrown up by her housekeeper leaving.

Try as they might, they cannot break the barricade to get into Michael's room. After three hours, Edmund is frantic, wanting to call the police. He doesn't understand Michael like she does, she knows he's cunning. He'll have realised that there is no better way of forcing the issue than being locked in a room until the truth comes out. Close to midnight, Michael allows them to open the door, just a fraction; the boy is still in one piece, which is more than can be said for the room. One of Diana's first jobs as the new house-keeper for Wynhope House is to disinfect it, but the truth is, nothing she does makes the room truly clean.

Even so, it is so much better having contract gardeners and the Spotless Angels cleaning agency, she says, when she finally returns one of Sally's messages; no personal relationships involved, just money. They come three times a week and say she is kind woman, boy is lucky. The rest of the time the house is pretty much deserted. The imposed quiet of those afternoons at Wynhope deafens her, like tinnitus, a relentless noise that no one else can hear but which makes everything else impossible. If being in the house is a night-mare, escaping the house is no easier. Her heart rate rises when she walks to the garage, she has to go back and check she has her keys, and then when she's out locks call out to her as she passes, padlocks on bicycles, keypads on office blocks. Once she passed a note Sellotaped to a lamppost, 'Found, set of keys', and a number to call. In the past she enjoyed her trips into town, swapping the rural idyll for the more familiar suburban hassle, overflowing car parks and crowded supermarkets, but even these streets provoke pounding anxiety in her nowadays. And it's worse when she's home. Keys appear in strange places: a box of them on the doormat, one on her pillow, and, worst of all, she finds a filthy old-fashioned key in her chest of drawers, its flaking metal hooked through the fine black-and-red lace of a thong, so repulsive it's almost erotic, rough teeth and the scent of freshly laundered underwear. Mrs H has gone, so it has to be Michael. He always looks as though he's plotting some-thing and physical, emotional, sexual aggression is in the boy's genes, she mustn't forget that. Her suspicions are confirmed by what happens next. At school Michael steals keys from a teacher's handbag. He is put on a part-time timetable. With Mrs H gone, this is a sentence which punishes both of them equally. Edmund sees it as an opportunity to give the boy more time to play outside in the fresh air, rehabilitation he calls it.

'Well, perhaps you'd like to come back early from London for PE,' Diana screams at him as he leaves in the morning. 'Why is this my job? Why? Women's work, is it? Show me a bloody job descrip-tion.'

For Diana, Michael's timetable is her timetable, his prison walls are her prison walls. Even the hours in the exercise yard do no more than confirm the height of the wire and the smallness of the square patch of blue. Day-release passes are few and far between, visitors, almost none. Sarah the social worker makes a final visit, bringing over some copies of the local authority carer's assessment and a box of Michael's things which she's rescued from Valerie's flat, Diana having passed on the opportunity to go there herself. The cardboard box is left on the table like a present at a wedding. When the social worker is gone, with the desultory interest of a rich woman at a jumble sale, Diana sorts through the scraps: a few books, a recorder, a remote control car with no batteries. It's all rather pathetic. When she opens the large brown envelope with the paperwork, two things fall out: a letter addressed to her care of Valerie's address and a small photo. The picture is of Valerie and Michael and a man she presumes is Solomon, all at some sort of garden party. There's a band, a long table covered in food, balloons and a banner which says something about Women's Aid. They're holding hands and dancing with each other, she can almost hear the singing.

The other envelope contains a letter written on rather cheap and childish A5 paper with ruled lines.

Dear Diana,

I know we have never met, so I hope you will forgive me for getting in touch, but I wanted to write about Valerie, both to offer you my condolences and also to share my grief, because it is the truth that I have no one else to share it with here.

Even as I'm writing this, I find it impossible to believe Val is gone and I have had to pray long and hard to find God's purpose in this. The two of you had not met for a long time, but she told me all about everything at what was her last visit, and she was full of hope for reconciliation and I am sure you found out so quickly what a special, special person your sister became. I pray you found peace between you before this happened. Even with all the troubles she had, she was so kind to everyone else and put their needs before her own. She was full of hope and trust and she believed in people, she believed in me when other people found it easier to be prejudiced against me. I am sure she told you that we were going to be married.

Most of all, of course, she was a mother. Mikey was everything to her. This is another reason why I write. That last visit I promised her that if anything should ever happen to her – and was God preparing us for this? – I promised her that I would take care of Mikey. He is like a son to me. You will know yourself by now what an incredible boy he is, everyone who meets him loves him, he is blessed with wisdom and empathy beyond his years. Actually he has had to grow up too fast and needs to be given the chance to be the little boy he is, to be loved and looked after like a child. The most bitter thing for me is that I cannot fulfil that promise now, but I am sure God has placed him with you so that he is safe at this terrible time in his life.

With your permission, I have included a card for him so he knows I have not forgotten him and again, with your permission, I would be so happy if you could write to me with your address so that I may visit him in September when I will be released. In truth, no prison is worse than the cell I am living in now with walls built of grief. I am sure it is the same for you and I do not forget that you have also lost your mother.

I pray that you will not judge me as a prisoner, but as the man your sister loved and who in turn loves Mikey.

I also pray that Jesus will be with you and your husband as you care for him and that He will watch over all of you at this difficult time.

Solomon

Blessed is the man that trusteth in the LORD, and whose hope the LORD is. For he shall be as a tree planted by the waters, and that spreadeth out her roots by the river.

With the letter, the card and the photo in her hands, Diana stumbles down the garden, through the arboretum, pushing the branches out of her eyes and tripping on the roots. These things cannot be thrown away, cannot be kept. Lie, lie, lie cries the buzzard overhead. Speak, speak, speak bleat the fledglings, open-mouthed in the nest in the ivy on the back wall. That's what they used to call her, at home, liar, liar, pants on fire, but at times it has been her best friend, her lying self. Edmund never lies. The first time Edmund ever brought her here the bluebells and wild garlic were out as they will be soon and they sat here, on this fallen tree, and breathed in the scent of limitless loveliness, and so she sits down, on that same fallen tree, and tries to find that same breath, but she is dizzy and sick with the pain of the photo and the letter and the thought of who she has become. Until now, it has always been the argument she remembers, the mess, but it wasn't all like that. She and Valerie had their time in the garden, and Solomon is right, there was hope.

It was all squandered. Here she is, squatting in the shrubbery like a tramp. The past is bitter at the back of her throat and she wretches, the leaf litter of the forest floor seething inches from her face, a million small things grown grotesque: twisted bark and broken twigs, shoots and soil and nettles and the tiny flowers of the wood anemone shining a white light through her shuttered gaze. The sickness is so deep within her, she knows she must purge herself before she rots from the inside out.

In Edmund's study, Diana chooses pen and paper for the connection it offers. The problem with speaking is that you are never in control, never know what the other person hears, or what they might say next: all conversation is an improvisation like that. Writing can be planned, redrafted, amended until it is right, and writing stays. When everything else moves on, there will always be a record, a true record of what happened that night when Valerie was locked in and she had the key. And even before.

An end to things seems so close. Diana draws the long, straight first line of the personal pronoun. I. The paper slides away beneath the nib, the pen is reluctant to spill its ink, the page lies white and unbroken as the nausea returns, and she cries out for help, but there is no one left between the echoing ceiling and the shuddering earth. The spasm starts in her right hand, she wants to swallow, but her throat is closed and dribble trickles from her lips that she cannot wipe away. Convulsions have ownership of her body, all control is lost – the floor, the falling chair, the dark.

A hint of a black eye, breath smelling of vomit, and Diana scrubbing at the blood on the carpet, that's what Edmund finds when he comes home with Michael at lunchtime. Is she all right, what does she mean she fainted, that isn't normal, should he call for an ambulance? No, not normal, not natural, she has fainted before, but Diana knows this is a loss of consciousness of a different sort. She doubts there is a physical remedy for this disease.

Chapter Twenty

'What the hell do they want?'

Edmund is patting his pockets. He thinks the police have come for him; recently it seems he is always waiting for the knock on the door, whether it's from the Financial Conduct Authority or planning authorities, who knows. The Spotless Angels are hiding in the downstairs cloakroom, they think they've come for them. Michael is hiding behind the cedar tree. They're all wrong. It's obvious who they're here for.

Once Detective Inspector Penn and another younger man whose name she has already forgotten are in the drawing room, Diana carries in a tray of tea. Wriggling on the sofa, Michael is fiddling with the handcuffs attached to the officer's belt.

'Don't touch those,' says Diana.

'No harm done,' says the policeman.

He touches them again.

'Edmund?' Diana nods her head towards the door. 'And the dog.' She calls after him. 'Sarah came yesterday with a box of his things. Maybe he'd like to play with those?' She turns back to the police officers. 'There's no point in him staying, I'm afraid he still hasn't spoken since that night.'

'Don't worry,' says D.I. Penn. 'If we do need to, we've got specialists who work with drawings, those sorts of things.'

'Why on earth would you want to put him through that? It's not exactly a mystery what happened to his mother.'

It is a bit of a mystery, it turns out. Edmund returns and the police confirm there were high levels of alcohol in Valerie's blood, but that alone did not account for why she was unable to get out of the tower, and Lady Diana was probably the worse for wear herself that night, isn't that the case?

'Yes, I was a little drunk, that's not a crime, is it? That bloody dog's back again. Edmund?'

It's easier when Edmund isn't in the room.

The detective resumes. 'So the difficult bit to piece together is why your sister couldn't open the door after the first tremor.'

They never get it right, do they? She was never her sister. 'Half' is a very small word. Little sister. Baby sister. Diana's mind wanders. Baby grand. There always used to be a little key in the walnut box on top of the piano, Diana is sure of it; it had a plaited yellow-and-red cotton thread tied around the end, what can have happened to it? Now she finds herself on the other side of the room, opening the lid, taking out the little glass and silver pots one by one.

'I understand you could hear her screaming?'

There is a button you push to reveal a concealed compartment beneath, maybe that's where the answer is.

'Diana, my darling, what are you doing?'

She does things now with someone else's arms, sees things with someone else's eyes, someone else's body on the bed, and her own face staring at the ceiling. Flushed in the face, Diana tries to pull herself together.

'I'm sorry, can you repeat that?' She takes her seat again.

'You could hear screaming.'

'I don't think I ever said that.' Diana begins to repeat her version of events, yet again, straightening the teaspoons into a line, but they're losing interest. Her words have no impact compared to the row coming from the top of the stairs.

'Oh, for goodness' sake, that's the child.' Diana jumps up, her knee hits the tray, the milk spills. 'I'm sorry, this place is a madhouse. It's impossible to think straight.'

To which the police reply that they are going to need to take a statement anyway so it might be easier for her to make an appointment and come down to the station.

After they have left, Edmund mutters something about not knowing what the hell is going on around here any longer and is she sure she didn't bang her head when she fainted because she certainly looks as though she's lost her mind. The study door is slammed shut. She hammers against the wood.

And would it be surprising if I've lost it? After everything that's happened? Losing my mother and sister within a week of each other? Locked up here on my own, you don't even talk to me any longer. You treat me like the nanny. I don't even know what you think any longer. You might as well not be here.

No reply. She wants to cry and she wants to cry in her own bed, but even that is impossible because something terrible has happened in her beautiful bedroom: shoes, handbags, jumpers and coat hangers with things on them and coat hangers with nothing on them strewn over the floor; everything swept off the top of her dressing table, make-up, scent, jewellery, photographs scattered and smashed; even the bed is disturbed – the bedspread crumpled and the duvet and the fitted sheet pulled off from three corners as if there has been a savage rape. Up until now it's just been keys and notes, faces sometimes, but whatever this is, it's out of control, wreaking a terrible destruction on her, breaking into her things, possessing her spaces. Diana falls onto the bare bed, exposed, as if she, like the mattress, is never meant to be seen like this. The boy is skulking at the door. Her fingers find the edge of the sheet and she pulls it up to cover herself.

'What were you doing in my room? Come on, tell the truth.'

Off the bed now, she moves towards him. He backs away, he has a face which is full of knowledge and planning and entirely blank at the same time.

'Go on, what were you looking for? Say something.'

As she pushes him up against the wardrobe, the boy is so thin and loose-boned that he rattles like a puppet, but his vow of silence is fixed, him and his mother, members of their own closed order. He's had his chance, she's tried to make her peace, and now it's too late.

'I've had enough,' she whispers. She's so close to him now she can smell Valerie. His face is between her hands. 'All this crap about not talking, just say it, you know you want to, you know you can.' Her hands tighten, fasten, lower, his neck. 'Go on, speak, speak.'

What she might have done next does not happen. Edmund is there. The three of them wrestle for and against each other, in a pitch-and-toss sea of chaos. Eventually the boy ducks away from her grappling hands and runs from the room.

'I can't go on.'

'I'm here now. It's the trauma of it all, it's the loss, it will pass.'

Even in her distress, she knows that Edmund is just looking for the stepping stones of his clichés to save himself from losing his footing and drowning; her madness is too deep a river to test.

'It won't, it won't ever be better because I . . .' He's holding her, not like a husband, but like some sort of jailer, gripping each arm too tightly. She cannot look him in the eye. 'Because I . . .'

Steering her towards the bed, Edmund sits her down and slides his grasp to her shoulders, arm's length. 'Because you nothing, darling. This has got to stop. Look at the state you're in. You're driving yourself round the bend.'

Having checked the landing to make sure Mikey is not listening, Edmund closes the door and leans against it. He doesn't know if he's trying to keep things in or out.

'It all started because of the earthquake. It changed everything,' whispers Diana.

'Did it? Didn't it start with your half-sister? Wasn't that what all this was about, you asking Valerie over? About things that happened between you long before the earthquake?'

'But I never got the chance, did I?'

Dominoes are actually what Edmund's thinking of, how when he was very young he used to line up columns of his grandmother's ivory dominoes on the hall floor because he loved the rattling, clattering sound they made on the tiles as they fell. Backwards dominoes. Valerie stayed the night, Diana's mother died, we dug the pool, some arrogant arsehole of an ancestor built a tower with money he made because the world had gone mad for sugar, in fourteen hundred and ninety-two Columbus sailed the ocean blue, ten thousand years ago the ice began to melt.

'When you think about it, it isn't really about the earthquake, or Valerie, it could have been anything.' Edmund moves to the window; from there he can see the trees that line the bank. 'You can't step in the same river twice.'

'What's that particular cliché meant to mean?'

'I don't know, it just came to me. That you can't go back, I suppose. Or that everything changes.' It's a beautiful afternoon. He could be fishing, the mayfly will be perfect this evening, the banks will be giddy with the smell of wild garlic, and when he stands in the pool and reaches into the river to release the fish, the water will be soft and slow with summer warmth. He talks with his face to the window and his back to the room. 'You see, when you stand in the water, you know that's just one moment, you, the rod, the fish, the fly, the circle of the current around your waders and all the things that have happened upstream drift past you, I don't know, fallen branches, feathers, rubbish even, and then it takes it all away downstream, even that perfect moment of you being there. It's gone and that's fine as well.' He turns round and shrugs, a little embarrassed. 'That's fishing as therapy. The miracle of the river cure, I keep saying you should try it one day.'

'I'm too tired for your Oxford philosophy, Edmund,' says Diana.

'Besides, people who live in glasshouses, or own them, they really shouldn't throw stones.' She repositions the radio alarm clock on the bedside table.

Taking his cue from her, Edmund starts untangling the coat hangers and finding pairs for the shoes. 'All I'm thinking is that Mikey needs therapy, that's what Sarah recommended, wasn't it? But so do you, Diana. Fishing or whatever else.'

The digital numbers are flashing 00:00. She focuses on resetting the time, hour by hour, minute by minute, until everything is caught up with the present. Does he have any idea what he's asking of her? Maybe he does. And he could help if he wanted to. Come home earlier, spend some time with her, and not just the boy and the river, massage her feet again like he used to, watch a box set together, sit at the kitchen table with a glass of wine and talk while she makes supper for God's sake. They're only small, ordinary things, but they would make a difference. He's locked her into this contract, he can help get her out. She's lost her voice but he's still talking.

'. . . before you do something . . .' He has a bottle of her Chanel in his hands and is breathing in deeply as if trying to find the words to describe the essence of it all.

'Something?'

'Something you'll regret.'

Later, as Edmund leaves the room, he speaks one last time before he closes the door behind him. 'I'll help in any way I can, Diana, but I'm no psychiatrist.'

An apology was presented the next morning on the whiteboard, no doubt under duress from Edmund who explains that Mikey was upset with the box of things from the social worker. Apparently there was no Elvis jigsaw, no Penguin, nothing from Solomon and no photo of his mum. Edmund can't imagine how awful it would be to have no photo of your mother. Diana just needs to look in Edmund's study to see how true that is, it's like a shrine in there. Anyway, what's done cannot be undone. After the bedroom episode, she burned the picture of Valerie, Solomon and Michael, and the letter and the card. It was wrong, but she was very angry and now they're just ashes in the wind. And, besides, she has more important things to worry about: today she's expected at the police station to make her statement.

The Fly and Salmon is a particularly pretty pub on the river out of town. Edmund agreed it would do her good to get out and have a chinwag with Sally. That's as close as Edmund gets to counselling; spending an afternoon teaching Michael to cast a dry fly is as close as he gets to surrogate fatherhood. Never mind. Diana is feeling much stronger today and in the mood for celebrating for the first time for a very long time.

'God, I love it here except for the effing name.' Diana laughs as she and Sally take their seats on the terrace. 'If someone mentions fishing again, and as for the chapel . . .'

'What about the chapel?'

'I wish that had come down in the earthquake. Edmund takes the boy with him, priest and bloody altar boy, for Christ's sake.' She is a little flushed from the wine and she can't feel her keys in the bottom of her handbag.

Checking over her shoulder, Sally whispers, 'You're not saying there's anything funny going on?'

'Oh God, no! Don't be ridiculous.' But now that Diana thinks about it, it is almost as if Edmund has fallen in love with the boy, and, of course, there is something funny going on. She orders a couple more glasses of fizz. The interview at the police station is over; she was dreading it, but it turned out to be something of a saving grace. Nowadays her downs are very low, but the rare moments of hope energise her into a manic happiness which instructs her to put on more make-up than usual and plays her speech on fast forward.

'Edmund got me a solicitor. That shows you how much or how little faith he has in me,' she tells Sally. 'He said it was better to be safe than sorry. I love that.' She dismisses Sally's attempts to defend Edmund with a wave of her hand – just wait for this, the important bit of the story is still to come. 'Anyway, I went through the same ghastly rigmarole with the police: Valerie was locked in, where was the key, who else was there, who locked the door et cetera et cetera ad infinitum to use Edmund's Latin. They mentioned Mrs H, of course.'

'They can't have thought she was a clandestine murderer. Grace in the tower with the arsenic. I can't think of anyone less likely.'

'Thumping up the stairs in her size nines, imagine it!' Diana laughs. When she has her breath back, she slows herself down. 'No, I think they were just checking out that the stories matched. What time she left, that sort of thing. Anyway, they've obviously ruled her out. But they did have another hypothesis.'

'What? Who?' Sally leans forwards, but Diana isn't whispering.

'Michael. Da-da.' Diana drum-rolls the table.

'Mikey?'

'Hear me out. It hadn't occurred to me, but they wondered if perhaps he'd been mucking around with the key. Remember I told you he'd been hanging around all evening? Well, he could have done something . . . locked the door to keep Valerie safe, or something like that, then later, when his mother's dead and everyone's going on about the key, he doesn't know what to do.'

'You're always saying he's obsessed with keys.'

'And it might explain why he won't speak,' Diana confides in Sally. 'He's dug himself into a terrible hole and can't get out. And the longer you leave telling the truth, the worse it is. Obviously it's a relief for me, but the trouble is, I'm not sure it's something you'd ever get over, killing your own mother, killing anyone, even if it is by mistake.'

Over a third glass and a light salad, they mull over the consequences of what quickly moves from theory to fact, Sally wondering if, although Mikey is one of the most gorgeous little boys she's ever met, he's going to prove too much. She's seen a documentary about those residential places where they put child murderers, not that she's saying he is a murderer per se.

'Per se' sets Diana off again, giggling like a schoolgirl.

Sally persists. 'Hundreds of thousands of pounds a year they cost, more than Eton. In the long term you might be doing him a favour as well as yourselves. You said yourself you think he's always dreaming up ways to get back at you. He might be dangerous, Diana.'

Before they leave, Diana allows Sally to hug her.

'You've been looking pretty frazzled, Di. I wouldn't be a friend if I didn't point it out. He doesn't hit you, does he?' She indicates Diana's eye. 'Mikey, I mean. Because it wouldn't be a surprise given what he's grown up with.'

Diana's hand moves to her cheek; she thought the bruise had gone or was at least well concealed. She explains her little fainting episode. Now is not the time to tell her one remaining friend that she fears she is turning into a fitting lunatic.

Not eating enough is Sally's conclusion. 'You're as thin as a stick. Can't get all the calories from Sauvignon blanc, darling. But perhaps things will look up now.'

Now that the alcohol is wearing off and her head is throbbing and the sun is weakening, Diana is running down like a toy with a flat battery. 'One way or another, the end's in sight,' she says.

Swans, gilded and deceptive, glide silently in the pond above the weir next to them. Someone told her they are mute, although Diana isn't sure that's true; she's certainly heard that they only sing when they're dying. Strong, ice cold and capable of snapping a man's leg.

'It's the only hangable offence left in Britain, isn't it?' Diana says, as she locates her keys. 'Beheading a swan.'

Chapter Twenty-One

It's almost as if someone has handed Michael the script. He certainly plays the part of the demented boy to perfection. Joking apart, this was a shocking incident, even on Wynhope's new Richter scale of disturbance. Edmund is very shaken by the whole thing, but Diana is neither surprised, nor upset. She sees it both as evidence of his capacity for evil and as something of an opportunity.

'Do boys his age get charged for crimes like this?' Diana wonders. 'I mean false imprisonment. He could get sent away to some institution just for this, let alone what happened with Valerie. What on earth's going to happen to him, Edmund?'

Mikey locked up a little girl. At the end of morning break, he volunteered to tidy up and told five-year-old Aimee to help him carry the play things into the equipment shed, and then he locked her in. It was a very long time before she was found sobbing on a bed of footballs, entangled in the nets. Neither explanation nor remorse was forthcoming from Mikey, but everyone was very understanding. He received an exclusion until the end of the summer term and the chance to start afresh in September providing Special Needs pay for extra support in school. No mention of a young offenders' place, quite the opposite. Sharing the police theory that it might have been the boy himself who inadvertently caused the death of his mother, everyone agreed it all made perfect sense and passed the story on like Chinese whispers until it became an accepted account of events for the teachers, the local authority, and the parents at the school gates. And, of course, Mikey didn't deny it, did he? There was no question of Mikey being prosecuted: aged nine, he was just below the age of criminal responsibility; the little girl's parents were not pressing charges; he'd never locked anyone up before; and there was no indication that he'd do anything like it again. 'Mikey needs help, not punishment. When things are as bad as this, it's a home we need, not an institution.' Those were D.I. Penn's very words, according to Edmund, who wholeheartedly agreed and decided that's what we're doing, Diana, we're giving him a home, whatever the cost.

In that home, Diana feels very much like matron.

'Mikey and I could do with a hot blackcurrant, we've both got the summer sniffles.'

'If you're making tomato soup for Mikey, that's just what I feel like.'

'I'm sorry, darling, I'm exhausted. I'll go up after supper at the same time as Mikey.'

The more they both need, the less she gives them. As often as not, supper comes out of the freezer, there are no clean shirts ironed in the dressing room, and despite the fact that July is marvellous and the borders are on fire with lupins and purple cranesbills and the orchard is a waterfall of roses, there are no fresh flowers in the morning room. The deterioration in standards is partly due to Mrs H leaving, partly due to money being tighter than it was before (although they are hardly on the breadline), but mostly due to the fact that she is so, so tired and why does any of it matter anyway? She can barely get herself up in the morning and hours pass with her slumped alone in front of daytime TV, watching the disasters watching her. There are very few highs, mostly a grey dragging decline, a feeling that they are all sliding inexorably downwards, helpless on a bank above a dark quarry pond, clutching at trees whose branches snap as they slip and whose roots are shallow in sandy soil.

No longer at school, Mikey spends even more time in the nursery with his circus animals, winding Sellotape around their bodies over and over again and spreading them out, flat on their backs, sleeping or dead. School initially proposed sending a teacher but are grateful when Diana offers to collect and deliver work herself; after all, over-stretched staff have more than enough to do at the end of the summer term. The boy completes pages and pages of maths, draws careful diagrams of plant parts, fills in the blanks in punctuation exercises, and everything is returned with green ticks and smiley faces. Against all odds, he is a very intelligent boy, which is part of the problem; a stupid child would be much easier to deal with. He writes a lot as well, and she reads the stories before handing them in, just in case, but they are also returned with banal comments: 'Great imagination, Michael. You have organised your story into a clear beginning, middle and end.'

A Story by Mikey

One day Solomon found a letter with his name on the front. The letter says that Solomon should climb a very famous mountain and when he got to the top he should tell everyone his news. Solomon had a lovely yellow flat with a cat and lots of jigsaws but he was bored because he did not have a school or a job or nothing to do all day except watch television or go to funrals so he decided it would be exciting to climb the mountain!!!

It was sunny and cold! It was very hard work because the snow was very deep and he nearly fell over a very perilous cliff. He ate all his chocolate so he did not have any food left so he kept going anyway because he wanted to go as high as he can and tell everyone the news then one night an iceman came to find him and said I will climb the mountain with you and I know everything about the mountain because I am an ice man. Michael was very happy to have a friend and he went everywhere with the iceman the iceman did not have any eyes or any mouth and was much bigger than him but he did have a dog.

In the end nobody knows if Michael got to the top of the mountain because they only found his lunchbox because everything else was made of ice but there was two sets of footprints on the top and a pool of water in his bedroom at home that never went away and then Solomon's mother was sad and so was his dog then they went to his funral but there was nothing to burn because you cannot burn water.

That one goes in the bin, the truth is starting to leak out of him. When August comes, the City of London sleeps, along with Westminster and anything decent on the television, the entire establishment still behaving as though it is on school holidays. Edmund certainly does. He is home most of the time at last, the summer evenings are long and light, and the two of them should have been on the lawn with friends, eating strawberries and drinking Bellinis, the glow of the low sun bringing warmth to their faces and colour to the old brick of the house, the marigolds spread at its feet like a cloth of gold. Instead she finds herself, pale and raw, cooking sausages which stink out the kitchen, and after supper it's fishing, another exclusive activity in their men-only club. In the dusk, they saunter down the drive towards the river, an ink etching, silhouette of man and boy, through the musk mallow and yellow mead in the meadow they wander, later leaving their dead fish on the kitchen counter in the way that cats leave baby birds for their owners.

Even the dog prefers the boy to her now.

If she were to walk with the boy to the river, she would push him in.

It's white hot outside. It hurts her eyes. She keeps the curtains closed.

If it rains, Edmund and Michael play inside. Sometimes chess in the study, more recently engrossed in a box of magic tricks Edmund brought home. Presents from town are no longer flowers and velvet-boxed surprises, but tacky gadgets from toy shops he has had no excuse to visit for forty years.

'Mikey's got a trick to show us,' says Edmund. 'He's written a series of instructions.'

1. I am going in the drawing room. When I bang three times on the door, you lock me in from the outside.

2. Leave the key in the door on the outside.

3. I will escape!

It is the tedious, age-old trick of the coat hanger, the key and the newspaper under the door.

'Encore, encore!' calls Edmund from his seat in the gods on the stairs. 'Bravo!'

'He does it on purpose,' says Diana.

'It's just a game, Di.'

'Do you think it feels like a game to me?'

Edmund catches up with her in the garden. Ever since the earthquake she lives in fear of thunder; it's close now, pulling on its boots. Deadheading the roses, she is aware of the steady throb of bees on the thyme and the way her head pounds continuously nowadays no matter what pills she takes. The scent of lavender, which once would have evoked memories of their holidays in Provence, now reminds her of the sachet in that drawer and all that it contains.

'I'm sorry about Mikey's tricks, perhaps you've got a point,' Edmund is saying. Something unusual in his tone of voice causes her to pause. He's not usually a sarcastic man. 'Does he ever talk to you about what he's up to? Because he does talk to you, apparently.'

Carefully, she resumes working, snip-snip-snipping away.

'You see, Sarah phoned earlier about the special guardianship date. We had a little chat, and she wondered how his therapy was going? I said fine, as far as I know, not that I'm ever told.'

'Yes, it's fine,' confirms Diana. She does not know how long she can get away with sitting in the public library every Thursday morning, Michael in the corner reading on his own while he is meant to be at a therapist she cancelled weeks ago.

'And,' Edmund continues, 'she was surprised, to put it mildly, that you hadn't told me Mikey talks to you. Long conversations, I imagine, all about the meaning of life.'

The boy is winning, the flag in the middle of the tug-of-war rope inching inexorably over the winning line towards Edmund, her feet sliding away beneath her.

Unable to differentiate between the bud and the dead, Diana is cutting blind. 'He doesn't talk to me, you know that. But I wanted it to be true. That social worker looks at me so critically, so patronising, I feel so ashamed and hopeless. Crapmother dot co dot uk, that's me.' She hopes he might love her for her apparent honesty.

'I don't know what to believe any longer, Diana.'

'What you mean is that you don't believe me, or should I say believe in me?'

'I didn't say that.' The loose mortar on the garden wall flakes as he picks at it.

'You don't need to, it's obvious.' Full house: mother, sister, husband, none of them believe. 'I'm not the only one who has been economical with the truth, am I?' she retaliates. She's holding one of the beautiful, undamaged roses in her hand and doesn't know what to do with it. 'Why were you so worried when the police came here? Don't deny it. I could see it in your face.' She chucks the yellow rose in the wheelbarrow, along with all the sodden petals and the thorns.

'So it's all about me, is it?' Edmund is walking away. 'Typical.'

'Well, it's not just all about me. If you didn't hide away in London, if you supported me more with Michael, instead of ganging up and undermining me maybe he would bloody well talk.' Diana screams after him, 'You aren't even listening to me now! I'm a nobody here now.'

Edmund has swung back and is face to face with her now. 'What exactly do you mean? Economical with the truth? I've never done anything illegal. Life's not black and white in business, Diana, you know that. It's all lines in the sand. People overstep the mark the whole time but as long as it's profitable and everyone wins, nobody minds. But then you get something like this earthquake and the whole thing comes down like a pack of cards.' He grabs her arm. Her wrist hurts, and she's frightened of him, for him. 'But, one, I'm not unfaithful to you. Two, I'm not a liar. Three,' he says, dropping her as if he's been holding a leper.

'Yes? What's number three? You might as well say what you mean.'

'Forget it.'

'Oh, that's right, run off back to Wynhope and your toys. Peter Pan in Neverland. And unfaithful, what's that about? And a liar?' Her voice is rising, higher and higher. 'So it's just me, is it? What about Michael? You think he always tells the truth on his little white-board? It's easy, isn't it, to hear no evil when you don't listen and to speak no evil when you don't talk. Come back!'

So he comes back. In the sunlight, his face looks like a caricature of confusion – grey round the edges, dark circles under his eyes – but he speaks very clearly and deliberately. 'He's a child, Diana, that's the difference – a child. And, yes, I do believe him. He's a very truthful boy.' Edmund pulls his jumper over his head and rolls up his shirt sleeves as he talks. 'I know he's not mine, I know it's not easy, especially for you, but you can't say I don't try. We go fishing, we take Monty out for hours, we go to the chapel, we play cricket.'

'Oh yes, your boys' own club.'

'There you are. If I'm around, you're jealous. If I stay away, you grumble. Heads I lose, tails you win. Listen.' His voice changes, maybe he's close to tears. 'It's silly because we've only had him a few months, but he's the closest I'm ever going to get, and I never understood how that would feel.' As he rubs his face with his hands, earth smears across his damp face. 'And forgive me if it doesn't fit in with your life plan, but I like to think of my parents having grandchildren, another generation, alive, here at Wynhope. Wynhope deserves it.' His gesture encompasses the park, the coach house, the whole estate. 'I'd like to think of leaving something good.' Taking up the handles of the wheelbarrow, he calls Monty to follow him. 'Something more than death and a pile of rubble.'

Death and a pile of rubble is exactly what it's all about. In a suffo-cating courtroom, the inquest asks all the same questions and fails to find the answers. The four-day hearing exhausts them, the tempo-rary nanny Diana reluctantly agreed to hire finds Michael delightful, but as soon as she leaves in the evenings he is defiant and abusive towards Diana, and they collapse into bed unable to find the words to process the day or comfort each other, night after night after night.

In summing up, the coroner's initial comments are, as expected, regarding the effect of the pool on the foundations: the survey was inadequate and this will be pursued by a separate investigation by the local planning authorities. Equally, there is nothing new in the account of the physical details, the fact that Valerie survived the earthquake and died in the aftershock. It is the final conclusion which shakes Diana.

'As the doors were locked by person or persons unknown and for reasons not established and as there is no clear indication as to why the key was not readily available to expedite the deceased's escape between the first and second shocks, and bearing in mind that had the doors been unlocked the deceased may have escaped alive, the conse-quences of the doors being locked are both significant and enduring and therefore the jury in this matter records a narrative verdict.'

A narrative verdict. Are you sitting comfortably. In the beginning. Happy ever after.

'Well, thank goodness that's over,' says Edmund, back at Wynhope. 'It's been hanging over us like the sword of Damocles. I'm not looking forward to the local authority snooping around, but at least they seem to think it's the surveyor rather than me who's at fault. And now we can get on with our lives. It might be a bit inappro-priate, but I've opened a bottle of fizz, Di.'

'It didn't answer anything.'

'Maybe not. But there'll be no more questions either. Closure, I think that's what Mikey's therapist lady will say and I agree. Here, raise a glass. To the future. To the three of us.'

Clink. Clink. Silence. Narrative verdict. As she sips the champagne, it strikes Diana that it is a contradiction. A verdict is a final act, a definitive line and a shutting down of options, but a narrative? Where a narrative begins and ends is a different matter, and wherever this particular story began, Diana is sure it has not ended. Valerie's death sits somewhere in the middle of a longer saga; like a box set, it has already outlived its original characters and future episodes are drafted, if not recorded. Edmund, of all people, should understand the long game.

Outside the lodge, the press love the present moment. It has it all, this story: family turmoil amongst the upper classes, a whole new take on the earthquake which ran out of steam months ago. Some of the reports move from Diana to Edmund, not only the property developer who failed to safely develop his own property but also the irony of his substantial investments in the oil company whose well is under investigation as one of the contributing causes of his own downfall. For two or three days a cluster of campaigners hang around the end of the drive with placards – hoot if you hate fracking. The horns sound a different song to Diana. She hears hoot if you hate wealth, hoot if you hate the upper classes, hoot if you hate me. Later, Edmund tells her the protestors are already behind the times, that he's sold his fracking shares and taken the hit. Somehow it no longer appeals, pressurising the past to fuel the future.

'In fact,' he says, 'apart from the Riverside Development, things are falling into place at last. What with that and the inquest being over, I thought the timing was ideal, but given the state you're in, now I'm not sure I should go away at all.'

Every year, Edmund makes a pilgrimage to an exotic location in search of the perfect fly-fishing experience. This year it's Mongolia.

It costs a fortune, which was never a factor in the past, but to some extent the pressure's off now the market's recovered and, anyway, it was paid for months ago, 'before all this', and it would just be money down the drain if he cancelled now. Just as he is hesitating, thinking he should stay, Diana is realising how very much she would like to be left alone.

'Just go,' she says. 'God knows we need a break. Not just from here and Michael, but from each other. It's all been too much and, yes, yes, I'll be fine with Michael and Michael will be fine with me.'

The school will have Michael back for the new term, she reassures him, she'll arrange for the cleaners to come more often so she can have a bit more support, and she might ask Sally to come and stay for a few days, or the temporary nanny, Michael got on with her so well. Yes, good idea to get back in touch with Mrs H, but he has more than enough to do, so she'll see to it, she lies. And when he comes back, they can start again.

He kisses her for the first time for a long time. 'I hope so, Di,' he says. 'I really hope so.'

Outside in the sunshine with Michael, Edmund prepares to leave. The two of them are sitting at the garden table examining his ten-foot number 7 rod, while, inside, Diana considers the possibility that she is in fact the one with the catch: the boy is hooked, she can reel him in. There will be no Edmund to release him, no visitors to Wynhope to see him flapping breathless in the net. Fourteen days. The silence cannot go on and he knows that. In a clear, undiluted way she allows herself the terrible thought that this heaviness she feels is the weight of hate: his face, thin and pathetic like his mother's, like his grandfather's; his latent sexuality with his feeble penis and sordid interest in her bathroom cabinet; his mutism, elective, deliberate and punitive. He is a thief, stealing Edmund away from her, and he needs to be caught. He will speak. They will sort it out once and for all. If she puts hatred at the top of her virtual reality flow chart and discounts carrots because she has nothing to offer, what sticks can she beat him with to break the silence? There is nothing she can take away that has not already been lost, except perhaps the dog. The threat to send Mikey away and the threat to keep him are both as self-defeating for him as they are for her. Long after he has left Wynhope and grown up, if he has not spoken, he will still hold all the trumps and be prepared to play them. Michael and Valerie, partners at the table in three-handed poker. However she solves the problem, it needs to be a solution which will hold. Be permanent in some way. If he was dead, for instance. Imagine that.

Footsteps on the gravel, they've finished their fishing game. In the mirror, she appears quite ordinary. Unthinkable things are helpful only in that they show where the full stop comes at the end of a sentence of spiralling thoughts. Or a comma, at least.

On the front of the card which Mikey has made for Edmund there is a picture of a fish, coloured in like a rainbow.

Dear Edmund

Have a nice holiday. I hope you catch loads of fish and take some photographs on your phone to show me when you get back.

Thank you for looking after me and taking me to the chapel and teaching me fishing. You are a very kind man and I love you a lot. I want to stay with you forever at Wynhope.

Mikey xx (and Monty woof woof)

A late summer storm is gathering, the back door slams shut in the wind, and the dog scratches at it restlessly, whining to be gone with Edmund. Children are like dogs, Mrs H said once, neither of them can cope with suitcases. Patting the card in his pocket, Edmund finds time to kiss Diana goodbye. He can't wait to get away from her and, given the state of their marriage, probably wants to stay away as well. He spends longer hugging Monty than her. He is only reluctant to get in the car because of the dog, Wynhope and the boy; all he will be looking forward to is coming back to the dog, Wynhope and the boy. She is an extra in this scene, a walk-on servant. Fuck you, she shouts silently across the lawn, fuck both of you.

Side by side, Diana and Michael wave goodbye, her hair blowing across her face and heavy splats of rain falling one by one onto the gravel. The anger in her retreats, gets smaller and smaller, until it is out of sight, and then her love curls, swells and breaks over her, tosses her and leaves her bruised and gasping. It laps at her loneliness, leaves her shivering on the shingle. Diana understands. All she wants is Edmund back, but she cannot have Edmund without the boy and it is impossible to lose the boy without also losing Edmund.

Checkmate.

Chapter Twenty-Two

At supper time, Diana and Michael circle each other in the kitchen, a macabre tribal dance where touching is prohibited. With Edmund gone, reality seems suspended. The boy puts himself to bed, she positions herself outside the door and listens; not for a reply, it's his breathing that interests her. Downstairs, wine in hand, she turns on the television because noise helps. It is a programme called *Dear Future Me*, in which people compete to have the opportunity to fulfil their dreams.

'I don't think about the obstacles,' says one of the contestants. 'They're just fleas on an elephant.'

Fleas have a way of biting in the night and Diana lies awake, scratching at her thoughts. The heatwave whispers with her paranoia and she grows feverish with fear. It seems to her that Valerie is back and playing fast and loose with space and time. Sometimes at 3 a.m. she's out on the landing crying as a child cries; other times, in the morning, as Diana sits at her dressing table, her half-sister is sitting on the end of the bed behind her, swinging her legs and waiting to play. Whether it is the house or her own soul that needs exorcising, Diana does not know, but after one particularly tortured night she falls to her knees in the morning and prays. She doesn't know to whom she prays, but she prays. She prays that she might be free from the past, from Valerie, from the guilt of what she has done, what she has not done, what she might do. She prays for someone to rescue her because she was wrong when she told Edmund she could manage on her own. Thought only in her head and not spoken, the prayers close over the room like ice on a pond, so she forces herself to voice them out loud and crack the terror open.

'Save me from Michael. Save Michael from me.'

Opening her eyes, Diana is embarrassed, as if the dressing gown on the end of the bed is mocking her and the fluttering curtains are giggling behind her back. She gets off her knees, creeps to the window like someone reaching dry land and squints into the fierce September sunshine. The oaks lining the drive are made sombre by the end of summer and even the grass in the park is thin and exhausted. Then she spots someone. He is a long way away, but he is definitely walking towards the house. She is not expecting anyone, no one comes to Wynhope any longer. The stranger reaches the cattle grid and seems to hesitate. She can see he is a youngish man in a short-sleeved white shirt and beige slacks and he is black, and therefore Diana concludes he is a Jehovah's Witness and hides behind the curtains. The bell sets the dog barking, but she waits until there is nothing left of it at all in the air. It rings again. Peeping out, she notices he is not carrying a Bible. Maybe she's wrong. On impulse, she decides to answer. After all, if nothing else, this is another human being. Cautiously, she opens the front door. The man is apologetic for bothering her and surprisingly polite; he actually sounds quite well educated for, well, for someone like him. He says he's looking for work, particularly gardening. If he wants to leave his name and a contact number, Diana says, she'll get her husband to call him if anything comes up. The pause is a fraction too long: Sonny is a false identity and the phone number is lacking a digit, of that she's sure. With Edmund away, she's vulnerable – the wealthy always are – and this man is obviously a foreigner. It's as though history and geography have slipped, seeing someone like him at Wynhope. Her hand hovers close to the panic button, but Monty is leaning against the man's crisp, clean trousers, looking up for affection and wagging his tail, and it's enough to make her hesitate.

'It's beautiful here.' He indicates the swing on the lawn. 'How many children do you have?'

'Just the one. He's not ours,' she explains. She should stop there. It's what fraudsters do, lure you into conversation, but the words blurt from her and she's like a child telling everything that's happened in a hurry. 'We've sort of fostered him. His mother was killed in the earthquake.'

His sadness seems genuine as he turns away, embarrassed by his emotion. 'I am so sorry.'

Stepping from the porch out onto the drive, Diana indicates where the tower was, tells him about the child she is left with, all that she is left with.

'Jesus said suffer the little children to come unto me and forbid them not: for such is the kingdom of God. Luke sixteen, verse thirteen. And that's what you've done. You will be blessed for looking after him.'

Religion. She was right after all, but nevertheless it's strange: she prays and then some priest comes up her drive? Mumbo jumbo. There again she believes everything else that trespasses into Wynhope from one world to the next, so why not this? In Edmund's study the landline is ringing; it jolts her back to the here and now.

'Please answer it, I can wait,' the man says. 'I'm not going anywhere.'

It's impossible to stop the scam calls which have proliferated recently. Edmund says it's because they've made an insurance claim. They all promise reconstruction and payouts on a scale she can only dream of. She hangs up abruptly and turns to look at the stranger. Something about seeing him framed in the doorway suddenly makes her recognise him from the photograph. Solomon. The prisoner. The illegal immigrant. He said in his letter he'd be out in September and here he is, come sniffing after his dead girlfriend's child. The thought frightens her, that someone just unlocks a cell door and people like him are free to do whatever they like, and wasn't he put away for attacking someone? This will be about money, she guesses, blackmail and unsubstantiated claims from the past. Well, he's not the only one who can be a conman.

'Solomon,' she cries. 'It's you, isn't it? Valerie's fiancé? Why didn't you say so?'

How sorry he is, he loves the boy so much, he promised Valerie that he'd look after him if anything ever happened to her, so he has come. 'I did write,' he says, 'but I never heard back. I'm sorry about the lies, I didn't know how I'd be received. I did not anticipate being welcomed like this. Forgive me for doubting you.' Then he adds, 'But one thing is true that I said, I prayed and God led me here to Wynhope.'

Oh, how she reassures him, regrets not receiving his letter, sympathises with his loss, agrees what a special person Valerie was, and would he mind just waiting there while she fetches Mikey? It takes her no more than thirty seconds to make the call. Has the boy heard Solomon? He's not come down. She asks her visitor to give them a few minutes, this is quite a shock for Mikey, he needs a bit of time, she'll return in a minute.

Clasping his hands together, Solomon closes his eyes. 'Thank you, thank you,' he calls back, either to her or to his god, who knows, then he backs away from the house, across the lawn. When he's parallel with the pond, he stands in a strange mirroring of the bronze boy with his arm raised. Taking advantage of his distance from the house, she bolts the front door, checks the back door, and waits on the landing just in case Michael makes a run for it. Why are they taking so long? She thinks she hears them, but the sirens are on the radio, it must be the news or some crime drama.

'Mikey.'

Suddenly, she can hear Solomon shouting outside, 'Mikey, don't worry. I'm here for you now.' There is an increased urgency and panic in his voice. 'Mikey. No. Stay back from the window, just wait. It'll be okay.'

There are bars across the window, aren't there? Now she thinks about it, she isn't sure. Are they on the front or back windows? Not both, she knows that. If he falls, he will surely die. It would be a hideous thing to happen, but it would be Solomon's fault and it would be over – the boy tumbling through the air, soundless, the body, thud on the mud of the flowerbed, crushing the crimson dahlias – a line drawn under this whole terrible saga and a new future possible, no, not even a new future, a return to the old present. Should she run up to the nursery or out to the garden? Once again she is frozen, only jolted out of her rigid passivity by the arrival of the police. Not just a car, but a van load of them, padded out and pumped up. Triple-letter score on this one: asylum seeker, offender, a man released on licence after assaulting a police officer. Against the van, Solomon is being held with his arms behind his back, black head flat on the white bonnet.

'One word, let me have one word,' he is begging. 'The boy, up there.'

The handcuffs are secured, confidence returns to Diana, and she unlocks the front door. 'He needs to go. He's trespassing and harassing us,' she cries. 'This isn't good for my boy, can't you see what it's doing to him?'

What they see is a child on the top floor with his head stuck between the bars and what they hear is a strange bleating, difficult to listen to, impossible to interpret.

'This man is not his father, he has no rights here, he needs to go. Please.'

Everything is hanging in the balance. The police are loosening their hold on their prisoner; the panic and the distress of the boy is shifting attention away from locking up Solomon to setting the child free.

'There's something not right here,' says Solomon, sweat, or is it tears, trickling down his face. 'Look at the boy, don't you see how desperate he is?'

The crackling radio conversations are inaudible to Diana, but she can tell the police are changing their mind.

'Jesus brought me here for a reason, to save the child. There's evil at work here.'

One mention of God is all it takes to convince the police that Solomon is indeed dangerous. With renewed conviction, they bundle him into the back of the van, all the time Solomon shouting that he'll make sure someone knows the truth. The doors are closed, the engine started. She's happy to give the two remaining police officers a few details and agrees to someone coming in the next couple of days to take a full statement, but what she's not expected is that they'll want to see the child. They do that, they explain, when there's been a domestic. With their hats off, they wipe their foreheads and wait in the shade of the cedar tree for her to produce the goods.

The body curled in the corner of the nursery does not acknowledge her. He could never have jumped; the bars at the front do go all the way to the top, it's only the rear windows looking out over the field that are dangerous. He's not going anywhere and he knows it. Back in the hall, she explains completely honestly that Michael is highly traumatised by this prisoner from his mother's dubious past turning up out of the blue, that he doesn't want to come down, so is it really necessary to add to his distress? No, apparently not. They remember the terrible tragedy of the earthquake and they only need to look around to see how lucky the child is to have her as his guardian. Goodbye and thank you.

No one is ever going to believe Solomon's word against hers. With a sort of hysteria born from relief and success, she starts to sing.

'Solomon Grundy, born on a Monday, christened on Tuesday.' Counting the stairs to the attic in time to the beats of the rhyme, she regains control. 'Died on Saturday, buried on Sunday, that was the end of Solomon Grundy.'

Chapter Twenty-Three

God. Religion. Even her stepfather crawled to church on high days and holy days for confession. Diana is furious with herself for so nearly falling for the smoke and mirrors, on her knees praying for forgiveness; she even took the arrival of Valerie's bit of stuff as the angel Gabriel. Enough. The boy is quite defeated, he complies with an early bedtime and lies like a rag doll.

'I know you're sad,' she reassures him, 'but he's not a good man. He only wanted money. Your mother always went for the bad apples. Now he's back behind bars, there's no use you hoping for anything else. Or anyone else,' she adds. 'That isn't how this is going to end.'

The next morning she decides she'll be the one who goes to church. Monty is a good enough babysitter, the boy is busy in the nursery and he's never going to try to escape. She assumes he's too frightened. He's hardly left Wynhope apart from going to school and he's certainly made no friends in the neighbourhood, adult or child.

Following the narrow path across the meadows, she puts her feet in their footprints, taking possession of their pilgrimage, through the brittle grasses scratching her bare legs, on past the lake which is stagnant and stifled by algae. The key to the chapel is easy to find. Intent on desecration and revenge, she barges inside like a drunk in a library, but stops short: there is no wealth to lay waste to, no sanctity to spoil, only a stained tablecloth on a makeshift altar and bird mess splattered on the pulpit. Edmund lights these candles, one, two, three; of course, the third is for Valerie and she feels indescribably sad for him, for them both, for all of them, clutching at false gods, grasping at straws, as Edmund might say. Shaken, she sags down onto the hard pew and weeps: such highs and lows, one minute all energy and fight, the next the drabbest of women, drained. Damp and dust and fungus sap her energy until an incomprehensible restlessness and the suffocating breathlessness of the place force her to her feet. She walks the walls. The faint inscriptions and his ancestors' epitaphs are impossible to decipher, even the leather on the front of the Bible on the lectern is marbled by mildew. The pages cling to each other, they weigh so much more than she expects. She heaves them from Genesis to Deuteronomy, Kings, Psalms. Here is number 137. By the rivers of Babylon, just like the little girl sewed.

O daughter of Babylon, who are to be destroyed; happy shall he be, that rewardeth thee as thou hast served us.

Like a kite snagged on barbed wire, she gets caught on that verse. Tearing the page from the Bible, she folds it and slips it into her pocket; she doesn't understand why, but destruction is on her mind. The scratch of the crow in the rafters drives her from the chapel.

Back in Edmund's study with a glass of wine, she takes inspiration from a text of a different sort, the framed cartoon on the wall showing a despairing man with his mouth gagged, his hands tied behind his back and a pen untouched on the desk in front of him. The caption reads: 'For all sad words of tongue and pen, the saddest are these, "It might have been."'

Like a bee, the unthinkable, once thought, loses its sting. Rivers of Babylon. Daughter of Babylon. The psalm in her pocket offers her another line: 'Happy shall he be, that taketh and dasheth thy little ones against the stones.'

Who would have guessed the Bible is so full of answers?

The other useful thing is the fishing map of the river. Edmund doesn't need to refer to it, he knows the lie of the river better than he knows their own bed, but he's dug it out of his estate paperwork recently for Michael. It shows every beat and bend and the average depth of every pool. She thinks of him now, casting around for the truth in Outer Mongolia.

The pretence is walking Monty. In the orchard, she picks up a small hard apple which has fallen too early from the tree. She knows it will be sour, but she bites into it anyway and then spits. The river is like a magnet, it draws her through the park, late summer low water, stones showing their skulls and wigs of green hair above the dribbling stream and islands joining hands with the bank. The putrid smell is that of a puffed-up body of a drowned lamb, but that's upstream and she's paddling downriver to the first pool, a favourite of Edmund's. Last year she brought a bottle of wine down, which they shared on the wooded banks as the sunset transformed the water into liquid gold. She doesn't understand the river like Edmund, everyone knows that. She tosses the bitter apple into the water and studies its journey; as Edmund says, the river carries everything away. Accidents happen, like if the boy had fallen from the window, for instance, no one to blame, just one of those dreadful things. Late evening would be best, with the mist whispering up the river, muffling the cries, blurring the lines. Here is a ledge where anyone might sit, squirming their toes in the stream and summoning the courage to swim, where anyone might lean over to count the trout, a ledge where anyone with a slip of a step and a scream might slither skinny-dipping deep, out of their depth while their aunty prepares the picnic.

This isn't so much a plan as a thing which might happen. She can sort of see it as it is when it has happened; her comforting Edmund as he packs up the circus animals in the attic, the two of them planning to spend Christmas in Cortina d'Ampezzo to get over it all, but the actual happening, that is divorced from her agency. Other things she tells herself as she treads carefully over the cattle grid on her way back, minding the gaps, holding tight to the rails: this child is never going to grow up and be happy; he is doomed to a lifetime of secrets and lies, of depression and self-loathing, because even if Edmund can create some false childhood idyll for him now, it will not last, not through the guilt of adolescence, not through the replayed pain in adult relationships. The truth is the rest of his life will draw on an infected tap root which will feed the sap with parasites and poison. If he could kill himself, he probably would. Like Valerie, who unlike her never got away, Michael is caught in a cycle; all she will be doing is setting him free.

The boy does not come downstairs the whole of the rest of the day. She hears him carrying things down from the nursery, but what he is doing or why is beyond her. She leaves a tray with his favourite toast and strawberry jam, a banana and a glass of milk outside his bedroom door, watched over, but left untouched by the loyal dog. When she wakes in the morning, it has gone.

All of the next day will have to be lived, with the Spotless Angels in the house, the contract mowers in the garden. The intolerable hours might wear away her stone resolve. The solution is a day out; she can upload pictures of the boy and her enjoying themselves and message them to Edmund for when he comes back from the wilderness and into range. They will form his memories and her defence.

In contrast to her wired enthusiasm, the boy sulks about the visit to the wildlife park.

'I've been there before,' he lies on his board.

'Go,' urge the cleaners. 'Get fresh air. Your aunty very nice to take you out for day.'

'You'll like it when you get there,' insists Diana, winking at the cleaners.

'Monty?'

'No.'

Oh, and what a thing she makes of it, popping little treats into a bag for the journey, promising pocket money to spend in the shop, saying he can take a photo on her phone so he can send a picture to his uncle. For most of the journey, Michael lies flat on the back seat so she can't even see him in the rear-view mirror, and in retaliation against his passive-aggressive stance Diana assumes a position of false jollity and sings loudly, working her way through her limited repertoire of children's music, getting louder as they get nearer, the one about the zoo, zoo, zoo and for he's a jolly good fellow and so say all of us, and so say all of us and Humpty Dumpty who even all the king's horses and all the king's men couldn't put back together again. Even she recognises the mania sitting on her shoulder, joining in with the chorus. Once she's stopped and switched the engine off, the silence is intolerable. She flings open the door so that the car can fill up with the everyday hum of the outside world, but inside, Michael slumps like an imbecile, kicking his trainers against the back of her seat. There are sideways glances from the family parked next to them, their children jumping up and down as children should.

'It's change, I'm afraid.' Diana sighs to the mother. 'Children with his difficulties find it very hard.'

The other woman softens, peers into the back of the Range Rover and encourages Michael – look how her children are excited, what fun it will be when he sees the animals. In response, the boy slides from the car and Diana whispers her thanks with the apparent gratitude of a harassed carer doing her best in difficult circumstances. It isn't that far from the truth. The day, her plan for the evening, her vision of the rest of her life with Edmund, it is all within her control and she is so credible, everyone believes her, there is nothing she cannot do. If anyone were to be asked if they saw anything that day, the family in the next car would bear witness to her dedication, her first and last day in the role of loving mother.

'Don't cry, love,' says the woman to her. 'It'll be all right once you get in there.'

Is she crying? Diana thought she was laughing.

Chapter Twenty-Four

But now she is crying. Michael is asleep in the back, ice cream smeared on his jeans, his face striped like a tiger, and an origami swan squashed on the seat beside him. In his hand, he is clutching the two plastic antelopes he chose in the shop where she was sure his lips moved as if he was saying thank you. And she is crying.

It's hard to drive in such a state of exhaustion; she's not safe, not really. The road disappears in a mirage of faces. It was a face which started it. Valerie's face in the booth at the ticket office taking all her money. Then there she was again behind the counter in the café, complexion as white as the cups and saucers, and again, behind the chain-link fence of the aviary feeding the screeching birds, and again, in the dark tunnel of the reptile house where a hand reached out for her hand and she took it. Out the other side into the fresh air and free from her, but then there were wolves behind wire on one side and swans on the lake on the other, and Diana remembered they only sing when they are dying and she had to hold tight to the railings to steady herself.

Everywhere there were children, hundreds of them, flapping their elbows and imitating the penguins, bigger children grimacing as they tried to pick up little children the better to see the animals, children in pushchairs with sticky lips reaching out their open palms to her as they passed as if they were offering pardons, and children half asleep, one eye open, thumb in mouth, draped across the shoulders of their fathers. It was all but impossible to stop herself touching the children; in fact, in the playground she did, she picked up a toddler who tripped in front of her and immediately the girl became a body, heavy and dead in her arms, and the mother was running towards her in a red anorak and Diana doesn't know why she has done what she has. She's not the sort of person who kills children.

'Don't worry, love. I was just saying thanks, that's all,' said the mother. 'Where are your kids?'

The screams in the playground were a jarring symphony played on broken strings and cracked pipes, animals noises snorting and roaring, birds as well, the sound of wings against wire, and children clapping their hands on the merry-go-round. 'The wheels on the bus go round and round,' they sang, 'all day long.' It's not possible to live like this. If only she could stop the faces, the noises, the singing – above all, the singing.

'Are you all right, love?'

Gathering up the disparate parts of herself, Diana organised words into a sentence. She's fine, thanks, her boy is up there on the castle, and she laughed, as women do, standing together in playgrounds with dry leaves and crisp papers swirling around their feet and nothing but love in their eyes. It was a brave attempt, but it would not hold. All around her, children were dying; they were falling from the slide, cracking their heads on the ground, pulled bleeding from the jaws of wolves, lifeless in the arms of fathers who found them with their legs broken, floating in the lake while the swans swam by and sang their song. It was she who pushed them, held their heads under water, dropped them wriggling with excitement behind the bars.

'He's the one on the top of the tower on the wooden fort. Can you keep an eye on him for a moment, while I pop to the ladies'?'

Once in the yellow cubicle, Diana shut herself in, squatted on the floor amongst the dropped toilet paper. Someone was knocking persistently – is everything all right in there, can you hear me? – but Diana's tongue was swollen, pushing against the membrane of her mouth, choking her throat, breath thickening, thought dumb. More banging. She observed the strange electricity activating her right hand, aware of a distance between her self and her fitting body. Open the door, they were saying, but they didn't understand the risk they were taking, unlocking her cage. The voices said they were coming in. Her face was pressed against the grime on the parts of the waste pipe which were difficult to clean, but the tremor was receding and then a man called Donald, who said he was from the park's medical team, but who knows, was unlocking the cubicle from the outside and later leading her past the staring holidaymakers to a room with a bed and a green blanket. Unable to answer their questions, she was given a pen and paper and asked if she could write something down for them, her name perhaps.

'My sister couldn't stop crying once,' Donald said a little later, over a cup of tea. 'It didn't stop until she told someone why. She was having a breakdown.'

The word is important to Diana. She tries hard to hold onto it as if it were a piece of driftwood in the sea and she is drowning. When she heaves herself up onto it, she remembers why.

'My dad died attending a breakdown,' she says. 'He was an RAC man. If he hadn't, none of this would have happened.'

'She got it all off her chest, talking to someone. Promise me you'll do that?'

Finally, Diana did talk: she talked about how she was alone, how she'd always been alone and her mother dying of a heart attack when no one expected it, too soon, too late; the earthquake and the falling tower and her sister, her half-sister, buried; the black man who came knocking at her door and her fear that the boy would die and Edmund and how far away he was and how far away he had been for a long time, further and further away, a man, barely more than a shape, someone small in the distance climbing the pink mountains, creeping over the horizon, everybody gone, taking their voices and their thoughts with them. Slowly, she felt the surges of grief for the ruins of her life subside and she looked around the first aid room and realised she was finally in the right place because she was ill. They were debating whether she was stable enough to look after the little boy who was waiting outside; she should have told them the answer, but she was not sure they would believe anything she said and with good reason. Besides, Donald had made his diagnosis – post-traumatic stress, understandable given what she'd told them. None of it her fault, they would help her to phone there and then to make an emergency appointment with her doctor.

The receptionist at the surgery offered a ten-minute appointment that evening. Donald said that he didn't think ten minutes sounded long enough to put things right, Diana wasn't sure there were enough minutes left in the life of the world to put her right, but they both agreed it would be a start.

'Strike while the iron's hot,' she said. 'Edmund's always saying things like that.'

'He sounds like a sensible man, your husband.'

Outside, Michael was waiting for her, his black eyes full of suspicion.

'Bless him,' said the other medic. 'We've been doing face painting and making paper swans, but he's been so worried about you, he hasn't said a thing.'

Because she did not know what she could do to ever make it up to Michael, she did the one thing she could manage and explained that he collects circus animals. With Donald's help, they negotiated the crowded gift shop and Michael chose antelopes, alert and beautiful, with sad eyes and long antlers and in the rear-view mirror she can see them now, being taken back to join the circus in the nursery.

Wynhope welcomes them home. It has been so hot, even the sunflowers planted by Edmund and Michael back in the spring are sagging from the shoulders. It is a parched place, the dog panting under the cedar and a dry dust spiralling up behind the car, and like a wounded animal Diana seeks water and shade. Her only thought is to put physical space between herself and the boy – two hours, surely she can keep him safe for two hours? He's taken the toy antelopes up to his room; it warms her to think he likes them. Once she imagined buying him a children's book of Greek myths for his birthday, a cake with candles on the kitchen table at Wynhope and the three of them singing together, later reading the stories with him at bedtime. If she gets better, these things are still possible. She never set out to be a monster.

So he goes to the nursery and she leaves the house to walk the time away. On the doormat she panics when she picks up a card from the local police, how can they have known what she was planning, but this is just the officer coming to take her statement about Solomon, sorry to have missed her, contact this number to arrange another time. There is so much to put right.

By the bridge, she edges uncertainly down the bank to the river, holding on to thin branches for safety. Blessed by the quietness and silence of the drops which fall from her hand onto her forehead, she sits. She just sits. This is Edmund's river, she wants to slide in and swim in him, trusting him completely to hold her head up so that she can breathe, trusting him to take her with him downstream, the two of them surrendered to the current and everything it's brought with it, and out into the ocean, believing in him and a wide, open future. This evening, someone, a nurse maybe, will find a sponge fresh from the seabed and dip it in cool water, gently strip from her these clothes which have been stuck to her body for so long and bathe her, wash her hands clean, lift her arms one by one, finding the raw places under her breasts, the sore places between her legs, then the nurse will lead her to a bed with clean, white cotton sheets in a room with no door and an open window where the sun comes in and there will be no more shaking or screaming, or footsteps, or keys or locked doors. And they will bring her food and they will bring her water and Edmund will sit next to her and he will say, I believe you, and he will kiss her and make everything better; only he can do that for her. And even Valerie and even Michael will forgive her because Diana is sorry, so sorry.

'I'm sorry,' she says, 'I am so sorry.' The river forgives her and the river believes her, it says so; this moment is one note and its song is a rhyme it sings from the source to the sea, made up of its stones and its strings.

A small glass of wine or two moves the grandfather clock through another thirty minutes until it's nearly time to go. From the hall she calls Michael, he'll have to come with her to the doctor's, maybe they'll make him better as well. No reply. From the landing, she calls again. Steeling herself, she climbs the steep, narrow staircase. She rarely comes this far nowadays, it's as though there's a dragon at the top and the nursery is his lair, and she has to remind herself that he's only a child, probably as frightened as she is, and when she reaches the top and peers into the room she notices how small, how thin, how quiet, how sad he looks, crawling round the room scratching at the edge where the wall meets the carpet, not a beast, more a baby rabbit in a trap. He is so engrossed in whatever it is he is doing that he doesn't notice her at first. The nursery looks different: the circus animals are all gone. Apart from an old box, a pad of paper and some felt-tips, Sellotape, miscellaneous things like that, there is nothing left. With a great welling up of hope she steps into the room. Like me, she thinks, he has realised he is not well and he is moving out of his prison.

'Have you lost something, Michael?' she asks.

Electrocuted, he springs to his feet.

'Mikey,' she says and smiles. 'Mikey, it's only me. I thought I could help. We need to go to my doctor's appointment now, but afterwards I could help you find whatever it is you've lost.'

Mikey runs towards her. She holds her arms wide as if to invite him in and he rushes into her embrace. She wraps her arms around him and he sort of falls against her and they stumble backwards into the nursery and fall to the floor. For a brief moment, they lie like that, him kneeling on top of her and when he climbs off, she sprawls on the carpet, catching her breath and laughing, and he is smiling too and then he slams the door and the last thing she hears is the turn of the key.

Chapter Twenty-Five

Mikey legs it. He stumbles, trips down the narrow stairs, falls onto the landing. Exhilaration powers him to his feet, eyes dart between the chessboard of a hall beneath him, the stairway up to the nursery above him and to his left, the wall where there was once a way through to the tower. His teeth bite his lip. He's as stiff and as still as if he was playing musical statues. He listens like a hare listens.

'Michael! Mikey? Can you hear me? I'm trapped and I need rescuing! Are you coming to get me?'

It's a silly sing-song voice like she's two years old. If he could sing back, he would. No. You're on your owny-oh. He's locked her in, he can't believe it, he's locked her in. He didn't plan to, it was just that she was in there and he was out here and it suddenly came to him that all he had to do to win was slam the door. So he did. Bang. Crash. Gone.

'Michael! It's a good joke, but you need to let me out now. It's not funny. I'll miss my appointment at the doctor's.'

But it is funny. It's very funny. In his bedroom, he jumps up and down on the bed, waving his plastic sword over his head in triumph, and he proclaims his great victory to the circus animals who now understand why they had to move house. Actually, that isn't quite true because when he did it he didn't even know this was going to happen, but looking back, it all makes sense. He's a fortune teller, or what was it Edmund called the sampler girl because she knew about the earthquake two hundred years before it happened? A prophet. He doesn't know what the difference is and he doesn't care, he's probably both. When they got back from the wildlife park he moved the circus animals and got loads of biscuits and stuff from the kitchen, not because he was going to lock her up, but because he was going to lock himself in. He was planning to hide in his room and barricade the door with the chest of drawers like he did once before. At least until Edmund got back. That way he'd be safe, because he wasn't safe with her; there was something cruel about her recently that he sensed. The only problem was he'd dropped Gorilla somewhere and that was why he was searching the nursery. Gorilla is very important, he is his bodyguard, and he needs one of those.

When Edmund went away, to start with she was almost nice and he was almost sorry for her, because she cried when Edmund left just like he did, but then she did the worse thing she could ever have done and he is never ever going to forgive her for that, and if she's the sort of person that tells lies just to get Solomon locked up then she must be the sort of person who could do anything. And lie about anything. He already knows what a liar she is, she's made everyone think it was him to blame for what happened. People like that stop at nothing, that's what his mum said except she wasn't talking about Diana. Although he spent a lot of time thinking of punishments for her, mostly based on Lockdown, he hadn't really come up with one that would work in the real world and now it's just sort of happened without him even thinking. She's in there locked up and he's out here, in charge of everything.

It was the trip to the wildlife park that did it. First of all, there was the nice woman who parked her car next to theirs; his aunt kept him away from people usually, but she couldn't do that, not somewhere like the wildlife park, and that woman was very kind, helping her little girl get her arm through the sleeve of her yellow anorak, and for one moment he thought he had found a way to escape and because it was so close and so possible, he realised how much he wanted to get out. He could say to the woman, this is my aunt who is horrible to me, can I come home with you? But he no longer had any idea if he could still speak. Sometimes he stood in front of the mirror in the bathroom, opened his mouth into a little O to see if anything came out, but someone always stopped it, calling up the stairs, or saying it was teatime. They stole his words. Even if the words came back, would anyone believe them? Diana hasn't actually done a crime against him. When they got back to the car, Diana was weird and the other family had left and he'd missed his chance.

The animals at the park understood him. The orang-utan squatting on the dead branch on the other side of the netting, playing with a piece of fruit in his long fingers, his eyes like the pool under the bridge, reflecting everything back at him. If you were an animal, which animal would you be? They did that at school. He said he would be a monkey, not a zoo monkey, but a king of the jungle monkey, hanging by one elastic-band arm from the tallest trees and hooting to scare the snakes away. That was in another school in another town a long time ago and he hadn't turned out to be that sort of monkey at all. They caught him and locked him up before he had a chance. In the reptile house, he didn't know why, all the way through the black tunnel, she held his hand, past the alligators pretending to be logs and the chameleons pretending to be leaves and the lizards as false as plastic toys; everyone was pretending, his aunt was pretending to be nice, he was pretending to have fun. Past great tanks of shifting weed they went and the luminous fish said O to him from the other side of the glass, and then from one world to the next, they were out in the light and dropped hands. There was a lake on one side where she stood studying the swans and a cage on the other where he stood studying the wolves, the she-wolf in particular, imagining the fleas feeding on her skin beneath the lank grey hair. Her eyes were green and mean, it didn't even really look like they were seeing you, but only the flesh beneath your T-shirt. Beyond the high fence, the other wolves were lying in the sun on the rocks and thin brown grass, but this wolf was on her own, prowling the length of the wire, teeth bared and biding her time. 'This she-wolf has been temporarily separated from the pack because she attacked her cubs. She will be reintroduced when the cubs are a little older. Do not feed.'

Since Edmund left, there was no fence left between him and his aunt.

One last chance he had, when she was ill and he was making swans with the man outside the first aid room, who went on and on talking to him even though he never talked back. Mostly he'd hoped she was so ill she would die and then Edmund would have to come back and look after him, or even if she was just very ill, someone else would be called, he thought they'd ring Grace. When the man called Donald came out with her, he was so sure that was what was going to happen, everyone must see that a woman like that couldn't look after children, and then Donald said that he wasn't to worry, his aunty was fine and they were going to buy some circus animals in the shop as a treat because he'd been so good. He burst into tears and everyone thought it was because he was happy. What if he'd said something then? Or even written something down? He didn't have his whiteboard, but there were felt-tips and paper in the activity box they'd found for him. I don't want to go home with her. That's all he'd have to write. Tell an adult, that's what they always said at school. But then they'd ask why and they wouldn't believe him and she'd be even more angry and when they got back to Wynhope it would be even worse than ever before.

In the shop it was like someone had turned the sound up, and for the first time for a long time Mikey was aware of everyone talking to each other. It looked so easy, like when you can't ride a bike yet and someone else can and off they go, pedalling, not even wobbling. He was jealous and he was frightened, all mixed up.

In the back of the car on the way home, she thought he was sleeping, but he wasn't. His heart was beating very fast. You don't get more than three get-outs on Lockdown and he'd lost of all them. They'd be home soon, she'd shut the front door, nobody would come to see them, she'd probably torture him and murder him because he's seen on the news that's what some people do to children, and then he'll be dead and no one will know and his mum will be sad and Edmund will come home and she'll probably have hidden his body so Edmund will think he's run away and he won't even come looking for him. On and on his mind careered into panic, gathering catastrophes as it went, and they clung to his fear so that the snowball grew until it was as cold and big as the whole world and bigger.

'Michael, come back. I know you're outside the door.'

But here he is all in one piece. The winner. She's shouting now. With his heart pounding, he wriggles out onto the landing like a commando then sits, leaning against the banisters, his knees pulled tight to his chest. She rattles the door handle then stops. Rattles and stops. In between, the house is very quiet, there are sounds, the ticking and tocking of the grandfather clock, the click of Monty's nails on the hall floor, the thud of blood pumping round his skull, but the silence is louder than all of them. He waits. He jumps. A short attack on the lock, rat-a-tat-tat, rat-a-tat-tat. Monty pushes his hands away from his face and noses his cheeks, and Mikey feels the warm and stinky breath of another living thing. The dog lies down beside him, head on one side, also alert to the invisible performance being played out upstairs.

'Michael!'

Breaking free from the boy's hand on his collar, Monty barks once, and getting no answer, turns a few circles and settles down again.

'I know you're out there with the dog. I can hear you.'

Monty's always been on his side.

'Michael, I know things have been awful, but I've been ill. That's what happened at the wildlife park. I've got an urgent appointment at the doctor's.' Her voice is coming down the stairs. 'I'm so sorry, I'm sorry.' A pause. 'I need to go to the doctor.'

Even Monty is worried, but it doesn't last long and he isn't taken in by it either, he rolls over onto his back as an invitation for Mikey to tickle him and as they rag and play she's up there banging her head against the wall like he does sometimes, so they play a little harder and she bangs a little harder until she starts up again as if she's pulled herself together.

'I know you're cross with me, but this isn't the way to sort things out. You can't just lock people up, you know. I'm not well, you can't.'

But you did. And I can. I have. Mikey is jiggling up and down, not just because he is triumphant, but because he really needs a pee and dares not leave the landing until he knows for sure that she can't escape.

'Let me out, Michael. I don't want to call the police. You'd be in a lot of trouble and I don't want that.'

Her phone. On Lockdown that would be a fatal error. It's on the hall table. Three messages. He's learned her password by watching her fingers, that's how people get your cash machine number and steal your money. The first message is something about winter fashion, the second is from the health club, reminding her to pay, and the last is from Spotless Angels. 'Hope it's OK, we will be at Wynhope at 10am on Friday, not 11. Hospital appointment.' That's tomorrow, which is ages away. He doesn't know what will have happened by tomorrow, but he knows he doesn't want them here, they come all the time and never notice anything. He texts back: 'Please don't come Friday. Thank you.' Dancing on the spot, he waves the phone in the air like a scalped head. She will be really, really, really unhappy not to have her phone, and he's really, really, really happy to have it because he can use it whenever he wants. As he puts it down, he spots the card with the word 'Police' on the top. Carefully he reads what it's all about then feeds it into the shredder in Edmund's study; they're no good either, arresting the wrong person. He's reached the next level. He can do anything in the world he wants to now she's in there and he's out here: his fishing rod is in the passage, he can go to the river for as long as he likes; the air gun is in the cupboard, he can just take that and kill things if he wants to. If he feels like it. Like this. He finds a packet of chocolate digestives and stuffs two of them in his mouth at the same time, gives one to the dog, stuffs another two into his jeans pocket. What else? Anything. Everything. Once he's certain she can't break out. Outside, he takes the long way round via the stables flat so he ends up hiding behind the swing tree. From there he can spy on the nursery. One front window is open, her head is poking out, her hands around the metal struts, and he remembers Gorilla, poor Gorilla. There are no bars on the windows on the other side, perhaps Gorilla could parachute his way to freedom. Picking at the bark of the tree, he waits and he watches. She must be thinking about calling out, but they both know nobody will hear her from there and nobody will come up the drive and rescue her, because nobody visits Wynhope any more, she's driven them all away. That's what he heard Edmund say once: 'You've driven everyone away.'

The best Greek myth in the book Edmund bought for him is the one about Cyclops. He can be like Odysseus and call himself 'Nobody', then when all the people ask Diana who locked you up in the attic, she will say 'Nobody' and they'll all say you've only got yourself to blame. This is boring. On television when police do surveillance, they have partners who sit in the car with them and smoke cigarettes, then one of them usually nips off for a burger just when the murderer turns up, but here it's just him on the job, except for Monty who appears at the back door, sniffs, then charges over the lawn wagging his tail and giving away his hiding place.

'Michael, I can see you there. Come up here now. The game's over now. It's not funny . . . please,' she screams.

In reply, he dances on the lawn in front of her like he's just won something huge and everyone is cheering and taking photographs of him and wanting interviews, then he runs for cover into the kitchen, laughing so hard he finds he cannot stop and he's not so far from crying. Having collapsed on the sofa, he turns on the television and what's on is a programme about what you can find in your attic. One woman is talking about jigsaws, how people don't realise that some of them are valuable and she shows an Elvis jigsaw, just like theirs. You have to have all the pieces for it to be worth anything. Their jigsaw was worth something. If Sarah had brought it back to him then he could have finished it, from the sparkly suit all the way down to the guitar in the bottom left-hand corner. People thought Elvis was dead but he probably isn't. Tears stream down his face. He suddenly feels so lonely that he finds himself to be like a jigsaw, sliding slowly to the floor and cracking into pieces – legs, arms, heart, head, brain, voice, falling apart. How he will never sit with her again to put the pieces together. How there will never be anyone to sit with him again. Not like that. Not like this. Not like anything. He's on his own.

The ring of Diana's mobile phone stirs him. Rubbing his eyes, wiping his snotty nose on the bottom of his T-shirt, it takes a few seconds to orientate himself in the sitting room, now lit only by random flickers from the television. He remembers what he's done. The curtains are open, but it's dark outside and the room is full of indoor shadows. Monty will know if she's out there, but the dog lazily puts a paw up on his knee and growls in a way that means it's past supper time. He loves this dog. The text message on her mobile is only from the cleaners.

'No problem. Thx for letting us know. We will come again next week.'

Having pulled the curtains so the night can't get in, Mikey puts on the lamp, turns on the chandelier in the hall, goes to each and every room, even to the drawing room, and lights up the house like Christmas, so the burglars and the crows will see someone's home, and then he creeps up the stairs and holds his breath. She's still in there. He'll have to let her out soon, at least before bedtime, but maybe not yet. The truth is he doesn't know quite what will happen if he lets her out.

Supper is everything he likes, except none of it tastes quite as good as he hoped. Afterwards, Mikey is brave enough to open the back door just a fraction to let the dog out. He leaps into the evening, barking at the place where the badger crosses the lawn. Monty's never scared of anything except for thunder, it must remind him of the earthquake. What if there's another earthquake? What if the house falls down? What if he is crushed and nobody finds him? The what ifs are running down the hill in his brain faster and faster, their arms waving, their legs buckling unable to stop.

'Monty! Michael! Michael!'

That puts the brakes on. Monty has triggered the security lights and they've lit up the bronze boy and woken her up as well.

'For God's sake, you can't leave me up here all night. I'm not well. That's what happened at the wildlife park, I realised I wasn't well. I know I haven't been very nice for a long time, but it's because I'm ill. Call an ambulance. Call nine-nine-nine.' Her voice is getting higher and higher like singing practice. 'There's no bulb up here. Please, don't leave me in the dark, I hate the dark. Oh God, oh God.'

He knows the bulb has gone; it popped soon after Edmund drove away. Edmund would have put a new one in, but he couldn't ask her so he's been playing in the dark. Paul used to take the bulbs out on purpose. He doesn't think his mum would like what he has done and for the first time he worries that she'll be cross with him. They said that, didn't they, the forensic people, that the lights were turned off on the spiral staircase.

'I can't sleep up here, there's no bed. It's not funny any more.'

She's right. It isn't funny any more. In the hall, he sits on the bottom stair where he sat once before, a very long time ago when he was just as scared as he is now except Edmund was there, even though he didn't know Edmund then, not very well. He has a plan. If he waits until she falls asleep, then he can open the nursery door very quietly, just an inch, then run as fast as he can down to his room and shove the chest of drawers across the door. He'll need to hide because she'll be like a beast, like something from the wildlife park when she gets let out, like the she-wolf with fleas and fangs and hunger and snarling. Two things occur to him: first, it would be a good idea to prepare his room now, to get the barricade ready because it's not easy to move the furniture, and to get more food and stuff, he needn't worry about water because he's got the little bathroom next door; second, he wonders if he might have time when she's asleep to sneak into the nursery and find Gorilla. When he was very small he used to play a game with his mum. She would put on a blindfold and curl up tight in the middle of the floor with a jam jar beside her. Then they'd say together: 'Isn't it funny how bears like honey. Buzz, buzz, buzz. I wonder why she does.'

It was his job to creep up on his mum and steal the jar and he nearly always got away with it. Just sometimes she'd catch him, grab him by the ankle and roar and chase him round their little sitting room and out through the French windows and into the garden until they had to be sensible because Paul would be back from work soon.

It's probably not possible to rescue Gorilla. Not today. What's worse is that Monty cannot hide with him either because Monty needs fresh air, and although that means both of them will be lonely, at least Monty will be his guard dog on the outside. He can trust him to do that.

Everything is ready. Each step on the nursery stair holds its fingers to its mouth and tells the next to be as quiet as possible; they are his stairs, they are on his side. At the top, he listens with his eyes as well as his ears; they scan the little landing and the wooden doors as if they can see sound. Because it's dark she's probably fallen asleep already, she won't know the time or that it's too early for bed. The key is in the pocket of his jeans, his hand is shaking, and he has trouble getting it to fit the lock. It rattles the door.

There is an explosion of noise. It seemed like a good plan, but the pounding and shrieking are the sounds of a prisoner this close to breaking out and he does not know what he will do if she escapes and beats him down the stairs. She is no longer just battling with the handle, she is battering the door itself. It's going to shatter, and he's trapped within a horror film of his own making.

And the words. Hate. You wait. Edmund. Never forgive. Police. Prison. Should have pushed you in the river. Better off dead.

The chest of drawers scrapes across the floor, inch by inch, so heavy, but finally the barricades are up and he waits for what he thinks is a very long time. He can never let her out, not when she's like that, he'd never get away in time. She's much, much worse than he thought she'd be. Now what? Somehow the now what slowly loses its question mark and becomes just a thing, maybe a row of dots like you get sometimes at the end of a chapter in a book. . . . Like that. And finally, at the end of the row of dots and with Monty whining at the door, Mikey thinks he can risk coming out. She might think he's a little kid playing a trick, but he's not, he's old beyond his years, that's what people say about him. He's made sense of things a little bit. He never meant to do it, he's not done anything wrong on purpose, he's only making sure she can't attack him.

When you've got such a long time and you don't know what to do with it, the best thing is the computer. In Edmund's study, he reaches level four of Lockdown and eats cold baked beans, but he does put them in a bowl because his mum says only slobs eat out of the tin. Some fall on the carpet, the dog eats them, but even so they leave little orange spots which smear and get worse when he scrubs at them with a kitchen cloth. Counting with the striking clock, he gets all the way to nine. He's going to have to spend the night alone, that's clear. He should go to bed, but how can he with her up there and him down here? He's got the computer, he likes the screensaver with its picture of the river, autumn, the trees on the banks are all golden and the heron is standing like a statue on the weir. Edmund says the salmon swim the wrong way up the river to get home, thousands of miles they swim to get home, and there are some who are not strong enough to jump over the rapids and those are the ones the heron is waiting for. Sometimes when he's by the river playing, he pretends he's the heron and sometimes he's the salmon. He wastes a bit more time checking his aunt's boring emails. None of them are from friends, they're all about things you can buy, but at least none of them say anything about anyone coming to Wynhope. Then he goes to Google and searches what happens to people locked up.

He knows a bit about prisons already. His mum took him to visit Solomon once, she must have wanted the company. He thought they might meet Paul if they left their new town, but she said when would he believe it: Paul has gone for ever. There were sniffer dogs, endless locked doors to get to the next level, waiting with nothing to do, and hardly any toys even though it was meant to be a family day, and how long now and his mum angry with everyone and everything and not much to talk about even when you got in. Who will visit Solomon now? Because of Diana, he must be back in that horrible place. His mum was right: no one did listen to Solomon's side of the story, no one believed him. The police just saw him at the window and looked the other way. It wasn't just his mum, he should have been able to rescue Solomon as well. Although he should feel bad about locking Diana up, he doesn't; it's his way of correcting the balance, and when she says sorry, then he'll let her out. That's a good idea. He'll put a piece of paper under the door asking her to say sorry for everything and then he'll let her out if she promises to be nice. He isn't sure when he'll do that, probably in the middle of the night just to be safe, or maybe first thing in the morning.

Some of the sites he finds on the internet are newspaper articles and easy to understand because he's got a reading age of 11.9; they tested him for everything when Diana took him to his new school, but they never asked any of the questions that mattered.

Woman, 37, free after 19 years of slavery.

Miracle: missing twins found in basement 9 years after their disappearance.

Most of the people locked up seem to be in America. The stories are all about good people locked up by monsters, none of them are about monsters locked up by good people. He can look for his mum for ever and never find her.

Other pages are more complicated. Experts writing about what happens to people who are held captive: how they go mad and start talking to themselves; how they imagine things that aren't there; how they might become violent or hurt themselves. Many of the peculiar P words are gobbledegook – psychosis, pseudo-hallucination, phobia – but it takes ages for people to go this crazy and start seeing things and killing themselves so he doesn't think the P things will happen to her in just one day, or one night, except she's got what Edmund would call a 'head start' as she's a bit mental already. The thought of her up there getting madder and madder is frightening. He types 'mad people locked up' into Google images and clicks on a black-and-white picture of a skull sort of woman behind bars. It starts moving, her hands come through the bars towards him and away, towards him and away. Mesmerised, he's drawn to the insanity. Maybe it's a film, maybe it's real, maybe it's a film about a real thing, he doesn't know, all he knows is that he understands it, and although the caption is complicated, it seems to understand him.

Madness, as you know, is like gravity. All it takes is a little push.

Torn between going to his bedroom and staying up all night downstairs with the television on, not just because he can, but because he isn't sure he can do anything else, he is simultaneously restless and paralysed. All the old DVDs are pulled out of the cabinet. This one is *Titanic.* Like an archaeologist, he lifts it very carefully and turns it over. It is an object which carries great meaning. He won't choose *Titanic.* There's nobody's hand to hold any longer when it gets too close to the end. On the television he selects the film channel. There are things he's not allowed to watch and he knows the password so he could, but in the end he chooses the family entertainment section and then *Jungle Book.* He watches that all the way through to the end and then creeps out into the hall, sees it's only 11.25 and that just like the alley running past the back of the pub at home, the night ahead is long and full of shadows, so he watches the film all over again, even when the music stops and the names creep down the screen and it ends. There should be someone to close up downstairs, tuck him in, leave the landing light on and the door not quite closed, someone to kiss him goodnight. He wants his penguin. Nothing that mattered was in the box they brought from home. These memories are not invited, but they're arriving anyway: dragging her bulging wheelie case down the stairs at home, his mum asking him if he wants to take Penguin and him saying he isn't having no snobby aunt thinking he's a baby. Perhaps if he had brought Penguin to Wynhope, none of this would ever have happened. Perhaps if he hadn't left Gorilla in the nursery, it wouldn't have turned out like this.

A solution to his wakefulness occurs to him. On the side table is an empty wine glass with her lipstick on it. Like the Cyclops she seemed a bit wobbly when he pushed her, which might be why she fell over so easily. Whisky is what Edmund has as his little nightcap. The light bounces off the glass as if it is made of diamonds, the whisky glows like Harry Potter magic but smells so strong the fumes slap him in the face and make his eyes water. Lifting the decanter with both hands, Mikey pours the whisky into the sort of glass that Edmund chooses and pours about the same amount that Edmund pours, but because it tastes like medicine he puts sugar in it and then drinks it all in one go and then has another for the road, like Edmund does, even though he isn't going anywhere. It worries him to leave all the lights on downstairs because when they argue Edmund shouts at Diana that they're not made of money and Mikey doesn't want the electric to run out. He wouldn't know how to top it up without a post office card, but he thinks just one night will be all right. Just one night. Much to Monty's delight, the dog is invited to sleep upstairs with him.

Mikey doesn't do his teeth, Mikey doesn't get undressed, Mikey doesn't read. The ceiling is treacherously thin and the creaking floorboards and incoherent muttering feed him information on her every move. When the noises stop, the bedroom walls torment him, lurching unsteadily around him, and the floor tips, as if the earth-quake is returning. Soon everything will fall in upon itself and his legs will be found sticking out of the rubble, pale and shiny like a plastic doll. The vomit goes all over his duvet. The dog jumps off and leaves him, curled up and shivering, a sick child. He is ill. He will probably die. Diana will die too. Edmund will come home and find both of them dead.

Chapter Twenty-Six

It is very late when he wakes; he can see from the daylight and the drizzle that time has moved on without him. The bedsheet stinks of sick. The radio is on in her bedroom down the landing; it comes on automatically every morning, though, so it doesn't mean she's in there. She's not, she's up there. She's not dead, she's pacing. With both anxiety and relief he reminds himself that today is the day that she'll say sorry and it will all be over.

The radio unnerves him. Feeling dry-mouthed and nauseous, he creeps along the landing, but once he has turned it off, the quiet is as creepy as the voices, like being in a classroom when everyone else has gone home, where you can do anything you like and nothing. You can stand on the chairs and pull your trousers down. You can look in the teacher's desk. In her bedside table, he finds a little gold watch which hangs lose around his wrist, some pills same as his mum has, other boring stuff, a torn-out page from an old-fashioned book. Cross-legged on the bed, he tries to decipher the words; it's more an Edmund sort of thing than a Diana because it's all about rivers to start with.

For there they that carried us away captive required of us a song.

The language and the layout make sense, it's from the Bible and Solomon taught him about verses with numbers like this. Solomon is good at explaining things. When they took him away, they took all the explanations away with him. It is a terrible evil thing to have torn a page out of a Bible and it confirms his opinion that she is a devil woman in disguise, just like Edmund's CD.

Let my tongue cleave to the roof of my mouth.

Tongue, roof, mouth: the individual words do not make much sense, but the meaning causes Mikey to lick the strange cave which opens up behind his lips, the smooth moulded dips and mounds, the secret sliding down inside himself at the very back. Cleave. He understands cleave as leave and knows one day his voice will break free. The Bible is important, Solomon would say she should have it. He decides to slide the page under the door to the nursery with his message written on the bottom (he hopes that this is not a sin, but he doesn't think so, it's not as if it's graffiti).

'If you say sorry for everything you have done I will let you out. Signed Michael. Wynhope House, Wynhope, Twycombe, England, Europe, The World, The Universe.'

He slides the page under the nursery door. Not long after, the screaming starts all over again, but later she quietens down, so maybe God's working his magic. He just needs to be patient.

It's past lunchtime, but he hasn't had breakfast, so he pours himself a gigantic bowl of cereal. He doesn't really feel like eating, so he drinks Coke instead because that's good for hangovers. So are cigarettes, but he doesn't smoke. He always thought smoking would kill his mum, but he's wrong; she gave up smoking, she hardly drank at all, she left Paul, she tried very hard to stay alive for him. Grace used to say it was his job to wipe down the table, so that's what he does, then he checks the nursery. No note back to him under the door, what if she doesn't say sorry? She'll have to. Everybody has to in the end, and the longer you leave it the harder it becomes, that's what his mum says.

Outside, he hangs around with the bronze boy, Hercules. They always talk about stuff like bikes and Lockdown. It's better out here in the hot sun with so much space. He knows she can see him but he's not going to even look up at her window, he's just going to look like he's happy and nothing's worrying him at all, so he throws sticks for Monty and stones for no one and kneels down to reach into the pond to play with the fish, and then he spots a piece of paper blowing across the drive. He runs, it swerves, he stamps on it. She's written a note with his red felt-tip pen on his pad of paper and dropped it out of the window. It was torn in half, but she's taped it up again.

He knew she'd want to get out and it would all be over by teatime.

The note is difficult to read, all the writing is a joined-up mess and not sticking to the lines.

Dear Mickey,

She started off writing Michael, but then thought better of it and crossed out the C and turned the H into a K so she has ended up with a spelling mistake.

I found your note. It was very naughty to write on a page from the Bible and you shouldn't be prying into my drawers. If you let me out, then I can say sorry properly to you and you can say sorry to me and we can start all over again.

Nothing will be solved if I'm locked in here. NOTHING. You must unlock the door otherwise you will be in trouble.

I missed my appointment at the doctor's yesterday. I must go. I'm not very well, that's why I've been like I have been. I promise I won't be cross.

The handful of gravel hits the house and shatters back onto the flowerbed. He picks up more stones, hurls them at the front door. She hasn't said sorry at all. She wants him to say sorry? What's she got hidden in her bedroom that she's so worried about? And does she expect him to believe her promises? She's a liar, and once she promised to leave the passage door open and she didn't. She should

202

have just done what she was told then it would all be over. Is she that stupid? It's time she learned to listen to him. Doesn't she understand anything he tells her? You are a thick, common little slut, you must never forget that, he rages. You're a nobody. When will you ever learn to apologise? And you can tell who you like, nobody will ever believe you. Who's ever going to believe someone like you?

The shaking turns to shivering then to exhaustion. All he wants now is to be somebody else and for it all to be over. On her phone there's a text message from the surgery saying she's missed her appointment, please call to make another one. So the doctor isn't coming up the drive to find her, and Mikey's face is twisting in the way it does when it wants to cry and he's trying to control it. It seems important not to throw anything away, so he puts the note in a brand new A4 file which Edmund let him have and slides it into a secret compartment he makes, taped to the bottom of his circus animals box. He hates her for not doing what she was told, he hates her for the fact that he doesn't know what to do with her, but most of all he hates her because of what she did and that's what gives him the idea. All he asked her to do was say sorry, but he didn't say what for. He could make another level with more challenges. No more secrets, no more lies.

How to write instructions was one of the things they did in literacy class and he got a smiley face for his work. For homework he wrote all about how to feed the cat and in school he wrote all about how to make a cup of tea for his mum. It was only ever a stray cat, but his mum said they'd give him home forever and who's looking after the cat now? Mikey's thumb finds its way to his mouth, these are difficult words. School. Mum. Smiley face. At the kitchen table he works hard. Two or three times he has to start again before he finally gets it right. Redrafting, that's what his teacher calls it.

To Diana. What you have to do to get out.
  1. Write an account of what happened the night of the earthquake.

2. When you have finished, throw it out of the window like you did the last one and I'll find it in the garden.

3. If it is good, I will let you out.

She must be hungry. On films, they send in food in exchange for hostages, but he can't do that, and anyway people live for years if they've got water and there's a sink up there, next to the toilet. She might not know how to write an account. They did lots of different types of writing at school but he settled on an account for this because it has to have facts. Sometimes in class he used to wonder whether he should write his own account, but they would only have thought he'd got fiction and fact muddled up, and, besides, the teachers are scared of him now because of what he did to Aimee. The last time he was in literacy in school they were doing narrative writing. Diana would be good at that, she was always making things up, but this was his story, with only two characters and him in charge of the ending. In his proper school, the teachers used to like him, they wrote nice things on his report like 'Mikey is a popular and helpful member of the class', and his mum took him to Pizzaland as a treat, he chose the one with pineapple and she had the one with, a different one, he can't remember what extra topping she chose, it is slipping away.

Because it is a long time since Diana went to school he copies a section out of the English book the school sent home.

Recounts are a way of retelling an important event you have experienced so that other people understand it. Remember –

First Person

Past Tense

Chronological Order

It didn't look quite enough, so he adds:

You have to tell the truth.

Sign your name at the bottom so everyone knows it's you.

(If there are any witnesses you can write about them too and put what they say inside the speech marks like this '. . .')

The door to the nursery is becoming a bit like a mouth, sucking in everything he feeds through the gap between the wood and the carpet. The instructions are not snatched, there's no shadow on the other side, not that he can see anyway, lying on his tummy and squinting. He can't see anything in fact, can't hear anything, but she has to be in there. She's just pretending, trying to trick him into opening the door, like she tried to trick him with her note. Let her out then she'll say sorry. She's always thought he's stupid, but he's not and he's got the upper hand now. Even so, he feels silly all over and scared as he slides back down the stairs, the rough carpet rubbing against his tummy, his knees going bump, bump, bump. At the bottom, Monty tells him he's done the right thing and he feels better, only Monty can do that for him.

The flowers on the hall table have dropped their petals and this reminds him of his promise to Edmund: he is chief in charge of the lilies. Come on, young man, says Monty, chop, chop. Inside the glasshouses, the green lilies line up in order like a school assembly, junior shoots thrusting up through the soil, the seniors tall with swollen buds and finally the full grown-ups, their heads wrapped in white scarves like the nuns in *Sister Act*, which is the only time he's ever been in a theatre and it was their best night out ever, him, Mum and Solomon. At the end two or three lilies have come and bloomed and spread their yellow seeds onto the stony floor and are left with their leaves shrivelling and the huge sticking-out bit, bare and drooping. The sweetness and warmth wrap him up and hug him, the smell of so many different things all mixed up, jungles and the sun, the cemetery, mums at the school gates, but mostly their very own chapel. He's not sure he's brave enough to actually take them to the chapel without Edmund, but at least they'll be alive for when he comes back. Outside, wedging the watering can under the tap from the rain butt and waiting for it to fill, Mikey examines the spider's web stretching all the way from the pipe to the gutter, threads of silk caught in the sunlight, and right in the middle, legs hunched and waiting, the spider. With a twig from the vine, Mikey pokes the web, provokes the spider into an even tighter ball. Incy Wincy Spider climbing up the spout. On tiptoe, he waves his stick to see how far he can chase it. Down came the rain and washed poor Wincy out. Balancing on a pile of old bricks, Mikey tortures the spider the length of the greenhouse gutter until he hears the water splashing onto the path, then, solemnly, he drenches the lilies in honour of Edmund. On the way back through the garden, paying close attention and hardly daring to hope, he covers the length of the flowerbed like a gardener, inspecting each plant, parting the dahlias with their huge bright pompom heads, examining the soil beneath their leaves. Perhaps her account has been blown away in the wind; the ink might run in the rain, maybe she hasn't written anything at all. In fact it's lying on the rim of the pond like litter. The wind must have caught it and played with it, probably didn't even realise how important it was, but Hercules does, he's kept an eye on it. Mikey squats down and reads it right there. The first thing that strikes him is that it's written in stupidly big letters as if he's in reception.

HELP ME
My name is Lady Diana Helyarr. I am locked in the attic room at Wynhope House, Wynhope, TW73 9KJ. 01981 877577
I am in urgent need of medical attention.
IF YOU FIND THIS NOTE CALL THE POLICE IMMEDIATELY.

The bronze boy tells him not to be such an old worrier, at least she's written something. He's got snakes in his hands, Mikey's got her stupid note in his; together they wave their arms triumphantly. Olé olé olé olé. Solomon taught him how to celebrate a goal, not that he ever scored any. Olé olé olé olé. If he's honest, he thinks he's losing this game as well so he doesn't dance for long. The soaked paper is spread carefully on top of the Aga to dry, like at school when they poured tea all over their history work so it looked like an ancient document, but that would be tampering with the evidence. On the counter, the red light on the answer machine is flashing.

'Darling Di, Mikey, it's me. We're just heading back out into the wilderness. I'll call you if I can, but there's probably no signal so don't count on it. I heard on the World Service that it's an Indian summer in England so you're probably outside having fun in the garden. The river should be perfect, catch a fish for me, Mikey, but be careful, don't go down there on your own even if it looks low. You'd love it here, Mikey, just to get to the camp we took a helicopter and then rode in on horses, like cowboys. Fantastic. And we saw a swan goose, beautiful. I'll bring you here one day. Lots of love to you both. Bye. Lots of love, Mikey. Bye bye for now. Bye bye.'

Mikey presses seven for save and then play, again and again and again.

What would Edmund say if he knew? What would his mum say? It's not his fault Diana's locked up there. It's her fault. In some ways it doesn't even matter whose fault it is, he can't let her out now. The truth is he can't ever let her out. It's not a game, but it is a bit like chess and this is checkmate.

As darkness slips into the house, she shouts even louder. Edmund has told him about badger baiters with traps deep in the woods and poachers with salmon rods down on the river, John says there are burglars who steal tractors from farmers, and Miss Coulson read stories at school about the ghosts at the gallows at the crossroads. They are all out there and she's upstairs. If his window is open because of the hot night, the screams come in, lit by the moon; if he closes the window, the howls crawl their way down the attic staircase or prise their starving bodies between the crevices of the old house. He creeps downstairs. As he opens the back door, just to make the security lights come on, a note scuttles into the house on the back of the wind.

What you don't understand is that you are a very sick little boy. I rescued you and all you've ever done is hate me in return trying to destroy everything that matters to me but you won't succeed. You are a monster you are very cruel unless you get help you will spend the rest of your life in prison. It's time you knew the truth.

your mother never wanted you
you haven't got a father
nobody's tried to find you
nobody will ever believe anything you say
We're all you've got.
DIAL 999 TO GET HELP. YOU MUST DO THIS NOW.
NOW.

There and then in the midnight kitchen he marks her homework in big black capitals.

THIS IS WRONG. MY MOTHER LOVES ME.
EDMUND LOVES ME MORE THAN HE LOVES YOU.

One by one, he presses the numbers to call his uncle's mobile.
'The mobile you are calling is temporarily unavailable. Please try again later.'
The circus animals are so cross they want to tear up her note, but he stops them and makes them hide it away with the other notes because it's evidence. He hopes she's not taking it out on Gorilla. The circus animals position themselves at strategic points around the bedroom: the tigers line the windowsill, their shadows much bigger than themselves; the monkeys work with the tanks and the soldiers as a first line of defence at the door; one elephant is stationed

at each corner, they are the most trustworthy of all and they remember everything.

At some point during the night, it rains so hard he thinks the glass in the window might shatter and there will be nothing in between him and all the things he doesn't understand.

Chapter Twenty-Seven

Like the tally charts they do in maths, he imagines Diana must be marking off the days on her wall, that's what prisoners do. He looks at the calendar in the kitchen. Two nights gone, which is a very long time. Today must be the last day. That's when he notices it's Monday and there is a V for the vegetable man who brings an organic box after lunch. If the organic vegetable man wasn't so huge and horrible he could tell him what's happened and he'd get help, but the organic vegetable man shouted at him once when his ball hit the van and laughed at him. Call yourself a footballer! So Mikey decides to write his own note to tell the veg people to stay away and everyone else. No one can ever know what he's done. The notice is typed up in font size 58.

Drive is unsafe. Please leave all delivries
at the lodge.

He spell-checks deliveries. Changes it. Prints it out in BOLD, UNDERLINED.

One other thing on the September page of the calendar catches his eye: back to school. It must have been written a long time ago because he was eavesdropping when Diana told the headteacher that he wouldn't be going back, he was going away to a special school, but that's never happened. There's no teacher calling out his name in the morning, no hook for his coat, no place at the table, no drawer for his things. At school they always talked about his aunty; he wanted to say she's not my aunty, she's only my half-aunty. Now he doesn't have a school of his own at all.

All the way down to the gates and back is a long way, helped only by the dog who is excited to be out, bringing him sticks and wanting to play; he doesn't understand how serious this is. They avoid the drive and take the long-grass way, which means his jeans get damp all the way up to his knees. Without Edmund beside him, the park is endless and unfamiliar. The trees have swapped places in the night, marching across the park like giants. If he runs, it's worse because nobody mows the grass here, it's lumpy and lays traps of rusty wire. In front of the stile a dead rabbit is blocking his way and the nightmare returns. Is it really dead? Monty's not interested in it, he's not the sort of dog who kills things, he's the sort of dog who brings things back. With a stick, Mikey pokes at its back legs and jumps away because it's still soft and its eyes are open. He has to go the long way round to where you can climb over the fence onto the drive and then, finally, there's the bridge. Down by the waterside, he calms down. The river is the only place in the park that has never frightened him; even in the beginning, he loved it. It's everything he wishes for all in one place, it's always there, coming and going, and it's never boring because of the things it brings with it and the things it hides, and if you want to, you can throw things in the river and imagine where they go next. You can spend hours trying to dam it, but it always finds a way through. You can spend hours just being you and doing nothing much and the river never minds. Bit high for you, today, young man. Just like Solomon once put pencil marks on the kitchen door to show how much he'd grown, the river draws lines up the trunks of the trees which lean out from the banks, and Mikey agrees that after last night's rain, today it would be way over his boots and nearly over

Edmund's waders, surging over the weir with such strength that even the stepping stones have disappeared and even the swans have left. Edmund told him that in the whole of England the only bird you cannot kill is a swan because that's treason and you'd be hung for it and your head stuck on the railings at the Tower of London. Sometimes, he pretends he is a swan.

These are the gates in and the gates out. Turn right for school and left for their silent sessions at the library on a Thursday. He's never understood why she takes him there and why she gets cross when he wants to borrow a book, that's what libraries are for. Beyond these gates is where all the other people are, shopping, driving, shouting, going to work. Wayside Electricians, M&M Mobile Mechanics, Wholesale Meat Products, they all speed past. It's mostly grey out there, he thinks. It doesn't have as many flowers as Wynhope, but it does have cinemas and bus stations and supermarkets and other people's nans who stop you in the street to ask after your mum and other people's mums who stop you in the street to ask after your nan. If he has to, he could probably get a bus home, go to his friend Ali's house and live with him. He'd take Diana's money and some food in case he got hungry and her phone (except they could use that to track him down), he would be okay. There is stranger danger, but no one is more strange and dangerous than her. Grace would be sad if she knew the lodge looked so left alone, drink cans and sandwich wrappers blown across her swept-clean porch, piling up against the front door with its orange warning tape and graffiti. If he knew where her grandchildren lived, he could go there, but he can't even find Grace or John under contacts on Diana's phone, they've been deleted. And maybe even Grace wouldn't want him, she's never even sent a postcard like she said she would. He could always move in here because the lodge is outside the gates strictly speaking and Diana's rules don't work here.

Whoosh. A huge truck rumbles past too close – Moving U Where U Want To Go – a glimpse of the driver, high up, one hand on the wheel, one hand on the phone. Two more cars, then a motorbike who slows up, glances in his direction and then speeds past. The noise, the blast of air is like enemy fire. He ducks, holds tight to Monty, because imagine if he got run over and he realises he no longer really understands the world and doesn't even dare ask it for help which is why they need to stay away, all of these cars and drivers and delivery men, which is why he has the notice. His Sellotape's in the nursery with her, but string is better anyway, it doesn't fall off in the rain.

DRIVE IS UNSAFE. PLEASE LEAVE ALL DELIVERIES AT THE LODGE.

Paul put so many signs on the gates at their old house that you couldn't see the number any longer: Do Not Park In Front of These Gates, No Cold Callers, Canvassers or Religious Groups, even a picture of an Alsatian, though they didn't have a dog, and a Neighbourhood Watch notice which meant he was watching the neighbours because he didn't trust them either.

It was the right decision not to make a sign saying KEEP OUT; if people saw that they'd only want to break in.

What if Solomon comes back for him? He wouldn't be put off by this notice, he travelled 3,000 miles to get to England with Jesus helping him.

Mission accomplished, Mikey saunters back up to the house, chucking oak apples at the sheep on the other side of the fence, scoring ten points for every hit and getting up to fifty. Only when he gets as far as the ha ha does he see her, leaning out of the window. Ha ha ha. That makes him laugh every time. The joke's on you. Nobody's coming to rescue you, I've sent them all away. Nanny nanny boo boo ya boo sucks. All in his head, of course.

Diana might be trying a new strategy, powerful, up there at the top of the house, never leaving her post, not saying a word, but Mikey can do better than that, he can do anything now. He devises a new military response in return: he becomes a spy. He has made a camouflage uniform by tying small branches to his baseball cap and wearing a green jumper, his face is smeared with chocolate and half a jar of green pesto sauce he found in the fridge, and when he looks in the mirror in the downstairs loo, he sees a warrior. Monty has to stay in the house because he's hopeless at keeping secrets. Dead pheasants are all that he's trained to find and that thought leads to the gun cupboard and what a real soldier would do. The key's in Edmund's desk, it's easy to open. Some of the guns look too big for him, but he has held the air gun before, so that's the one he chooses.

'Never, never let your gun
Pointed be at anyone.
That it may unloaded be
Matters not the least to me.'

Edmund made him learn that off by heart and Mikey recites it to himself as he skulks round the back of the garages, darting from cover to cover. He hunkers down when he reaches the ditch and points the gun away from himself and towards her.

'Michael,' she calls. 'I know you're there.'

Heads down, men, below the parapet.

'Someone will come soon. It's better you unlock the door now. Michael. Mikey.'

Brazenly, he stands up in the trench, tries to swagger like a soldier except the gun's a bit heavy.

'There you are. Listen to me, darling. I love you, really, I'm sorry about what I wrote. I've done everything all wrong.'

He waves the gun at her.

'That's really dangerous,' she cries.

The gun is pointed up at the window. She disappears. The gun is lowered. She reappears. In out, in out, shake it all about. Up goes the gun again. You do the hokey cokey and you turn around. With the gun pointed at the clouds, Mikey pulls the trigger, the crack of the shot punches him in his shoulder, but she's the one who's crying. That's what it's all about.

Suddenly she retaliates. There is a thud on the drive and there is the packet of felt-tips.

One thing leads to another, that's what Edmund says. Like he pushed her in and slammed the door and now look what's happened, except it started before that, she started it on the night of the earthquake. Anyway, she's thrown out the pens so she can't write the account so he can't let her out so she'll die in there and what will happen to him then? Without the felt-tips, his plan is worthless. A great disturbance grows deep inside him, it heats him up so that he sweats, it clenches his fists and turns him into an alien who crashes through the house, smashing everything he finds with his gun, the little blue sugar basin, the china hen with eggs in it, even the mug with an M which Grace gave him as a secret present when she left. When the alien's gone, Mikey screws himself up under the dining-room table with Monty, who has licked up all the eggs and the sugar, and it's quite some time later that he locks the gun away again. Edmund is right, you never know. Then he re-examines his packet of felt-tips and realises the orange one is missing.

So the next note is orange.

You want me to write an account of what happened. Where do you want me to begin?

Duh. He doesn't want some long story, all about herself, she's really old and it would take her ages to get to the bit that matters. That would be a biography or an autobiography, he can't remember which; it's something to do with who was telling the truth. He just wants her to get it over and done with.

I will begin with where you came from.

So now she thinks she can tell his story, she has no right to do that. This note is written quite carefully, with bits corrected and full stops added in afterwards.

You have a right to know where you came from. Your mother and I had different fathers. My father was a gentleman, her father was a beast. That's your grandfather. He was an evil man. He was a bully and a liar, he spoiled people's lives.

Do you recognise yourself? Because when you are older you will understand that this is what he did, planted his evil in you, like a seed, and as you grow, it will grow as well until it has spread throughout your body and your mind.

Without his clothes on, Mikey examines his body. What would it look like if she was right? Pressing his finger into his tummy button, into his ear, into all the other places where bad things can get in, he doesn't think he can defend himself. He wonders if that's why his willy does what it does sometimes, like now, like someone else is controlling it from inside. On the end of his bed, Mikey winds a jumper round and round his neck and stays like that for a long time. Even the circus animals are hiding, they don't want this note in their box.

The sky is changing, the weatherman says the heatwave is coming to an end and there are warnings. Squeezed between the low cloud and the sulky ground, Mikey feels there must be thunder somewhere; it will be difficult to make it down the drive and back for the vegetables before the storm, he would rather be anywhere in the world than here when the thunder comes. In a crazy way, hurtling very fast down the drive as if he is a racing driver, further and faster than anyone ever before, he collects the box. The cars swish past, nobody waves back. A siren comes and goes in the distance, he waits, but it's not coming his way. Dark stains on the tarmac mark each individual raindrop. The box is too heavy, so he throws away the cabbages and the cauliflower, gets half way home, ditches Diana's disgusting yoghurt drink, and struggles back with the rest of it just before the thunder stamps its feet on the doorstep. For some time it hangs around out there, clearing its throat and cackling, before suddenly, without warning, it roars and the whole of Wynhope trembles in remembrance of the terrible shaking that was the start of all this. The doors bang, the curtains in his bedroom flap in panic, and all he wants is someone to count the spaces between the lightning and the thunder in sevens like his mother did and tell him it is marching away, mile by mile, across the globe and on out into space, but now he's the one who has to be brave because Monty is shaking, scuffling to get under the bed.

Lying on the floor, reaching his hand past the lost socks and the dust, finding the fur and the clink of the tag on the collar, he comforts the dog so the dog knows he'll always be there for him, that he can make everything better, only he can do that, that he loves him and that he's not really horrible with bad seeds in him, he's just a child.

The thunder stays close, prowling in circles around Wynhope like a tiger, swiping at the house with its paws. To make Monty feel better, Michael gets his animals out and arranges them throughout the castle. When the earthquake comes again, the castle is shaken, the sides buckle, it loses it shape, the animals tumble from the battlements, the bricks crush them, even the tanks and the soldiers seem powerless against it, but nobody gives up. When the storm is over, gently he lifts the Lego off the bodies of the circus animals, encourages them to stand, bandages their limbs with paper and string, and then there is an awards ceremony for bravery for all those who stayed at their posts, which is everyone, and a special medal for Monty and a bit of a ceremony for Gorilla, who had to survive it all on his own.

If she's died in the thunder storm at the top of the house, there would be a sign, like the sour smell of the rats which ate the poison in the woodshed and rotted under the floor.

Time is going so very slowly; he thinks all the clocks have stopped, maybe he's meant to wind them up. It must be nearly supper time, but who knows, who cares.

With the new organic loaf on the kitchen table, Mikey gets out the bread knife, his hand barely stretches across the top of the crusty bread and he struggles to keep it still as he saws away for a piece of toast. The first slice gets wider and wider at the bottom so it won't fit in the toaster. He tries again, the knife slips and there is blood all over the bread. That's my scream, he thinks, I have cut off my finger and no one can hear me and there's no one to help me. I'll bleed to death. With his left hand held in his right hand, his right hand gets covered in blood and so does the bread board and the counter and the floor. He stands at the sink on tiptoe, but the blood keeps coming, running red all over the white basin, his life pouring out of him, spilling away down the drain. There is someone upstairs he can go to, knock hard and say I've cut my finger and I don't know what to do, but he no longer knows what he might find behind the door.

He could call 999, but how would he ask for help? Without his voice, nobody can hear him. He has become Nobody.

On the floor with his head between his knees, he knows he's going to die because the world is fading away. There's a voice. We can stick that back together again, it's saying. His mum, it must be his mum, of course she'll be here when he dies. A memory of being on his mum's knee and her winding a white bandage round and round his hand, round and round the garden, tickle you under there, the scratch of her jumper on his bare arm, her hair soft as nothing on his face, that's how close she is. Reaching for the kitchen roll, he winds it round and round his finger, most of the paper falling away on the floor and unravelling, and the bit round his finger red to start with, then only just a bit red, then plain white. He kisses himself better because she can't. There are no signs that the red is seeping through the white, so after waiting a long time just to make sure he butters the fat-bottomed piece of bread one-handed and feels better. He has saved himself.

Because he's still alive he runs outside. The evening feels as if it might float away, light as the balloon he can see drifting above the park, striped like the big top on the lid of the circus animals box. A little boy in the garden of a big house, playing all on his own, that's what the balloon travellers must see. They're waving at him, he waves back with one white finger.

'Hello,' he calls.

His word is taken from him, carried all the way up into the sky and given like a present to the people in the balloon. They unwrap it and throw gifts back down to him.

'Hello there, little boy,' they cry. 'Hello and goodbye!'

'Goodbye,' he calls back, goodbye to you and your balloon and Mummy and Nanna, goodbye, goodbye, goodbye.

Higher and higher climbs the balloon, skimming its way through the sea of a sky, waves of white foam and blue, and they take his word with them, wherever they sail, they pass on the message to whoever they meet.

His word.

It's going through a curtain to another world. Maybe it's all magic and everything is make-believe. The test is if he can do it again. Monty has brought him a stick, it's his way of saying go on, try. The dog speeds after the stick thrown far into the long meadow grass.

'Come,' he cries.

And the dog comes.

'Fetch,' he cries.

And the dog fetches.

Deep down in his tummy, his name wants to be next, pushing, its tiny hands reaching for the surface, its very own lungs looking for air. With closed eyes and screwed-up face, he clenches his fists; it's in his mouth now, it's coming, mmm . . . Mum, me, Mikey.

'I am Mikey,' he says. 'Hello, everyone. I am Mikey, Mikey, Mikey.' The balloon is barely a speck in the sky. 'Help,' cries Mikey. 'I am Mikey. Can you help me?'

The bush that climbs up the house is covered in them. He can see from as far as away as the swing tree, hundreds of them in the dead branches flapping to get free like trapped doves. The first piece of paper he picks up from the drive says 'Dear Mum'. The next he pulls from the leaves, just 'M'. He tears down those he can reach; they're all the same, or nearly the same, they have nothing written on them except 'Dear Mum'. Mikey stares into the sky as if for answers, wonders if the balloon man dropped them for him, but they're to his mum, not from his mum. Then he realises, they're all orange; it's not his mum at all, it's her. Gathering as many as he can, he understands that she is writing letters to the dead. Even though they're meaningless he can't really throw them away, but he can't keep them either. She must have gone mad, so what does he do now? Not long after, another 'Dear Mum' note floats down from the nursery. If you catch a leaf, you can make a wish.

Dear Mum,

I wish I'd written to you before. You used to say never let the sun go down on a quarrel, but now it's too dark and too late.

I don't know what to say except to ask you questions. I loved you so much when I was small and you loved me, you and Dad both loved me, but after Dad died, where did all that love go? Most of it disappeared when you married the bastard. The last little bit went when you had Val. I suppose you loved them more than you loved me. Or were you scared of him, like I was?

I had to leave, but I wanted you to call me back. Even when I was packing stuff, I wanted you to come in and say don't go. Maybe even if you had begged me, I would have gone. I was in an impossible position. Why didn't you believe me? Was I supposed to wait until it was too late?

I've done OK for myself, I want you to know I have been happy at times. I love Edmund so much and he did love me, so you mustn't worry.

I've been thinking about our family holidays in Minehead. That's because from up here in the attic I can hear the rain pattering on the roof and it reminds me of the caravan, the smell of the gas heater and Dad's homemade beer, the grey waves and tea at Gran's on the way home. She had a door

knocker in the shape of a boat, didn't she? Because Grandpa
was a sailor. I think I've remembered that right.

I was so happy when I was small and it was just the two of
us. There was no need for anyone else.

Diana

It isn't what he wanted, he can hardly bear to read it; to know
she had a mum and that she loves Edmund and that she'd had a
holiday in a caravan in the rain just like him. He can talk now and
maybe she can talk too, someone like this Diana has to be able to
talk. Maybe he can let her out and they can sort things out and it
will all be over and be their secret before Edmund comes home. He
did promise no more secrets, no more lies, but this is different. If
Edmund loves her as much as she loves him, then Edmund will be
cross if he knows. It's a frightening thing to do, but what else is
there?

'Hello, it's me, Mikey. I'm talking. I'm just outside.'

There is no reply.

'It's me, Mikey. I can talk now. Do you want to come out?'

He didn't mean to ask that, he's forgotten how words just jump
out sometimes on their own, but there's still no reply.

'It would be better if you came out now. In case you get ill or
something.'

'Are you in there? I went on holiday in a caravan as well. I just
thought I'd tell you.'

Is she in there?

'Can you hear me?'

Is he really talking? Perhaps he's just imagining it. After all, who
is there to hear except Monty, and the internet said people who go
mad think they see things and hear things. He thought it would be
her who'd go mad, but maybe it's him because he's locked up as
well in a way, if you think about it.

'I'll let you out if you promise to be nice and to tell the truth
and not tell Edmund.'

221

Nothing.

'I'm going now.'

Maybe she's asleep. Maybe it's her who's lost her voice, she doesn't shout much any longer, she just makes noises. Maybe she's . . . What if she's . . . For some reason, he finds himself fleeing not to his bedroom, but to Diana and Edmund's room, almost as if he might find them there. There are photos of her in here, like this one of her in a long dress and jewellery, but she won't look like that when she comes out of the nursery and they zip her up in a black plastic bag and put her in a coffin and push her out the back door of the cemetery. On the little tapestry stool in her bedroom, he studies the boy in the mirror who no longer looks like a Year 5 school photo either. There is a gold box with a lid on a spring and inside treasure on a bed of red velvet. He slides rings on each of his fingers, one by one; he takes a purple silk purse with a drawstring top and finds a silver chain with a locket with no photo, he hangs it round his neck all the same; bracelets, he slips onto his thin wrists; a pink butterfly, he clips in his hair. With his lips painted crimson, he leans forwards like his mum used to and the mascara goes all over his long, dark eyelashes and everywhere else as well. He can't pull off his T-shirt without all the jewellery falling off and all the make-up smudging, so he just threads his arms through the bra he finds and lets it hang over his shoulders, empty-cupped. Grinning back at him is a mad queen of a boy, with feathers and butterflies and jewels like a celebrity, and he makes faces at the goddess and practises saying out loud, 'I am Mikey.' One by one the contents of the drawer are examined and dropped on the floor: tights, false fingernails, dry shampoo, teeth whitener, then comes a packet he recognises, YourNews. His mum had this, she dipped the stick in her wee, and he asked her if she wanted a baby, and she said one day and Solomon will be the daddy and you'll be a big brother. Now he knows that he would be a half-brother but he wouldn't have let that matter, he'd have just had a brother like he'd always wanted. Holding the box, he remembers that Diana's the one who didn't want babies so he doesn't know why she'd want YourNews. The box feels heavy and rattles a bit; he opens it, unwraps the instructions. There he discovers the key to the tower.

Piece by piece, Mikey dismantles the queen in the mirror. The bra falls from his arms, he unpins the butterfly from his hair, and the bracelets and rings slide onto the floor. With wet wipes from the shiny plastic pouch, he scrubs at his face until his skin hurts, until he no longer smells of her. Breathing faster than fast, hotter than hot and clammy, he vomits into the toilet, then rests back against the bath, his legs trembling at the knees and his mouth sour. After some time, he knows what he's going to do. He was weak before, but he's brave enough now, he was right all along.

At the bottom of the stairs, the dog circles and waits like a set spring.

'I've found the key,' he says to the nursery door. 'And soon everyone will know that you did it, that you . . .' This is a hard sentence to finish, so he uses the speech from the policeman on telly. 'You have the right to remain silent, the whole truth and nothing but the truth and anything you say will be used to punish you.'

No doubt she'll write the truth tonight. Suddenly he doesn't feel so bad about locking her up because soon she'll be locked up for ever anyway and he won't have been lying. People will think he was a hero and that he did the right thing, locking up a dangerous criminal and keeping her there, even though he was all on his own, until someone came to rescue him.

Clearing a space on the floor, on his hands and knees, he gently opens his cardboard box and greets the circus animals.

'Hello, zebra, hello, horses, hello, cars, you're all free to come out now.'

How happy they must be to hear him talking to them. He arranges his circus animals in a beautiful spiral, starting with a small circle of the monkeys and the clowns and working outwards with the lions and the tigers and the tanks. Soon Gorilla will be back in the middle of the circle. Even some of the broken people are allowed to join in. He plays for a long time. The circus animals carry out raids and acts of great daring and come home safe at night to a hero's welcome, until they're tired out and he lays them on their sides to sleep and he curls up beside them on the floor.

'Goodnight, Monty, goodnight, circus animals.' He leaves the light on, but closes his eyes. It has been a long, long, long day. 'Goodnight, Monty. Goodnight, Mummy. Goodnight, Mikey.'

Chapter Twenty-Eight

It is a windy, back-to-school sort of morning when you wear long trousers and a sweatshirt and winter shoes which are too big and too heavy and it feels like a new start. Mikey lies on the floor and cries and cries. He hurls his circus animals at the wall and sucks his duvet and his stomach heaves until, exhausted, he sleeps again. Later, his head is heavy, and he knows the jeans he has slept in are damp and cold. He doesn't know what time it is. Sitting up in bed, he writes a timetable because the circus animals are getting bored and badly behaved.

Get up
Eat breakfast
10 o'clock Maths
11 o'clock Break
11.20 English

And so on. It doesn't tell him what time it is, but it does tell him to start the day. He reads it out loud just to check he can, but he doesn't stick to it because the grandfather clock tells him it's already later than when it was meant to begin. Instead, downstairs, he sits at the piano in the lonely room and presses middle C once and sings a bit, but the notes are too lonely and the black notes sadder still, so he closes the lid and moves to the study and logs on to the computer instead, but even Lockdown fails to hold his attention. Aimlessly he tries Facebook. He wasn't allowed an account and when he tries to log on as his mum, he finds she's disappeared. Everything that was on her page, her photos with him and Solomon and everything she ever was, gone. He would have liked to have sent her a message, to have said I miss you and maybe asked her what to do now he was in a muddle, but she's gone, even from Facebook, gone.

Ali is still on there – even though it's illegal, his brother signed up for him – but they chose a stupid picture of him with his bike and it's obvious he's not thirteen. Mikey touches the picture. Ali is still on Facebook, so Ali is out there somewhere. He posts a message.

Hello. It's me Mikey.

He waits in a sort of stupor. Eventually, he notices a reply has been posted.

Hello Mikey. Are you coming back to school?

Four people have liked it.

Someone whose name he does not recognise has added another message.

I thought Mikey S was dead.

Four people have liked that as well. Maybe the same four people.

Help

Mikey looks at the word. Just one word. Just one click. It would all be over. Help what? What could he possibly say? No one believes what they read on the internet. Even if they did believe it, who knows what might happen next? There are horrible people online who read your messages and they would know he was on his own and come to Wynhope. Burglars or murderers or Paul could track him down and get him locked up, and now his mum's dead there's no one to visit him in prison.

Here might be a horrible place to be, but at least he knows it well.

The backspace key deletes the four letters. X closes the page. It's probably time for play, even if he hasn't done the work.

There's a dry, cold wind bending the poplar trees and it slams the door behind him. Some green leaves have been tugged from the trees, there are twigs, even little branches on the lawn. Hercules is playing footie with a ball which has been blown across the garden and landed on the pond. It's Monty who finds the next note, hooked on the thorns of the last yellow rose. Monty must be able to smell her. Right there and then he reads it, shivering from the cold and the not understanding it, not just the tricky words or the scribbly handwriting or the long sentences, but what it all means. The account is a waterfall, it takes away his breath. He has no sense of which way he is facing or what it is that is pulling him down, he can no longer even see light at the surface.

Dear Michael,

It is dark and probably the middle of the night, but I have a very clear mind, it's important you know that. There is no point in writing an account of the whole thing – there's only one bit that needs explaining. I did want to tell people what happened, but the longer I left it, the harder it was and no one's ever believed what I say anyway. But this is the whole thing.

It's very long, this note. It doesn't need to be, all she needs to write is 'I did it'. She knows he's found the key, so his voice was working after all and she was listening. There's a lot of stuff about her being a liar, but he knows that already. He skips the weird bits which don't make sense about Chinese whispers and candyfloss and goes instinctively to the bit that really matters and that's usually at the end. He skims for the important words like he's been taught to at school. I. Kill. Mother.

This is the truth.

I didn't mean to kill your mother, I just wanted her to know what it felt like when your last chance of rescue is gone. To scream and for nobody to listen. It was an opportunity, that's all, and I took it. One moment. I had the key. I can't describe it properly, it was like I mattered. It was almost worth it but nothing is ever over and done with.

Diana

The words themselves are tricky, but on some deeply instinctive level Mikey understands Diana completely. It isn't so different as to how he felt: the slam of the door, the turn of the key, the tumbling down the nursery stairs, that feeling in his body when he locked her in. He relives it now for a reason he does not comprehend, deep down, stirring inside, the pulse, the push, the scream of pleasure, the fall on your back and a laughing-crying-spinning sort of excited that makes you grow bigger and bigger until you think you'll burst. She's telling the truth. You could do anything for a feeling like that.

It doesn't last, though. She's a grown-up, she should have known it would all end in tears. It has all ended in tears.

How different it might have felt if there was someone else to show this to. It's like unwrapping a parcel, layers and layers of paper which won't tear and string tied up in tight knots and your fingernails are bitten down to the skin, then reaching the middle and it's something much heavier than you thought at first, you can't even really make out what it is, don't even know whether to be pleased or disappointed. If there was someone else to say it works like this and here are the instructions and this is where you put the battery, it might be different.

Up until now he's been the only one who knows for sure that it wasn't him who killed his mum, and Diana blamed him just to get out of it herself. Up until now, he didn't know why she did it, but he's not sure how important that is any longer. What matters is that he has her letter and the key and proof and people will have to believe him.

This account is his prize, but he doesn't feel like a winner or a loser; he feels a sort of nothing, or at least something which he doesn't have the word for. It's not satisfaction, not triumph, not sadness, not guilt.

The adrenaline ebbs away. He is empty. On the wet grass, surrounded by nothingness, motionless, a tiny amount of energy maintains his sitting position and keeps his head on top of his neck, but otherwise the muscles in his face slowly sag, his eyes are open but blank. He's disappearing back into the earth, becoming nothing. Exhausted, in the beautiful garden in the autumn morning, he lets go.

The dog is worrying his body, licking his face. He's so stiff and cold. Bewildered, as he wakes up clutching the thing he's been waiting for all this time, Mikey wonders what he has won and what it means for what's next. Does her note actually change anything? He's still alone. His mum's still dead. He cannot name a single person who has stayed around, except maybe Edmund, and when he finds out he'll probably take her side. When people find out, they won't bother about what she's done, all they'll think about is what he's done. Social services will take him away from Edmund, even if Edmund doesn't send him away. He's spoiled everything for everyone. Paul was right: he's nothing but trouble. Diana's right: he's a monster. Grace and John pretended, but even they've given up on him. It's all his fault. What will his mum think of the terrible things he's done? If she didn't want him to do terrible things, she shouldn't have died. This is all her fault.

There is no other choice but to go. There will be room for him to take just a few of the circus animals in his rucksack, although he doesn't know how he'll choose and he knows that the most important one is still locked in the nursery with her. Poor Gorilla, he never did anything to deserve this. Since Solomon tried to find him, he'll try to find Solomon, even if that means going to Solomon's country which is in Africa. He read a book once about a boy who escaped from a prison and walked all the way across Europe to find his mum and when he reached her house, she opened the front door and recognised him straight away, even though she hadn't seen him for years and years and they probably didn't have photos in the war. She loved him straight away. All the boy said was his name.

I am Mikey.

The dog places its head on his knee. He can't take Monty because Edmund loves Monty even more than he does. Mikey sobs noisily into the dog's warm, familiar fur until finally Monty makes him get up and go into the house and get warm by the Aga. There's nothing else for him in the kitchen, food is no longer of interest; in the sitting room the television is always on because he leaves it that way for the company, but the words and pictures blare over him. He wanders aimlessly into the morning room and spins the globe until he finds England, then all the places Edmund has showed him: Mongolia, Africa, Antigua, all the way round there and back to here again. On the wall is an old map which has Wynhope at the centre of everything. Back to the globe, Mikey sets it spinning violently on its axis and leaves it blurring the world as he moves on into the study. He opens a Word document to write something to someone, but ends up with his finger pressed down on the X; on and on it runs over the lines and back again, a black river of love.

There is one thing he can write. Edmund mustn't come in with his suitcase and fishing rod and just find Diana, who might be dangerous by then or worse, and get all upset on his own with no one to help him, so Mikey types out another of his giant notes.

STOP!
DO NOT GO ANY FURTHER WITHOUT READING
THIS NOTE.
CALL AN AMBULANCE.

His mum wrote exactly that once and put it on the bathroom door, but Paul took it down and everyone just thought she'd slipped in the shower, even though Mikey knew that wasn't the truth. Perhaps if you say you want to die, you do eventually. He could try that, say 'I want to die' out loud and close his eyes and wait. Print. Shut down.

Maybe it would be better to take her phone and when he's far enough way he can tell the police and they'll come and then Edmund won't have to be the one.

The house is completely quiet.

The only person left now to tell is Diana.

Having changed out of his smelly clothes, Mikey brushes his hair and cleans his teeth. He puts Diana's final letter in the circus animals' box with the others; he'll take them with him when he goes as proof. The key to the nursery must go with the note for Edmund, he'll leave it on the stairs and that will be the last thing he ever does at Wynhope. In the hall, he stands with one foot on a black square, one foot on a white square, listening to his friend the clock ticking out the time. He doesn't want to leave, this foreign palace has become his home. Wynhope is a lovely house, it isn't to blame for what happened, it's been quite kind to him and might even be sad to see him go, but it'll probably get on better when he's gone. Will the bronze boy miss him or notice he's left? Nobody even mentions the tower any longer.

Today the tears do not seem to stop. Everything he does, thinks, sees, feels, smells brings a welling up and spilling over of grief from somewhere very far down, even the thought of saying goodbye to Diana is twisting him inside out. He loves Wynhope, he loves Monty, he loves Edmund. Step by step he creeps up the stairs and stands outside the nursery door for the last time. She must know he's there, she's developed some sort of sixth sense, but there's no banging or shouting. He clears the leftover crying from his throat.

'Hello,' he begins. 'It's me, Mikey. Michael.' It doesn't even sound like his voice, it's coming from the wrong part of him. Perhaps she's asleep. 'I've got a message for you. Can you hear me?'

Now she's being annoying, probably regretting writing her account and wondering how she can get it back off him. He hammers loudly on the door. 'I know you're in there, so you have to listen to me. I got what you wrote and I read it.' His mum used to say how you feel better if you say sorry. 'Maybe you'll feel better now you've said what you did.' But she didn't say she was sorry, did she? Not once in her writing did she say she was sorry and he's not going to say sorry either. Never let the sun go down on a quarrel, Mum said, but that's what has happened ever since coming here, the sun getting up and going down, up and down, up and down, day after day, and no one ever saying sorry, so everything has gone wrong and his mum is dead and he has nowhere left to go.

'You're a witch. The police will put you in prison when they know. I'm going to call them. They'll lock you up. Fuck you, fuck you, fuck you.'

Spinning, round and round in circles, dizzier and dizzier, he can't stop even if he wants to and if he giggles he'll never stop giggling and if he cries he'll never stop crying and the only way to stop it is to fling yourself on the ground and batter the unmoving earth until it remembers you're still there and that is what he does, banging his head against the wall and banging against the wall and banging the wall, until the pain makes the wall go away and he is free.

There's still no reaction from the nursery.

'I'm going now. I'm not coming back. I'm never ever coming back to your horrible house because I hate you. I've left a note.'

Nothing.

'I hate you.'

Nothing.

'Hate, hate, hate, hate' in time to his thumping on the door, as if it's he who is locked away, not her. It's like teasing someone who doesn't rise to the bait, all you can do is say more and more horrible things until they crack.

'You're not even my aunty. You're only half an aunt.'

And if that doesn't work, you say lies if you have to.

'Oh, and by the way, Edmund left a message on your phone. He's not coming back either. He's going to live in Mongolia for ever with the swan goose and the horses and go fishing, and he's invited me so I don't know what will happen to you, locked up here all on your owny-o. I expect you'll die.' He kicks the door and screams. 'Everybody dies.'

Now the silence is beyond understanding. Mikey begins to wonder what has happened behind the door. He can just run away anyway, but never to know? Monty whining on the landing gives him an idea; he'll see what the dog thinks has happened.

'Come on, come here.'

The dog bounds up the stairs, barks, goes straight back down again, back up the stairs and back down again.

'Don't be so stupid, Monty.' He does what the police do on the telly. 'Who's there? Who's in there?' he asks, pointing to the crack beneath the door.

But Monty isn't interested in the nursery. He doesn't scratch at the door or snuffle underneath it or anything like a proper sniffer dog would do, he wriggles against the boy's grasp and finally frees himself by slipping his collar and then he's back down on the landing, barking. When Mikey goes down to the landing, the dog runs down to the hall, when he gets to the hall, the dog runs out into the garden. Enough. Picking up Edmund's cricket bat from the stand in the hall, he returns to the nursery.

'I'm going to see if you're all right,' he declares to the emptiness. 'But if you attack me, I'll lock it again and I'm armed. Are you ready? Shall I count down from three?'

Nothing.

'Three . . . two . . . one.'

How loud it is, that slight sticking, click of the key. When you get through to the next level on Lockdown, they're always hiding behind the door and you go in with your gun in two hands, sweeping the room, watching your back. The door swings away from him, far wider than he intended, and he steps into the nursery. There's something awful about doing that, as if the room has nothing on. He whirls the bat against the unseen demons of the place, but finds only air.

She's not there.

One orange felt-tip, a pad of paper, a roll of Sellotape and a set of instructions on the floor, but she's not there.

It smells of her, but she's not there.

The nursery is empty.

Chapter Twenty-Nine

Fitted television showing CNN, fitted fridge with minibar, fitted cupboard, fitted hangers in the wardrobe. The blinds filter the neon lights of Ulaanbaatar, flickering an unintelligible code onto the king-size bed. Edmund is finding it difficult to sleep. After days of feeling light like water, concerned with nothing more nor less than the drift of the fly and the tug on the line, after nights of sleeping as deep as the pools he waded, this overnight stopover before his last four days out in the wilderness is deeply depressing for him. His reluctance to return to the UK stirs like sickness in his stomach. Compared to the calm monasteries in the hills and the fast-flowing waters of the Eg-Uur valley, the printout of his life from the esteemed City of London is stained with the spilled wine and greasy fingers of a thousand deals; there's no such thing as a free lunch, the cost lies hidden behind the number of zeros on the end of the bill and cannot be offset against tax, only against some final accounting procedure, the rules of which are unclear even to priests. He is certain he will be judged and found wanting. Guilt. For a few days after his father's suicide, people – the press, society, the police – wondered if he killed himself out of guilt because guilt seemed to be the most obvious reason to make his lordship take a shotgun to his head in the bottom of a tower in the east wing of his country house. His finances, dealings with his staff, his private sexual behaviour were all examined and found to be beyond reproach; his father lived an exemplary life, except perhaps in the manner of his leaving it. It was not out of guilt, but out of love that his father killed himself: he loved his wife too much. In comparison, in all manner of ways, Edmund reflects that he has been an incompetent lover, not once, but three times over, if he includes Diana.

The photos on his phone are nearly all of Mikey: Mikey fishing, the river so low and slow it barely laps his boots and the flowering irises on the islands midstream higher than his head; Mikey captured flying higher and higher on the swing hung by a blue rope from the boughs of the Cedar of Lebanon in what is, of course, a silent movie. Is this sharp yearning what fatherhood feels like? Mikey draws him into an extraordinary world which everyone else seems to inhabit quite casually, but the child has quite the opposite effect on Diana. Looking at it with the benefit of hindsight and distance, it is obvious Diana was becoming more than a little mad and he should probably have said something to someone, should probably not have left them alone. This unequilateral triangle cannot maintain its shape. If he wants to stay with Diana, Mikey will have to go; if he wants to keep Mikey, he will lose Diana. The first scenario seems less and less appealing, the second, quite impossible; they probably wouldn't let a man like him have Mikey anyway, whoever 'they' are, so all three of them will go their separate ways and be lonely and that will be that. God knows where Mikey will go. Out of sight out of mind. To distance yourself from difficulty is almost a genetic trait in his family. He supposes if it wasn't for the earthquake, he would never have met him. As Diana says, it was a watershed of sorts. The coroner's verdict might have brought things to a close, but the story runs on.

The hopelessness of what awaits him on the other side of customs at Heathrow in a few days' time is unbearable. The leaning lines of people in the arrivals hall waving their expectations over the barriers; he isn't expecting a welcome home banner, Diana barely leaves the house with the boy any more. Pushing aside the blinds, Edmund opens the window as far as it will go, which is not far enough. Beneath him the city looks and sounds like hell: shouts and horns and sirens and commerce and pollution and motherless boys picking pockets on Peace Avenue and fatherless girls for sale in bars. He will go home and sort things out once and for all, but he will not stay. Wynhope has been mothballed before. In his mind's eye he imagines himself retreating to somewhere quiet, a clean, uncluttered space, a whitewashed cell in a monastery on a mountain, one window looking west over a snow plateau. *Desert Island Discs* gives you the Bible and Shakespeare and that would be fine for him; he would be a very British hermit.

Pen and paper in his suitcase, wash bag with two packets of paracetamol and a bottle of sleeping pills in the bathroom. He isn't man enough for that, although there is something fitting about a mediocre mid-lifer such as himself taking his curtain call in an anonymous box in a hotel chain. He could never have carried off the tower. Never put off until tomorrow what you can do today, no time like the present; his father had an inexhaustible supply of prov- erbs. Well, he'd lived and died true to those. The cartoon in his study at Wynhope gave Edmund his own motto, it was a sort of pointed present from WNT, a man gagged and bound by the blight of what might have been. Mikey is what might have been.

The screen on his phone lights up against the yellow ochre bedspread. Message from Diana. The only email he's had from her sounded peculiarly positive and cheery – something about a trip to a wildlife park with Mikey, which seemed very unlikely. Anyway, that won't have lasted and he can't face talking to her; she'll want to Skype if she knows he's got a signal and there'll be some long catalogue of Mikey's deficiencies as if he was a child psychologist and could suggest a solution. This time last year he missed her when he was away, missed the unconditional way in which she loved him physically with no expectation or disappointment. It was something he thought he'd never know again when things went downhill in that department; he missed the quiet evenings together in the drawing room when neither of them felt the need to talk. He had thought that was a measure of love between people, the quality of the silence between them. He missed what fun she was, always game to have a go at things that were new for her: racing, opera, getting to grips with the estate and its little ways. She became more like his mother every day as if, despite all the differences in their backgrounds, she was born to belong to Wynhope. And even stranger, although he always revelled in having time to himself without her fussing over him, he did miss fussing over her; for all her executive competence, he cherished the infinitesimal part of her that craved a bit of TLC.

But now? The hotel window is still open, he is on the eleventh floor. It might not be a big enough gap for a man, but it is wide enough for a phone with an unread message.

'Help me.'

The room tilts around him. Help me. Diana? Help is not a word in her vocabulary, unless of course that is all she can manage. Possible scenarios: attacked at Wynhope during a burglary, his study turned over, paintings ripped from the wall, spaces where valuable things had been, he couldn't quite think what; a car crash; some sort of breakdown, her, not the car; and as his thinking slows, that seems to him most likely, a descent into unfamiliar vocabulary and incoherence. If she needs help, why doesn't she just try calling and speak to him? He has not heard from her as often as in previous years when there were dozens of messages waiting for him when he returned to the city, and he wonders what has really been going on back home in his absence. He shouldn't have left her there with Mikey, she was already too close to the edge.

Mikey. If Mikey needed help, he would have to text. What if it's Mikey? That, at the very moment when he is thinking about leaving him, the boy reaches out to him for help? As if a gun has cracked and a race has started, his heart rate speeds up and his stomach tightens; he has the physical experience of not being able to run fast enough to save the thing that matters most.

'Who is this?'

While he waits for a reply, the radio alarm switches from 21:07 to 21:08. The television follows a warplane flying low over a burning city, he does not know if it is fact or fiction. Keeping the phone in one hand, he opens the fridge with the other, takes out the mini vodka, pours it, tops it up with Coke, shuts the fridge with his foot, throws the can in the bin. 21:09. Surely online messaging should be instantaneous despite the 5,000 miles between them. It must be afternoon in England, light, raining maybe, only the stubble left on the hills and the sweet smell of wheat straw blowing in on an easterly wind. Everyone lives almost simultaneously these days, almost, but not quite.

'It's me.'

'Mikey?'

'Yes.'

Despite the drink, Edmund's mouth is dry. Something is wrong at Wynhope, but he is so far away he does not know what it is or what he can do about it and, although blood is pumping through his muscles, there is nowhere to fly to and nothing to fight. Another earthquake? Everyone said it was just a question of time, Valerie's skirt crumpled up above her thigh and her white leg sticking out of the rubble. The boy could be trapped. How come he's got the phone?

'Hi Mikey,' he types, 'everything OK?'

'No.'

'What's wrong?'

Diana is typing, it says at the top of the screen, but it's lying.

'Diana.'

Diana is what's wrong. A shaky sort of hysterical laugh breaks the silence; this is probably yet another fallout between the two of them and he is being expected to mediate from the other side of the world. It's not funny, but at least it isn't a catastrophe. He downs the vodka and Coke in one and leans back against the pillows, chuckling to himself.

'Oh dear. What's happened now?'

Mikey is probably scrunched up in the nursery, his circus animals guarding his stolen mobile phone, he can virtually hear Diana screaming up the stairs.

'She had an accident.'

Not awful, not laughable, something in between.

'Are you on your own?'

'Yes.'

Edmund swings round to the edge of the bed.

'Well done for texting me. Can you ring 999?'

'No.'

No? He can't even call 999? Why the hell not? Edmund and Mikey's relationship is based on silence: apart from maybe two or three words on that terrible morning, he has never heard the boy talk and not only has he become comfortable with his mutism, he realises he has been more than a little in love with their secret ways of understanding each other. But now at this greater distance in terms of both time and space, Edmund experiences the stubborn dumbness as if for the first time – why won't he just bloody well speak?

'It is very easy. Press 999. Say three words. Ambulance. Wynhope House. You can do it.'

Two ticks. Message received. No reply.

'Are you still there? Press 999. You don't have to speak to them. They will trace the phone. Mikey? Let me know you're okay. I'm worried.'

The phone rings until it goes to Diana's voicemail, composed and efficient. He leaves a message anyway, Mikey is always listening even if he doesn't talk. Impotence and anxiety, his twin torturers, are back, cornering him. Nothing he can do, no one he can turn to. Contacts. The names mean nothing, spiralling past, the police are a last resort. You never know with Mikey, and Edmund is reluctant to further professionalise his family's crimes if it is not necessary. It is shocking to him that out of all the people captured in his list, so few, if any, can be called upon in an emergency like this; the whole village would have turned out for his parents. There is one he can select. Despite the fact that John and Grace were his lifeline in so many ways for so many years, he has been too embarrassed to contact them since 'letting them go' and surprisingly Grace hasn't even kept in touch about Mikey, but he is certain they will do whatever needs to be done, for Wynhope, if not for Diana – there's no love lost there. Grace answers. It takes no more than two minutes. He imagines her untying her apron, rattling through her bag for her car keys. Neither of them knows what she will find.

Chapter Thirty

Ulaanbaatar to Seoul. Seoul to Heathrow. The arrival is delayed by fog. Carried downstairs by the escalators, sucked by the moving walkway into the baggage reclaim hall, Edmund has the sensation of having been prematurely recalled from paradise and transported against his will back to a world he had decided to quit. On the coach from the airport, squashed against a suntan lotion and aftershave man, waiting at the bus station with a busker playing Elgar and a pop-up selling Lebanese which smells of mornings in Damascus, and a homeless man with a cardboard box he's given to his dog, he feels everything too clearly. Like a neap tide, it is all creeping back to him, saltwater seeping up the estuary in the mist and him realising, too late, that the banks are too steep for a fisherman who is in too deep. In the taxi queue, a woman in fishnet tights and leather shorts asks him where he wants to get to, sometimes, you know, it's cheaper to share. It was in a bar in the Caribbean that he lost his virginity to a woman like this, another escape at another time and he was as high as the waves then, as full, as strong, nothing like the limpet, low-tide man he has become. Everyone in the queue waits for his answer; he hears himself saying something about needing to get to the hospital urgently, wife, accident. Now they are all on his side, no point in a taxi, less than five

242

minutes' walk, he'll be stuck in a cab for hours in the one-way system. It's a wonderful hospital, they hope everything works out all right, God bless, smiles the girl in the fishnet tights.

Descending into the subway, he is relieved to lose the psychedelic album cover of a world beyond the tunnel, to reduce the traffic to nothing more than a rhythmic throb far above him. England knows him too well. In their own peculiar tight-lipped way the people are too kind. Down here it is easier to be himself, a tired man dragging himself and his awkward luggage back towards his dying wife, an unspoken acknowledgement that her death would be the simplest of solutions slung over one shoulder, his prayer that he will not lose her so heavy it makes his lungs ache. Having climbed and counted the steps to the hospital, he places his feet on the painted line that leads to Intensive Care where a sign directs him to disinfect his hands with the alcohol gel in a dispenser. How many people like him pause at that entrance wishing they could wash their hands of the whole thing?

The consultant is well known to Edmund, not personally, but from dinner parties and other people's daughters' weddings and charity auctions where people bid highly for things they already own. Both pull their trousers up slightly as they sit on easy chairs designed for difficult conversations, both lean forwards a little, hands clasped. They understand not only each other's body language, but the requirement for minimalist, polite responses to devastating information.

Diana has sustained significant injuries to her spine, multiple fractures and severe head injuries. The apparent delay between the trauma and medical attention was not helpful, but they operated successfully to reduce swelling to the brain and she is now in an induced coma and will be kept that way for the time being. At the moment they have no way of knowing what level of consciousness might be regained or when. It is too early to talk about a long-term prognosis.

Following the neurosurgeon, Edmund is the car-sick child in the backseat: how much further now? The genre changes from drama to science fiction. The neuro ward is a future factory, it is hard to tell where the power lies between the machines and the people or what extraordinary experiment is being conducted that can necessitate such extravagant technology. As the workers cluster, part, regroup, Edmund glimpses beds and heads and the bent backs of visitors, then the charge nurse says here we are and here he is and here she is, apparently, and he becomes the bent back of a visitor. Once, on holiday in Siena, he stepped out of the heat into the cathedral, found himself in front of the mummified head of Saint Catherine, two and a half yellow teeth in a dumb mouth, a nose nibbled and moon craters for eyes. It was imprisoned behind an iron grille, and according to the information sheet it took three separate sets of keys to open it; a lot of trouble to go to, to unlock the dead. The saint's thumb was preserved in a separate shrine of its own. Carefully positioned on the white sheet, Diana's right hand is also a thing apart. Edmund turns his attention back to the nurse.

'I'll explain a couple of things.'

There is a ventilator because she cannot breathe on her own. He thinks instead of the grey plastic pipe in the laundry room which the rats gnawed through last winter and how the smell lingered a long time.

There are lines in and lines out from a stack of machines which resemble the sort of sound systems they had as students. His was a Sony. The trustees released the money for it on his seventeenth birthday.

There are monitors recording her pulse, heart rate, oxygen levels, pressure on the brain, but there is no indicator of self, of how much of Diana is there.

The nurse offers him a chair and a few well-worn phrases.

'Just sit with her,' he says. 'I know it's hard, but don't be afraid. Talk to her, you can't do any harm at this stage. I'll be right here if you need me.'

This is an unknown country, although Edmund has seen documentaries about it while flicking channels, heard its soundtrack, the steady whoosh of the ventilator, the insistent beep of a monitor and beyond that the airless silence. There was a boy at school who hid in an old freezer while playing hide and seek; his bed in the dormitory was taken by some boarder from Japan who didn't understand its provenance. It must have been something like this, thought Edmund, hearing the voices counting down from ten, the never being found. Or like being trapped under an avalanche, that's how his friend's uncle died in the Alps, with the weight of the snow crushing your chest and no hope of rescue. So many white deaths coming to mind now, in this half-life place. That is what it feels like to him; what it feels like to Diana, he has no way of knowing. Like pheasants beaten out of the covers for the shoot, his thoughts fly randomly in all directions. He forces himself to focus. With her head bandaged and her nose and mouth encased in plastic, it is only her eyes which are recognisably Diana, and even so, he rarely sees her without make-up. At night she takes it off sitting at her dressing table by the green Chinoise lamp, leaning into the mirror, while he sits up in bed and finishes the *City Digest* on his tablet. If it seems likely they might try, she keeps her make-up on and he turns off the lamp, then afterwards she slips into her bathroom and he is aware of the light shining under the door, of her taking just a little too long if all she is doing is removing her lipstick – and who can blame her? In the mornings, he is always up first and out and about, so for their hours spent together she is eyebrow-trimmed, eyelash-perfect, her foundation smooth and flawless, but here she is with eyelids as grey and flaccid as the gills of a dead fish. It may be the light, but her flesh is tinged purple. Reaching for her free hand, he repetitively smoothes her thumb with his thumb. Even her nail varnish is chipped. No bracelet but a plastic identity band, the skin nourished by years of expensive hand cream now blemished with marks of injections and surgical tape. How she would hate this ignominious ugliness. It is passive and heavy, this wrist in his, but it has a pulse.

As time passes, a confluence of rivers swirl in unnatural eddies around unspeakable thoughts. As he should be, he is incapacitated by the awfulness of what has happened, by the warm woman who he has loved, by the stone senselessness of what she has become. But here is a colder current from a foreign glacier, bringing with it a chill wish: less than forty-eight hours ago he admitted to himself there was no life left for him and Diana, and now there is no life left, or almost no life left, just enough life left to lock the door on any other ways of living. Less than forty-eight hours ago he had not loved her enough to want to live with her. Only then does it occur to him that Diana's fall from a great height might have been intentional. He should not have left her alone at Wynhope, he knew that at the time; that knowledge will now be forever linked with the smell of the back seat of taxis. There was a glimpse of something across her face as they said goodbye. Not tears. Hatred is the word that comes to mind. Living together was not an option, but dying together? Here he can crawl into her bed, lie himself out under the sheets, disconnect them both and they will be together as equals in intent and outcome, removed from choice, remembered in marble in the chapel in the park, an Arundel couple.

'Will you be back later?' asks the nurse.

No doesn't seem to be an acceptable answer, he will have to come back, maybe not today, but every other day and every day after that.

'One day at a time, that's what we say. Come any time, but try to avoid between one and three. It's important your wife gets some uninterrupted rest.'

By her bed, he envied her rest as he envied the dead; only now does the possibility occur to him that beneath the flat green horizon of calm, she is in turmoil. One Boxing Day morning when he was too young to ride out, with the hounds parading across the frosted lawns and the huge horses pawing the gravel, he asked the kennel man what they did with the dogs when they were too old to hunt.

'Boy, one day you'll learn that some questions should never be asked.'

The doors will not open. It says exit but he cannot get out.

'Here you are, sir.' A cleaner puts down his mop and the yellow triangle warning of danger ahead and pushes the green button for him. 'You'll get used to it all, don't you worry.'

Dithering outside the main entrance, Edmund hesitates amongst the smokers, the foot stampers, those on the phone passing on the news. The axis has tilted, but the world looks the same. In the end, he gets a taxi and says the first word that comes to him: 'Mikey.'

With a pocket full of Mongolian tughriks, for an awful moment he thinks he is going to have to ask John to pay the taxi like an incompetent teenager coming home at one in the morning. The bell on the front door of the modern, semi-detached house has a sing-song electric tone, the sort Diana describes as common because she believes that's a posh joke. The thought makes him angry; he is very angry with Diana. He should have gone to Wynhope, he is in no fit state to be here, with a mind like a cesspit, but then the frosted-glass door opens and Grace is there, clapping her hands and showering icing sugar onto the sparkling tiles. Behind her, a shadow. Hardly trusting himself, Edmund hangs back in the porch, trying to think strength back into his voice.

'Mikey,' he whispers, 'is that you?'

The boy rushes at him, hits him with such force he almost falls over, clasps small hands around his neck so tightly he can hardly breathe.

'Edmund,' he says. 'My Edmund.'

Chapter Thirty-One

In the front room, Edmund perches sideways on the end of the sofa with Mikey very close to him, leaving an expanse of leather stretching round the corner and on underneath the window which looks out on the street, passers by, men unloading furniture, someone moving house. The boy hasn't spoken again. Edmund acknowledges how he must have had a horrible time, but it is all over now; it's not, of course, Mikey is always knife sharp at slicing through stale platitudes. The front door slams. Mikey jumps. Edmund puts his arm around him, kisses his head; he needs a haircut and a good night's sleep.

'Louisa,' calls Grace. 'Come in here a moment, love.'

A skinny teenager peers round the door, blazer, tie and heavy eye make-up, and takes her headphones out of her ears.

Grace introduces her granddaughter, Louisa. 'You remember Sir Edmund,' she says.

'Yeah,' says the girl, and Edmund wonders what has been said in this house about the arrogant arseholes who live at Wynhope to provoke a look like that.

'Mikey and I have been doing some cakes for Sir Edmund, they should be ready now. Can you give him a hand decorating and bring them in?'

Grace's face is indicating she needs Mikey out of the way.

'You all right then, Mikey?' says the girl. 'You should be at school, you should. What's these cakes you've made?'

The voices fade. He and Diana were mad to offer to look after the boy. They could never give him anything as normal as this; apart from anything else, neither of them ever had anything as normal as this themselves.

'I can't believe he spoke, he hasn't said a thing until now. Maybe this is the beginning,' says Grace.

She pops out to the hall. 'You all right in there, Louisa? We won't be a minute.' Closing the door firmly behind her, she takes a deep breath and tells him what they found at Wynhope: the strange notices stuck to the gates, the front door wide open, and Mikey curled in his cardboard box, the state of his room, you've never seen anything like it.

'And Diana?'

Dreadful. At the back of the house, by the railings, a nightmare. And Mikey had put a blanket over her and there was a little cup of water, bless him; hours they reckon he must have been there, alone with her. Doesn't bear thinking about. It was John who realised she was still breathing, what with being in the army, he's good at that sort of thing. The ambulance men were wonderful, you couldn't fault them. For the first time, Grace looks him in the eye, flushed with the relief of not only having passed the story on to him, but also having left it with him to finish.

It is as if he is standing at the back of Wynhope, the bottom of his trousers getting wet in the long grass, the carcasses of the squirrels hung from the railings and the sheep bunched suspiciously against the far hedge. His wife is there, spreadeagled on the ground. He raises his eyes from her body to the windows on the top floor.

'It was the nursery then? I don't understand.'

'It's a mystery,' agrees Grace, 'and of course Mikey can't say.'

'How she could have fallen. Just fallen.'

'Oh, here you are. And what lovely cakes!'

Bearing a plate of cupcakes with ludicrous amounts of butter-cream icing and splatterings of gold stars and hundreds and thousands, Mikey enters the room, intense concentration on his face as he offers them round. They all make noises about how wonderful the cakes are, how you can't possibly eat two, then they are left with just the sound of swallowing. The girl's phone beeps, she checks it and says she's off out.

'Who's that, dear?'

'Liam, isn't it. I told him about' – she indicates Edmund with her head and raised eyes – 'so he won't want to come home here, will he?'

'Not now, Louisa.' Grace stares pointedly at her.

'When then?' snarls the girl. 'Never?' The door slams behind her.

Teenage girls, hormones, feminism, anti-capitalism: there can be a thousand reasons for her apparent hatred of him and all his type represents, most of them possibly legitimate, but none of them seem sufficient. The sound of John's van pulling into the drive is probably a relief to all of them, not just him.

'Edmund,' says John, brushing his palms against his work clothes before shaking hands. 'Dreadful thing to happen.'

The thing, whatever it is, is clearly dreadful and perhaps all the more dreadful for not knowing what sort of thing it is. Edmund nods his appreciation. Thanking him for all he has done, Edmund says something about having taken up enough of their time and kindness and how he and Mikey better be on their way, he's ordered a taxi. Grace and John exchange glances. Why doesn't he go back to Wynhope and get some rest, sort a few things out, come back in the morning? He is obviously not a safe pair of hands, although they don't say that, not explicitly.

'What do you think, Mikey?' Edmund asks.

'No.'

What is anyone meant to do with a boy who never says anything and then says no?

'Goodness. It's good to hear that voice of yours at last, young man.' John gets down to eye level with him. 'But you need to be grown up about this. Edmund's very tired. He's going back to Wynhope now and he can come with Monty in the morning and pick you up. All right?'

Huge tears roll down the boy's face. He kicks the coffee table violently, the cakes slide onto the floor, their stars face down on the carpet. Sagged on the sofa, the child moans, more the sound of a no, rather than no itself, but it is unbearable to Edmund. Every no an expression of everything he has felt since leaving the wilderness: the harm that existence brings within itself, the intolerable ache of living, the irresistible appeal of no. He too wants to snuggle up on the sofa with his thumb in his mouth and cry no, no, no, but John and Grace and the consultant and the nurse and his business partners and the estate manager and the taxi driver who is booked to arrive in five minutes' time, they are all yes people with expectations of yes and he drags himself back to adulthood to meet them as Grace scrapes the buttercream back onto the plate.

'I'll be here at midday tomorrow and I'll take you home with me,' he says. 'And that's not a fisherman's promise.'

There is a trace of a smile on Mikey's face as he lets go of the cushion and stretches both hands out wide.

'What's a fisherman's promise then?' asks John.

Matching Mikey's gesture, Edmund winks. 'I promise you, it is this big! Not quite the truth, not quite a lie.'

The red lights of the taxi disappear down the main road. Edmund specifically asked to be dropped at the bottom of the drive, the man who creeps back to his lover without turning on the light, the better to feel his way into her arms. Wynhope wraps herself around him, and he rests his head on the smooth slope of her shoulders, careful not to disturb her siesta. He is home and home smells of harvest. The late afternoon is perfectly still. Picking up his bags, he mentally times the moment when his footsteps will set the dog barking, smiling when they do. Even now it takes him by surprise, the absence of the tower. He pats his pocket for his keys.

With the burglar alarm off and Monty fussed over and loved, Wynhope settles itself down. In every single room downstairs, Edmund checks the status of the things which act as his tide time-table and Grace has hit the nail on the head: nothing is wrong, nothing is quite right. The kitchen is not a mess, but the counters are smeared, crumbs on the floor, a splatter of jam congealed in the sink and a white bowl with an encrusted orange rim of baked beans, unwashed. The dining room is a *Mary Celeste* sort of set, all the ornaments dancing in the dust, but the sitting room is the opposite, overly familiar. Diana, the minimalist, never lived anywhere so fully as this. There is a heap of DVDs on the sofa, Mikey's coat dumped on the floor, mud on the carpet, a glass with the remnants of whisky congealed at the bottom – but Diana never touches the stuff. The smell is that of an absence of polish.

Instinctively he takes the pile of post he has collected from the box by the lodge into the morning room; he has no idea why Diana has not bothered to collect any of it for days. At this time, early evening on a dull and breathless day, the room is drab. There is a hymn Edmund remembers from school. The day thou gavest Lord is ended, the darkness falls at thy behest. He remembers also the day the shadow fell on them. He was sitting right here in his armchair reading the paper when Diana came in saying Valerie had called with the news that her mother was dead. It was the first time they had to connect over something big, maybe they just didn't have the vocab-ulary. Perhaps if she'd said she needed him to be there for her he might have found the strength, like he did for Mikey with Valerie's funeral; then he would have been at Wynhope the night of the earthquake and that might have made a difference, although he doesn't quite know what. That's another incident shrouded in confusion. He has never been one hundred per cent convinced of the theory that it was Mikey who locked the door to the tower. If he'd ever met Valerie, the infamous half-sister, maybe things would have made sense.

What might have been. The cartoon in the study hasn't moved, even if the rest of the place looks a bit of a tip. Edmund picks up the screwed-up bits of paper from the floor and puts them in the bin. Diana probably let Mikey mess around in here for hours; after all, it can't have been easy being left alone with him twenty-four seven. Upstairs, the light is on in Mikey's bedroom, revealing quite a different room from the one Edmund remembers before leaving. All the things which usually lived in the sacred nursery – the cardboard box, the castle, the circus animals – have all been brought down to his bedroom, which now resembles a squat. The floor is covered in junk, biscuits, clothes, mud, empty cereal packets, felt-tips without their tops on; even the furniture is out of place. The model animals are jumbled in a haphazard pile beside his bed, a funeral pyre of zebras and tigers and smiling acrobats. How Edmund used to hate this clown when he was a boy, from the moment he opened the box on his seventh birthday, how it laughed at him throughout, how he never had the courage to throw it away, in case, like the tin soldier in the story, flat on its back and poker-faced in the gutter, it refused to die quietly. Sitting cross-legged on the floor, Edmund works through the rest of the animals. His hands remember how the elephants can be linked up as a family, trunks looped around the tail in front; the room warms with the song his mother used to sing to him as he played with them, 'Nellie the elephant packed her trunk and said goodbye to the circus.' He hums it quietly to himself.

The head of the herd was calling, far far away,
She left one night, in the silver light,
On the road to Mandalay.

The leavings that have been and the leavings which might come suck him deep into himself, into the lightless hollow at the bottom of the wave. He becomes trapped, turned over and over again in a perpetual cycle of fathomless grief. When finally he is exhausted from weeping, he heaves himself up onto the boy's beach of a bed where he cramps like a child with a tummy ache and falls asleep, clutching a plastic gorilla.

Chapter Thirty-Two

The wall is inches from his face. As if the process of unfurling will open up the memory of the day before and the prospect of the day to come, and survival relies on being able to cling curled to this unformed state, he lies motionless. Only the gorilla digging into his back reminds him where he is and why. The Khoridol Saridag mountains are known for their beauty, Lake Khövsgöl is meant to have the purest water on earth, the nomads there are said to be amongst the most hospitable in the world, and he is here with the stones of his house heavy around his neck; beyond the cities, no one owns property in Mongolia.

The bath is full, it foams over his tanned arms and neck like snowflakes, but when he finally lets the water out and everything is drained from him, his exposed body is defined only by the dry white edges of the bath and the cold air, legs peculiarly redundant, pale flesh already puckering. If Monty was not whining at the bottom of the stairs, he might stay that way for ever.

There is no milk, but there is coffee and bread; it looks as though the organic people came, if nobody else. His body clock is all over the place, but breakfast always has been important to him, ever since he was a boy fishing plastic toys out of the cereal box. He should make some calls, but he is so tired and when it comes down to it, he can't really think who will be genuinely interested. Sally cares, she can spread the news locally; his secretary can tell people in London; it isn't as if there is family left alive to call on either side. It is a bizarre conundrum, who the undead call to let the dead know they are dying.

Edmund does visit Diana, but he doesn't collect Mikey. Nothing has changed at the hospital. He doesn't know if she is living or dying, and that physical uncertainty disorients him. Time is equally distorted, this present could last for ever. Having bought a KitKat, a pint of milk and some dog biscuits at the garage, he drives home. Smoothing out the silver foil from the chocolate bar into a river, he lies on the phone to Grace, says the doctors have asked him to be back at the hospital later and can she keep Mikey for one more day. Then he falls into a heavy unconscious state and wakes when it is dark. Routine is meant to help both jet lag and trauma, but he hasn't been given a timetable so he spends most of the night drinking whisky and watching television. The chaos of their own bedroom repels him, the dressing table trashed, the bed unmade. Maybe this is what it would be like to be the man who cleans the theatre, standing on stage at the end of some modern play, broom in hand and not a clue what the whole thing is about. Both he and Monty are drawn to Mikey's room, but his adult body feels intrusive and out of proportion on the child's bed; downstairs there is a rare edition of *Gulliver's Travels* with a colour picture of the mean and armed little people tying down the ropes and using their spears to prod the body of the visiting giant.

The anonymity of the spare bedroom is more to his liking, until Diana materialises: the black beads on the faces of the embroidered parrots on the bedspread are her eyes, their crusted claws clutch at him. But this is where he eventually sleeps, throughout the witching hours he is both Gulliver and a Lilliputian. When he wakes at midday, he is aware that he smells stale.

There are things to do – post to open, private health insurance to check, endless unread emails in his inbox – but he does nothing.

There is a sour stench of things rotting in the fridge so he closes the door, vaguely aware that he is hungry. People phone, he doesn't answer, they leave messages, he doesn't listen. He isn't thinking. He just is. Is, he likes the word, feeble and lumpish at the back of the throat refusing to swallow the past or let the future breathe out freely. When he calls yet again to cancel collecting Mikey, he is relieved to get Grace's voicemail because it makes it easier to lie and he doesn't answer when they ring back. The third day, he doesn't even visit Diana. The dog is the only one who can motivate him, so towards the end of the afternoon, he sets off for the river. The water is running fast over the weir, carrying with it golden leaves like candles on the Ganges. Months he spent in Varanasi as a young man; he remembers the meditation, the understanding of things glimpsed between the white smoke at the end of joints and the sweet grey curl of the funeral pyres. Only last week, he found enlightenment of sorts in the shallows of the Tuul. Perhaps his ashes can be scattered here, rivers are good places to wash away the past.

On the bank of this, his English holy river, Edmund sits dry-eyed, remembering all that is Wynhope and wishing he could cry. It is a perfect evening for fishing – muggy, the threat of a storm luring the fish to the fly – but he hasn't even been able to bring himself to thread the reel. He will miss this perhaps more than anything, because through it all, there has always been the river: he threw stones in this river, each pebble a counted prayer for his mother to live, while he waited for his mother to die; he swam in the three-fathom pool the day after her funeral and wondered if it was a sin, to still love the slide of his naked thighs into the icy water and the wonderful wet wildness of it all; he smashed his father's treasured salmon rod and threw the pieces in this river, watched the fragments drift away on a slow summer stream, snagged by a fallen sycamore. But more than all those moments are the unnoticed, unnumbered days, as a child, a teenager, a man, with the murmur of turning water for company, the drifting fly, the wading stick to read the riverbed and the rod held low and lightly, waiting, always waiting for the tug on the line. For him, fishing has always been a spiritual experience: complete attention to the moment co-existing with complete absorption in the imminent future, a fusion of deep peace and heightened suspense, all that is past part of the stream around him. Sometimes he still prays here, in a way which is different from the prayers he offers himself in his chapel.

Perhaps more than anything it is the way the river speaks to him. Wading out, aware that even his presence in the water changes the conversation, he listens to the steady rush of the weir behind him, closer to him the gentler lilt and babble of stones in water. It is as though there is a child hidden in the water, playing with words and laughing at all the amazing sounds and infinite songs he can sing. Sometimes when Edmund fishes, if it is warm, he hangs his coat from one of the low branches of the willows, and at the end of the evening, he hands back his soul in exchange for his coat. This evening he is not looking for baptism, but for confirmation of his new creed.

He has decided to leave. It was ridiculous to think Wynhope could ever be anything other than a perpetual graveyard; it was equally ridiculous, once he decided never to have children, that it could be anything other than a historical dead end. And on the question of children, it was ridiculous that he ever thought he would be good enough to look after Mikey. He is a very unsuccessful man.

That is the saddest thing. He was just beginning to teach him to fish. How surprised he was that this boy, taut and suspicious as a terrier from a rescue home, was able to spend hours standing right here, waiting and watching, then walk away not having caught a thing, but still happy. Talking didn't matter when it came to the important things in life like cricket or gardening or reading or listening to music or fishing, nor when they ambled back over the park, where the trees were too old for gossip, the rooks too busy for small talk. They only dropped hands when they spotted Diana scowling out at them from the kitchen window. She wanted Mikey and she didn't want Mikey. He never understood it, but now it doesn't matter; she will never care for the boy again and nor will he. Surely

Grace will have him, she won't be able to say no and it will be better for the child that way.

In a shower of water, Monty leaves the river, barks expectantly, but Edmund is leaning over the old stone bridge staring into the pool, deep in thought, planning the mechanics of his departure and where he might go. Over the years, he has tried many ways of living in many different countries, leaving Wynhope to take care of itself. Money lets you do that, turn into some parody of a wandering minstrel: a bar in the Caribbean, a yoga retreat in the Himalayas, a job in a safari lodge in South Africa, studying in Cairo, a bank in New York; all punctuated by periods of staying at Wynhope usually associated with marriage and moments of leaving Wynhope usually associated with death or divorce. Perhaps he could learn from the nomads he saw on the steppes, moving on with their yurts and their horses, taking their selves with them as they go.

Not just himself, Edmund isn't so stupid to think that they won't all be with him on the empty seats beside him on the bus: his parents, his wives, his half-dead wife in particular, the boy he hasn't looked after, the children he hasn't fathered, the house and the slaves who built it, and the history he will put on the market. All tattooed on his flesh, but even so, he tasted freedom on his fishing trip and he feels an adolescent lurch of excitement at the idea of walking away down the drive on his own two feet. He turns in the direction of the main road and salutes the gates. He'll have nothing more than a pack on his back. A gap year. A gap life.

Already back at the house, Monty is waiting for his supper with the absolute certainty that it will be provided. Edmund can't allow himself to think about leaving the dog. He and Marguerite took in a rescue dog once, adored him, then he savaged the sheep and they had to return him to the kennels. Edmund is still haunted by the look in his eyes as the volunteer clipped the chain on the collar and led him back to his cage.

Having closed all the doors and turned off all the lights, he restricts himself to the sitting room for the evening. Although the chimney is cold, last year's wood is dry and the fire catches quickly. Monty settles tired and happy on the hearthrug. With a bottle of expensive Burgundy, Edmund streams the soft porn film on mute and turns up Bach's *St Matthew Passion* to full volume. Sometimes, when he is all by himself, he can manage it this way.

The slam of a car door. Monty cocks his head, barks. Edmund stops what he is trying to do. Who calls this late? The police? Perhaps the hospital sends someone to tell you if someone dies, then he realises how ridiculous that is. People die in their thousands every night, there would hardly be enough living to read out the telegrams for the dead. The bell rings again, louder, longer. Whoever it is does not seem to be prepared to go quietly so Edmund sorts himself out and goes to the front door.

In the porch, the silhouette of a man with his back to him, hands in the pockets of a dark outdoor jacket, a black beanie pulled low over his head. It was Diana who insisted on security lights. He always hated the way they set themselves up in opposition to the moon so as soon as he realised she might not be back, he turned them off. This fear is his punishment for being presumptuous, to peer into the darkness and not recognise the night visitor at the door.

'Edmund.'

'John!' The immediate relief disappears as Edmund senses bad news and cold air fills the hall around him. 'Is there something wrong with Mikey?'

'I don't know. You tell me.'

John has had a drink problem in the past – ex-army, didn't they all? – and he looks as if he is spoiling for a fight. For that matter, they are both probably drunk. There is something going on with Grace and John which he doesn't understand, how they walked away from Wynhope as though they were glad to escape and the antagonism from their granddaughter when he visited.

'Are you going to invite me in? Or should I go round the back to the tradesman's entrance?'

It is an unnecessarily caustic comment from someone who

Edmund believes he has always treated as an equal, but, letting it pass, he leads his unexpected visitor into the sitting room. The fire is almost out, the bottle is empty, the room is a tip. On the television, a black woman is licking a white woman's nipples. Edmund snatches the remote and the screen goes blank.

'Do you want to take your coat off?'

'I won't be here long.' Glancing around the room as if he is looking for something, John picks up the DVD of *Titanic*, opens it, snaps it shut. 'I'm not going to mess around. I want to know what the fuck is going on with Mikey.'

So that's it. Edmund does not want this conversation. He had planned to say whatever needs saying over the phone in the morning, when he can think clearly, not now, under threat, under the influence. Spreading his arms wide, John sarcastically reminds Edmund of his fisherman's promise.

'Every morning, that boy gets up, packs his rucksack and sits at the bottom of the stairs, staring at the front door, waiting for you to come. Can you imagine that, Edmund? So we call and you don't answer, we leave messages and you don't reply. And at bedtime, we have to tell him that you're not coming. Again. You're a selfish bastard, do you know that? How can you do that to a kid?'

As Edmund doesn't know how he can do that to a kid, he doesn't answer.

'Well?'

Edmund shrugs in a gesture of helplessness. 'I know what you're thinking.'

'No, you don't,' says John. 'But I do know what you're up to. This is not about me and Grace. We can look after him, we have been looking after him, as you well know. I bet you're thinking, oh, they'll have him, they'll never say no.'

An involuntary turn of the head gives Edmund away.

'I thought so. It's a speciality of your type, isn't it? Taking advantage of other people on a grand scale for hundreds of years, and more recently as far as our family's concerned. Oh, don't pretend you don't know. Anything goes, as long as you get what you want. I, that's your favourite letter, isn't it? I for idle rich.'

Edmund tips up the empty wine bottle. 'Whisky?'

'You've had enough, and I haven't popped round for a drink before dinner.'

Turning his back on the sneer, Edmund takes some time in the dining room, gets himself a whisky, downs it in one, wonders if he should just tell John to go or threaten to call the police. In the end he pours himself another and one for his guest, and despite what he said John takes it from him without a word and sits down. Edmund remains standing. The alcohol helps him to say what needs to be said.

'I've screwed up, I don't mind admitting it. I've coped pretty badly since coming back and finding Diana, well, finding her like she is.'

'It can't have been easy. I'm not saying that and I'm sorry about Diana. I didn't like her, don't like her, you know that well enough, but I wouldn't wish that on anyone. But all I want to know is whether you're coming to get Mikey tomorrow or not.'

The fire spits, and Edmund scuffs at the spark with his shoe, leaving a black stain on the rug. With great effort, he speaks straight to his former gardener.

'No,' he says. 'I'm not. I was going to call in the morning. I've done some thinking and I know, however fond I am of Mikey, I can't look after him. Not on my own. So the answer's no.'

Having taken a large swig from his whisky, John puts the glass down slowly. He crosses the room towards Edmund. 'You were going to call? What, leave another voicemail? Like Tuesday? Because you're not man enough to have the conversation face to face, with us, or with Mikey? You've got no balls, have you?'

He's so close to him now, Edmund can smell the disdain.

'You don't fool me, Edmund. Grace gets taken in by you, but not me. You're not planning to look after Diana, or Mikey, are you? You're planning to look after yourself. Number one. Like a spoiled brat who never grew up. Little Lord Fauntleroy.'

Hands against his chest, whisky on his breath, John is right in his face.

'Packed your pigskin suitcase already, have you? Booked your first-class flight out?'

Even in the playground, Edmund always stepped away. 'Oh, sit down, John, for Christ's sake. You can hit me, I wouldn't care.'

'Well, thank you. I will.'

Out of nowhere, all at once, shirt grab, whiplash, crack, blood, black. Staggering backwards, Edmund's hand goes to his nose. No pain, not immediately; that comes minutes later as he leans over the washbasin, wondering if he is going to vomit. Finally, firm enough on his feet to let go of the sink and reach for the towel, he runs it under the cold tap and holds it tentatively to his face. No one has ever headbutted him before, let alone a man twenty years his senior. He had no idea it was so painful, but even he can't stay locked in the toilets until the end of break.

Bending forwards, breathing out noisily, once, twice, John is sitting down with his head in his hands. Edmund recognises the techniques; he tried the course himself once at Marguerite's suggestion. She was a great believer in therapy, but, as she admitted, he had enrolled at the wrong level. It was all about how to manage your anger, not how to allow yourself to be angry to start with. Slowly, unsteadily, he selects a log, places it on the fire and pushes the ashes with the poker, just to buy time.

'Where was I,' says Edmund, 'before I was so rudely interrupted?'

'You were telling me about your plans. Tell you what, you can apply to go on that programme, *Dear Future Me.*'

The words batter Edmund, but he deserves it so he doesn't protest. He is so very tired now, he's never been so tired. He wants to go to bed. He wants to tell John to bugger off, to tell them all to bugger off, but John is still there, his unrelenting inquisitor.

'So what do you imagine is going to happen to Mikey now?'

It is a ridiculous question. How is he meant to know? The future always has been a dropped pack of cards. 'I don't know. You're right,

I was going to talk to Grace and see if there was any chance of him staying with you. I can pay, like they do for fostering. The money isn't a problem.'

'It's not the answer either, though, is it? Didn't you ever buy the record? Money can't buy you love and all that . . .'

Flicking the crystal glass with his fingers, Edmund listens to the chime, then the silence, and in that dead space he finds it within himself to stare the counsel for the prosecution in the eye. 'I didn't mean it like that and you know it.'

Suddenly it is John who looks exhausted. He pulls off his hat, runs his hands through his hair. 'Well, you need to know something. We're not keeping him. Grace and I have been over it again and again, because we guessed this might happen. It's not fair on Naomi. They've got Liam and Louisa at home. There's no room, it just won't work, not long-term, and anything else wouldn't be good enough. So you know what that means.'

Edmund does know, but he cannot let the thought form in his mind, let alone voice it.

John fills in the gaps for him. 'Social services, that's what. They won't find a family, not for a kid with his problems, so it will be some residential home, with a load of paedos and a different social worker when the wind blows and, believe me, I know what that's like. Why do you think I joined the army at sixteen? Can you really do that to him, Edmund? Can you?' John swirls the remaining whisky round and around and lowers his voice. 'Grace says she's never seen you so happy as when you're with Mikey.'

Happy. If you're happy and you know it, clap your hands. It is such a childlike word, head and shoulders, knees and toes, knees and toes. Skip, that is another one. Play. Going home time. Stories. Closing his eyes, Edmund finds himself telling John a story, all about the decisions he has made, to move abroad, to sell Wynhope, leave enough for Diana to be cared for and for Mikey's education, and give all the rest of the bloody money to charity if that will put things right. That seems about the only way to fit through the eye of a needle.

'I don't know if Diana meant to kill herself or not, but I've thought about it myself,' he confesses. 'What sort of father would I be? History repeating itself, Wynhope series two. Christ knows, we could make a box set before long.'

John says it wouldn't have to be like that.

'You're a man's man, aren't you, John? As you've just so aptly demonstrated.' Edmund's hand rises instinctively to the bridge of his nose. 'I've seen the way you used to look at me, like when I had to ask you to, oh, I don't know, mend the mower or something like that.' Something registers in the handyman opposite him, the glance at the door, the pulling down of the sleeves. 'I bet you're thinking what a pansy, with his public school education and City millions and he can't even mend a fucking mower. Isn't that right?'

'Maybe.'

'Well, as you've seen this evening, that's just who I am. An all-round, one-hundred-per-cent-guaranteed disappointment. Even my own father saw no future in me. I'm rock bottom now. I can't do it.'

'Can't or won't?'

'Can you see me, a single dad, doing the school run, cooking fish fingers, at my age?'

'Yes.'

Yes. The word takes flight in the room, a kingfisher in a rookery. Yes. Edmund repeats it silently to himself and then out loud.

'Yes?'

'Yes, if you choose to. You're a bright bloke, you've got the money, a spare bedroom or two, the time on your hands, and you're kind, really, aren't you? It could be the best thing that's ever happened to you, let alone Mikey. That's what Grace thinks anyway.'

But if I say yes, Edmund is thinking, if I say yes, there will still be Wynhope, ghosts under the catalpa tree, shots in the tower, and if I say yes, there will still be Diana, or what's left of her. But if I say yes, there might be other things as well, things I dare not name. Like love, for instance.

'And what about Diana?'

'I only care about Mikey,' John replies. 'I'm sure a man of your means can find a solution for Diana . . . if it comes to that.' He gets up. 'I need to be going. I told Grace I'd only stay five minutes. She didn't really want me to come at all.' He pulls his hat back on. 'So, to make it clear, we've told Michael you're not very well, which isn't so far from the truth, looking at the state you've let yourself get into. You've got until Friday. If you haven't let us know by then, we're calling social services.'

At the front door, Edmund is grateful for the fresh air. He watches John getting into his van, then suddenly he calls out, like a child about to jump off the top diving board. 'You really think I can do it?'

With the driver's door half open, John nods. 'I did it,' he says. 'Rock bottom as well, I was. Bankrupt, lost the pub, on the point of losing Grace because I was such a drunken, violent shit to her, would have lost the kids as well. I retrained, didn't I? And I don't just mean the job. And not everybody would have employed me, but you gave me a chance, I haven't forgotten that.' The headlights light up the bright colours of the dahlias in the long border, moonshine on rubies. 'Best thing I ever did, rescuing this garden, bringing it back to life after all those years. If I can find a silver lining, Edmund, so can you. If you want to.' He closes the van door and lowers the window. 'Thanks for the whisky. Sorry about, well, you know. And by the way, a wash and a shave always helps.'

Leaning into the van, Edmund has one last question. 'Do you think Grace would help me? Paid. You could even move back into the lodge when I get it repaired.'

'You still don't get it, do you?' John turns on the engine. 'We're never moving back to be your staff or your tenants. We've got our independence, our family. I got a lot of work out of this earthquake. Winners and losers. Grace is her own woman, but I reckon if you ask her, she'd jump at the chance of helping the kid. She was heartbroken leaving him. And I almost forgot, I was meant to give you this.'

And then he's gone.

An envelope. It is starting to drizzle again, the soft pattering of raindrops falling on old tiled roofs, the drip of the gutters and the chime of water in an empty tin bucket, it plays like a xylophone in the night, and Edmund turns the envelope over and over in his hands as he listens to the night orchestra.

Inside, a card, a picture of mountains and black birds, a river and two stick people fishing under a huge yellow sun.

Dear Edmund,

I am sorry you are not very well. I hope you get better soon. I am looking forward to seeing you and Monty again.

I am not feeling very well either.

Love Mikey

Chapter Thirty-Three

Did the sunrise mean nothing to her? Or did it mean too much? The dressing-room window, Mikey's bedroom, the back windows of the nursery, they all face northeast over the agricultural fields behind the house rather than over the landscaped park. The architect designed it that way so that the smiling face of the front looked south and invited the sun in through its elegant windows, turning its back on the cold winds and slanting rain which sweep in from the hills. But for all the glamour of the sundowner lawns, it is these windows which frame the sunrise; luminous clouds, mottled and flecked and ribbed like salmon, awaken in Edmund the aching passion he feels for his home, whereas only yesterday he was besotted with his whore: distance. In the space between, he feels the need for guidance.

Outside, it is cold for the end of September, the spice of autumn bringing back the feeling of a new term, stiff shoes, blank pages in the exercise books, write about what you did in your holidays. The iron railings which encircle the park are laced with silver cobwebs. As he walks he checks the saplings he has planted and tended and with his hand he measures the length of this year's growth, new life on old wood. These trees won't make much difference in his lifetime, but in the next century the landscape will be changed because of this commitment and he is proud of that. Further on, a large branch has recently split from the trunk. He lets dying trees stand as a rule; they provide lookout posts for owls, hollows for nests, homes for scavenging beetles and false scorpions, crevices for fungi and parasites and millipedes and mites – so much life vested in one decaying host.

The chapel is dark. The old candles have burned out and the new ones have the waxy shine of feverish flesh. There are not enough left in the box to mark everything that has been lost, but he lights three of them anyway and then plays with a fourth before putting it back. Light for the dead, darkness for the living, none of it really made sense. Sitting in his pew, Edmund fixes on the space where the crucifix once hung. Even if it was still there, he would not be able to think of anything to say to the man hanging from the tree, nor did he imagine that man would have much to say to him. As restless as the rook stamping and scratching on the beams above him, Edmund pecks at his usual routines but finds little nourishment. It strikes him that he has constructed his own religion in this chapel and that prayers offered here are nothing more than introspection. Aimlessly, he deciphers the inscriptions to his forefathers carved on the flagstones beneath his feet and on the war memorial above his head: 'Greater love hath no man than he lay down his life for his friends.' Heroes all of them. At the font, he dips his fingers in the deconsecrated dryness of the bowl. He's never paid much attention to the verse that the stonemasons chose to carve onto the rim in the twelfth century.

'Suffer the little children to come unto me.'

He feels it as he reads it. The words speak to him.

When he parks outside Grace's house, he does not get out immediately. People walk past, pushchairs and shopping bags and scooters and skateboards, it must be the end of school. His visit to the hospital has exhausted him. What the nurses made of his recent absence, he had no idea; they live too close to death to be in the position of making judgements on the living, but they did comment that it was helpful for her to have visitors, and there had only been one or two. He was advised to set up a rota to take the pressure off him, but he doubted it was needed. Diana must have been lonely after the first few months at Wynhope. She'd always seemed so busy, with lots of invitations on the mantelpiece to start with, but there's no queue now at the door to Intensive Care. He should have paid more attention.

There appeared to be no change in Diana's condition since his last visit, but it was hard to know for certain. Edmund explained to her how he'd been tidying up at home, how the sweet peas were still flowering, that the private health insurance covers rehabilitation . . . As he talked to her, he could feel her coming back to him, the old Diana coming home through the dusk and settling down beside him until it was a shock to remember where he was and everything that had happened and then, and only then, did he realise how sad it all was, what was lost. Because, regardless of the medical terminology and the guarded use of the future tense, it was clear that a lot was lost. He always was a poor mathematician and his accounting in recent days had been faulty, but if he did the figures, surely they had spent more time in love than out of it? When the nurse appeared with a bowl, he took it from her and washed Diana's hands with the warm water, gently, so gently there was barely a ripple on the surface. He sponged her palms, her fingers, one by one, and then the delicate flesh between one finger and the next until the whole hand was cared for. That is such an intimate part of someone's body, the spaces in between and the webbing. To bathe all of her, that would be something, to massage her feet with oils, to stand and raise her arms high above her head and let the water trickle down between her shoulder blades, to sponge her softly underneath each breast and lie her down and tend to the most private parts of her, for her. When her hands were dry, he laid them back on the soft, rolled towels, loosely curled around nothing but the air, as if there was no need to worry about a thing, everything was going to be all right. Even if he could not envisage loving her back at Wynhope, he could at least love her here, where it was just the two of them, where it was safe enough to love.

With a jolt, in the wing mirror Edmund notices Louisa getting her keys out of her school bag and letting herself into the house. She has not spotted him. He can't see Mikey at the window, but he's probably there watching, behind the net curtains.

He hadn't mentioned bringing Mikey home to Diana, but he did tell one of the nurses.

'I'm on my way to collect our nephew,' he said.

She asked if he was going to bring him to visit and he queried if there was an age limit, like a film, a point at which the nightmare merited a 15 or an 18, death being mistakenly thought of as a matter for adults.

'For a lot of children the fear of what they'll see is worse than the reality,' advised the nurse. 'Are they very close, your wife and the little boy?'

They are not easily separated, Edmund is sure of that. They are enmeshed, like when you try to unroll barbed wire and all the spikes get caught up with each other.

This time Edmund is invited into the kitchen where he sits with his coffee at the table opposite Mikey with his milk, Grace doing this and that at the cooker. No recriminations, he doesn't think she is a woman who holds tight to hard feelings or past injustices. Everyone else is out doing things, Grace explains. John is on a rebuild job at the health centre, Naomi does afternoons at Brean & Walters – the solicitors are busy, there's been quite a surge of claims since the earthquake, most of them trying their luck, she reckons – and her son-in-law and Liam are on lates, and Louisa's just got in from school. Edmund is painfully conscious that he does nothing useful. Other people have phrases that are not really part of his vocabulary. He overhears them at the hospital: take a morning off, what with work and one thing and another, no holidays left for the year. If he owned those words, then he might have been part of it all, propped up by the pillars which keep everyone else in a state of mutual support; as it is he has his own language in his own castle in his own country, some distance away and the court interpreters have long fled. He is as good as unemployed, he just doesn't need to sign on.

'Busy people,' he acknowledges to Grace.

'And that's an understatement.' She laughs.

Mikey is staring at him. Edmund has forgotten how the child unsettles everything around him, wobbling the kitchen table until the milk spills from the cup and a clementine rolls onto the floor. A couple of minutes later and he has his rucksack on his back and is waiting in the doorway. Edmund thanks Grace, says he can't find the words to express how grateful he is that she'll be coming to Wynhope to help out and Grace says she's thrilled to be asked.

'It isn't that I didn't enjoy it before, it's just that Diana . . . Never mind, that's all in the past now, isn't it? Bye!' She waves. 'Bye, Mikey, you be good!'

In the supermarket on the way home, they go a little mad, both of them overexcited and silly: vanilla sponge cake with jam and cream in the middle, sugar cereal, fizzy drinks, sausages, baked beans, tubs of chocolate-coated flapjacks. Comfort is chucked into the trolley and piled high, with Edmund adding some bananas and natural yoghurt as a responsible father should. At the burger place next door, Edmund explains that tea is not going to be like this every day so Mikey shouldn't get his hopes up, but he admits it feels like a bit of a treat, squeezing the mayonnaise out of its plastic pouch, dipping his chips in it and tasting Mikey's strawberry milk shake, sucking from the same straw.

When they get home, Mikey is pulling on the door handle, but Edmund keeps the child lock on. He has rehearsed this. 'You know I told you my mother and father died. Well, I thought I'd never be able to walk back in here again, I thought it would be horrible, but do you know, it isn't. It's home. Wynhope is home.' Sometimes with an audience this inscrutable, it is difficult to know how well your speech is going down. 'And horrible things have happened here. I don't understand them, but maybe one day you'll be able to tell me about them.' Not a flicker, Edmund ploughs on. 'But this is your forever home now, Mikey. Nothing will change that. This is where you belong.'

It would have been nice if there was a hug, a smile, even a nod, but as soon as the door is released, Mikey slides to the ground and is gone. Edmund knows he is going to have to get used to small rewards.

'Monty!'

Such a warm welcome for the dog. Words, apart from anything else.

'It's me. Mikey.'

'So, you talk to Monty and not me,' says Edmund.

'Yes.' In the Jekyll and Hyde way the boy operates, the smile drops and he disappears to his room.

'It's only the cleaners who've been in here,' Edmund reassures him as the door is shut in his face.

Only Monty is allowed in. It is noticeable how the dog seems to feel responsible for the child; Edmund can speculate on the reasons, but has no answers. In his study, he can't concentrate. He is writing emails with an eighth of his brain, he isn't quite sure what they will do next; Mikey has a strange way of contorting time so that it feels urgent and endless simultaneously. If this is what one evening is like, what the hell is going to happen seven days a week, three hundred and sixty-five days a year? What did he do at that age, all day every day, between one death and the next? He was packed off to some obscure relations in Salcombe, dispatched to cricket camp – generally the solutions seemed to have involved being sent somewhere some distance away – but when he was at Wynhope, he hung around on his own, painting his model army and setting up battles between the Orgs and the Undead (and whose side is he on now?), fishing, of course, and mucking around down at the river. And he waited for his father to come home from the hospital. And he counted the days for school to start again and when he got there, he counted the days until he could come home again.

Diana was meant to be arranging that while he was away.

'Didn't you go to visit the school?' he asks Mikey.

Shake of the head. Apparent intense concentration on Lego.

'Why not?'

Shrug.

'What did you do while I was away?'

Second shrug. Lego back in box. Grabs the remote. Television on. Inappropriate programme. Taking a leaf out of John's book, Edmund takes control and turns the television off.

'No, don't argue. Listen to me. I've no idea what went on here, but I wish you could tell me. It might help. But if you won't tell me, you'll have to tell the police. They're coming round. Will you talk to them or at least write something down? Shall I find your whiteboard?'

'No,' says Michael.

It is a start.

Chapter Thirty-Four

It was bad enough knowing they were going to try to talk to Mikey, but Edmund had not anticipated them wanting to interrogate the computer. Just when the pressure is off on the pool and the planning permission, now this. Watching the police car head off down the drive, he wonders if they are going to 'take things further' as they hinted. He is not surprised they are concerned. So is he.

The state of things in the house when he got back from his fishing trip was disturbing enough, but nothing compared to the state of the search history on his computer. It was a strange and perverted list; when Edmund read it he was glad he had been in Mongolia because it was the sort of browsing which could get you into trouble.

Someone had visited a range of sites – online newspaper reports, Wikipedia, YouTube and strange image searches – and what they had in common was that they were all about prisoners: solitary confinement, Stockholm syndrome, confession, torture, how long it took to starve to death.

Someone.

Your wife or the child, sir? The thought that it was either of them was ridiculous. Kids nowadays might get ideas from violent games but how would Mikey have even understood half of it, and as for Diana, why would she have looked at sites like that?

'Besides, she never made spelling mistakes,' he added. 'She was' – he caught himself – '*is* a very precise woman.'

Maybe Diana wasn't well, D.I. Penn suggested; he remembered her from his first visit, concerning the death of her sister. It's as though they can both hear Diana standing in the doorway to the study, correcting him.

Edmund speaks for her. 'Half-sister,' he says.

'Narrative verdict, wasn't it? Well, it's what I say to my colleagues in the force: we can close a case if we want to, but it's never the end of the story for the family after a trauma like that.'

And D.I. Penn didn't even know the half of it: her temper, how manic she could be, her increasing obsession with keys, the terrible rows they had when all sense deserted her. How she'd turned him into the sort of man who shouted at women. But he also felt some sense of loyalty to Diana.

'I wouldn't say she was mentally ill.' Not out loud, anyway. Not to you.

People jump from windows usually for one of three reasons, according to the police: they are attempting to commit suicide, they are attempting to escape from someone or something, a fire for instance, or they are suffering from hallucinations, often drug-induced.

'For Diana, drink, yes. Drugs, no, never.'

'So we come back to the question of whether there can have been anyone else.'

'If anything, Diana seemed to be keeping people away from Wynhope, not inviting them in. Even the cleaners were cancelled apparently. You've seen the phone.'

That was when D.I. Penn consulted his notebook and referred to an incident with one Solomon Namutebi. He was at Wynhope some days before the incident apparently, and there was an allegation of harassment, an arrest.

'Solomon? Valerie's boyfriend?'

'Fiancé, I believe.'

For reasons which were all too obvious now, Diana didn't follow up the complaint. She wasn't in when the officer called to get a more detailed statement and she failed to contact them afterwards. They hadn't been able to hold Mr Namutebi any longer so he appeared before the magistrates and got three months, suspended for a year. More important, they imposed conditions of no further contact with Michael and that he could not come within ten miles of Wynhope. That included direct or indirect contact, online, social media, pigeons, the lot.

'Have you ever met this man?'

'No. I mean I heard about him from the social worker and I think Valerie must have spoken about him to Diana, but beyond that, I don't know anything about him.'

'You've got no history there then?'

'None, as far as I know.'

'The duty sergeant reported that he had a lot to say for himself when he was taken in, shouting about this, that and the other that had happened in the past, but don't worry, Sir Edmund, you shouldn't hear another word out of him. Oh, and the DV team reported that all was well with the lad at that time although they had no direct contact.' He double-checked. 'That's not best practice, to be honest. They should actually speak to the kids if there's been a domestic. Talking of which, can we try a chat now?'

The conversation, if you can call it that, went like this.

'We've been looking at the computer, Michael. Did you use it when Edmund was away?'

'Yes.'

'Do you know why there are all these searches about prisoners?'

'Yes.'

'Can you tell us more?'

'No.'

'Were you afraid while your uncle was away?'

'Yes.'

'What were you afraid of?'

Shrug.

'Were you afraid of Diana?' asked Edmund.

'We try not to ask leading questions, sir.'

Mikey looked at Edmund before he replied. 'Yes,' he said as he left, dragging the dog behind him.

The police offered the opinion that he appeared to be a very unhappy lad, for sure, bottling everything up. As if to prove the point, Mikey appeared on the other side of the study window, between the glass and the dry and flowerless branches of the light-starved side of the wisteria. It was difficult to disagree with the police's conclusion that something pretty disturbing went on while Edmund was away, and given the state of Mikey's room, not to mention the incriminating evidence on the computer, it seemed likely that Diana had indeed locked him up at some stage, for an unknown length of time. The best thing to do in the circumstances was to wait and see if there was any improvement to Diana's condition in the hope that she herself could provide some answers.

Just before they left, the policewoman spoke with Mikey directly.

'You know that man who came to visit when you were here alone with your aunty?'

Mikey nodded energetically.

'I know you were very scared because the policemen who came said you were hiding upstairs and too upset to come down. I want you to know that the bad man is not allowed to come here ever again and he's not allowed talk to you. That's the law, the judge told him. If he tries to get in touch, even on the internet, you must tell your uncle immediately and we'll deal with him.'

Bursting into tears, Mikey ran back inside; they could hear him sobbing from where they stood awkwardly on the drive. The policewoman opened the car door. 'That'll be relief,' she said.

Solomon. Valerie told Diana something about his being Mikey's unofficial guardian angel, that if anything happened to her, he'd always be there for the boy. But he hadn't shown that much interest, had he? Even if he was in prison he could have written or something.

Later, when Edmund tucks Mikey up in bed, he asks if he can give him a hug. His pyjamas hang loose like a jacket on a scarecrow, he has lost weight in the last few weeks. Abused. Victim. These are words Edmund is sick and tired of hearing on the news. He thought half the stories were probably made up to get attention and the other half were blown out of all proportion, and on top of that there was often some absentee father who appeared out of the blue, mourning and accusatory, and Edmund would shout at the TV screen, if you loved him that much, why didn't you stick around to look after him? Yet Solomon had stuck around apparently. The social worker's words return to him: 'Solomon would have made a wonderful father.' He imagined him searching, finding Wynhope, walking up the drive between the heavy summer oaks. A solitary black man. Edmund sees him as a man who came to reclaim what was rightfully his, and what truth was it he discovered when he finally got here? No one will pay attention to Solomon's version of events; he has been truly gagged and bound. It is all too complicated to say anything to the boy, so Edmund decides to let bygones be bygones. Besides, what would be the use of a criminal for a father, in and out of prison all the time?

The police visit drops poison into the well from which Edmund has been sustaining whatever love he has left for Diana. Now when he visits he has to reconcile the abuser with the wife, the hands that locked the child in with the hands that sometimes helped him be a man again, the hands which he had taken such care to bathe. When he drives home, let her live, let her die beats in time with the windscreen wipers until he is so mesmerised he has to pull over. He turns off the engine. Let her die. As a child, he was never able to admit to anyone that sometimes all he ever wanted was for his mother to die and for the waiting to be over. A man hangs out of the passenger side of a scaffolding lorry and calls him a wanker for blocking the bus lane; he sees an old woman struggling to put out the rubbish.

It was Grace's idea that letting Mikey visit the hospital might relieve some of his anxiety. She didn't know the half of it and Edmund didn't intend to tell her, but Mikey's insistence won the day. Now Edmund is full of doubts as to the wisdom of that decision. The head bandages are off and a line of stitches mark where her skull has been prised apart for the operation. Even if you haven't seen *Frankenstein*, it is a shocking sight.

'You needn't come all the way to her bed, if you don't want to,' Edmund told him, but now they're here, Mikey wants to know everything. Transfixed by the inert body of his aunt, the boy studies every artificially enhanced breath, registers every monotonous bleep of the machines. Of course, the last time he saw her he must have thought she was dead or dying; wasn't there something about a blanket and a cup of water? Perhaps his presence will trigger some visible response in Diana. Are her lips moving? Whatever the medical facts, it is undeniable that the room changes, something between the hypervigilant child and the comatose body on the bed, as if Mikey, like Doctor Frankenstein, might become the monster maker and spark her into life, or that in some as yet unwritten script, Diana's hand might reach out and unplug the boy.

At the window, Edmund peers through the blinds at the ambulances queuing outside A&E. Beneath them ventilation shafts are sucking the germs out of the wards and pumping them back out into the low grey sky, round and round, round and round. Beyond the hospital is the rain-streaked concrete and glass of the 1960s town centre; the crane brought in to rebuild the multi-storey car park is still there, a solitary skeleton of a prehistoric bird bent over the civilisation which succeeded him. Strung across the dual carriageway, the banner which declares the town open for business is torn at one end and flapping. Is it for this she is clinging to life?

Mikey joins him at the window and pulls on the nylon cords.

'I don't know if we're meant to open the blinds,' says Edmund. 'Maybe they keep them shut for a reason.'

Returning to the bed, Mikey pinches Diana's wrist, picks up her hand, drops it, picks it up again, drops it, eyeing the monitors like a scientist in his laboratory. Resisting the urge to stop him, Edmund tells himself it is natural for a child to want to make sense of this living death, most nine-year-olds would be fixated with the technology, but he also feels profoundly uneasy, witness to some communication he cannot understand, and he dare not ask for a translation for fear of what it might tell him.

'We'll be going now. I'll come again the day after tomorrow. Mikey will come again one day, won't you, Mikey?'

'Yes,' says Mikey.

'Did you hear that, Di? Mikey's talking. That's something, isn't it?'

'Yes.' Mikey repeats as he skips away. 'Yes, yes, yes.'

By the nursing station, he finds a whiteboard and a marker.

'Don't scribble on there,' says Edmund. 'It's got important information on it for the nurses.'

A young doctor grins and tells Mikey to carry on, if he has something important to say.

When is Diana going to start talking.

The boy reads over what he has written then adds the question mark.

When is Diana going to start talking?

Edmund understands: if Diana can talk, then she can confess. As for the doctor, her apology that they do not know the answer to the question is obviously unsatisfactory and when she adds that Diana might not be able to talk but there are other ways to communicate, and then tells the miraculous story of a very famous man who wrote a whole book just by blinking, Mikey rubs out the message with his sleeve and heads for the exit.

'My question,' says Edmund as they get back in the car, 'is when are you going to start talking?'

'Now,' says Mikey and sits in silence the whole way home.

It isn't a lie. There is a steady increase in a number of monosyllabic words Mikey chooses to use. Yes and no, as before, but now a lot of questions, as if he is a toddler again. When? Who? Where? What? And most often, why? When he thinks no one is listening, he speaks to the dog or to the bronze boy or to his plastic gorilla, at length and in sentences. But even though he now insists on accompanying Edmund to the hospital every time he goes, he never again talks in front of Diana. Edmund quite likes having his company on these visits. They develop a silly little routine of stopping for a drink and a pastry at the coffee shop and then treading the line painted on the hospital floor like tightrope walkers, one foot in front of the other and arms out wide, all the way back to the other side.

Chapter Thirty-Five

The radio is a blessing. Edmund is grateful for anything which serves as a distraction on the journey.

'Was that Elvis?' asks Mikey.

'No. Cliff Richard.'

'What woman is he singing about?'

'No woman in particular,' says Edmund slowing down, looking for the turning to the school.

'He is. He says she's the devil.'

'Oh for goodness' sake.' Edmund turns off the radio. 'Five minutes and we'll be there.' But the rest of the journey takes place to the soundtrack of Mikey's personal version of the iconic hit single and Edmund wishes he'd never heard it again in the first place, songs like that stay in your head whether you want them to or not.

Edmund doesn't know who is more nervous, him or Mikey, but he is glad he spoke to the local authority and asked for help. He never did think that Diana's policy of keeping all professionals at arm's length was a sensible one, although he can see now she had her reasons. School is necessary for all sorts of reasons, not least the fact that, although Grace is a godsend, he does need to get some work done and find his way back to the office and everyday life.

'Westerhaven. Healing. Learning. Thriving.' They have arrived.

In terms of architecture, this may be a school for children with emotional and mental health problems, but it looks remarkably like Wynhope. Even so, he can't leave the 4x4 in front of the pillared porch, so Edward follows signs to the visitors' parking. Fire assembly point signs are erected at the entrance to what must have been the old kitchen garden, keypads are bolted on the doors to the converted barns, and the windows in the main house looking out on the playing fields have neither curtains nor shutters and look curiously ashamed of themselves. Edmund's instinct that it is a terrible thing to do to a listed house is confirmed as they wait in a reception area where history and character and art and style and beauty are all trumped by function: plastic chairs are pushed up against the oak panelling, decorative floor tiles covered by carpet designed for 'high traffic areas'. In the brochure it recounts how the house was handed over to a charity by the last heir, who himself had a troubled childhood. A bell interrupts Edmund's uncomfortable thoughts about the current state of his will and the place comes to life like a show. Children thunder down the grand staircase, others bundle in from the wings, bringing with them fresh air and basketballs, a tone-deaf band strikes up to their left in what must have once been the drawing room. Sound. Movement. Energy. Essential components of what you might call life.

'It's a bit like home,' he whispers to Mikey who fidgets beside him.

'Yes and no, yes and no.' Mikey mutters the mantra as he touches everything around him, the visitors' book, the exit button, the fire alarm.

Working through the home life questionnaire, Edmund wants to lie, but the truth is it is a relief to tick boxes and write comments which lay bare in plain English what a strange boy he has inherited.

Self harm? Yes. He circles ligatures and head banging, hesitates over cutting. There is a recently healed scar across Mikey's finger which he refuses to explain.

Isolative? Yes. Spends hours sitting in a cardboard box (but can be sociable, cuddles up on the sofa, loves fishing with me, holds hands on the way home, adores the dog).

Uncommunicative? He is going to put no – after all Mikey is starting to talk – but the man on the Clapham omnibus would certainly not consider a few monosyllabic words and a whiteboard the living language of a healthy tribe. Yes.

Physically aggressive? Yes. Kicks people and property (but doesn't bite, much, any longer).

Stealing? No. (There was the thing with keys, but that seems to have stopped.)

Verbally aggressive? No. Unless you include silence. You should include silence.

'I know it sounds silly' – Edmund is handing over the form – 'but this doesn't feel like Michael to me. He's had some terrible things to cope with.' Will he be forced to tell them everything? Not now. 'Most of the time, he's fine with me.'

'It was mainly with your wife then, before her accident . . .'

On the guided tour, Westerhaven reminds him of his prep school but without the price tag, the parents and the pressure that went with it. He doesn't share this thought with the headteacher who undoubtedly has already identified him as an idle, rich bastard.

'What do you think, Michael?' asks the head at the end of the tour. 'Do you think you could give it a try?'

'Yes and no.'

'Is that more yes than no?'

'Yes.'

'Good.'

When Mikey starts going to school, it is as if there is a signpost in the house pointing in the direction of normality and the road ahead looks passable. Grace irons Edmund's shirts and Mikey's shorts. Edmund loads his laptop into his case, Mikey packs his school bag. Every morning Edmund tells Mikey to be good at school and Mikey tells Monty to be good while he's gone. Edmund doesn't achieve so much, but Mikey comes back with gold stars and certificates; it turns out the problem child is not only good at things, he can also be very good.

'I did singing.'

Edmund has learned not to overreact. 'Are you any good?' he jokes.

'Yes.'

Once he settles, the school say he is ready to start therapy again.

Again. 'Do you remember the name of the therapist you used to see on Thursday mornings? I can't find it anywhere,' Edmund asks Mikey.

That inscrutable look.

Edmund persists. 'You went to a therapist in Twycombe on Thursday mornings with Diana, remember?'

'No.'

'No what? You don't remember? You never went?'

'Never.'

'Don't be silly. I know you went with Diana in the car. Where did you go if you didn't go to counselling?'

'To the library.'

Sometimes Edmund wonders where he was living for the past six months, although in truth he knows the answer: he was hiding, buried away in London, turning up at meetings where he wasn't really needed, long lunches at the club, streaming videos at the flat having 'missed the last train', anywhere but with Diana at Wynhope. He knew a long time ago that Diana had not made good on her promise to get help for herself – he let sleeping dogs lie on that one – but to deliberately deceive him about Mikey's therapy as well? She had more than enough reasons to be paranoid about a child trusting a professional. It isn't just the thought of what she did to Mikey that provokes a fierce anger in him, it is the way he himself has been given the fool's lines to learn. Hours he spends in the yard when Mikey is at school, splitting wood, letting the axe fall on the splintering logs with a terrible force, stopping only when he can trust himself to be tired; it is what he does when he's not in the City and it is what he does when he should be visiting Diana.

When Edmund's mother was in hospital, he was not allowed to

see her. His father drove there and back every day, followed by door-slamming homecomings and whisky-sodden evenings. He could spend time with Mummy when she came home, they lied, but when she came home, on New Year's Day, they sent the wrong lady by mistake. They had shrunk her, sucked away her cheeks and shaved her head, painted her face and dried it out, green and grey like her alligator shoes, and it was hard for him to touch her in the way he used to. And the solution after her death? Boarding school. Naturally. On his last night at home, he hid on the landing, looking down between the banisters onto the balding heads of unfamiliar grown-ups in the hall, and eavesdropped.

'It must be awful for him, having a son who's the spitting image of his dead wife.'

What was awful about that? The promise that the two of them were in it together, that he would be as much a comfort to his father as his father would be to him, that turned out to be an eggshell April Fool, tap it and it splits into emptiness. Out of sight, out of mind. Five days late for the start of term he returned to school. No hook left in the hall for his outdoor coat and the trials for the Under 11s over and done with, he became the boy who took the oranges out at half-time. For the first time for a long time, Edmund allows himself the thought that his father's grand gesture was far from being a selfless act.

When he does force himself into the Intensive Care Unit, Edmund sits at Diana's bedside scratching constantly at the scab of their relationship. Other relatives tell him how the ones they love are still there, just locked away for a while, but when he slides the grille to one side, he has no idea who it is behind the cell door. Another questionnaire is given to him by the speech therapist; this time it's all about Diana. It seems he is required to spend his life summing up people with yes and no and the numbers one to five. Apparently, it helps to have a record of what the patient was like before the accident so they can have meaningful communication, if and when that becomes appropriate. Edmund couldn't agree with them more, but their questions are more mundane than what he has in mind. Favourite TV programmes? Pets? Car? Work? Friends? People often get together when they are young, like him and Marguerite for instance. You have time to create your own shared footpaths of the mind, but God knows before he and Diana even met they both had years of mud tracks stamped across the wasteland, thick with brambles and nettles, and neither of them ever really wanted to retrace their steps or share the view. But even on this short walk they have undertaken together, he has been losing sight of her for a long time, since the earthquake anyway, catching glimpses of her round the next corner or loitering behind in the valley – and now she is nowhere to be seen. The other option, of course, is that he can't find her because he doesn't want to. The path is too narrow for two, so why should he walk hand in hand with a woman who locks children in their rooms and researches how long it will take before they try to kill themselves? Surreptitiously he leaves the form blank on the end of the bed; they'll probably assume he is too distressed to bring himself to complete it.

Every visit is worse than the one before. He can't talk to her about Mikey, can't think of anything else to talk about. A nurse says some people find it helpful to bring something in to read and share, a newspaper, for example: 'Inquiry finds car park developers responsible for poor construction' – we'll leave that well alone; extraordinary picture here of a man who they said would never walk again and now they've rigged him up with some sort of electronic legs and he's just climbed Snowdon. Behind that impassive face is she wondering, like him, if they might at some point in the future take these leaden limbs and fit them with electronic chips, plug her in and watch her walk and talk and tell?

Shaking the creases out of the paper with force, Edmund continues again out loud: 'That TV presenter, he's been found to have over a thousand images of tortured children on his . . .'

Sometimes he resorts to the crossword.

What about twenty across? Spy tracks down hidden communication system in strange land.

Fantasies often preoccupy his well-trodden route from the car park to the ward. He imagines a solemn nurse taking him to one side – the consultant would like a word; variations on a theme of the announcement of the deterioration or death he secretly craves for his wife. And now, on a weekend visit with Mikey, with a catch in his breath, he believes his wish is about to come true. Here is a doctor who wants to have a chat. Please God, he prays with his fingers crossed in his pocket, please God.

Diana is stable enough to see if they can withdraw the sedation and start to bring her out of a coma.

Mikey kicks off when he tells him. 'No, no, no.' There is a struggle, fingers scratching, the bed moves, the high-pitched monitor is screaming for attention and Mikey is punching him, baring his teeth. Staff are running from all directions. Then the alarms are switched off, the crowd disperses, and the space settles down again, leaving the squeak of shoes on clean floors and reassurances about faulty connections.

The nurse puts her hand on Edmund's arm. 'I expect the alarm frightened him.'

That happens a lot with Mikey. People misread the sequence of the chicken and the egg.

Twelve hours later, Diana opens her eyes. Later that night, had Edmund been by her side and had he held a mirror to her mouth, he would have seen the clouded glass.

The timing of the start of Mikey's therapy could not have been better. At exactly ten o'clock, the therapist opens the door to her room. Sofia is small, but conveys simultaneously a sense of great energy and great calm. Her speech is accented, but Edmund can't place it. French? Italian? Instinctively, he feels he'd like to know her better, but acknowledges that he never will, nor does he understand his momentary reluctance to hand over Mikey. In the waiting area, he cannot concentrate on the papers he's brought to read while he waits; it's the geological report on the Riverside Development so it's pretty important, but all he wants to know is what's going on in there. He wants to be in there with them, he wants to be in there on his own.

Someone mentioned something called life story work. That would be something.

Suddenly, Mikey appears, half way in, half way out of the therapy room, opening and closing the door. Unseen, Sofia is talking from the other side.

'You seem very interested in the door.'

Again, Mikey comes out into the waiting room, and this time he stays out, pressing the keypad with different combinations of four numbers over and over again, pausing at the end of each attempt to try the handle beneath.

'Looks like you really want to crack that code and be in control of the door.'

Immediately Mikey jumps back inside and slams the door behind him.

A magic trick comes into Edmund's memory – keys and newspaper and the drawing room – and yet another row with Diana in the garden.

'Do you think it's a good rule, only adults knowing the code?'

Once again Mikey is outside, this time with the door propped open with his foot.

'Maybe part of you wants to be here and part of you wants to leave.'

Wriggling, Mikey takes off his school sweatshirt, gets his elbow stuck in the sleeve, then uses his top as a doorstop. Now Edmund can hear everything, see nothing.

'I'd prefer it if we could work with the door closed, but I can see you have left a way open so you can get out. Or perhaps it is for other people to come in.'

Giggling, something is knocked over.

'I notice you haven't said anything and now you've got your shirt over your face, you can't see either.'

. . .

'And goodness me, now you've got your hands over your ears, you can't hear either. I suppose the only thing left is touch.'

. . .

'You're good at not bumping into things, perhaps you can see more than people might think.'

. . .

'Would you like me to take your hand?'

. . .

'It looks as though you do want me to take your hand, so that's what I'm going to do.'

Has she held his hand?

'Oh, now you've taken it away. I wonder how it is to want to hold my hand and to want to stay away, both at the same time. Like speaking, I suppose, sometimes you say things, other times you say nothing.'

. . .

What's happening now? Bizarrely, Edmund finds himself not just wanting therapy to help Mikey, but for Mikey to be good at therapy; he feels that a lot nowadays, the burning sensation of wanting other people to see in Mikey the unique and talented and loving child that he sees, for things to go well for the child, and the physical pain of realising he cannot do it all for him.

'You can go ahead and explore the room and the boxes.'

What does it look like in there? Are there toys? At a meeting, Sofia explained something about the therapy room, but he found it hard to listen and now he can't remember, can't imagine it. Something is being dragged across the floor.

'Go ahead. You can stand on the box to look out, but the window doesn't open, not the whole way. It's fixed that way to stop people falling out.'

A terrible noise, a frightening noise, banging on the glass, over and over again.

'Michael, it's a safety window. It won't break. It must be very painful to think that your aunty fell from a window and nothing or no one was able to keep her safe.'

The hammering continues. Edmund gets to his feet. He wants to burst in there and rescue Mikey. Safety should be that woman's first priority, shouldn't it? He'll take Mikey home and not come back if she can't even keep him physically in one piece.

'You look as though you really need to break that window. I wonder what it is that you need to get away from. It must be a very frightening thing if you want to break the glass.'

Forcing himself to sit back down, and covering his ears, Edmund leans forwards and rocks slightly. The point of therapy may be to get it all out, but what happens when it all comes out? It had not occurred to him that this therapist might discover the truth just like that, in the first session, that she will discover that Diana did terrible things to the boy and she will have to tell social services. That was made clear at the introductory meeting. And would they let Mikey continue to live with a man whose wife was a torturer? With a man who might have guessed his wife was demented beyond the point of safety, if only he'd taken the trouble to look and listen? With a man who did guess, no, more than that, a man who knew, but got on a plane and left to save himself instead? He knows why Mikey is obsessed with escaping and it is only a matter of time before the therapist puts two and two together and makes four. Inside his head underwater sounds reverberate, the roar of water over a weir, heard in darkness, from a distance. Abruptly, he takes away his hands, struggles to reconnect with the therapist's voice and a less frantic banging.

'That's better. Perhaps it's helpful if someone notices how frightening things can be for you.'

Something strange is happening, the mad hammering is developing a rhythm, like a football chant – de de dedede dedede de, de de – then the glass is abandoned in favour of clapping.

'So all those scary feelings have become a song, a game? That's fine, but it's also okay to feel angry or scared or sad. You've had hard times over the last year.'

. . .

Is he sitting? Hiding? Crying? Mikey nearly always cries silently, even now. Even when he speaks, he doesn't really say anything. Why doesn't the woman say something? She shouldn't leave him like that, alone with his silence. Edmund has such fear that Mikey will slip under the surface and he will lose him again to that underworld.

'Maybe you're very tired, with that blanket from the playhouse pulled right up to your chin. You can sleep if you want to.'

. . .

'Is Michael asleep? I don't know. Sometimes memories and feelings spoil sleep and give us horrid dreams, but Michael really does seem to be fast asleep.'

Six minutes . . . six minutes of silence. One. Two. Three. Four. Five. Six. How can the therapist just sit in there with this deafening absence. The little hand of the clock on the wall of the waiting room hauls itself uphill as though it takes all its energy to reach the top.

'There is one minute left of our time, Michael.'

Fingers grab the sweatshirt, Mikey careers out of the room, and the door slams behind him. He swings round and kicks it. Sofia appears behind him.

'Goodbye, Michael, I'll see you next Thursday.'

Mikey runs at her, tries to push past her to get back in the room, or tries to push her into the room. Whatever he wants, he looks out of control. Edmund is going to hold him back, but Sofia's words are apparently more powerful than his hands.

'Our time is finished now. Here's Edmund, he's been waiting here for you.'

The long drive home happens with the mute button on.

The next day, Edmund phones the therapist from the office.

'I'm sorry, I had to call. I found it so hard just sitting in the waiting room. I could hear bits of what was going on, but I couldn't make head nor tail of it.'

'It's early days. Michael did well. He stayed in the room for nearly the whole session, which is more than a lot of children do to start with. I think he'll make very good use of therapy.'

'But what did it all mean? All this toing and froing and banging on the window?' Therapists are probably wise to fishing expeditions, but he has to cast.

'Well, he's preoccupied with entrances and exits, but so are a lot of people when they start therapy. It's part of being unsure about the process itself. And . . .'

'Yes?'

'And it would be easy to draw conclusions about his mother being unable to escape the earthquake and the blame attached to him for that, perhaps even his aunt being in a locked-in state. He may have heard that phrase. But it's early days and it's as much about the transference of emotion in the room as what he actually does. It wasn't all fear and hopelessness, there was also a sense of a battle for control. We have a lot of work to do.'

Sofia thinks it's definitely worth continuing, she believes Michael may even be able to share some of what has happened to him.

'Can I just add one more thing?' she says before she rings off. 'He is a very unhappy boy, but I also get a sense of great warmth deep down in him, that he has been very much loved in the past and will therefore hopefully be able to allow himself to be loved in the future, in fact may already be letting that happen. You're doing a great job, Edmund. I could see that when I saw you both walking hand in hand to the car park, when I heard the two of you singing.'

Chapter Thirty-Six

Edmund has chosen a more mundane route to sanity. His GP is prescribing him something to help him sleep.

'I don't really care about myself, to be honest,' he says to the doctor, 'but I owe it to Mikey. To stick around.'

'No one can really look after anyone else if they can't be kind to themselves,' says the doctor. Having gone for medication, Edmund is ill-prepared for wisdom or sympathy. He puts on his coat and feels for his keys.

'I wondered if you knew that your wife made an emergency appointment at the surgery before her accident.'

His mind is kicked sideways into touch. She didn't attend, apparently, didn't respond to a reminder either, and, no, the doctor did not know what prompted it and no one would ever know if it might have made a difference. Edmund remembers suggesting to her that she should see a doctor; her reply was that a marriage counsellor would be more help, or an exorcist (she hadn't specified whether the latter was for her, for him, or for Mikey). Or a support group for women with passive-aggressive husbands, that's the other thing she said once, which was very hurtful. Driving home from the surgery, Edmund pauses for some teatime trick-or-treaters, skeletons and ghosts holding hands with their mothers under the fluorescent lights at a zebra crossing. He does a three-point turn and heads back to the supermarket where he buys the last two pumpkins on the shelf.

Self-consciously he plays with Mikey at the kitchen table, stringy heaps of scooped-out flesh on the chopping board, pips discarded like baby teeth the fairy forgot. They are sculptors, of sorts.

'Be careful with that knife,' says Edmund.

Mikey touches the point of the blade to the scar on his hand.

'When did you do that?'

'When you were gone.'

That's his favourite sentence at the moment. He speaks as usual without looking up, concentrating on the gaping mouth, then the knife slips, the serrated fangs are severed and swallowed by the pumpkin. There is little point in Edmund saying it doesn't matter, these things are always catastrophic for him. His face flushes with rage and the pumpkin is stabbed over and over again in a frenzy, then the pulped body is taken into the garden and kicked like a football under the floodlights until it disintegrates entirely and Mikey disappears up to his room, hands down his tracksuit bottoms.

Later he presents Edmund with a printout of a Google search and a picture.

'The tribe played soccer with the head of their conquered opponents.'

There is no denying he is very competent on the computer.

The one remaining pumpkin is finished by them working together and the shared talisman is placed outside the front door. Mikey arranges the elite of his circus animals in a circle around it. Either side of the curious shrine, they cup their palms against the wind and hold the match to the wick. The candle flickers behind the eyes and the light catches the bronze boy, whose muscles quiver.

'The pumpkin's meant to keep away ghosts,' says Edmund, then regrets it.

Under the catalpa tree, the flame has become sunlight filtering through the huge leaves and his mother is resting in her wheelchair, only half asleep. If anything is true, it is that time and history and memory and chronology are unreliable partners and that ghosts lose their faces.

'Do you believe in ghosts?'

'I believe in souls.' Edmund is aware he is whispering.

'Why?'

Because if not, what's the point of the candles and the lilies and the prayers and the chapel? Because he experiences his parents as the people on the far bank watching him cast over the river. Because, before turning back, he himself has seen the ferryman, hand out for the silver.

'Diana did.' The boy's voice is coming from behind the yew hedge. 'She believed in ghosts.' There he is back on the edge of the lily pond, dancing for the bronze boy. 'No more secrets, no more lies,' he sings. 'That's our song. Me and my mum.'

It's nearly midnight when Edmund puts Monty out, and the candle in the pumpkin is just holding its own against the rising wind. That's the first time Mikey's mentioned Valerie; it's almost impossible to believe that he might have caused her death. From the park there's a muted rumble like faraway thunder. Edmund wonders if it's another tremor, or maybe time itself is rolling over in its sleep, as well it might on a night like this when the living and the dead are too close.

In the broad light of the next day there is a battle over what should happen to the remains. Edmund wants to throw the pumpkin on the compost heap. Mikey pokes the sagging cheeks and one eye collapses, and he insists on having it in his room. And there it stays until Grace calls time several days later when the smell of decay has got as far as the hall and Edmund goes upstairs to seize the hostage. There are good times, then there are times like this, when the feral child is back. As soon as he touches the circus animals' cardboard box in an attempt to tidy up, there are fingernails in the flesh, boots against the ankles. Edmund is too tired for this right now: climbing a mud-sucking footpath up the side of the mountain, the sliding back makes the summit look more and more unachievable. He too has a temper if he chooses to lose it. Part of him wants to shout at the boy, why do you think you're the only one who has the right to kick and scream and bite? I want to. We all do. Every one of us on this earth, we are all full of rage, we just make an effort to control it. In the bathroom, he checks his hand and is relieved there is only a faint imprint of tooth marks on the skin, no blood. The staff at the office might notice, but they won't comment, at least not to him; new excuses for his injuries are becoming harder to invent.

'Do it yourself then,' he says to Mikey, 'but that pumpkin has got to be out of here by teatime.'

The grave is dug and marked with two pieces of kindling tied up with string. Mikey writes a name in biro on a piece of paper which he Blu-tacks to the cross. Cyclops. He then prints out a notice which is Sellotaped to his bedroom door, in font size 58: KEEP OUT.

The next therapy session starts as badly as the first ended, with Mikey holding tight to the fire door in the waiting room, rattling the bar. When Sofia welcomes him in, he deliberately thumps his fist against the glass in the alarm box, not quite hard enough.

'He's cross,' Edmund explains. 'He knows I'm going to visit Diana. He wants to be there because they've done more tests and hope to be able to tell us how she's doing, but I've said no.'

For ten minutes, Mikey crouches with his back to the fire exit and the therapist waits in the room. Edmund hovers between them, dry-mouthed with anxiety about missing the meeting with the consultant although he dreads the good news they might have. Elective mutism is a weapon Michael uses well. Edmund copies him; they stare each other out with silence. Eventually the boy knocks on the door to the room.

'Hello, Michael.'

Mikey bends down, looking at the floor.

'You look as though you've lost something.'

'Yes,' says Mikey.

Sofia and Edmund catch each other's eye. Mikey is speaking. Sofia is smiling. She says she'll help Michael to look for whatever it is he has lost, but as soon as she steps outside, Mikey slams the door. Everybody is on the outside now. Calmly, Sofia enters the numbers into the keypad, but as she opens the door, Mikey pushes her violently. She stumbles into the room and Mikey shuts her in, triumphant. Then, quite calmly, he lets himself in using the code, the one that only the adults are meant to know.

Driving to the hospital, the scene replays itself in Edmund's mind with the sickening realisation that this is what Diana must have done, tricked him into going upstairs before violently locking him in the room. It was all being acted out in front of them so that what could not be said could at least be understood. Worst of all, finding his fishing map spread out in the study now makes sense: Diana must have realised at some point that she could not keep the boy locked up for ever, that eventually he would have to come out and then he would tell someone what had happened. The fishing map must have represented her final solution, her guide to the places on the river where the pools were deep enough and the current strong enough that a small boy learning to swim would not survive long.

And was that going to be her final revenge? Not enough for her to have taken away his child, but to have poisoned his river as well.

One day soon he will be able to ask her himself, because the consultant is delighted to tell him that Diana is conscious and able to respond to simple questions. Like did you plan to murder Mikey? And what sort of woman are you exactly?

Chapter Thirty-Seven

'Can you see the Christmas card, Diana? Michael has drawn you a Christmas card. Can you open your eyes, Diana? She's sleepy today, Michael,' explains the nurse. 'I think she's tired.' The staff are frequently having to remind Mikey his aunty needs to rest; to them, his over-eager interrogations are manifestations of his love for her.

Visits are like this now. Diana moves her eyes in response to the doctor's questions. To the right for yes, to the left for no. Sometimes it looks as though she is smiling, but unwitting babies do that thing too, the physiological grin.

'Can you hear me, Diana?'

Eyes right.

'Where are you, Diana? Are you at home?'

Eyes left.

'Are you in hospital?'

Eyes right.

'I'm hopeful she'll be able to talk, given time,' says the doctor.

In the meantime, all the information on the questionnaire which Edmund finally completed is being used to establish her credentials as a fully paid-up living member of the present tense, but history is another country and no doubt the future is also a challenging concept. With great bitterness Edmund concludes a life sentence is little punishment at all if lived in the moment.

At the school Christmas concert, Mikey shines playing the piano and singing a solo. Edmund has to take some time in the car before he collects him, checking his red eyes in the rear-view mirror. Grace incorporates the boy into her shopping, her granddaughter's carol service, their family trip to Santa. Together, all three of them choose an enormous tree for Wynhope from the same place that has always provided an enormous tree for Wynhope. The minimalist white snowflakes Diana bought in her first year at the house are discarded, and instead Edmund blows the dust from old cardboard boxes and they decorate the tree with the garish reindeer and faded Father Christmases of his childhood and finish it off with a tarnished angel. Booted and coated, they stomp through the frost-whitened park searching for holly with berries and mistletoe; the wreaths Mikey makes with Grace turn out to be for the head of the bronze boy and for Monty, who is less than impressed with his festive costume. The mistletoe is hung from the chandelier in the hall.

'That's so you can give someone a kiss,' Edmund jokes.

'Who?' asks Mikey.

Not Diana, obviously. It should be hideous – the red and green trimmings of the season while his wife is trussed up in a neuro ward, paraplegia confirmed and a mind as soggy and stinking as a heap of Brussels sprouts – and there are still times when he weeps, late at night watching Christmas Special re-runs with Monty, but Edmund acknowledges that, if he is in mourning at all, it is for himself. The only other reason for weeping is this fear of her living.

The New Year has begun. It is almost 2 a.m. when he gets back to Wynhope, the taxi having gone the long way round to avoid the flooded roads. With Grace having offered to have Mikey, Edmund was free to be a grown-up and go to a proper party. He is quite pissed. Everyone there knew his wife was in hospital, but it didn't stop several women coming on to him. Being a surrogate single father seems to have given him some sort of added appeal;

he even felt something like a stirring of attraction in return. Nobody blamed him for anything, in fact quite the opposite: Sally draped over his shoulder – no use crying over spilt milk, darling, that's the last thing Diana would want and everyone thinks you're a wonderful father . . .

The rain is turning to hail, sweeping into the back porch, bouncing off the tiles, shining white and crazy in the light. Edmund leans unsteadily against the door. In the distance, the bass throb of a party in the village vibrates through the storm. He is alone. Diana comes and takes her place beside him, slips her cool hand under his shirt. Of all the occasions she loved New Year's Eve the best, dressed up to the nines and choosing her jewellery, and the kissing and the vintage champagne and good times they had. Relatives were probably allowed to stay on the ward for midnight, he hadn't even asked. Unlike the café and the entrance to the children's wing, there is no tinsel in neuro. It is more of a Good Friday ward, but there has been a Christmas sort of feel to the place all the same. People love other people despite the wheelchair and the incontinence and a future of tapping out of wishes on adapted keyboards.

Edmund took his festive celebrations elsewhere, with a few drinks parties in the city as usual. The highlight was an outing to London as a Christmas/birthday treat all rolled into one for Mikey; it was a bit of a con, but at least the absence of birthday cards was less painful that way. As Mikey pointed out, Solomon wasn't allowed to send one, and as Edmund thought privately, who else was there? The trip took the boy back to the past anyway; he pointed at the map on the underground, that was where he lived with Paul, he said. Mikey's history was like reading the middle part of a trilogy and not quite knowing the plot or the characters from the beginning; the story could stand alone, as it said on the cover, but there was always the disconcerting sense that you were missing something. Particularly Valerie. More and more Edmund wished he'd known her the better to understand her son. All the little things he'd gathered indicated she was a rather brave and lovely lady, who did after all produce a rather brave and lovely son.

The first Christmas is always the hardest. He did the best he could: the lights in Regent Street, a visit to Hamleys where Edmund bought three brown bears as a stocking filler and a calendar that was on the Father Christmas list. He viewed it as a positive thing, Mikey being able to look ahead. He found the perfect one with a different musical instrument for every month – it was always music now with Mikey. He'd chosen a bright red boombox for his birthday present, having told Edmund that music was just a better way of talking. In the evening, they went to the pantomime. *Beauty and the Beast*.

'And are there any children out there who think they can wake up the beast? Because the beast has gone to sleep and we need to wake him up for Christmas.'

'I can sing,' said Mikey and he climbed over the backs of the seats and the coats and bags and other people's knees before Edmund could stop him.

Feeling physically sick, Edmund was terrified Mikey would commit himself to something impossible and make a fool of himself. No one ever made allowances, and he didn't look like a child who had problems. On stage, the giant white rabbit was hopping between the children whose hands were up so high they were coming out of their sockets, confident girls in pantomime best and swaggering boys belting their names out to roars from their families. It was inevitable that he would settle on Mikey, this child with a magnetism that drew people to him then terrified them with its force.

'The beast has promised he will wake up if we sing him a Christmas song. Do you think you can do that?'

A nod.

'And what's your name?'

'Mikey.'

'Can Mikey do that?' the rabbit asked the audience.

'Yes,' they all roared.

'I can't hear you,' the rabbit danced in a frenzy. 'Can Mikey wake the beast in time for Christmas?'

'Yes,' they roared even louder, spectators in the gladiators' arena.

'Then Mikey, my boy, we're all relying on you.'

The pantomime squirrels with gigantic tails climbed down from the trees (and even the trees had hands and faces), the owls flashed their luminous eyes from their perches, the grasshoppers and foxes and badgers gathered round the boy in the surreal woodland paradise, feigning anticipation on their masked faces and nose-snuffling paws.

'What are you going to sing, Mikey?'

Mikey whispered to the rabbit and the rabbit whispered to the conductor and the conductor whispered to the violins who picked up their bows. The cellists leaned forwards in their seats, the oboist and the flautist and the bassoon raised their instruments to their lips, and the opening bars of 'In The Bleak Midwinter' swelled and filled the auditorium. Everyone clapped and called their approval and then fell silent. Quietness in a theatre is as complete as quietness can be, thought Edmund, because everyone is holding their breath.

One thin boy, swamped by his hoodie, ignored the offer of a microphone and crept towards the beast and bent low to whisper in his grotesque ear.

'We can't hear you,' called the white rabbit, waving the microphone towards the boy, but Mikey wasn't listening to him. He was keeping his promise, he was singing to the beast.

'We can't hear you,' chorused the audience as they roared with laughter. The conductor looked from the rabbit to the boy to his players and back again, then took matters into his own hands and finished the scene with a drum roll and a flourish.

There was the briefest suspension of time before the audience rose to its feet and cheered the dumb show. Beside the boy the sleeping beast rubbed its eyes and stretched, heaved its huge bulk from the forest floor and turned its monstrous head. With claws matted in hair, it reached into its sack.

'A present, a present,' screamed the white rabbit in delight.

Off the stage, down the steps, up the gangway, out of the exit, Mikey fled. Edmund's response was instinctive. If he runs into the street, he'll get run over, if he runs away, I'll never find him, if I never find him, I'll have lost everything.

'I think he was a bit overcome by it all.'

An usher was standing very quietly at the entrance, her hand in his. In the street, Christmas lights swayed in the wind above the rain-shimmering pavements – illuminated planets this year, blue Earth, red Mars, silver Neptune, a universe of wonder – and behind them, in the theatre, the distant throbbing of 'Rudolph, The Red-nosed Reindeer' and all the other children, bringing the house down.

Falling into Edmund's arms, Mikey sobbed. 'I sang,' he said, 'and he woke up. Why were they laughing at me?'

'It's just that they couldn't hear you,' whispered Edmund. 'You did sing and you must have sung beautifully. If you stay to the end, you'll see that the beast changes because of the song you sang, because somebody loves him.'

Unsteady on his feet, Edmund is sheltering in the porch hiding from both the storm and the New Year. He sings as he remembers: 'What can I give you, poor as I am?'

Diana's Christmas offering to him was a guttural, primitive greeting of sorts. The single, apparently involuntary sound came from deep within her throat and was impossible to interpret. The nursing staff thought it must be the greatest gift of all, although unlike God's offer at this time of year, Edmund was not raising his hopes. He takes no gifts for Diana. No gold, frankincense or myrrh, no hope, no love. At some level she must sense his urge to slip away, turn out the lights and leave her in darkness, and his visits to her prison are no better than a torturer peering through the spyhole, his footsteps and jangling keys his orchestra.

New Year. A favourite quote of his father's comes to him. 'I said to the man who stood at the gate of the year, give me a light that I may tread safely into the unknown.' That's what he sees in other visitors at the hospital, the hand outstretched, the light in the eyes. 'Go out into the darkness and put your hand into the Hand of God.'

So Edmund goes, out into the darkness.

Like pale ghosts, the sheep scatter from him as he leans into the spitting sleet and stumbles drunkenly across the park, boots sinking into the sodden ground and slowing his progress. Monty is close to him, fretting. Never has the chapel felt more like a refuge, high above the rapidly flooding pasture, its back turned against the wind. He has not been here for some time. At Christmas he took Mikey to the crib service in the village church instead and afterwards the vicar showed them the Christmas tree where people could write the names of people they'd lost on paper stars and hang them from the branches. It was a memory tree, he explained, because Christmas can be difficult. So many stars, so many lost. Mikey wrote 'My Mum' and Edmund helped him slip the cotton loop over the needles. It was something about the hovering vicar and the women at the back of the church handing round mince pies, but Edmund could not bring himself to hang his own stars, and then later he couldn't bring himself to light candles in the chapel either. So now he is reading inscriptions in the dark, using the torch on his phone to search for affirmation of a New Year's resolution he has already made.

Where, O Death, is thy sting? Where O Death, thy victory?

They asked all the wrong questions, these ancestors. What about the pyrrhic victory we call life? All of us, driven by the cruel biological imperative to go on living, regardless of the cost. Diana, ambivalent and hesitating in her shadowland, what does she choose? Diana, goddess of the crossroads. Edmund, protector of wealth. Were they both damned even as they were christened?

Yea, though I walk through the valley of the shadow of death, I will fear no evil.

To the right of the door one of the earliest carvings in the chapel leers at him from the shadows: a primitive demon with a gaping mouth and lolling tongue, pinned down by a pentagon. A scholar once told him it was a sort of medieval graffiti. Edmund remembers taking Diana to the Rijksmuseum in Amsterdam, the two of them hand in hand laughing at the Bruegels. The other side of this pillar has a very different picture scratched into the stone, difficult to make out even in daylight, but he can see the simplistic upright lines which are trees, the repeated horizontal lines which is the water, and the disintegrating roman numerals beneath, CXXXVII, the very earliest representation of his Wynhope Psalm. Even then everyone liked the bit about the rivers and the songs and forgot about the ending, which tonight strikes Edmund as the only bit that counts. 'Daughter of Babylon, who are to be destroyed; happy shall he be that rewardeth thee as thou hast served us.' Death as revenge, death as punishment, eye for an eye, this Old Testament thinking does not usually feel comfortable to him, but in the third hour of that New Year it slips into the pew beside him and he finds himself taken with its company. When the chapel calls time and sends him back out into a black magic sort of night, there is no moon, only a thick and secret silence.

Shaking the rain from his coat, Edmund gravitates towards his computer and to a favourite site which seems particularly apt for a disoriented man on this, the first day. From its lonely orbit, the space station livestreams its unique view of the world. He finds its perspective soothing; how very slowly, slowly we are turning, turning; he imagines a vast pair of hands rotating the globe. It takes imagination to see the people on the planet ride, heads flung back and clinging on for dear life to the brown bits of land cast adrift amidst the flooding oceans, strapped into their hurricane and wildfire and mudslide experiences, their faces distorted by the calamitous wind, screaming for the cameras trained on their suffering. He's seen their pain often enough on the news: the crowds fleeing their villages with torn shirts and masks across their smoke-blackened faces and bare feet and bicycles and the bodies of children amongst the bloated goats and matchstick huts and single shoes floating. It never seems they have much choice. Things happen. But tonight the vast disasters in the circling world have come down to this one act: him, Edmund, at a desk and a decision made to snatch the future back.

Chapter Thirty-Eight

The head waiter at Goya's is very sorry to hear of Lady Diana's accident. Edmund thanks him for his concern and suppresses an ironic smile when he is guided to their 'usual table'. His old mate Dominic has not yet arrived. Edmund sits, as he always sits, facing the door. Diana would be opposite him, straightening her wine glass, ordering the sea bass, counting off the pearls he brought back for her from a business trip. In front of him everything turns to white: the tablecloth, her neck, the lifeless shells, her bloodless skin. It is only ever her head that he sees now, on its pillow, sliding left and right like a tipped doll, revealing the whites of her eyes, sometimes accompanied by growling the way his teddy bear used to rumble when he tipped him. The other morning at the hospital he lifted the sheets as if he no longer believed that the rest of her existed. The plaster had been removed, he felt the dead flesh of her legs, noticed the redundant skeletal structure of her ankles, the bones doing nothing but maintaining the shape of the flesh, the flesh doing nothing but maintaining the appearance of life. He knew from talk in the family room that with some patients doctors worked towards being able to ask them if they wanted to live. Would it be eyes right or eyes left for Diana? Once, she despised herself enough to try to kill herself; it is difficult to see if God has offered her many additional incentives to stay alive. Perhaps she will choose to live so she can seek forgiveness for the monster she has become? Or perhaps she will choose to live, simply to ensure that neither he nor Mikey will ever be free to enjoy their lives, choose to live to be the better monster? It doesn't matter. Since she has regained consciousness the medical focus is on rehabilitation. In theology Edmund studied the story of Eutychus, a man who fell asleep during a sermon and toppled out of a third-floor window. Everyone thought he was dead before Paul brought him back to life. That was the beginning of outsourcing the business of resurrection, and although he can see it could be a profitable enterprise, Edmund always had doubts.

It's not quite Dominic's job, but as good as, as Edmund understands it. At Oxford, he and Dominic partied hard, Edmund having to work hard to overcome the hangovers and essay crises which followed, but Dominic, he managed it all, the drink, the drugs, the women and academic success, and now he is one of the top neurosurgeons in the country and adviser to the government's medical ethics committee. And what do you do, Edmund asks himself, oh, a bit of this and that, nothing very much and nothing very well, he replies, and the empty chair laughs politely at what is apparently a joke.

A fly-on-the-wall documentary would have shown Edmund always in company at university, but friendship was never really his strong point and he notices the groups and couples around the restaurant, touching over the tables, leaning to one side to catch whispered conversations with their neighbours. Diana is not so different from him. He is surprised how few of her so-called girlfriends have visited more than once, and the cards he receives on her behalf are corporate, bought by other people's secretaries and rarely followed up with phone calls of concern. Her funeral would best be held in a small church. A shared experience of the absence of love or friendship is not the firmest of foundations on which to build a relationship. Dominic, however, he does count as a friend. On the rare occasions they meet up, the three decades past mean nothing compared to the three years they spent together. And here he is, looking good, looking bloody good.

'Don't tell me you've joined a gym,' Edmund says as they clasp each other, man to man. 'You look disgustingly well.'

'And you look disgustingly haggard,' says Dominic, handing over his coat to the waiter, 'although understandable. I'm sorry about Diana, I really am.'

The well-practised nod from Edmund gets them past that, and they meander through a bottle of wine, order another, exchange news of old friends, the City, the FTSE, Mongolia versus Patagonia.

'Which isn't why you suggested meeting up, is it?' says Dominic. 'I'm guessing what you really want to talk about is Diana . . . about what happens next.'

He always can see right through me, thinks Edmund, which is a relief. Diana could too, most of the time; he misses that, having someone to whom you don't have to explain everything, someone who knows more about himself than he does, like a parent with a child.

He blows his nose. 'Sorry.'

Although he deals on a daily basis with patients with the sort of injuries Diana has, Dominic says he cannot for the life of him really imagine how it feels to be sitting where Edmund is sitting now.

'No, but you do have knowledge, and knowledge, as they say, is power.' Edmund presses ahead. 'The team at Twycombe have been fantastic, can't fault them.'

'Anderson's very good, he was at Jesus College, you know, then at the Royal,' says Dominic. 'She couldn't be in better hands. I taught him myself.' He nods and the waiter tops up the glasses.

'Well, he doesn't beat about the bush in terms of how Diana is and what the likely prognosis is . . . and that's pretty bleak.'

Having ordered coffee, Edmund catches himself sweeping the crumbs from the table into the palm of his hand and the action sends a shiver down his spine but he continues. 'Despite all the talk, what I can't really get from them is what happens now. What are the choices?'

Dominic has taken the liberty of updating himself on Diana's status. He isn't sure he can add a lot more to what Anderson and his team say: long-term care, life-altering paralysis and possibly reduced brain function. There are aspects of her case which are medically interesting, he tells Edmund, some paralysis which makes sense neurologically, the legs for instance, other impairments which are harder to account for, the apparent impaired function in her right arm for example. Edmund should understand that the management of trauma is a dark art.

'But,' he says, 'that's not what you're here for, is it?'

Grateful for the reappearance of the waiter, with his cups and cafetière and side plates with chocolates and hand-made macaroons, Edmund doesn't respond. He wills the man to take his time with the coffee spoons and the sugar crystals, forget something, return, interrupt them again and again so he doesn't have to utter such words in this three-star Michelin altar. Dominic holds his gaze. That's why he must be so good at his job, to be able to stare hopelessness in the face and operate all the same.

'I'm guessing, Ed,' says Dominic, 'that the questions you want answered are to do with pulling the proverbial plug. Am I right?'

'God knows I loved Diana but . . .' The tense doesn't go unnoticed by either of them. 'Okay, love her. That sums it up in one, doesn't it? Jesus, I'm better at tenses in Latin than in my own language at the moment. Because, to be honest, I know I'm meant to hang around that bloody rehab ward saying how much I love her whatever happens, but, frankly, that's not true. Other people might think that, and I don't doubt their honesty, or if they're lying, it's only to themselves, but when it comes down to it, was it really a marriage made in heaven? You were at the wedding, what did you think?'

'I'm not really in a position to offer any judgement on that front, Ed. Mine wasn't exactly an amicable divorce.' Dominic checks his mobile, puts it back in his pocket. 'And to apply to the dilemma the analytical thinking in which you were so rigorously and expensively trained, in this case, the past is not strictly relevant to the future.'

'Point taken,' Edmund says. 'Present tense, then. To apply your logic, whether I love her now or not is not strictly relevant either. Agreed. But what is relevant is that she's not there, it's not her.' Edmund pre-empts Dominic's objection, holds up his hand. 'Hear me out. There's no one else I can say this to. I turn up, prattle away to her, read the paper, ask for her suggestions on the cryptic cross-word for Christ's sake. It's madness. It's like some Beckett play. As if she's going to suddenly say, oh, I think four across is Scandinavia. It's not going to happen, is it? Is it?'

'At this stage, it's impossible to say.'

'Even if there is a, what, one per cent chance, okay, let's look on the bright side, a ten per cent chance it might happen one day, a ten per cent chance that she'll sit up and say "Scandinavia" at the right time, what does the ninety per cent look like? Just a living death, for her, for me, for Mikey.'

Dominic pours the coffee. 'I wonder if you realise how much you've talked about him tonight. For a bloke who never wanted kids, it seems to me you've found one you'd quite like to keep.'

'I haven't even asked about yours,' says Edmund. 'I'm so sorry, I'm becoming selfish. Some godfather I am.'

'Forget them. They're all fine, up to a point. Expensive, but fine. And don't apologise, you've been a great godfather to Josh, through the divorce and all that. You always said it was in the genes, that you'd be a lousy father, and I always disagreed. If that's how you can be with this nephew of yours, well, he's a lucky boy, and, maybe, he's the best thing that could have happened to you.'

'You're not the first to say that,' admits Edmund, 'but don't you see' – the urgency in his voice is attracting attention, the group on the next table are glancing their way – 'we're trapped, all three of us. Mikey is unable to move on, to use the jargon, while she's still alive.'

Dominic raises his eyebrows.

Edmund lowers his voice. 'Between you and me, Dominic, some weird stuff went on when I was away. I think Diana completely lost it, she was pretty vile to the boy, and that's putting it mildly. I've found things on the computer, a map of the river . . .' It would be a relief to tell someone. 'Well, that's for another time, but I believe he's terrified of her, scared witless that she'll live. Now everyone's refusing to let her die. It's ridiculous. And apparently I don't have a say in the matter.'

'And what about you?'

Emptying the glass, Edmund has the sensation of being on the other side of the window, standing on the pavement, tapping on the glass, looking in on himself.

'What do you mean, me?'

'You say you are all trapped – Diana, Michael – but I'm asking, what about you?'

'Me? Of course I'm trapped too. What's next? Twenty, thirty years of waking up next to a . . .' Edmund struggles to find a word which is acceptable to himself, let alone to his oldest friend, a doctor. Vegetable? Basket case? Living corpse? Monster. 'You know what I mean,' he concludes. 'And on top of that . . .' He turns the plate with the four macaroons round and round in his hands, pauses, pushes the sweets towards Dominic, who shakes his head and waits. Edmund unwraps one, puts it back down again uneaten. 'Thank God it's not a fortune cookie.'

'On top of that?' prompts Dominic.

'On top of that, I'm pretty sure she was trying to kill herself. You know Wynhope, Dominic, you can't exactly fall out of the nursery window.'

'You can be pushed.'

'Who by?'

'I don't know. Who else was there? Could Michael have done something? Could that explain his behaviour and what you found when you got back?'

Someone's coat topples his wine glass. Edmund catches it, but even so, red wine spills onto the white table cloth. Almost imperceptibly, the stain is mopped up, the glass is topped up; that's what you pay for in a place like this, the invisible hand that makes everything better. The waiter slides away into the wings, there are apologies from the people leaving, then closing handbags, kissing and partings in a language he doesn't recognise. The taller of the two men throws his car keys to one of the women and they all laugh, over there, on their way out into the world, together.

'Michael,' prompts Dominic.

'Mikey,' says Edmund, taking a deep breath. 'I grant you he's a weird kid. He put up with years of living with some domestic violence pervert, and he's screwed up by the death of his mother and, yes, it seems likely, or possible, he unwittingly had a part in that. Then all the business with Diana, he's hardly going to be Mr Normal. But is he a murderer? No. I know him pretty well now and he wouldn't have been capable of it emotionally, let alone physically.'

'She didn't leave a note, though, did she?'

'Not exactly.' Edmund envies people who smoke. They have an excuse to walk away, to hunch their shoulders and hide their faces. 'But I can be pretty certain that by the end, she didn't like herself any longer. She didn't want to live with that person.'

Leaning over the table, Dominic speaks quietly, but with authority. 'You think if she was mentally in a state to make a decision, she would not want to live, but, despite that, she might do the whole eyes right thing and say yes. Don't interrupt me . . . you asked me here, Ed, so let me say it like it is. You think she would not want to live, partly because of the state she is in now, partly because of what life is likely to look like for her in the future, and partly because of how she might feel about what she's done in the past. You think you have evidence that she already wanted to die.'

'Yes. It's called jumping out of a second-floor window.'

'We need to discount that last point. The world is full of people who have tried to kill themselves, failed and gone on to live happily ever after, if, and it's a big if, that's what happened. As you know, suicide is a complicated matter, and given your family history, you are certainly not the best person to make judgements on what people may or may not want from that. Let's focus on her prognosis, what you assume would be her feelings about that quality of life and' – Dominic looks him straight in the eye, unflinching – 'what you assume will be the impact of her living on the quality of your life, more specifically your life with Michael.'

Edmund pushes back his chair, screws up his napkin. 'For God's sake, Dominic.'

'Oh, sit down, Ed. This is the conversation you wanted all night. It's just a little harder than you thought. You want to know if, how, when, she can be allowed to die.'

Edmund's phone vibrates in his pocket. He checks to make sure it's not Grace. 'Yes,' he says. 'I want to know. Is there any way out?'

Shaking his head, his oldest friend sounds just like Mikey. No No. Diana has not made her wishes clear, and, in the light of that, the doctors have no option but to treat her, to feed her, to ensure the safe functioning of her organs and to try their best to ascertain her wishes. It's been how long since the accident? Three or four months? And already she's breathing independently, showing signs of being able to respond to questions, making sounds, possibly regaining some movement in her upper body? No one would countenance even beginning to think about any alternative until at least a year has passed, and that would be assuming she regresses in either her cognitive or physical functioning, and, he emphasises, counting the points off on his fingers, 'even then it would be a lengthy legal process, highly unlikely to succeed. So the answer to your question is no. No.'

If Edmund could hit something, he would, but he can't, not in Goya's, not here, not now. It is what he expected Dominic to say, it is what they all say – Google, doctors, magazine articles in the Sunday papers – but that cannot be the end of it. He seizes his old friend's sleeve.

'Are you telling me,' he hisses, 'that there's no way round this?' Releasing his fingers, he stares at them as if they do not belong to him. 'Sorry. Look, we go back far enough, we always found ways round things, that was our trademark. How many summer balls did we gatecrash? Nothing was impossible. I know what you're telling me is correct, legally speaking, but I can't believe it's how it happens in practice, not when it's morally obviously crazy, or ethically, I don't know, I never did know the difference.'

People have come to Edmund in the past, not good friends, but people who thought themselves close enough, asking for share tip-offs, merger information, a bit of economy with the truth on the environmental assessment for the planning permission, personal email addresses of people in influential positions in compliance departments. It's how the world works. Now Dominic is the one with insider knowledge and access to the technology and Edmund's the one who's come knocking.

'You're the only person I know who can . . .'

'What you need to do, Ed, is stick with it for the next six months or so. It might seem like eternity, but time will pass. Do what you're doing, focus on the boy, come to London a bit more often, we'll meet up again. Time will pass, fishing starts again in March, and before you know it, by next summer, the position may be clearer. Things happen. And' – Dominic finishes his coffee – 'I'm not talking about bolts of lightning and miraculous recoveries, but the other side of the coin as well, pneumonia, blood clots. Nature sometimes has her way, regardless of what us doctors do to stop her. I know you'll find this hard to believe, but I've met patients who swore when they were alive they would never want to live like that. I've met families who have been equally sure their loved ones would not want to live like that, that they did not want to live with them like that, but then somehow there they are, living like that, and they all say they wouldn't change it for the world, that it's worth everything just to have them alive. Did you see that neuro work in Switzerland that was in the papers? Every single patient with locked-in syndrome who they managed to communicate with said they wanted to live. Actually, to be accurate, all except one. And Ed, you were in love with her once . . .'

Dominic pays. Maybe he thinks his financial problems are so bad he can't even put a card on the table for dinner, or feels sorry for him, or maybe he looks incapable of doing something as simple as getting out his wallet or remembering his PIN. Edmund does feel disabled. It is not unexpected, what Dominic says, just so unwieldy he cannot carry it home.

Outside the restaurant, they rub their hands and pull their collars up, make jokes about weak bladders and make promises to meet up again at the College Gaudy. The taxi pulls up, Edmund says he can do with the walk, and Dominic confirms his address with the driver, but before he climbs in, he turns back to Edmund.

'One word of advice,' he says. 'Don't go taking things into your own hands. It very rarely works out well.'

The taxi nudges out into the stop-start traffic, the world and his wife heading home. Dominic has some new woman on the go. He hasn't said much about her, but Edmund guesses that she's the source of the messages during dinner, imagines him unbuttoning his shirt, kicking off his shoes and getting into bed. Poor bugger, he'll say to his woman as he slips on top of her, what a fucking awful position to be in.

From pool to pool of light, Edmund creeps unsteadily along the Embankment. The pavements are slippery with ice and everybody is either overtaking him or coming the other way. Nobody is walking beside him. His father tried to teach him bridge once; he had this phrase, 'There's many a man walking the Embankment because he didn't lead trumps.' He is no good at bridge either, never seems to have the right hand. A thin layer of snow has already settled on the benches, so he leans on the wall and studies the abstracted reflections on the mudflats on the other side of the black low-tide river, no reason to it other than the swallowing current. Sounds tune in and out around him: a girl screaming incoherently into a mobile phone; reggae booming from a passing car; sirens; a group of young men all dressed as Elvis – a stag night, maybe – drunk, but definitely not dead. Dominic read his mind. They put away a lot of booze tonight. The wine of life is drunk and only the dregs are left. He's been thinking a lot about Macbeth recently. And Lady Macbeth. He struggles to remember another quote, something to do with plucked babies and brains.

Taking poorly judged decisions on speed and distance, Edmund crosses the road carelessly and is drawn to the entrance to the underground where he swipes his card and accepts the invitation of the tunnel even though he has no business there, nowhere to go. This is his sort of place tonight, littered and angry; these are his sort of sounds, mechanical and deafening, leaving no space for anything else, no air to breathe when the train blasts into the station and then pulls away, sucking the people and the life out of the place. He lets one, two, three trains pass; they all have different destinations but he isn't sure where he is going. He can't face the flat. He really thought Dominic might have had answers, or a set of instructions at least, though with hindsight that was unrealistic. The electronic board gives him a three-minute warning: train terminating at Angel. It is strange, staring down at the tracks, appreciating their offer, realising there would have been times, not so long ago, when he might have accepted their invitation, but he has Mikey now. If he is contemplating anyone's death, it is not his own.

Angel train: one minute.

'Are you all right, sir?' A man in a fluorescent jacket is reaching out his hand. 'I'm sorry, I didn't mean to surprise you. I was just wondering if you're feeling unwell.'

Stepping back from the yellow line, Edmund apologises. 'Just a little queasy,' he mumbles. 'Too much to drink, I expect.'

Train approaching. Staying close to him, the maintenance worker is obviously only partially convinced. The doors open.

'Is this your train, sir?'

Doors closing.

'No, I think I'd be better off walking, don't you? Fresh air.'

The roar of the departing train muffles in the tunnel. Just the two of them are left on the empty platform.

Embarrassed, Edmund takes a few steps towards the exit, then turns. 'Would you have stopped me? I mean, if I had been going to jump, which I wasn't, would you have stopped me?'

'I would've tried,' says the man.

'Why?'

'It's a beautiful night out there. Other people grumble, but I love the snow, it makes everything look so clean. My grandfather tells a story about when he came first from Pakistan and saw the snow. He thought the world had ended, but then he realised it had only just begun.' He smiles. 'No matter how bad things are, show me a man who doesn't laugh if he's throwing snowballs with the children.'

Edmund has to acknowledge the truth of that.

'They say it's the little things in life, don't they?'

'They do,' says Edmund, 'and they're probably right.'

'We all do what we can with what we have been given,' says the man.

'We do, we do indeed.'

Edmund holds out his hand and the maintenance man shakes it.

'As-sālamu 'alaykum.' 'Wa'alaykuma, as-salam.'

At the top of the stairs, Edmund stops in front of the transport map for southeast England, remembering Mikey's retracing his past the night of the hideous pantomime. You are here. With his finger, Edmund tracks the overground network due south, on over the Thames and through the suburbs, across the South Downs until he can almost smell the sea. The line arrives at a station whose name is familiar from a leaflet in the family room at the hospital. Eastham-on-Sea. Less than two hours' drive from central London. That makes it well over three and a half from Wynhope. The Angeline. Pictures of caring staff and the grateful smiling sick. You are here and she is there. Long-term care. A home away from home.

Chapter Thirty-Nine

'Are you going to bring her back to Wynhope?' Sally has popped round for one of her moral support visits and a glass or two after Edmund has attended the patient planning meeting at the hospital where there was welcome news, with certain qualifications. Diana is making such good progress: she sits up (with the help of an adapted chair); she smiles (although like a baby, sometimes it's hard to tell); she makes noises (of sorts). It is time to think about next steps.

Sally makes helpful suggestions. 'You could put her in the coach house, couldn't you? Plenty of room for live-in staff and it's all on one floor for the wheelchair. There's the downstairs bathroom for all the ghastly paraphernalia – bags and what have you. Ideal really.'

Lots of people have put 'idyll' and 'Wynhope' together, but not in this context. 'To be honest, Sally, I don't think I can manage it, not quite yet.'

'Quite right, darling. Far too much on your hands with Mikey. Isn't he doing well? God knows you've got enough cash in the attic to splash out on some luxury rehab place. Property's on the up again, isn't it? Earthquake dead and buried. You could flog a cottage or a field to pay for it. And my ex always used to say the FTSE 100 had a very short attention span. Look, don't beat yourself up about it. All she wants is for you to be happy.'

'She says that?'

'In an eyes right sort of way, not in so many words. But I know. It's all she's wanted ever since she met you.'

'It's what she did,' says Edmund, responding to Sally's suggestion and reaching for the crutch of historical precedence to support him. 'She had poor old Aunt Judy shipped out before you could say Jack Robinson.'

It's what one does when the going gets tough. The tough don't get going, they stiffen the lip and stand their ground and send their problems packing instead, usually to highly expensive residential establishments where someone else can sort them out. His estate manager has looked into the price he can get by selling a couple of outlying fields for development; they can't be seen from the house so it won't spoil the view and the income should finance Diana's care for a very long time. Nobody would be able to say he hadn't done everything he could. Some people might ask if it wouldn't be better to choose somewhere closer to home, but there isn't anywhere local even half as good as the Angeline. He'll claim to have researched every opportunity. Dominic's throwaway comment about not taking things into his own hands was irrelevant; he could never do that, but if he sends Diana to the Angeline he will achieve an absence almost as permanent and a distance almost as great, without the cost or consequences. If the land is going to be lost, it should be for affordable housing – he knows the village needs it – but he's opting to maximise the profit and save the here and now instead and roll the dice on the endgame. On the phone, the manager at the Angeline expresses surprise that Sir Edmund doesn't want to visit first, it's such an important decision and Lady Diana's so very young. In reply, Sir Edmund makes it clear that he has every confidence the Angeline can discuss his wife's needs with her specialist medical team and every faith that the care she will receive at their hands will be first class. The deposit has already been transferred. When he puts the phone down, it occurs to Edmund that online banking is helpful like that, you can pay for all sorts of things at arm's length.

Outside, the overnight snow has topped the yew hedges and the low morning sun casts sharp, geometric shadows on the white lawn. The bronze boy stands stoically above the frozen pond and Edmund's are the only footprints crossing the yard to the coach house where he checks the locked door. Because of Edmund's early start, Mikey has stayed the night with Grace so the scene before him is one of great calm: all the red mud ridges and erupting molehills in the park are buried under the even hand of snow; each tree revels in its very own sky, each bud wrapped safe against the frost. Edmund loves the lakes like this, snow on ice on water, and he feels the quietness as a pause between movements, only the intermittent drip of icicles measuring the slow thaw. It is Wynhope as it was always meant to be: a white world apart.

The winter conditions have brought chaos to the motorway. It takes him for ever and Diana is already in situ when he arrives at the Angeline with his shop-bought flowers and exclamations of what a nice room it is, even if she can't quite see the sea, and how homely it is, even if it isn't quite the same as Wynhope. Maybe they upped her meds to help her cope with the transfer in the private ambulance, or is it seeing her out of the ward and somewhere just a little bit more normal which makes her appear more incapacitated than ever, pushed in, put down, propped up, then arranged like a doll with stiff limbs, staring out from the middle of the bed when everyone rushes off to play with more interesting toys. Even the eyes right thing doesn't seem to work here.

No, it's kind of them to offer, but he won't stay for lunch.

'I'll come again very soon, Di. You sleep now, it will all seem better later.'

With the restrictive neck brace off, she has more movement, and it looks like a shake of the head, rather than a nod, but it could just be another involuntary spasm.

While with her, in her room, he can hardly even imagine leaving her there, leaving at all. But he does. Leave. Along the carpeted corridor, past the reproductions of Monet's lily ponds which line the walls, he walks as quickly as he can without actually running, hearing her voice pleading with him to come back, her paralysed legs pounding down the stairs after him, her mechanical fingers gripping the bottom of his coat as he slips out through the front entrance. Please don't go. Come back. That is how he used to be, a little boy in shorts on the first day of term outside the boarding house, looking the length of the long avenue of chestnut trees also still dressed for summer, despite the long winter term ahead. And did his father recover as quickly as he does now, because by ten, certainly no more than twenty miles along the motorway, Edmund has convinced himself that it is the right decision for everyone. She will be safe and well looked after and should make good progress and he can almost imagine her happily waving goodbye from her first-floor window overlooking the garden. By four o'clock he is back at Wynhope and school is over. In the park, Mikey and Monty and Edmund throw snowballs.

How time flies and how often he has to be at the office or at a meeting for Mikey or at the Riverside site. Edmund only makes it down to Eastham twice before the first care review: the first time he couldn't stay long and the second time she was being whisked away for a scan, silly of him to have forgotten when it was in his diary all along. This time, with forty minutes to kill, Edmund parks in the centre of the small town and wastes time on the main street with its predictable chain stores, the mass of people spending and getting and losing, the drab-coloured coat of the capitalism which keeps him warm.

The coffee shop looks out over the estuary. It isn't the sort of thing he does usually, but upstairs he finds a table free in the window and experiences the same degree of pleasure he used to get as a child claiming the front seat on the top of a London bus. From here, the tops of the masts are visible, the boats grounded and tilted at low tide, and safe behind glass he can study the monstrous seagulls, sentry soldiers of the sea wall. It is hot inside, mothers are unwrapping their toddlers and a man bustles in with the wind and a boy about Mikey's age who's been to the doctor and will soon be as right as rain, and Edmund is loath to leave this café and its humid hum of the living.

At the Angeline, the manager, the charge nurse, the liaison nurse from the hospital, the physiotherapist, the speech therapist, Uncle Tom Cobley and all – shall I find some more chairs? – introduce themselves and call him Edmund and suggest having a few words before Diana is wheeled in to join them. How easy it is to hand over your problems to a team and for those problems to become polished and professionalised, how good they look on the shelf. He chooses a custard cream, changes his mind and takes a Bourbon, noticing the hair on the back of his hands and the size of his shoes as he crosses his legs. He is the only man in the room and he makes a conscious effort to talk about Mikey as if being a good father might give legitimacy to a husband who never visits his wife. They sit on chintz sofas and armchairs, balance their coffee on sturdy side tables. The small lounge where they are meeting is designed to look like a room in a grand house, with its *Country Life* magazines and a piano and expensive shades of paint, but he recognises the ways in which it is unnaturally clean and subtly adapted for those who will no longer be riding horses or passing the port and there is no sheet music on the stand. The team are so pleased with Diana's progress: her strength is returning, she has much better control of the neck muscles and even some slight movement in the fingers of the left hand. The last medical review – such a shame he couldn't be there – reiterated the difficulty in ascertaining the cause of some of the upper body paralysis, the right arm for instance. Scans had confirmed that there is no physiological or neurological reason for it to remain paralysed, and the charge nurse thumbs through Diana's file and reads sections out loud, as if to emphasise her role as messenger rather than message: 'at some point in the future, it may be helpful to give consideration to possible psychogenic disorder'.

'You mean she's making it up?'

Of course not. Psychosomatic illness is a complex field, pain is genuinely felt by the patient, but our minds and bodies are inextricably linked, especially if there has been trauma. And there has been trauma, Edmund acknowledges silently, there has been a lot of trauma, and curiously he notes that it has been a long time since his IBS has flared up. He tunes back into the meeting. They are saying how this links to their other concerns: how isolated Diana is, how she resists any form of communal activity, how she still chooses to eat all her meals in her room, that she can't really be said to have made herself at home at the Angeline.

'The same with interaction skills,' adds another professional, a language and communication something or other. 'She's still reluctant to engage in speech therapy and refuses the enhanced laptop which could make life so much richer for her.'

'Oh, she can talk a little and she does sing.' This comment comes from an older woman, the only one who has had to fetch her own upright chair from the dining room next door. She sits on the edge of this circle of professionals.

'Sorry, Margaret? Do tell us.' The manager turns to Edmund and explains that Margaret is a care assistant, a gem, she probably knows more about Diana's day-to-day presentation than anyone, but it's said with a patronising smile that implies Margaret's understanding of emptying bags and wiping bottoms is nothing compared to their professional competencies.

'She sort of sings, when she thinks no one's listening.'

Edmund is not the only one surprised. What does she sing?

'She sings the Psalms.'

'The Psalms?'

'Maybe not quite. The Psalms reggae style if you like.' With a big smile, the care assistant hums the popular reggae song for the benefit of the meeting. 'By the rivers of Babylon, where we sat down.'

When Edmund suggests she could add 'Red Red Wine' to her

324

repertoire, they laugh politely, probably on account of his title, probably because he's the one who settles the account, either way he realises his sarcasm has not got down well.

As if neither Margaret's insights nor the singing count for much, the speech therapist brings them back to the agenda. 'There are some memory issues. Are you familiar with PTA?' She turns to Edmund and doesn't wait for a reply. 'Post-traumatic amnesia. Complicated, but all about what the client's capacity is, not just to remember, but to form new memories.'

Edmund is aware that he is thinking of Mikey, how together they are knotting and knitting new memories, and that almost trumps the resentment he feels for Diana's pick'n'mix recollection policy.

'We could do some very useful work around memory if she would talk.'

That's the professional opinion. That, and the summary conclusion that Diana presents as very withdrawn and depressed.

'Depressed,' says Edmund. 'Yes. She is a woman used to being in control. I imagine as the extent of her problems have become clear to her she must be very depressed. I thought about her mood last time I was here, I worried about it all the way home,' he lies.

The remaining discussion revolves around the fact that Diana is refusing antidepressants and whether or not an ethics committee meeting should be convened to overrule her wishes and administer them anyway, just to break the cycle. In which case, thinks Edmund, there are plenty of other decisions the ethics committee can make and plenty of other cycles it can break.

'Now, let's invite Diana in and see what she has to say.'

Chapter Forty

The waves queue up in straight lines along the length of the coast, inconspicuous little arrivals, hurrying through life with their heads down until their time comes, finally making it to the shore only to be broken against the beaten brown of the breakwaters, losing all identity amongst the million shards of shingle who have gone before. Death is not unusual. Every second across the world, untold numbers of people die. In the scale of requests, it is not such a big thing: it would cost nothing, or everything.

The beach is almost empty. Edmund walks because walking usually helps. To his right, a windsurfer has caught the keen breeze and allowed himself to be spirited towards the sly horizon, but now he is struggling with the sail, straining his bodyweight against the bar to bring himself back to land. He said no, Diana, no, she shouldn't think like that, life would get better, just see how he is holding her hand, and he can feel her fingers almost closing on his, listen to how she can speak, it may be a croak or a rasp, but there are memories, aren't there, and words, whispered words loud enough to scare the sandpipers picking for a living along the edge of the surf.

Further on, the beach is trimmed with bungalows, shells in the front gardens and painted pebbles and one with a For Sale sign leaning in the offshore wind in the way that black widow trees turn their backs on the cliffs in Cornwall. The curtains are pulled and the paint is peeling – it was somebody's home, once. Edmund imagines the grown-up, married and moved-away children putting the house on the market, everything going in the skip, her recipe books, Mother's Day presents from the old days, her odd stockings. Home. He brought some Chanel for Diana today. When he kissed her cheek, the smell of home was stronger than the smell of air fresheners; it was the scent of Wynhope, early evening before heading up to London for the opera, fastening her jade locket around her long white neck, his swan, he called her, at times like that. She didn't actually say that what she wanted was to return to Wynhope, that if that was not possible then death was the next best thing, but surely that was what she meant. She said very little, but she said enough. At the window in her room, which only opened so far, he looked down on the ordered rows of bedding plants and lurid forsythia bushes which lined the immaculate paths through the Angeline's terraces, a little like Mikey's plastic plants, each pressed into the correct Lego slot. Those sterile beds are no substitute for the richness of the gardens at Wynhope; they are like the nursing home itself, modelled on a country house, but with no soul, no history. He often thought that the English obsession with the past was unhealthy, but to live without it? Maybe that is how Diana feels, a contemporary structure of a woman, empty inside, memory uncertain, history denied, future defined, in which case, who can blame her for asking? When you tap the Angeline, it is hollow, it has taken the word 'home' and abused it for its own ends. He has done the same with the word 'husband'.

Stepping to one side to let an old man pass him on the boardwalk, Edmund has his own moment of illumination as the sun temporarily transforms the sea into white gold: the pensioner has a Dachshund in one hand and a plastic bag in the other. We are all of us looking for somewhere to dump the shit.

He cannot – will not – bring her back to Wynhope. He is not

prepared to lose Mikey in order to save Diana. It is as simple as that. Nor did she expect him to. It was her selflessness which was the most painful thing about the whole hideous conversation. Her lips blurting the words and her tongue getting in the way, short splurges of speech and saliva, each one apparently exhausting her, and any platitudes offered in reply ignored as Diana summoned yet more energy from her depleted reserves.

'Sorry.'

'Just the two of you. Happy.'

'This is the way I want.'

The stones he skims across the sulking sea barely skip more than once. He used to be the best, collected the smoothest, flattest, roundest pebbles from the beach in Cornwall where they went on holiday and brought them back in his suitcase to Wynhope where he could make them dance from one side of the lake to the other. Perhaps he can take Mikey there one summer, teach him to skim, to swim, to hit the tennis ball for six and send the fielders wallowing into the waves, to fall asleep with the window open and hear the roar of the surf in the shell at your ear. There is a whole world of happiness waiting for them both if they are allowed to inherit it. Wet shoes. Edmund jumps back. Without him noticing, the tide is flooding in, pools of foam leave scallop patterns in white lace all the way along the canvas beach. A childhood poem comes to mind: 'King Canute sits down by the sea, up came the tide and away went he.'

With Diana propped up in her specially adapted chair, he tried to talk to her. Her head rocked against its cradle continuously, it made it hard to know where to look. He crouched opposite her, close to her, leaned in towards her, touched her senseless knees.

She isn't to worry.

She's been unwell ever since the earthquake.

He should never have left her.

'Listen, Diana. Are you listening? If you're worried about what I'll find out,' he said, 'then you mustn't be. Because I know everything already. I know and I understand everything.'

Spasms engulfed her upper body.

He thought she might no longer be able to smile, that the system of pulleys which heave our cheeks into position were snapped, but he was wrong. She smiled that proper Diana smile which had always won him over no matter what, and that was when she asked. Out loud. Quite audibly, quite clearly, no doubt about it.

'Help me die.' Then, as if to rule out any possibility of misunderstanding, she repeated her request. 'Help me die, Ed. Please.'

Entering the neuro ward he used to wish for her death, he prayed for her death as he knelt in his chapel, he condemned the medical profession for failing to let her die, he blamed her for struggling to survive and fantasised about dealing with her himself, but not once had he realistically considered doing that. Not once. The wind is picking up, the swollen waves are sucking the shingle down the beach. Reaching a smooth swept patch of sand, Edmund squats down and lets the grains run through his hands. Ovid. The classics always had a lot to teach him: the Sybil who asked to live for as many years as the grains of sand she held, but made the terrible error of forgetting to ask for eternal youth, her body withering until it was so small it was kept in a jar and only her voice was left. I yearn to die.

Doing nothing is always an option. The sin of omission appeals to Edmund. He can pull the waters over his head night on night, year on year, allow himself to be washed up with the driftwood, a flotsam and jetsam sort of human being, tangled in orange rope and hung with seaweed, an ordinary man of whom too much was asked and so did nothing. Nothing except hopefully keeping his boy on an even keel and visiting his shrivelling wife from time to time until the visits become so few and far between the past is no longer enough.

Stone after stone, Edmund the fielder, the rock the stumps. Miss. Miss. Hit and split and bounce in to the water. Howzats. Another hit, another. He has his eye in now. The other option is do as she asks. If she had muscles to hold tight, as tight as his hand grips this pebble, she would do it herself, dash herself against the stones; all she is asking is that he will be her right-hand man.

Once there may have been absolutes: thou shalt not kill, for example. Today there are only lines in the sand, gone for good with the last wave, but back again tomorrow. The sea thrashes its history against the shore again and again, relentlessly regurgitating, recycling, reliving; its only future to repeat, its only outcome, the grinding down of stones. Edmund feels he has lived too long in the ocean, swimming against the tide; he has always preferred the river.

Turning his back on the coast, he finds his car and sits for a moment, reluctant to start the engine. A driver looking for a space calls out, 'Are you moving, mate, or what?', so Edmund crawls out of the car park towards the main road, past a garish notice board welcoming everyone to a Sunday service at the Baptist church on the corner.

'In my father's house are many mansions,' it says.

As usual, it is a question of interpretation.

'Is she talking? What did she say?'

The three wise men, as he calls them – Mikey, Monty and the bronze boy – are lined up waiting for him when he gets home. The report card reflects a bad day at school, and Edmund kicks himself for not having let the staff know he was visiting Diana. It's no excuse, he tells Mikey, you can't have a meltdown every time I go to the Angeline.

'But did she talk? What did she say?'

'No, she didn't talk, not properly,' he lies. Some truths are too difficult. There must come a point when if you fold darkness upon darkness you will leave a child blind. 'I suggest you go and do your homework to make up for today's performance at school and we'll catch up over supper. Take Monty with you, go on.'

Getting his coat out of the car, Edmund feels in the pocket. 'Hang on. Come back here, you. A present from the seaside.' The stone is a perfect oval, thin as silk and as smooth, one of the best he has ever found. 'It's for skimming,' he explains.

Examining his gift more closely, Mikey observes and reads. 'M for Michael, how did that get there?'

Edmund did that, the old childish habit of getting one stone and using it to chalk your initial on another. The writing never stayed, but at that moment he always used to feel he was worth something. He was wrong.

'You look worn out,' says Grace, once they are alone in the kitchen. 'All that driving up and down to see Diana, you'll make yourself ill.'

'It's been a long day,' says Edmund. 'Do you want a cup of tea? I'm making one.' It sounds so casual, but fails to conceal how desperately he needs her to stay.

'I should be off in a moment,' she says. Grace avoids talking about Diana, Edmund has noticed that before. 'Still, a few minutes won't hurt. Is Diana worse then? Mikey was wondering if she's talking?'

Taking his time, filling the kettle, getting the milk from the fridge, Edmund replies from the larder, 'Yes, she's talking, but I haven't told him.'

Grace plonks herself down at the kitchen table.

'Well, very few words. But she's lucid. She asked me a favour.'

There is some sort of non-committal grunt from Grace, who no doubt thinks Diana is capable of being a grasping woman even from a wheelchair.

'She asked me to help her finish it all.'

'Finish what? Oh, you don't mean . . . Have I got the wrong end of the stick?'

'No, you haven't. She doesn't want to live any longer.'

'It's so gloomy in here today and it's not even that late.' Grace turns on the lights and hovers close to the switch as if everything might suddenly go dark. 'Oh, Edmund.'

'I'm sorry,' he replies, 'I shouldn't have said.'

'No, don't apologise. Poor you. But I suppose with her disabilities and all, you can't blame her. I wouldn't wish that on my worst enemy. And not being able to live here with you at Wynhope, that must be the worst. Having to be in a home.'

Grace is not making things any easier.

'Anyway, there's nothing I can do to help her. The medical profession won't oblige, Dominic made that clear enough, and I can't exactly go taking things into my own hands. I wouldn't know where to start for one thing.' Edmund allows the Aga to warm him as he sips his tea, he felt chilled to the bone all the way home.

'I hate to say it, and I know you can't or anything, but it would be a release, wouldn't it, and not just for Diana, but for you and Mikey? He worries the whole time about her, doesn't he? But, as you say, it's a non-starter. Listen to me, rabbiting on.'

From here Edmund can see the railings through the kitchen window and beyond them the field, the pale pregnant sheep and the white flowers in the blackthorn trees by the winter wood, iridescent in the fading light. Diana used to stand here like this, talking, often with her back to him. If he had been here then, he would have seen her fall. Did she stand here and see herself falling?

'I hope that young man's not eavesdropping, he's a devil like that.' Grace checks the dining room, pokes her head out of the back door. 'All clear,' she says. 'He's not doing his homework but he's playing with that little Down's boy who you said could keep his pony here, bless him. They're quite good friends. The mum's there too so he's quite safe.'

The remains of his tea go down the sink, the mug in the dishwasher, the milk in the fridge. His one pathetic act of local charity is not going to weigh much against manslaughter when the scales are brought out.

'Thanks for the company, Grace,' he says. 'Life is so busy now Mikey's here we never seem to have the time to chat. You should head off.'

He shouldn't have said anything. Diana would hate him for it, and Grace is a very moral woman, she will think less of him for it.

The television allows news of worse things happening elsewhere to fill the space left by her leaving, but then unexpectedly Grace is back, a few things from the washing line over her arm. She drapes them on the Aga rail.

'I forgot these,' she says. 'They needed a good airing, but now they're damp.' Feeling one of Edmund's shirts as if to check it's dry, she presses it to her cheek. 'I don't know how much you know, but I've plenty reasons for hating Diana. But I wouldn't wish a life of suffering on anyone. I'll have a word with John.' And before he can object, she's gone.

Searching the corners of the past few years, Edmund fails to come up with anything which might have led a woman such as Grace to spit such a commitment with such venom. Her relationship with Diana appeared to sour after the wedding, some time during that summer anyway. He had put it down to differences of opinion about the house – Grace's sense of ownership, Diana not being used to managing staff – but none of that accounted for this outburst. Nor does he really want Grace talking to John. True, John is a man not unaccustomed to death, but it hasn't done his mental state any favours pulling soldiers out of bombed-out buildings in Northern Ireland, patrolling the killing fields of Afghanistan. It's left him always with one foot in the past. Killing is not even the right word for what Diana is suggesting. If Edmund is considering anything it is from a different genre: painted yellow rather than splashed in red; played out to piano music heard from a distance over a spring garden, not to the rattle of war; it is barely physical at all. In the clinics in Switzerland, they use chocolates to sweeten the pill. If he loved her, it would be easy; it is the hating that damns him.

Chapter Forty-One

It never rains but it pours. February is heading towards being the wettest month since records began. The river floods the meadows, its dull thunder thudding out the soundtrack to Edmund's aimless walks through the sodden park; it is so far out of its banks it is impossible to tell where it begins and ends, and he keeps Monty on a lead for fear of him being swept away. Even when the rain stops, Wynhope echoes to the persistent spluttering of blocked gutters and water butts. Everything is wet, the kitchen floor permanently filthy with paw prints and pools shaken out of Mikey's soaked coats. Last night's deluge has even carved a miniature stream through the gravel and water is seeping under the front door and pooling around the feet of the grandfather clock. The main line to London is out of action. Edmund has nowhere to go but here, and here is a difficult place to be. Grace has not followed up on her hints of help, but she has planted a seed which is growing as living things tend to do. On top of that, there is now some palaver at therapy and he is expected at school for a review meeting.

It started when Mikey insisted on taking something into the therapy room with him. It looked pretty innocuous to Edmund, just a yellow plastic bag with a book or something in it which he refused to show him. Edmund was surprised when Sofia made such a big thing of it. Apparently, the agreement is that children take nothing into the therapy room and take nothing out. As a result, Mikey didn't go in either and cemented himself in the waiting room for the entire hour. To Edmund, the child and the therapist were both as stubborn as each other, but he didn't say so. The next week, having given it great thought and consulted her supervisor, Sofia allowed him to take the mystery bag in after all, and that, Edmund hoped, would be that. Except nothing is ever simple with Mikey, and Edmund has been summoned to meet Sofia himself because something went on in that session and Mikey has refused to attend since.

'Is it something he said?' he asked on the phone.

'More what he hasn't said,' Sofia replied.

They meet in her office, not in the therapy room, which is a disappointment for Edmund. This is too ordinary a room with its computer and phones and dirty mugs. In carefully arranged easy chairs, at ninety-degree angles to one another, they take their seats. On a little coffee table to her left is a box of tissues and Mikey's therapy notes in a bound blue A4 book, which, however hard Edmund tries, he can't read from here. They start with an offer of coffee, as well as a few words on the ubiquitous subject of the rain, and as she puts the kettle on, Edmund comments that Mikey never tells him anything about therapy except one occasion when he was asked to tidy his room at home and he'd replied that he'd already tidied up in therapy. Sofia laughs, she remembers that session very well; he'd created chaos in the room, all the art stuff everywhere, the sink overflowing, the playhouse wrecked, then he tidied the whole lot up. It was very hopeful, Mikey having the experience that things can be messed up and then put right. What can Edmund say, except that he can see that must be so. She must be a bit of a mind reader, this Sofia; God knows she'll probably have him arrested if that's the case. The water has just boiled when a high-pitched alarm goes off and Sofia needs to pop out and see if any assistance is needed with the children.

The temptation is too great. By leaning forwards and swivelling the notebook round, Edmund is able to read her accounts of the therapy sessions. At first it's hard to make sense of the transcript, but then he works out that most of it is a literal description of what the patient does: anything Sofia says is in italics and her comments are underlined. He scans quickly, conscious that at any time he might be caught cheating.

Session 7

M repeated what has become a familiar pattern, going straight to the sink and filling it with water. He took the soap dispenser and squirted some into the water, swishing it around until it made bubbles. He sang as he played. He scooped the bubbles into his hand and brought them over to show me.

You've made something beautiful this morning. Interesting, as well.

This account is recognisable. Edmund heard Mikey singing a carol that day when he came to collect him; the window was open. At the end of that session, Mikey cried for fifteen minutes and refused to leave. He had to be physically manhandled out of the room. Edmund knows that already; it's what Sofia made of it that interests him.

This session held extreme contrasts. It seemed that for the first time M admitted the possibility of fun and beauty in his playfulness with the bubbles, also able to accept something of the transitory nature of good things. His singing felt like a performance, rather than a communication, but perhaps he was also showing me he could communicate and would, when he was ready.

It is not clear to me what prompted the extreme emotional response and collapse into tears. As he cried, I was made to punitively experience helplessness, an inability to understand real sadness, powerlessness. I also had the strong sense of things that were not able to be spoken in words, only in tears.

I was not surprised that M found it painful to leave. He exposed more of himself in today's session – both highs and lows – and must have felt very vulnerable.

These are difficult words for Edmund, to see in black and white the boy's pain, which he knows he feels but which is rarely expressed to him directly. In fact his increasingly normal behaviour at home, for want of a better word, sometimes worries Edmund. He doesn't know where all the difficult thoughts go. He does now.

The door swings open. Sofia looks flustered. 'I'm so sorry.'

Hastily getting to his feet to disguise his snooping, Edmund turns the book around.

'There's a bit of a problem, I need to stay and help. I may be another ten minutes or so before someone can relieve me. Would you mind waiting?'

Of course. As soon as she has closed the door behind her, Edmund picks up the notebook.

Session 8

M arrived at therapy on time and came straight into the room. He sat down on the armchair opposite, swinging his legs and smiling.

You seem happy to be here.

Yes.

(This is the first time M has said yes in these sessions. He has spoken in the two previous sessions, but only to say no.)

Yes?

Yes yes yes yes yes.

He laughed, quite spontaneously. He got up from the armchair and opened the box.

What shall we do? (speaking to himself?)

I don't know if you're speaking to me or not. Are you talking to me?

337

He did not respond.

This one.

He got one of the plastic figures from the tin.

This one will do, you can be her.

He got another plastic figure from the tin.

<u>The sense in the room was that there were two other people in the room, but I was not one of them.</u>

M found some tissue paper and Sellotape.

You.

He picked up one of the figures, apparently indiscriminately, wrapped it up in tissue paper and wound the tape around the small parcel before lying it on the edge of the table.

That looks like a present for someone.

M turned round as if surprised that I was there. He returned to his play. He repeated the same procedure, saying 'you next', picking a model, this time a man, and wrapping him up. He struggled to break the tape and turned again to look at me and said, 'Scissors please.' I took the scissors out of the high cupboard and gave them to him.

It feels nice for me to be able to help you.

He put his finger in between the blades and made a cutting motion, looked at me and stopped. Then he put a piece of his hair between the blades and cut off a small amount and held the hair out to me.

That's your hair, whether you've cut it off or not.

He threw his hair in the bin under the sink and held his hands under the tap for a long time. He came towards me, took some of my hair in his hand and made as if to cut it. I stayed still. He was leaning over the chair, very close and I experienced a strong urge to protest.

No, don't do that . . . I won't, don't worry.

He sat back down at his box with the model figures.

Thank you. I didn't like the feeling that you were going to cut my hair without my permission. I'm happy you didn't.

No response. During the following ten minutes, he wrapped up all except one of the figures and laid them in a row on the edge of the table. He said, 'Now what?' I repeated the question, I was ignored. He took the blanket from the doll's cot, but then said sorry and returned to the cot with a cushion to cover up the doll.

That's kind, to think the doll might be cold and you can help her.

M did not even appear to hear me any longer. He laid the blanket out on the floor, next to the toy box. He took the first figure selected and made that figure push all the wrapped-up models off the box and onto the blanket, one by one. He then folded up the corners of the blanket and rolled it up so that all the models were inside and then he put the entire package in the toy box and closed the lid. The remaining figure was made to dance on top of the box.

You have put all the people except one in the blanket in the box. What will happen now?

I've got circus animals at home.

That's the first time you've mentioned home in one of our sessions.

Haven't I? (surprised) **They've got their own box. It's nearly time, isn't it?**

When I agreed, he put the remaining model figure in his pocket. I reminded him of the rule that everything stays in the therapy room and will be there for him at the next session. He hesitated then handed the remaining model figure to me.

You look like you trust me to keep this safe.

He nodded.

I'll put the figure back in the tin for safekeeping.

He shrugged. He waited at the door and left quietly at the end of the session.

<u>This was a very painful session for me. M took the decision to speak, but I experienced great difficulty in replying as if he could still not be understood or responded to. I felt I could not meet his needs. On top of that, the difficulty I felt in commenting</u>

339

on his game or joining his play was debilitating. There was a strong experience of more than one M in the room and of being excluded by both of them. There were also poignant moments such as covering the doll, which seemed quite spontaneous and confirmed what people report, that M has a very kind and loving nature. Having said that, the threat of a potentially violent child was strongly experienced when he approached my hair with the scissors.

I struggle to bring meaning to his play with the models. Each one was wrapped carefully, deliberately, the predominant sense of the action was of silencing, burying. The omnipotence of M identifying himself with the last model standing was typical of many of his gestures, but mitigated by the need to hand himself over to someone else to keep safe. There were two occasions in this session where M asked for help for the first time and he mentioned home. It would be interesting to note whether this is mirroring increasing trust of his uncle and an increasing faith in the stability of his home placement.

As it is now half way through the planned therapy sessions, I plan to meet with Edmund soon to review progress.

Edmund does not struggle to interpret Mikey's play. The triumphant figure is not Mikey, but Diana. Diana, who successfully drove everyone away from Wynhope and ended up dancing over the buried bodies of both her sister and her nephew. It's Diana who locks people away in boxes. It's Diana Mikey wants to hand over and make sure she can never hurt him again. It's Diana who must have felt omnipotent to him. With one eye on the clock, Edmund skips over the session where Mikey took his plastic bag and wasn't allowed in and moves on to the most recent notes.

Session 11

As I anticipated, M brought the plastic bag to this session. In the waiting room I told him that I had been thinking hard about the bag and about how important it seemed to him and had decided to let him bring it in to therapy.

M came in immediately. He stood inside the room looking around, then put the bag under the cushion on the chair where he often sits so that it could not be seen. He then sat on top of that cushion.

Well, you've brought the bag in and you've hidden it, but not very well. I can find it pretty easily. But it's your bag and you're in charge of what happens to it.

The start of the session repeated the game, filling the sink. Then he wandered around the room fiddling with various toys, the house, the model figures and then the catch on the window. He did not settle. At the table, he scribbled illegibly on endless pieces of paper, screwing each one up before standing on top of his chair and throwing it into the air, watching it fall to the floor, beginning on the next. He ignored all my interpretations, comments or offers of help. He looked repeatedly at the chair with the bag hidden under the cushion.

We are half way through the session now. The bag was very important at the beginning and I notice you keep checking it's still there. Do you want to open it?

No.

This feels like a game. Do you want me to guess what's in the bag?

No.

M tidied up the models, cleaned the table, put all the pens back in the case, all the paper in the bin and emptied the sink until the room looked the same as when he arrived.

You've made everything clean and tidy just like it was at the beginning of the session, almost as if you haven't been here, as if nothing's happened. All that's left that's different is the bag under the cushion.

M retrieved the yellow plastic bag, pulled out a black A4 ring binder and put it on the floor besides the door.

It's a file. I can see it's got paper in it. And now you've put it by the door so neither of us can go in or out without touching it. Someone's going to have to do something with it.

M sat on the chair, holding the cushion to his chest, rocking slightly, making occasional moaning sounds. This lasted four minutes.

No, no.

Maybe it's enough for you to know that you've brought it here, I know it exists, and we've shared that. I won't read it unless you hand it to me and ask me to. It feels like a private thing. This is your choice.

M took himself into the house, with the cushion, closed the door. I was aware that he was not asleep, every now and again he peeped out through the cloth.

I can see you're checking that I haven't touched your file. That you can trust me. Well, I haven't touched it or read it. And I won't, I promise, unless you give it to me.

M remained in the house like this until the end of the session. Once I had counted down the time, he came out, picked up the file and put it back in the yellow plastic bag. He then vomited violently and the session ended.

After he left, I was aware I felt furious with Michael, for the mess on the carpet, the lingering smell of sick, for having allowed him to bring the bag into therapy and then having tortured me with it and then having regurgitated my decision. Torture was a word which came into my mind often. That and repeated questions: why didn't he give it to me to read, why didn't I take it, why bring it in if I wasn't allowed to see it? I wondered why I hadn't just offered to read it, but that felt ungenerous. I concluded I was becoming something of a torturer myself, obsessed with getting Michael to tell the truth. It is more important that Michael is able to express himself, not rely on short cuts or gimmicks like the file, particularly as he was not able to ask me to read it. The onus was being passed to the therapist, when it should lie with the patient. I felt I had made the right decisions, but was left with the unsettling concern that by not reading the file I had thrown something vital away. When I looked again at my notes, it was interesting to note that while I was waiting in silence I had drawn several pictures of keys.

I was right (see above). M has refused to attend any more therapy sessions. To be reviewed re plans for future therapy. Meeting with EH to be arranged asap.

There are earlier sessions recorded, obviously, but Edmund does not turn back. He closes the book, holds it tight to his chest and paces. There's really nowhere to go. The room is little more than a converted cupboard in this old house, with four white walls and one small window looking out at a high fence. The books on the shelves might have answers – *Psychotherapy, Silence and Shame, Put Me Back Together Again: Psychotherapy and Severely Deprived Adolescents* – but there again so might the pictures drawn by children and displayed on the walls. There is an elephant with a balloon (by Ellie), a waterfall surrounded by flowers and parrots, (no name), a boy and a snowman on top of a mountain (by Michael, another Michael presumably). The pain from the therapy record is physically felt in Edmund's chest. The file must be a secret diary kept during his terrible imprisonment and the pages a record of torture and pain and isolation. He thinks he has been building such a bond, but Mikey is not able to share this with him; it has to live taped to the bottom of a cardboard box, only the circus animals trusted with its safekeeping.

'What should we do about this file of Mikey's?' Edmund asks when Sofia finally returns, apologising profusely that they've run out of time and will need to reschedule. 'He's hidden it away again. Shall I ask to see it?' Despite the terrible repercussions there may be if its contents are revealed, enough is enough. It is time for the truth to be known.

'You can ask Michael if you feel that's the right thing to do, of course,' Sofia replies. 'But don't be disappointed if he says no. And don't, whatever you do, take things into your own hands and break his trust by trying to read it when he's at school. That way always ends badly as mothers of teenagers know only too well.'

'I think I have some idea what this might all be about,' Edmund begins. 'It's not an easy thing to talk about, but . . .'

'Then let's give it the time and space it deserves when we meet again.'

The therapy notes are slid back into the filing cabinet. Another appointment is made. The moment has passed and Edmund knows before it is out of sight that it is too late to catch up with it.

Sofia shows him to the door. 'What I think is that Michael will come back to therapy and bring his secrets to us when he is ready. We're getting there, Edmund, we really are.'

Driving home cautiously along flooded roads, the spray making it impossible to see where he is going, Edmund reaches the conclusion that Sofia is wrong: Mikey will never be free to share anything with anyone while the omnipotent figure is still dancing on top of the tower. Edmund is making his mind up.

Chapter Forty-Two

Grace wants a quiet word while Mikey is at school. She suggests they sit on the bench outside the back door, you don't often get a chance at this time of year, do you? The sun has burned through the mist and Monty lies stretched at their feet in the unusual warmth. The garden is getting ready for the forthcoming anniversary of the earthquake, plump buds in its buttonhole and primroses in its hair; as poppies are to Armistice Day, so the magnolia and the cherries and the weightless scent of heaven from the Silver Chimes narcissi have acquired a new, ill-fitting solemnity.

'I can't believe it's almost a year,' says Grace. 'In some ways it feels like yesterday, in other ways, like a different century. It changed so much. Especially here.'

To Edmund, the daffodils which Grace has picked and left on the bench between them look as if they have been laid at a shrine. 'The garden's still as beautiful as ever, now that spring's coming,' he says.

'Makes you glad to be alive, doesn't it?'

Edmund tells her he has been wondering if Diana might be able to visit occasionally, how that might cheer her up, although he was never sure when he was a boarder whether it was better to have the occasional weekend leave or not. He is dipping his toe in the water.

'Oh, I don't think so,' says Grace. 'I don't think so at all.'

'Why not?'

'It's . . . I can't think of the word . . . tantalising, that's what it would be. You know, to just have glimpses of the one thing you want more than anything and not be able to have it. That would be torture in my book.' She gets up. 'Give me a moment, it does those flowers no good left like that.'

He can hear her clattering in the kitchen. Does Grace know what Tantalus did to deserve his punishment? Murdered his son, fed him up to the gods for dinner?

'But that's not really the point, is it?' she says from the back door. 'If she can't come back properly, and don't get me wrong, I don't blame you for not having her at Wynhope, not at all. I mean it's impossible, isn't it, with her disabilities, not to mention you having your hands full with Mikey. It's more than anyone can take on. And when it comes to Mikey . . .'

'When it comes to Mikey, what?'

Disappearing back into the house, Grace throws the comment over her shoulder. 'You know what I mean, Edmund.'

At the lily pond, the bronze boy gleams. Drops of moisture are evaporating from his skin like sweat, his body no longer rigid and encased in metal but as fluid as the element from which he rises. Playing with the water, Edmund watches the fish take cover in the shadows. Maybe Grace is right; to be able to dip your hand in this paradise, but never swim, that would be the worst punishment, if it is punishment he's after. Inside, he finds Grace in the morning room, mopping up a bit of water spilled from the flowers.

'These look a treat in here,' she says. 'Yellow always brightens things up, gives you a bit of faith in the world.'

'You said you wanted a word?'

Having wiped her hands on the cloth, Grace perches on the edge of the sofa.

'Is it too early for a little damson gin, do you think?' says Edmund with a smile.

Retreating to the dining room, he dithers, finally fetching two small glasses and the bottle after rummaging for the little wooden inlaid tray from Sri Lanka, although it's hardly necessary. He hesitates in the hall before carrying it in and pouring the gin.

'I shouldn't really,' says Grace.

How happy the room is now that it's spring. The sunlight shines through the long windows and then reflects off the mirror and the silver photograph frames so that the walls look like dappled streams. For the first morning for a long time, he hasn't lit a fire.

The dog nuzzles up to Grace, places his head on her knee and growls for attention; for a moment they both welcome the distraction. 'I had a word with John. About Diana's request and the difficulty for you.'

'Grace, you shouldn't have.'

'I thought he might be able to help and I was right.' From her trouser pocket she pulls out a piece of paper and reads it to herself, as though she's checking the small print before handing it over. 'If you're still thinking along the same lines, he says to tell you he knows people, people who can get hold of' – she sips her drink – 'something that will do the trick.'

Picking up yesterday's newspaper, Edmund shakes out the news with its headlines of murder and terrorism across the world and folds it all up neatly, following the creases. 'Why would John stick his neck out for me? Let's face it, Grace, he doesn't have a very high opinion of me.'

With her empty glass back on the tray, Grace starts to tidy up. 'That's true,' she admits. 'But something changed after that night he came over here. He admired you for not walking away. Not' – she busies herself plumping up the cushions – 'just taking your father's way out. And on top of that, I think John sees life and death a bit differently. Well, you would, wouldn't you, after what he's been through.'

'And?' says Edmund.

'He understands the position you're in. We both do. We want to help. He says to give him a call. Monty, get out of here.' Grace picks up the tray, leaving the note on the table. Just one word on it, as incomprehensible as the situation he finds himself in.

'Wait, Grace.' As if to physically stop her leaving the room, Edmund moves towards the door. 'That's not the whole story, is it? You've both got reasons you've never told me about. I've never seen you so bitter as you were when we first discussed this.'

The world witters on around them, the radio in the kitchen, Monty outside now, barking at the Spotless Angels who have just arrived.

'You really want to know why?'

There is only ever one answer to that question.

'You were married in May.' Grace readjusts her grip on the tray to prevent everything sliding off. 'That summer, after your honeymoon, our Liam came here to do some odd jobs in the garden to earn money before college. Do you remember?'

'Of course.' The boy did a few days before giving up, which Edmund thought typical of kids like him. Edmund bangs on the window to get Monty to stop barking.

'Well, I may be getting on a bit and I know times change, but as far as I'm concerned if a man did what she did, it would be called rape. He was fifteen. She was nearly forty. It was disgusting.'

'Rape?'

The glasses on the tray clink against the bottle as she leaves the room. 'There. Now I've said it.'

In the porch, they stand side by side. Hiding in the ivy on the coach house wall, the wren waits impatiently for access to one of his many cock-nests built high up on the pillar above them.

'You're telling me she never said anything to you?'

'Look at me.' Edmund physically turns her towards him. 'I promise, Grace. I don't know what you're talking about.'

'I didn't think so, she's a sly one like that,' says Grace. 'Truth is Liam bragged about it to his sister, Louisa told her parents, they told us. Eventually. I wanted to resign there and then, but what with living in the lodge and everything, it wasn't that simple. Our Liam was crying, bless him, he never knew if she'd told you, or anyone else. He felt used, ashamed. Neither of us will ever forgive her for that. John says it's a class thing, I say it's nothing of the sort. It's just the type of woman she is. I'll tell you a funny thing . . .' Grace pulls her cardigan tighter around her.

'Yes?'

'You know your Psalm, the one the little girl embroidered that used to hang in the drawing room before she took it up to the tower? Louisa's doing Psalms for her RE, she had her books out on the kitchen table, and I was telling her about the sampler and even recited it to her – I know it off by heart after all these years – but then she pointed out that in the version they use nowadays it doesn't say "cunning". Oh no. It says paralysed. "If I forget Jerusalem, let my right hand be paralysed." I'm no churchgoer, Edmund, you know that, but I can't help wondering if what's happened is God's way of punishing her. And one more thing . . .'

There's always one more thing.

'John doesn't want me to have anything more to do with it, if there is a plan. He says if you want any help, you're to call him direct.' She reaches down to pull up a young nettle which is pushing its way through the gravel. They sting at this age, but she doesn't seem to notice. 'And we both agree, if there's anything to be done, sooner rather than later's best.'

On slideshow mode, his laptop tells the story of his marriage, starting with that first hot, heavy summer at Wynhope. Diana, sunglasses on her head, perfecting her tan on a lounger under the catalpa tree – she always hated strap lines, not that they'll concern her now. Here's another: a lunch party they held, small marquee and caterers in black and white, and forty of their closest friends, only three or four of whom have been in touch since he fell from grace in the City and she fell from the window at Wynhope. Himself and Monty in the orchard with the wild rose tumbling through the fruit trees.

Finally, the screen presents him with a photo of Diana taken by him; she is wearing very little and blowing a kiss at him, but looking over her shoulder, and in the background the tower is still there, of course, and Liam is cutting the hedge. Long shorts, brown legs, a bare-chested, beautiful boy. Having pressed pause, Edmund studies the picture closely. Dancing with Flacido Domingo, that's what Diana called his little problem, and suddenly it's clear that everything his wife ever said about not minding, about there being other ways of feeling close, that his lack of physical competence was in some ways a relief for her, was all a lie. Her list of sins was damning enough already before this; what she has done to Mikey on its own is reason enough, but this! It isn't the infidelity in itself – he tells himself that he could live with that – it's the lies. Lies upon lies upon lies, the fact that he can never again believe one word she says. She had good reason to want to kill herself, and he has good reason to help her. Bitch isn't a word he normally uses, but it's the only word that has enough spit in it.

Google confirms that John's one-word remedy is indeed very effective. It is a drug legally prescribed in some Eastern European countries and the risks which prevent its use in the West include the difficulty of working out a safe dose and brain haemorrhage – a quick, painless death, not unusual in people who have suffered cata-strophic head injuries, sometimes months even years after the trauma. It is almost impossible to trace, although there are docu-mented, if rare, cases of it showing up in blood tests in post-mortems. Now he's turning into the sort of person who should delete his search history.

Ask and it shall be given unto you. It will probably take her by surprise; she'll assume he isn't man enough to see this through. She is wrong.

The first message is to John: 'Thx for offer of help. Let me know further details asap. E.'

The second is an email, sent only a few hours later when he has had time to plan ahead and that is sent to Dominic.

'Hi. Following up on your idea of taking Diana out for the day. Can you bear to come with me? Pathetic, I know, but I'm a bit daunted about the idea of doing it on my own and can't face having that enormous care assistant dragging along. Diana always did love flirting with you, it might do her good! How does a visit to Stourhead appeal? Gardens are her thing. Let me know if Easter Monday is any good? It will be busy there, but it might be nice for D on the holiday weekend, if you're not on call. You could always bring along whoever it was who was texting you throughout dinner . . . I'm sure she's gorgeous, as always. E.'

Using his best friend as a doctor in situ who can witness the death and act as an alibi is perhaps a greater crime, ethically at least, but this is how it happens, one thing leading to another, no simple solitary act. There is no way the drug can be administered to Diana at the Angeline without suspicion falling on him, but if they are out and about, who knows what might trigger a stroke? The stress of unfamiliar surroundings, late medication, the cold? Grace will have Mikey for the day, obviously.

Was he half hoping Dominic might say no? He doesn't. Then John confirms in a note hand-delivered by Grace that the order is placed and he'll bring it over when it arrives. Was he half hoping it might be like online shopping, out of stock? Who are the men behind this supply line? They must meet in small towns and slip bags into pockets of leather jackets left over the backs of chairs in shabby pubs, but Edmund has no real idea, only images based on film and fiction, stories he is now part of. On the Monday, the weekly pay envelope on the sideboard with Grace's name scrawled in biro on the front is thicker than usual. She tucks it away in her handbag and makes no comment other than to say that John will pop in next week, probably on the Tuesday. Liam is never mentioned again. It is like the stories of war crimes and exploitation Edmund hears on the news, when victims, their families, their descendants, even whole nations demand apologies from visiting heads of state. Maybe he should say sorry for what Diana did to Liam, for use and abuse of various sorts over the generations, for this will not be the first time the lords and ladies of Wynhope have exploited their servants. If you went back far enough the whole place was founded on slaves. It is difficult, if not impossible, to think of how one might make amends.

The delivery is left for him in the glasshouse. The packet is tiny and unlabelled. What is he expecting? 'Once opened use within seven days and keep out of the reach of children'? Stepping out from the oppressive glasshouse into the fresh orchard where the boughs are brought low with blossom and the grass, spring lush and long, he feels the future is both butterfly and ogre, paradise lost and possibly regained. It is not safe to leave the pills among the flowerpots where Mikey sometimes plays and the contract gardeners keep supplies. In the drawing room, the walnut box on top of the piano offers its services. It is after all her box for her valuables, and, he must remind himself, this delivery belongs to her. The tiny brass button on the side is pushed, the secret compartment slides out, the packet is slipped inside, and the box is locked, guarded by the silver key and its telltale twisted thread.

'What are you planning?' asks Mikey at supper time.

'I'm not planning anything.'

'Are you planning what to do with me? Why haven't you eaten your supper?'

Scraping his untouched portion of Grace's shepherd's pie into the bin, Edmund replies without looking at him. 'I'm not hungry, and I've said I'm not planning anything.'

'Yes, you are, you've got planning eyes. Like the Enormous Crocodile.'

As he brings yoghurt from the fridge for pudding, Edmund says he can't remember that book. Roald Dahl, isn't it?

'Yes, and the Enormous Crocodile has secret plans and clever tricks,' says Mikey, and Edmund snaps at him with his teeth and snarly face and the boy screams with delight.

Later, Edmund stretches out on the sofa in front of the television. He has a full glass of wine beside him and he watches a film as a distraction from the fear churning his stomach. Alone in the green room, all set for the opening night. Even Monty senses the occasion, restless, getting up, turning, scratching at the carpet repeatedly before he can settle to sleep. On the ten o'clock news nearly all the images are of murder of one sort or another, bombs and battered toddlers. He will be adding one to the grand total, but it is nothing like these killings, the brutal, unnecessary culling of the innocent. This is a different sort of killing: requested, not inflicted. This is what she has asked for, and it's hardly a death at all – more of a passing, a release, a slipping away. What is it about S words – serendipity, surreptitious, sanctimonious? Their lovely, long Latinate deceptions. Anglo Saxon has simpler words. Sorrow. Sad. Sin. Sleep.

Chapter Forty-Three

The night helps. In the end the spring warmth could not hold its own and a bitterly cold wind has driven it away. The sky is fathomless; ice-white stars shine against the restless blackness out at sea and only the faintest smudge of light pollution is visible in the north, towards London. This is an impulse visit to the Angeline. There will be no opportunity for goodbyes on the Stourhead visit, he has not even decided whether or not Diana should know it is planned for that day. Would he want to know if it were him? To have the chance to pack up his soul and prepare for its long journey? One last visit, that is all he craves. He was up in London anyway; there is good news on the financial front and the possible prosecution over the Riverside Development has been dropped, and, with Mikey staying over with Grace, he was in no hurry so two or three of them gathered in the name of the Index to share a bottle of champagne to celebrate. For him, Dutch courage maybe, but it is certainly true that his stock is rising. He shouldn't be driving, he keeps one eye on the rear-view mirror for the police. Visit any time, that is the policy, but the staff are surprised to see him so late nonetheless, probably surprised to see him at all. Diana is very tired today, the night nurse says, unlikely to wake easily. Perhaps they are using similar tactics to those he has planned, drugging her for the sake of a peaceful life. He doesn't mind, he reassures them, he just wants a few quiet moments together – one last time, he almost says, but stops himself.

In her room, the television is on mute. A man is pounding the streets in the rain in a foreign city, someone chasing him. He's bleeding, staggering. It isn't the sort of thing Diana watches; he guesses a member of the care team would have planned to slip in later and see how it all ended, and he's put paid to that.

At the bedside, he pushes a strand of hair away from Diana's eyes. There is a skilled hairdresser here, but as he runs his fingers through the sparse, thinning strands, he knows she must hate it, the lurid colour, the puffed-up ugliness of it. The drugs they've got her on are bloating the character from her face. She was such a beautiful woman. He traces her cheekbones and, beneath his touch, time slips. Despite everything, they never stopped kissing and he will kiss her now. Here. What is it Macbeth's porter says about desire and performance? He never lost desire. Nor did she, apparently. But certainly they are both knocking at the gates of hell. Sssh. With his forefinger on her chapped lips, he envisages forgiveness not incrimination. She does not stir again. It could be done now, quickly, quietly, with a pillow, she wouldn't suffer at all, wouldn't know a thing, but what would happen to him? He'd pull the cord, there would be light, action, fingers pointing at him. Her collarbone is sharp beneath his cheek. He moves his head to her breast, her heartbeat drums and summons him from its lonely watchtower. Nothing is infinite any longer, but numbered, limited, the clock and the lock, and the step by step on the stairs, counting all the way to the quiet end.

If someone were to paint this picture, it would be called *Husband Awaits the Death of His Wife*. The dark oils on the canvas would be lit not by candles, but by the flickering glare of the dumb television, the winking red light above the alarm cord, the luminous clock moving relentlessly from minute to minute. At midnight, not so far off, it will read 00:00. She is straight like a corpse, he is bent double, supple like a lover. So very rarely alone with her like this, just the two of them in the night, holding hands, slipping apart. And if he goes ahead, this is indeed what this is, a last night together. If he goes ahead, he will never sit alone with her again like this, she will be gone for ever. He was foolish when he said in the hospital that there was nothing of her left, that she was as good as gone. She is alive. If he goes ahead, she will be dead. A terrible, binary clarity. Edmund turns to music to soften the equation. Someone once said it was helpful in restoring memory. He can understand that. A single note held is like a moment in a river. He took CDs to the hospital quite soon after it all happened and they were packed up and delivered here along with her nighties and her grey cells in the hope that someone would find the connecting leads which seemed to have been mislaid. All their favourites, *La bohème*, for instance.

'Diana, can you hear the music?' She is still sleeping. 'It's *bohème*, Diana, our favourite.'

Maybe she squeezes his hand, maybe she doesn't. At least now he is honest enough to recognise that this is only partly about Diana, or for Diana; it is also his own need to punish himself. Deliberately he selects Act IV, the final unbearable farewell when Mimi and Rodolfo sing of candles extinguished and keys lost. It is important for him that this hurts.

'Ho tante cose che ti voglio
dire, o una sola,
ma grande come il mare,
come il mare profonda ed infinita . . .'

Mirroring the performance, he takes Diana's small, cold hand in his. It seems to him that these lines were written for the two of them, for this moment. 'I have many things I want to tell you.' But the time for telling is over. He will never know or understand.

What he has forgotten is the awful silence when Mimi dies, how even the instruments are paralysed, and all that can be heard through the vast, choked auditorium are footsteps on stage and weeping. The absence of music seems to him to stir a response from Diana. It is not physical, no turned head, no smile, no speech, but a warmth felt like slipping into the gentle lapping of a still, warm sea. And he swims with her back into the night on an empty beach on the Gulf coast, moonshadows of palm trees on sand and the hot touch of her; and their bed is crumpled cotton in a hotel room in Siena looking out over the burned road and orange hills; and the white sheets are like snow on a smooth slope in Cortina d'Ampezzo, the only tracks in the snow behind them, theirs. Now, there is room enough for regret. If he had spent more time loving her and wishing her life and less time hating her and wanting her dead, it is possible this warmth would have been like music, like the river, enough to unlock the tight imprisoned throat, and they could have talked about all the things that have gone wrong, not just the earthquake, but before that, deeper histories and childhood stories with sad endings, and mothers and fathers and sisters and why they are like they are and who they could be. Diana is not a bad person; there was neither malice nor greed in the woman he loved, maybe anger and insecurity somewhere underneath that cool exterior, maybe a lack of trust in the future, but he had not recognised it for what it was. Is it now too late? Outside, even at this time of night, the tubers are feeding, the sap is rising. Earlier in this opera, Mimi feigns sleep because she wants to be left alone with Rodolfo. I have many things I want to tell you. O una sola. Well, just the one. As large, as profound as the ocean.

'Are you awake, my love?'

No. Diana is not pretending. She is not going to wake up and tell him.

She has made a terrible request and he has made a terrible decision to grant it and, yes, it is too late.

When the music finishes, with great care, half-lover, half-undertaker, he replaces her right hand on the sheet and creeps from the room.

There is no one else alive. Driverless cars pass him and are gone. Occasionally, two red lights appear in front of him like a will o' the wisp. He does not undress, does not sleep, and in the morning he ignores the stubble and sweat and takes his dishevelled self to the village church, abandoning his chapel for a reason: he found there what he wanted to find, the candles were also false guides in this swamp in which he lives. He saw in their flames the images he wanted to see, the miracles worked were those he already believed in because he made them himself.

Here, in this public place with its mundane protestations of faith, the Sunday School map of the world, the half empty basket with tins of peaches for the food bank, yellowing postcards falling from the board giving advance notice of things that have already happened, pancake day, a fundraising coffee morning for victims of a tsunami, here, believing is much harder. In front of this crucifix and this Lenten altar, stripped of all colour, nothing but the plain white silence and wood, faith might be worth something.

Thy will not mine be done.

Other phrases take their seats in the empty chancel of his mind, cross themselves and leave.

It is harder for a rich man to enter the Kingdom of Heaven than for a camel to pass through the eye of a needle.

With the bones in his knees pressing against the kneeler, his head on his hands, Edmund is accusatory mood. You did it, he says, you sacrificed the one you loved so that others might live and be free. How can you condemn me, made in your likeness, for doing the same? Because I am guilty. We are all guilty. Forgive Diana, for her hatred of the boy, for whatever it was that happened with Valerie, for the thing with Liam, surely she too must once have been more sinned against than sinning to have done the things she's done. Bless Mikey, he has been through too much, he is the only innocent victim in all this. Forgive me, whatever I do next, I only ever wanted the best for everyone.

And that's a lie in itself, he confesses. How far back do you need me to go, there is too much to be forgiven?

The click of the latch of the door, heels on stone; behind him an elderly woman is unpacking her dusters and polish. He has been caught. She is getting everything nice for Holy Week, she tells him as he leaves.

Easter Monday was a poor choice for Diana's final trip, Good Friday would have been a better day, with the sun eclipsed at three o'clock and darkness over all the land.

Before you go, the cleaner calls after him, here, this has all the service times on it and there's a glass of wine after and nibbles, and she offers him the parish newsletter with its forthcoming events and a sentence from scripture.

And about the ninth hour Jesus cried out with a loud voice, saying, 'Eli, Eli, lama sabachthani?' Then, behold, the veil of the temple was torn in two from top to bottom; and the earth quaked, and the rocks were split.

Edmund pulls the weight of the door closed behind him. This is a God who can play tiddlywinks with tectonic plates, but for him? There'll be no deus ex machina, never has been, never will.

With the Stourhead visit less than a week away, the tightness in Edmund's chest slowly becomes less about the sentiment and more about the act. He reassures himself that he has said his goodbyes. He is doing the right thing. He is only doing what she has asked for. She is never coming home. Spring cleaning is what he calls it when Mikey wonders about his fervour and new-found addiction to decluttering.

'You need to sort things out,' says his solicitor.

'Oh, but I am,' says Edmund.

Hours are devoted to getting rid of the unpalatable, as if you've smelled in advance the seafood you are about to serve for dinner and realised it is off, scraping it into the bin before the guests have even arrived. It is premature to take most of Diana's things to the dump – people might wonder why – but some things can justifiably go: espadrilles for the beach where she will never swim again; silver flip flops for the little restaurant on the quay in Santa Maria di Castellabate where they danced after dinner, where she will not dance again; ballet pumps, walking boots, brand new bright red slingbacks he has never seen her wear. Maybe it's something to do with the earthquake, that's what he says to Mikey. Anniversaries do funny things to people; you look back at the past and into the future and need to find a way to put the two together.

The queue at the recycling centre snakes back past the hazardous materials help point. It provides secure employment, working at a dump; people never run out of things they want to get rid of. The last rubbish bag splits as he is carrying it, spilling all the financial information he has cleared from his desk – annual reports on the fracking drills in which he no longer invests, glossy brochures for holiday complex developments in the Caribbean with architects' impressions superimposed upon glorious headlands. He now feels uncomfortable investing in this new imperialism. The wind whips up the paper and a couple of people chase it with him.

'Thank you,' he calls after them, 'thank you. What a mess.' Suddenly, he spots something which shouldn't be there, the Babylon sampler which all those months ago he rescued from the ruin and put in the third drawer down for safekeeping, now swept up with the rubbish by mistake. 'No, not that,' he shouts after a woman who is clutching the grubby cloth between her gardening gloves. 'Sorry, that isn't meant for the dump at all.' Just in time, he stuffs the sampler into his coat pocket and closes his fist tightly around it.

'Is it worth a bit then?' asks the woman.

The first day of the holidays is also the first anniversary of the earthquake. Maundy Thursday. On breakfast television, footage shows the Queen handing out pennies to the poor.

'What does Maundy mean?'

'It comes from the Latin. Mandate. A command.'

'What command?'

'Jesus' command at the Last Supper.'

'What was that?'

'That we should love one another.'

'That's what Solomon says.'

It could be described as a loving act, a mercy killing, to use the common phrase. After all it's not so different from examples he's seen in the press. The mother smothering her pain-riddled baby. The replacement of an antibiotic drip with clear fluid, allowing the pneumonia to finally claim the beloved husband of thirty years in a way that the motorcycle accident had not been allowed to. Nearly always women. Did it look different if it was a man? More aggressive? Less loving? In the end it all comes down to motive and that is what plagues him. The news has moved on to a new item: one year on from the earthquake, an expert is hypothesising that a big tremor in London is overdue, and they run the standard clip of the car park collapsing and then move on to the sport. Would that it were so easy.

'Do you want to do anything special to remember Mummy?'

'No.'

'We can go to the chapel and light a candle, or better still go to the village church with some lilies for her grave?'

'Monty thinks we should clear out my room,' he says. 'Like you've been doing with yours.'

'Grace could help you do that on Tuesday.' Next Tuesday. The day after.

'No. Now.'

It is an unlikely request, but Mikey is an unlikely child and now he is possessed with a frantic energy. He raids the cleaning cupboard and loads Edmund up with everything he can find: polish, bleach, cloths, dustpan and brush, bin liners. It is impossible to carry anything else. Even the dog is given a duster, tucked into his collar. The hoover is thudded up the stairs behind him, chipping the skirting on the way. Once in the bedroom, Edmund notices the musical instruments calendar on the back of the door, nothing on it to mark next Monday. Flicking forwards, Edmund traces the year to come: July, holidays, in capitals, just like he used to; August, a blue squiggly line the length of a week with 'seaside' written with a question mark;

September, one date coloured in yellow highlighter.

'What's this one?'

'I'm very good with calendars, I got good when you were away.' Standing on the bed with his recorder, Mikey toots a fanfare. 'That's for when Solomon can see me. One year, that's what the judge says, so I worked it out.' He jumps down. 'You don't mind, do you?'

Picking a pen up off the bedroom floor, Edmund asks permission to write on the calendar and the boy says it is okay by him. 'Solomon for tea.' The boy can never be all his; maybe that was the mistake, thinking fatherhood was something to do with ownership.

'Will that be enough?' asks Mikey.

'Enough?'

'Nothing.' Mikey replies. 'Let's start. You can do the bed.'

As Edmund strips the sheets, Mikey hurls out all his clothes from the chest of drawers and then everything is sorted into pairs and piles, socks and school clothes, things that are too small, things that he does not like, things that are for summer which is coming, things that are for winter which has gone. The books have to be put in alphabetical order, the shoes and trainers lined up in the bottom of the cupboard, the Lego put back so that the top of the box shuts properly, the batteries on his old remote-control car tested, declared dead and replaced. Even his cardboard-box castle is squashed flat and put out for the dump.

'Are you sure?'

'Yes.'

On his allocated tea break Edmund gets them both a drink and a packet of biscuits from the kitchen. She always chose the custard creams. It is these unexpected things which knock him off his feet, enfeeble him with the anticipation of grief, sick to his stomach with the anticipation of guilt. Back upstairs, Mikey is standing on the bed with his hands behind his back.

'Swapsies,' says Edmund. 'You give me whatever you're hiding and I'll give you the biscuits.'

In exchange for the custard creams, Mikey hands over the key to the tower. Confused, it takes a moment for Edmund to even recognise what it is. Slowly, he pieces it together. So Diana and the police were right: Mikey had the key all along. It was him who locked his mother in. That was his unspeakable act, not hers. In the now immaculate room, there is no place to hide, so Mikey stands like a statue, tears running down his stone face like rain. It is not such a surprise, it has been the working hypothesis for a long time, and there is no need to panic, Edmund reassures himself. There was no intention to harm his mother, he could never have known there would be an earthquake, he is still innocent. No wonder the child was silenced.

Edmund knows better than to try to hug him. 'It's okay, Mikey. I understand. It isn't your fault, none of it is your fault. Where was it hidden? We all looked everywhere.'

Like the fool in blind man's bluff, Edmund allows himself to be led by the sleeve along the landing to their bedroom and to be seated at Diana's dressing table. The drawer in front of him is pulled open and a pregnancy test kit taken out and placed on the top. Taking the key back out of Edmund's hands, Mikey slides it into the box and closes the lid. How, why did the child hide the key there, where anyone, Diana certainly, would find it? And what is she doing with a pregnancy kit? As if a magician has handed the box to him and challenged him to discover the secret mechanism by which it hides the truth, he turns it over in his hands, opens it, shakes out the key once more. He's got it. The boy is not the magician, these are her tricks.

'Diana.'

Mikey nods.

All those months, the police interviews, the inquest for Christ's sake, even under oath, she said nothing, she confessed nothing. All that hysteria and protestation about the narrative verdict. Since that last night in the Angeline, he has been trying to redeem Diana, to put the pieces back together to rebuild the face he knew once, loved once, the better to bless her journey which he has booked and paid for, but here she is again, the devil woman. No wonder she cannot face the future here, although God only knows, Edmund stumbles on the thought, what other judgement will be passed on her. The boy wraps his arms around Edmund's neck.

Back in Mikey's room, sitting side by side on the clean bed, Edmund says he is sorry, he thinks Diana is sorry too. 'She didn't know there was going to be an earthquake, none of us did, she didn't mean to hurt Mummy, she didn't want her to die.'

'She did.'

'No, Mikey, she didn't.'

'She did.'

'She loved her. Mummy was her sister.'

'Her half-sister.'

'Listen, I think Diana wanted to tell us the truth about that night, but do you know what?'

'What?'

'The two of you have something in common: when you've dug a hole, you keep digging.'

'But I haven't buried anything,' pleads Mikey.

'When you've done something wrong, you don't know how to tell anyone, how to say sorry.'

With his attention turned to the one untouched item in the room, the circus animals box, Mikey gets down on his hands and knees. 'It's all right, you can come out now,' he says to the clown.

'That's the thing about grown-ups,' says Edmund, 'sometimes we're just like children. We haven't really grown up at all.'

'How sad,' says the clown.

Out trots the zebra, stood up on all fours on the now spotless carpet. The caged gorilla bosses everyone else around. 'Come on out, hurry up.' Tarum-tara goes the trumpet call on the mouth organ.

So they all emerge: the ponies, the family of elephants, the brown bears, the three lions and the sad antelopes. Eventually, the box is empty and all the animals, plus the cars and the fire engine and the tanks and even the legless acrobats and the ringmaster and the pink ballerinas who are never usually allowed out, are arranged as if waiting for a show to begin.

Managing something close to a laugh, with relief Edmund takes this as the end of the cleaning. The revelations are shocking, but they change nothing; if anything, they confirm everything. 'Well, that's that then,' he says as he gathers the mugs and the unopened biscuits, but, like a kidnapper, Mikey darts for the door and blocks his exit.

'Now what?'

'One more thing.'

'You can put the circus animals away on your own, you don't need me for that.'

Eyes staring, fists clenched, Mikey kicks the box and kicks it again and again until its sides cave in, but it does not split. The animals scatter, are trampled underfoot; some snap, others are pushed into the dark under the bed. Exhausted, Edmund puts everything down and waits for whatever it is the circus animals are going to deliver. Sofia always said Mikey would do this in his own time.

'I know you've built a false bottom in the box.'

Immediately the kicking stops.

'But I've never looked at it. It's your box, your secret, but it does seem today is the day for – what did you and Mummy call it – no more secrets, no more lies.'

Squatting on the floor, Mikey rips at the box. The tape has been wound round and round until it forms a second skin and is impossible to tear. With growing frustration, he picks at it, strips it, pulls sections which come away but reveal nothing, until finally he climbs into what is left of the box and stamps so hard the bottom falls away and there is the yellow supermarket plastic bag and, inside, the black ring binder. Private. Do not Read.

The warning is unnecessary. Edmund does not want to read it; whatever it is has been hidden because it is ugly and unpalatable. Two small white hands place the shiny black file on his knees. With the caged gorilla clasped tightly, Mikey waits at the door, half in, half out.

Noticing the slip of his sweaty skin on plastic, Edmund opens the file. Inside is a set of instructions in different-coloured felt-tip. The first line reads like this:

To Diana. What you have to do to get out.

1. *Write an account of what happened the night of the earthquake.*

He turns the page.

You have to tell the truth.

Sign your name at the bottom so everyone knows it's you.

Chapter Forty-Four

'Mikey?' It is late afternoon when Edmund finally leaves his study, the grandfather clock has just struck five. Closing the door firmly behind him, he calls up the stairs again, 'Mikey?'

No longer ringmaster in his own circus, Mikey is at a loss. He has given everything away and is now empty-handed. The circus animals are all over the place in his spotless room and they need a new home, but he has not found the energy to build anything for them. He will need a new home as well, he will need to save himself. He has been listening. He thought perhaps Edmund would be so angry that he would go away, but he hasn't heard the tyres on the gravel. And here he is, calling up the stairs. Mikey cowers on the floor between the chest of drawers and the bed, gorilla in hand.

'Mikey, I know you're up there. Do you want to come fishing with me? You and me, first time out for the new season?'

Sensing trouble, the dog has not deserted his post on the landing since Edmund left, but now he is tempted, nosing at the boy, wagging his tail and eager for a walk. He lures Mikey out and the boy appears in his pants and T-shirt, lurking between the banisters and looking down on the head of the man who once offered everything. Edmund sounds stern, so he obeys, pulls on his jeans and a jumper and creeps downstairs. He fetches his waterproof coat and boots and waits. The fishing gear is ready by the back door, along with an old hessian bag and some string.

Mikey lags behind, and even when they reach the river, he crouches further up the bank, pulling tufts of grass from the bank, watching, waiting. He does not know what he is waiting for, but from deep inside himself to the ends of his fingers, he is charged with a fierce energy.

With the rods and nets laid to one side, Edmund opens the hessian bag and pulls out the black file. The boy looks away, he knew they weren't going fishing. It does not belong here, at the riverbank, its hard plastic and metal clips which nick your fingers. Now Edmund knows everything, he must hate him. He will send him away. He sent Diana away, didn't he? Like other boys with foster parents, he will probably have to be a boarder at his school, even during the rest of the holidays, just until they find him a prison. Diana said they would lock him up; she was right, everything she said, everything she wrote in that file, that he is mad, that he is dangerous, that nobody's ever loved him, she is right. Even the stuff about being full up with evil seeds growing deep down inside him is right. The days he spent here at Wynhope on his own with her in the attic, they are a muddle, like they never even really happened or were just a film or a game on his computer, but something bad did happen, he knows that, and it was him who did it, although he never meant to. All he did was slam the door and then there was no way back. Maybe Edmund has brought him down to the river to drown him. She was going to do that. That's probably what the river's for. Maybe that is what he deserves, but no one stands around waiting to be drowned. His instinct is to run. Behind him the drive leads down to the gates, to the empty lodge, to the main road, to the lorry drivers and the swish-swish-swish of the cars, to Ali, to Africa. He should have run away long ago like when he put the notice on the gates. He should run. Run.

The dog bounds ceaselessly between the two of them in a figure of eight, as if he can bind them together in an invisible knot.

'Wait, Mikey, wait.'

It is just enough to stop him, but the hold Edmund's words have on him are only as strong as a moment that doesn't last long. The heron has flown the water, the ducks retreat to the shivering pool above the weir, Edmund is begging him to slow down, wait a minute, come back, climbing up the bank towards him, slipping, reaching out to the low-hanging branches to pull himself up. Edmund gets bigger as he gets closer, mud on the knees of his waders, and breathless, catching hold of the bottom of his waterproof coat.

'Wait. Please don't go. Listen to me.'

Mikey remains standing, but Edmund kneels down, catching his breath. 'Thank you for giving me the file. I understand. I do, I understand.'

This is what Edmund understands. He understands that Mikey locked Diana in the nursery. Constructing a mental flow diagram, he tried to work out what this meant in terms of who was guilty of what, who did what to whom and why and what happened next, but events would not stand in line; they jostled for first place, refused to sit quietly and make sense. For a long time he sat in his study and stared at the wall, wary of the desk where the file lay unopened. He played with the corners of the pages, saw enough to recognise Diana's writing, the way it was different on different pages: sometimes the writing was recognisably hers, controlled and neat; other pages were more childish; at times the hieroglyphics looked quite mad. He could burn the file, not that there was a fire in the grate any longer.

Not everything that is written has to be read. Not everything thought has to be spoken. Not everything spoken has to be heard and taken as for ever. Words, like everything else, are seeds and plant themselves in the past where, if you are not careful, they spread their tubers underground and store up guilt to feed the future. They are the product of their times, but times and circumstances change and they do not. No doubt there were dreadful things written in this file and maybe there were also sad or hopeful things, but they were transient, and if he should read them, they would achieve permanence long after the letters faded. The epigraph outlasts the corpse – like the narrative verdict with its present tense, thinking it can sum up the past and close down the future, when all along it was just words. He ran his hands over the pages and could feel no meaning. Just words.

On the other hand, if he did not read the file, the saga would be incomplete and he would fill that vacuum with fear, constructing a thousand stories in order to bring about an ending.

There was no decision to be made, not really. Like so much else, it was an inevitable future. Edmund took his familiar place again, pulled his chair up to the desk, and turned on the reading light, because this was indeed work. How else could he bear this story unless he became a reader and the handwritten paper torn from a child's colouring pad became the pages between the covers of a book, one of a million unpublished real-life stories? As readers have done since there was parchment and ink, he made the story his. In the vitriol which burned through the paper like acid, he found relief because he had to. This bitter anger must spurt from some polluted history of which he knew nothing and it confirmed his suspicion that Diana was not well. If it ever went to court, it would certainly be a case of diminished responsibility. He also found relief in that Mikey was not himself at that time either. Disconcerting that a child could have planned such a meticulous revenge, certainly, but on reflection Edmund can see that Mikey was driven to an extreme childish solution to an impossible situation: he became the prisoner of the prisoner. No one could ever have expected the whole thing to last so long or end as it did. So many secrets. So many lies.

Like readers do, he focused on some bits more than others, and it was Diana's letter to her mother which made him mourn the loss of his love with a pain he had not felt for many years. That she told her only now that she loved her. That she asked her only now the questions which could no longer be answered. That only in her letter to the dead did she capture the voice of the child she was before

370

and the woman she might have been. And then that one terrible sentence. 'I love Edmund so much and he did love me.' What was it he said to Dominic all those weeks ago, something about being better at tenses in Latin than English? Well, even in her madness, Diana had paid attention to the detail and taken care with the grammar. It was easier for Edmund to move on to the final, long-awaited explanation than to stay wedded to those ten monosyllables.

To Michael,

It is dark and probably the middle of the night, but I have a very clear mind, it's important you know that. There is no point in writing an account of the whole thing – there's only one bit that needs explaining. I did want to tell people what happened, but the longer I left it, the harder it was and no one's ever believed what I say anyway. But this is the whole thing.

The nights in here alone have dragged me back down to a dark place, I thought I'd never get out, my hands pushing the weight heavy above me suffocating me feet kicking the wall face flat against the damp places. I remember things. I told my aunty what my stepfather did to me and the Chinese whispers passed it on to everyone, my mother, my teachers, the social workers, the police and the story at the end was nothing like my story. So I said to them all ask Valerie, she knows, she'll tell you the truth, but she never did, did she. Your mother was only half a sister, she had divided loyalties, I can see that now.

I don't believe a single word you say

Liar liar pants on fire.

And I told a half-truth about her father. What I said wasn't true but it wasn't a lie either. He hadn't done what I said he'd done but he was going to one day. When I was small, it was the way he kissed me goodnight when he thought I was already asleep and his look up my skirt when he did up my laces. When I was old enough to know, I felt him hard against me in the queue for the candyfloss at the zoo. He came between me and mum so she couldn't even see past him. What was I meant to do? Wait around until it happened and be believed or lie and survive? I spent so long waiting for something dreadful to happen I couldn't take it any longer. So I left home and now you know.

This is the whole truth.

I didn't mean to kill your mother, I just wanted her to know what it felt like when your last chance of rescue is gone. To scream and for nobody to listen. For nobody to take you seriously, nobody to believe you. It was an opportunity, that's all, and I took it. One moment. I had the key. I can't describe it properly it was like I mattered. It was almost worth it but nothing is ever over and done with.

Diana.

Sorrow stood behind Edmund soft with the scent of lavender and the whisper of those unspoken words. 'I love Edmund so much and he did love me.' Unable to move from his desk, alternately Edmund read and wept and wept and read. There were things left unexplained, he was sure of that. No story is complete; choices are made, things put in, left out, beginnings, middles and endings imposed upon the slippery chronology that is history. What Edmund knew was that these texts that did remain were sufficient, that they changed everything, and that for the first time the pieces were sliding into place and he was beginning to understand.

Which is what he says now to Mikey, on the riverbank.

'I understand.'

Chapter Forty-Five

I understand. Diana's not good at remembering, although she's getting better, but she is not mistaken about this. It's what Edmund whispered when he visited and she asked him to do her that one final favour.

'I understand,' Diana says out loud.

Diana is talking. Out of all the expensive professionals at the all-inclusive Angeline, it's this one lady who she can talk to, the one who bustles in and brings the outside with her, and once she is here, they are intimate. This lady lifts her breasts, one by one, parts her legs, moves across her body with fingers which can read the damage and then sponges her sore skin with warm water and massages her lumpish feet with fine oils until she is smooth again. The expectations of the speech therapist silence her, her muscles contract in the face of the physiotherapist, but Margaret is a care assistant, and it strikes Diana that this is all she's ever needed and all she ever wanted: care.

'And what was it he understood?' Margaret is emptying her bag. The biological processes of staying alive dominate Diana's days and nights, but conversation has at last become possible, even alongside such indignities.

'Long story,' says Diana, and it is. The plot has brought her here, to this window, in the distance the hint of a calm sea and a blue sky, and there have been worse places. 'Is it cold outside?'

'Much colder than it looks. The ocean out there, it looks like Antigua but feels like the North Pole.' Margaret looks up from the end of the bed. 'You want to go outside today? We could wrap you up warm and go in the garden. Give me half an hour to get some things done and I'll be back for you.'

The room is hers again, until the next interruption. Knock knock. They always say 'just', they just want to check this, they just want to measure that. Thinking is so hard. Like a child practising cartwheels, she needs space to turn things over in her mind without the risk of smashing things. Along the corridor the chapel service has started, and she can hear the edge of the hymns – 'There is a green hill far away, without a city wall.' She has been wondering about attending, but hasn't made it yet.

I understand. What was it Edmund understood? Is Michael talking? Has he told Edmund the truth? It seems unlikely. Perhaps someone found the things she wrote in the nursery. So be it, she can't remember all of it, but she does remember that it was the truth. Edmund won't help her die, it isn't his way, even if he does know everything, and she means everything, which is a good thing, because the more she has thought about it recently, since language has made thought more possible, the more Diana has realised that what she asked for is not what she wants. She's not actually sure death was ever what she wanted, not when she asked Edmund, nor even when, in the nursery, she stepped up to an open window and recognised a familiar way out. There have been times since then when the pain and the loneliness and the ugliness and the clumsiness and the impotence – yes, most of all the impotence – have made her want to throw in the, throw in the, the cushion? These phrases do not come neatly any longer, she needs Edmund for that. Margaret has been building a pile of dirty laundry by the door; it is a dirty business being disabled. Towel. Throw in the towel. But since she has begun talking to Margaret, she is not inclined to be so hard on herself, finds herself in touch with the ordinary things, made it down to the dining room for instance, started reading again, stupid things like the newspaper, even attempting the simple crossword.

4 across (12) Declaration of I___pe____ce (12)

Since she has been talking to Margaret, she grips her feeder beaker in her own right hand, like she does now, just the trace of dribble on her chin.

'Take this cup,' says Margaret. 'Here, you can do it, drink.'

Sitting in the little summerhouse, out of the wind, Margaret on the bench, her in her chair with the rug slipping from her knees, Diana wills her fingers to grip the fringe and tug it slowly back up over her dull legs.

'I asked Edmund to help me die.'

'You did, you have told me more than once, and you know my opinion on that.'

'Where do people go from here?' asks Diana. 'When they jump?' Not the right word at all. There was a time when she wondered not whether she'd ever smile again, but if she could. She can, if a little lopsided. She laughs as she searches through the alphabet on her tongue. L. 'Leave.'

'All sorts.' Margaret opens her arms wide as if the multitudinous residents of the Angeline might take to the sea in front of them and set sail to the New World. 'Some stay. Some go home. Some go to different residential accommodation. Some go to supported living.'

'How does that work?'

As Margaret explains the ins and outs of sheltered housing, specially adapted for the disabled, and living allowances and live-in carers and the expense of it all for the average person, there are words which find purchase in Diana's precarious thinking. You are free to live life as you choose, that's what Margaret said. Free. It is cold out here, but it's very beautiful. There are daffodils lining every path and tight tulips waiting their turn in huge Tuscan pots on the terrace; even the handrails can't spoil the eyeline to the windswept hawthorn hedge at the bottom of the grounds, the first green leaves iridescent against the winter wood, and beyond that, the clattering shore.

'Gardening,' says Diana.

'And gardening. What's to stop you now?' Margaret ignores her when she indicates the feebleness of her hands, her inability to kneel or dig or weed or plant or prune. 'Knee-high beds, that's what they have at my aunty's place in Bracknell. Lovely flowers all chosen for their scent because none of the residents can see a thing, God bless them. There are ways, Diana, God always shows us a way if we are looking and willing to listen.'

The way, the truth and the life. That would be something.

'Did they tell you your husband phoned? Just confirming he's coming to collect you on Monday. Easter Monday. Now won't that be lovely? He's planned a trip to Stourhead. I think that's a big house with gardens, maybe that's why he chose it.'

It's written all over Margaret's face that she struggles with the Christian policy of forgiveness when it comes to Sir Edmund; she considers his lack of visits a sin, and maybe it is. Diana wonders if perhaps she forgave him too much too easily in the past.

Stourhead. Why suddenly all this fuss and attention? Suddenly it occurs to Diana that Edmund would choose a time and a place like that, if he was going to actually do it. A substitute Wynhope, because Wynhope itself was already full.

'Joke?' queries Margaret.

What is the colour she is looking for? Blue? Blonde? 'Black joke, Margaret,' Diana replies.

When she conceived the idea, she envisaged it here at the Angeline. He'd probably play *bohème* and lean over and kiss her goodnight, his face this close to hers, his body heavy on her breasts and sharp against her collarbones as the pillow presses on her and the breath leaves her. It is such a clear image that she wonders if he came one night when she was hostage to her sleeping pills and tried and failed and left. There are solutions on the internet, but when she thinks about it, she's sure Edmund isn't the type of man to take this on himself, and money buys distance. Maybe that's why Dominic is coming on the trip? Or Mrs H? She wouldn't even need a fee. Mrs H, who made lasagne with yoghurt on the top and stuck notes on the fridge – instructions, were they, or warnings perhaps? Anyway, she did things Diana didn't like and Diana did things she didn't like, and, oh, the world is a hedgehog and she is tired of needles.

'We went there once,' remembers Diana.

Margaret leans in to hear her. 'To Stourhead?'

It was a *son et lumière*. There were friends, or acquaintances as they turned out to be, they brought tartan rugs, although they all sat on expensive folding chairs so what was the point of the rugs? Perhaps the rugs are a false memory, because in books and films and other lives people take tartan rugs to picnics, not because that's what happened in her life. The same with the champagne and fireworks. One picture does feel like hers and hers alone: a disappearing point at the end of a long avenue of trees, a hilltop horizon and a clear black sky, then a magic trick, out of darkness, out of nothing, a blaze of lights and a tall tower appeared like a shining vision and everybody gasped. When the music stopped, it was gone and someone said it was a folly.

'I don't think I'll go, Margaret.'

'Then that's your choice, Diana. I would say a trip out would do you good, but you make up your own mind. Don't let yourself be bullied into things you don't want to do. Shall we go back inside?'

The pain in her neck is relentless and her brain receives scrambled messages from parts of her that have given up communicating sensibly, but her body panics and translates them anyway and she sweats. In the afternoon she accepts more medication, drifts in and out of sleep. Once or twice, half awake, she thinks Edmund is with her, or maybe they are in a garden somewhere and he is asking her to come home to Wynhope. The scene replays on a loop, coming and going, barely changing; she never seems to get round to answering, but the next morning she feels stronger and her reply has come to her in the night in a way she doesn't understand, but with a degree of conviction which surprises her. If he ever asks her to return to Wynhope, she'll say no. Not because she doesn't love him. Not because of Michael, although even to think of the child frightens her. Not because she hates Wynhope, because she doesn't think she does, despite all that has happened there. But because she does not want a gilded prison. She does not want to implement her bowel-control programme in a newly adapted guest bathroom where the sun used to light up the morning room. She does not want someone else to operate her stair lift, hauling her past the peeping eyes of generations of men – imperialists and perpetrators, every one of them. The thought of the three of them handcuffed to each other and to Wynhope makes her thin wrists sore.

The leaflet Margaret brings shows a smiling woman in a wheel-chair and dark glasses planting a rose. All around her are roses, Ballerina, Tranquillity, Anne Boleyn. 'There is no horticultural task we cannot do, we just have different ways of doing things,' it says. Inside are quotes from people who she now knows are people like her. The other booklet looks as though it used the same woman to demonstrate the newly built flats in southwest London. Diana comments wryly to Margaret that she could forget the gardening and have a new career as a model for disability brochures.

'And a very beautiful model you would be too,' says Margaret.

She's not beautiful any longer, though; it took a long time before she could look in a mirror, but she knew before she looked, the looking was just the proof.

'And don't go telling me you're not beautiful. I'm sure you're different. I never knew you before, but beauty is on the inside and you get more beautiful every day.'

That's another thing, thinks Diana, she does not want to be surrounded by people who only see what she is no longer and only notice what she has lost; if she is to live, she needs to belong to a present-tense club. She would like to decorate her own flat, she used to be good at interior decoration, she had a job like that once.

When Sally visits her, they had planned to venture out into Eastham for the first time. Her friend has identified a little café looking out over the harbour, very old-school, darling, but loads of room for the wheelchair and they serve evil-looking brownies. Unlicensed, unfortunately. They were going to have a cup of coffee (that sounds easy, doesn't it?) and count the masts of the mud-marooned boats and then come back to the Angeline. But Diana explains that she needs all her energy for talking, does Sally mind staying here?

'You're asking me if I mind talking? We used to talk for England, darling. I can't tell you how happy it makes me to hear you say that. So what is it to be? Just a minute? Shall I pick a topic?'

'No. I talk. You listen.' Diana wills the forefinger of her left hand to point to the miniature fridge. 'Wine. Like old times.'

Sally pours herself a big one and Diana a thimbleful. Go on, treat yourself.

'Edmund is coming on Monday. To take me out. There are things I want to say to him, I get in a muddle, I want to practise.'

'Be my guest.' Sally rolls up her sleeves, spreads her legs and leans forwards in the manner of a man, if not exactly Edmund.

Diana closes her eyes and concentrates. 'I do not want to return to Wynhope.'

Silence used to be so difficult, but she doesn't mind it now, she needs conversations to be slow.

Finally, Sally replies. 'I hope it's not because of Mikey, or Grace with her broomstick frightening you off.'

'I've nothing left to be frightened of,' says Diana. 'And look at me, I'm not a threat, am I?'

'I wouldn't put it past you, darling, you're armed and dangerous. The amount of metal plates they've stuck in you, one swipe and she'd be out cold. And you could always secrete poison in the arms of your wheelchair, Bond-style.' Sally sings the theme tune.

'I want Mrs, Mrs A? Mrs thingy to stay to help with Michael. We can put things right one day if she'll let me.'

'Don't do this to be a martyr. Ed still loves you, Diana, he'll do anything for you. There were a few old tarts giving him the eye on New Year's Eve, but it's obvious it's you he wants, you and Mikey. He'll want to look after you. It's all he's ever wanted.'

Edmund has clearly not confided in Sally so Diana concludes there is no reason why anyone should ever know what she asked him for and what he was going to give her. She stays with explanations of how she wants to live, rather than how she wanted to die. She wants to see Edmund, she explains, and Michael, just visits, short, taking things slowly.

'I'm not the only one who needs to learn how to walk and talk,' says Diana.

Uncharacteristically quiet, Sally moves to the window and stands with her back to Diana. If she could, Diana would embrace her. Before she leaves, Diana has one more favour to ask.

'Will you come to Stourhead with us? I might need help.'

As her friend bends over and kisses her goodbye, she is christened by the tears on Sally's face.

'I will count it as an honour to be your interpreter.' Sally buttons up her leather jacket and winds her scarf around her neck, then winks. 'I'm very expensive, mind you, but I do accept cases of Merlot if you can't get to the bank.'

There is an Easter feel to the Angeline. Everything is yellow: the primroses on the tables in the dining room, tiny bags of chocolate eggs in gold foil tied up with yellow ribbon, great bunches of daffodils and forsythia and euphorbia at the entrance to the chapel. Margaret has given her an Easter card, she won't be working the weekend, Easter Day is the most important day of the year for her and the church will be full to overflowing, and not just with people, but with joy. Margaret thinks yellow is the colour of joy, and if she ever got her own place, she would paint it yellow.

Diana offers her one of Sally's expensive truffles. 'You said your aunt lived in Bracknell. Do lots of your family live there? Do they all go to church?'

Because if they do, Diana wonders if they might know the man called Solomon who was her sister's partner. She thinks he had a job with a church in Bracknell. It would mean a lot if he would visit her.

When Margaret has left, Diana manoeuvres her way to the little dressing table and studies the small array of miscellaneous things which were returned to her by the hospital when she was transferred. Her wedding ring is in there; it was sawn in half to get it off her finger and has not been repaired. There is also a folded-up page torn from a Bible, with the bottom ripped off. It was in her pocket when they found her and someone must have thought it important and they were right. Diana reads it again now, as she often does. She knows the beginning off by heart and it feels like a poem which has been everywhere in her life and nowhere. She thinks that when she can place it, things might become clear. It's something to do with rivers and there is even a tune to some of it; she has a memory of someone singing it, although that seems unlikely, not Edmund, not Michael. Valerie. Yes. Valerie. This memory is a true memory, the two of them singing and dancing in a tower, just her and her little sister.

Chapter Forty-Six

It is getting dark. Mikey can make out the patterns on the other side of the river, but only because he knows what they look like already. This should be the best time, when the baby trout play over there by the fallen tree or behind him under the weeping willow, but this evening even the fish must be scared. No one can know everything. For a start, Edmund does not know what he's thinking right now, and he'll never know, not if he doesn't tell him. A circle of ripples disturbs the pool beneath him; the trout is hungry after all, the flies never stop dancing.

Mikey surfaces. 'I didn't know she was unhappy.'

Edmund looks up towards him. Mikey can't tell what he's thinking either, his face is in the shadows, but his whisper is very loud and clear because everything else is so quiet and wrapped up in the evening.

'Nor did I,' says Edmund.

'Or that she was sorry. She never told me.'

'She didn't tell me either, Mikey.'

Mikey's bottom lip is distorted. 'I wanted her to be dead.' He holds his hands to his ears and closes his eyes, screws up his face so the truth can't get in.

Sandpaper words these, for Edmund. 'And so did I.'

As he reaches out, the boy struggles to escape his grasp, but then gives in, folds up on himself. 'I almost killed her,' he whispers.

'And so did I,' says Edmund, keeping hold of him as best he can. 'Do you know, I wasn't entirely truthful with you? Diana did speak to me when I visited her a few weeks ago.'

Sliding towards Edmund, Mikey crouches down close to him, finds a stick and pokes the ants which scurry away but always return to their chosen route. He will concentrate on the ants.

Edmund ploughs on. 'Do you know what she didn't say?'

Shake of the head.

'She didn't say anything about what happened when I was away. About any of what's in the file, or what you did. That's very brave of her, isn't it? I think she wanted to put things right, she took all the blame herself.'

Nod.

'Who do you think is to blame for everything that's happened?'

'Me,' says Mikey. His stick cracks in two, and he breaks it into three pieces, four, five, six.

'And?'

'Diana.'

'And?'

Mikey throws the splintered fragments into the water.

'And?'

Hanging around close to the bank where the river goes nowhere, the twigs turn circles on themselves until something invisible calls them into the mainstream and off they sail, one after the other in a line, a little bit like the ants, all moving off together past the safe-as-houses islands and the snagged branches and then they'll slow over the top of the three-fathom pool and then they'll skim over the glistening weir and . . .

'And you,' says Mikey.

'Yes, and me. Everyone except Monty, everyone except your mum.' Edmund tries a smile and Mikey hugs the dog who lies chewing a stick beside them. 'I've got it all wrong. All along I've been thinking that there is not enough love to go round. It has to be me and Diana, and not you. Or you and Diana here at Wynhope, while I go away. Or me and you, with no Diana, she has to stay at the home. But I've got it all wrong, Mikey.'

He is talking to himself, but he can see the child finds his words soothing, in the manner of their speaking if not their meaning. Mikey strokes the dog, over and over and over again.

'The challenge is not in how to find ways to live without each other, but how to live with each other. I've done a lot of thinking this afternoon. Do you know what I think should happen next?'

'She comes home.'

'Diana comes home to Wynhope. It's a terrible punishment to be banished, it's like a sort of death, Shakespeare knew that,' says Edmund. The quote is just out of reach, it is something to do with walls – no world for me outside these walls, that's it. 'And do you think that's the right thing to do?'

Nod.

'I can't hear you, Mikey.'

'Yes.'

'And do you think you can manage that? Living here, Diana and me and you. And Monty. Do you think we can make a go of it?'

Mikey is doing the maths. Does it mean he will only have half of Edmund? Because from what he's seen, half of things is never enough.

'Mikey? I asked if you thought we could make a go of it.'

'I don't know.'

It is perhaps the most honest thing Edmund has ever heard Mikey say.

'Now we have work to do.' Awkwardly Edmund pushes himself to his feet. 'Fetch me some stones, go on, two or three big ones.'

Stones for throwing, stones for skimming, stones for damming the stream, he dare not ask what these stones are for. Mikey has a terrible feeling he gave the wrong answer to the question. He should have said yes, he can manage Diana coming home, then he'd definitely be staying at Wynhope as well. In class, the teacher stares around the room with that expression on her face which says has anyone else got a better answer? Wading into the shallows, he reaches into the water, soaking his sleeves; the cold numbs his hands as he grasps a stone and heaves it to the bank. Back in again, stumbling, he almost loses his footing. What if he falls? Would Edmund come in after him and save him? He's never been frightened here before now, but the current is pushing at his legs and the river is creeping up over the top of his boots as he tugs on a second, heavier rock, his fingers scratching into the gravel until he prises it from its bed and the water turns cloudy with all the thousands of bits of stuff which have been stuck underneath it for years and years, all free and floating now like they are in space. He will go back in one more time, if he's brave enough. For the last stone, he searches for some thing special and he finds it, the perfect stone. Smaller, smoothed and rounded and polished, it fits in the palm of his hands like a miniature globe.

The stones are not for keeping. They are to go in the bottom of the sack. This is how people drown kittens, Mikey saw it in a cartoon once, and his mum said he shouldn't watch things like that on the telly, not with the cat in the room. In the low light, Edmund's shadow is huge, his enormous hands are holding the mouth of the sack open wide; behind Mikey the river rushes away into the dusk. Paul put his mum's head under the taps in the bath one night, he saw through the door, hair held, face down, shouting, the smell of soap and the splatter of water. Edmund has got rid of people before. He had two wives before Diana and where did they go? At times like this, there has only ever been one person who could make everything all right again and even though she is gone and cannot hear, it is her name he calls inside his head as though he could summon her out of the tower. Gripping onto Monty's collar for dear life, his heart beat-beat-beating, he has never felt so small and so completely powerless. He has never wanted his mother as much as he wants her now.

A man's arm across your shoulders is a heavy arm, a man's breath this close to your neck is hot. Edmund is crouched beside him, pulling him close, pointing at the file.

It is the file he is going to drown.

The file.

Picking it up, sideways, Mikey checks Edmund's face for confirmation, receives a nod. It is the file that's going to die.

This is the child's process, Edmund is not going to interfere. He forces himself to wait in silence and to wait with patience as behind him he hears the click of the metal clips being snapped open and shut; he wonders what Mikey is going to leave and what he is choosing to keep.

'Ready now.'

All the pieces of paper are dropped into the bag; only the empty file itself is left out, the label peeled away from the front.

'Why?' asks Edmund.

'It isn't biodegradable,' says Mikey. 'We did that in science.' Sometimes Edmund is quite stupid.

'True,' replies Edmund, twisting the top of the sack.

With Mikey holding the twine with his finger and thumb and Edmund tying the knot, tight as you can, they close the bag. It is too heavy for a child, so Edmund carries it for him and together they scrabble back up to the drive to the edge of the old bridge. Beneath them, the water is over thirty feet deep, even in the hottest of summers. All sorts of things have probably met their end in that pool, thinks Edmund; we will not be the first or the last to ask the river to take things away for us.

'One, two, three.'

Together they heave the bag onto the ledge.

'Are you ready? Are you sure?' asks Edmund.

A nod.

'I can't hear you, Mikey.'

'Yes, I'm sure,' says Mikey. 'Are you?'

'Yes, I'm sure too.'

It's quite hard to push it, it's an ungainly, ugly thing, this sack,

386

and the hessian snags on the stonework before it topples and tumbles in slow motion like a man from a roof, but there is no body, no questions, no siren, even the ripples last only a minute or two of waiting. Edmund realises that time is not linear; these are the patterns not just of what has happened, but of what is going to happen, of what might have happened, different dimensions contained in a series of perfect, concentric circles.

'All gone,' says Edmund. 'Shall we stay down here a while?'

Everything else is preparing for night. It is a violet dusk, too pale to allow the thin moon to shine, too hesitant to convince the rooks to roost in the pines. They settle, rise and swoop and scatter and re-form in unison to some unknown music. Lying on the bank, Edmund feels the roots of the overhanging sycamores digging into his back. He shifts his weight. The sunset has faded, colouring in the sky through the jigsaw pattern of the bare branches over his head, the only stars the fragile white wood anemones under their feet. The difficult, ordinary here and now, this is where they have to live. Grand gestures of the past, like that of his father, are not what is called for. It is how to live honourably with the people and the places God has given to you – that is the challenge. How to live with them, not how to live without them. How to sleep easily, spooned with your history, your family, your story. How to live easily with your self, your God.

If he sits up, Edmund can just see the roof of the chapel and he hears that cry, that prayer, a second time: *Eli, Eli, lama sabachthani?* They are not forsaken, they have all been given a second chance, and for that Edmund is grateful. He will restore the chapel, chase out the crow, request that it be reconsecrated. The house is also visible in the distance, two lights on upstairs; he imagines a third lamp shining in the months to come, maybe even this summer. He has pushed Diana up the long drive after a picnic at the river, walking and talking about this and that, she has finished the glass of wine he brought her as she rested under the catalpa tree, her rug is slipping so he pulls it up over her cold legs, and the shade is as soft as silk falling on her shoulders. The piano music is Mikey, the front door to Wynhope is open, she is ready for bed and he carries her upstairs and the smell of meadow hay sweetens their bedroom. His mind wanders on into a future: he will employ a couple to live in the coach house, Grace won't want to look after Diana, even if she ever agrees to come back at all, everything might be explicable, but that is not to say everything will be forgiven. It turns out Grace is a complicated lady after all. The drawing room has been converted and it has become Diana's dayroom, opening out on the front lawn where they have built raised beds and he helps her tend them. He does the hard work, he digs in the compost in the winter and plants new roses in the spring, she picks the tulips and yellow daffodils with her left hand. Wynhope has been restructured to accommodate the sick before, in a different time, for the casualties of a different type of war. It is all very idealised, he acknowledges, but if it is to work at all, there has to be hope.

Monday he will go to Stourhead with Dominic as planned. His friend will never know what the original purpose of the day out was, nor will Diana. He'll unlock the walnut box with the silver key and destroy its contents, put the little key with the yellow-and-red twisted cotton tag back in its rightful place, and it will be as if none of it ever happened. Monday, there will be a sort of second proposal to Diana, to come and live with him at Wynhope, and she will say yes, yes, please, and he will do something of value with his life at last, pay his long overdue debt to the dead – he will rescue her. He will change the tenses: Diana loves him and he loves her. What if she turns him down? The evening has become cold, Edmund is stiff from this blind groping with the future unreal conditional, and he sits up, pulling his coat around him. Does she still love him? How could she still love him? He cannot force her to do anything; he fears he has been something of a bully over the past year.

'Penny for your thoughts,' says Mikey.

Edmund shares his dream.

'She might say no,' says Mikey, the world expert in no. 'She probably doesn't like me or Wynhope any longer. Or she might not want people fussing.'

An element of wishful thinking, to put it mildly, thinks Edmund. 'Well, we will have to listen to what she wants.'

'And I've been thinking too,' interrupts Mikey, taken up in a hurry of thoughts. 'We still need to go to the seaside in the summer holidays like you promised and her wheelchair won't work in the sand so she'll have to stay here and someone will have to look after her.' He pauses. 'Sally is her best friend. She can come. I think Grace might not want to. She'll be too busy.'

'We'll work something out.'

'Diana could come in September instead when I'm in Year Six and Solomon will be here as well. He can come and stay, not just for tea. He's good at helping. He helped Mummy and Mummy helped him. And there's John, he's strong enough to carry people.'

'Come here, you. Snuggle up to me.'

Edmund hugs Mikey to warm him up and hold him still and keep him close and in one piece. He does not fool himself that this is going to be easy, but despite everything that he has read about the future prognosis for boys like this, Mikey does not frighten him. He never has, he has only ever stirred up feelings of great love; if Diana has finally met her childhood self, then perhaps, in a roundabout way, the same is true for him. He feels Mikey's hands rummaging in his pocket.

'What are you looking for?'

'Gloves. I'm cold. What's this? Your hanky?'

How extraordinary, thinks Edmund, in my pocket tonight of all nights. 'I'll show you.'

Having turned on the torch on his phone, Edmund hands it to Mikey. It is a very white light, Edmund's face is all lit up and luminous. Mikey flashes the beam down the river, listens to everything running away into the night with a rush and a rustle, then he shines it on the ground between them where the Wynhope Psalm is laid out on the damp moss, weighed down with pebbles from the river.

'You look surprised,' says Edmund. 'Do you know it?'

'Yes and no.' Edmund helps him with the difficult words like Zion, captive and mirth, and Mikey reads it out loud.

'By the rivers of Babylon, there we sat down,

yea, we wept, when we remembered Zion.

We hanged our harps upon the willows in the midst thereof.

For there they that carried us away captive, required of us a song;

And they that visited us required of us mirth, saying.'

Edmund joins in the last line.

'Sing us one of the songs of Zion.'

So they don't rush off, they don't fish, they just sit. They don't talk, they listen to the songs the river sings. The trout rise to the fly, flashes of silver twisting high over the black water before swimming away free, deep beneath the weeded ledges, until a kind darkness comes with the coolness of a cloth held soft against the forehead and the still earth reminds them both that this feverish day is done and that Wynhope is waiting.

Acknowledgements

With thanks: to everyone at Canongate, in particular to my editor Francis Bickmore; to The Arvon Foundation for the one week every year where I can disappear from view and write; and finally, to all those in the NHS, in social care, in education and in charities who believe in the potential of every vulnerable child and who work tirelessly to help them achieve it.